THE INNOCENTS

A cop pursues a violent felon to avenge his father

NATHAN SENTHIL

Published by The Book Folks

London, 2021

ISBN 978-1-913516-73-4

www.thebookfolks.com

For Dr. Aarthi,
a rockstar surgeon who saves babies for a living.
You are a hero in its truest meaning,
and my inspiration to live with purpose.

Part I: Lolly

Chapter 1

July 27, 1967. 02:01 P.M.

A determined kick thumped inside Iris Durant's stomach and rescued her from a near-death state. As her eyes fluttered open, she discerned that she lay on her side, facing the caved in head of a man she had lived with for a decade. The gash, deep and messy, exposed pink brain within the crushed cranium that oozed dark viscous blood.

Another kick pushed her into reality even further—a reality filled with a myriad of unpleasant noises: the distant sounds of assault rifles being fired, military men barking orders, sirens wailing, glass shattering, and people yelling.

A deafening boom stunned her already feebly beating heart. The explosion not only reverberated through her shop, but also shook the very ground she lay upon.

It's the tanks.

When the electricity still powered their TV, the news had reported that the forty-ton war-machines had arrived to finish the job which men from the National Guard failed to.

Witnessing the carnage, a stranger would have been forgiven for assuming he was smack-dab in the middle of a battlefield. In a way, he would have been correct, but this was not Vietnam or Stalingrad. Iris's ransacked shop, along with her dead husband, was located on the 12th Street, Detroit.

Talk about being in the wrong place at the wrong time. What had started as a relatively simple raid in an unlicensed bar on the West Side turned into a full-blown riot between the blacks and Detroit PD. Though skin color played a vital role in inciting the incident, the riot later became a free-for-all plundering fest. Iris's store, 'Goodwill Electronix', was in fact robbed by a variety of criminals, including whites. Together.

And the victims weren't of one particular ethnicity either. Iris was white, and Lawrence was black. Both of them were thrashed with baseball bats wielded by browns. Thankfully, the hooligan who'd hit Iris was only a boy, barely out of adolescence. He had swung the bat from an awkward angle with little force and a lot of hesitation. She just hated it when kids were forced into a life of crime.

Iris moved, trying to get up, but the bump in her stomach prevented her from turning over. Getting her bearings, she planted an elbow and then a hand. The billing counter provided help; she grabbed its ledge and heaved herself up. Her knees shook and threatened to collapse. When she stood straight, her world slipped under her feet. If not for the grip she had on the table, gravity would have triumphed.

Dizzy, while hammers battered within her temples, Iris reckoned her vision was completely black on the right side. She dared to peel a hand from the table and brought it to her head. Trembling cold fingers traced her face. There was a craggy lump, where the eye should have been, but she felt no pain. Hand still holding the table, she stumbled to her left and looked into the shelved mirrored back wall behind the counter, where the radios used to be. The lump was her right eye bulging out of proportion; the blood and vitreous fluid ran down her dust-covered cheek.

As Iris digested the horrible image in the mirror, something tinged in her lower abdomen. Before she understood what happened, warm liquid ran down her inner thighs.

No, no, no!

Accumulating all her strength, she cried out for help but her voice failed, and the desperate scream came out with a gasp of air. Did it really matter, though? She knew no one would come to her rescue. Good people had already fled the neighborhood, leaving it to the mercy of wolves.

The shortage of options disheartened Iris, and the grim situation sank in: she must deliver unassisted.

She bent down, pulled up the hem of her long skirt, and secured it in her mouth. Locking a thumb on the strap of her underwear, she shoved them down but couldn't get them past the knees. So she stood up, wriggled them further down, used her feet to remove them completely and flung them across the floor with a toe.

Something happened inside, and she felt the contents of her entire body being vacuumed out. Her throat let out another groan, and this time there was no air. It was all pain.

The contraction eventually unclutched her from its stinging grasp, and her heartbeat decelerated, blessing her with the few moments of clarity she needed in order to plan.

She doubted that she could be in the second stage of labor, not having been conscious except for the last phase of dilation.

Pursing her lips and remembering to use her lungs, she waddled to a corner peppered with shards of a broken beer bottle, remnants of a Molotov the rioters had thrown. The walls were burned, and soot covered the ceiling.

Iris neither had the energy, nor the audacity, to walk to any of the other corners. So she swiped the glass pieces with her feet, and when it was relatively clean, she held her knees and slowly sat down.

Okay. Now to the next step.

Panting, she propped herself on the nook and tilted her hip upwards so that the path for the baby was clear of the floor. She didn't know when she had last eaten or how long she'd been out cold but she definitely didn't feel dizzy, not one bit, not anymore. On the contrary, every element of destruction around her was crystal clear.

She waited for the next contraction, and when it came, she grabbed the dirty rug, her fingernails breaking off.

And began counting.

Her insides hurt as if someone had inserted a hot knife into her and twisted it. Whenever a grunt or a scream broke through her, she added five additional seconds to her count. The final number, when the contraction gave her a breathing space at last, was fifty-seven.

Iris relaxed and rested her head back against the wall. Her heart burst in agony, body screamed in pain, and mind in fear, but she would not succumb. She needed to deliver the boy. An overwhelming sense of responsibility enveloped her and gave her the strength to brave through the scariest hour of her life. Alone.

She began counting again. Just as she reached two hundred and forty-two, the contraction returned. The world around her slowed, as if she was underwater, and small stars danced in front of her eye. But when the last thread of consciousness was about to slip and let her drown, she held it tightly and pulled herself back up to the surface.

She slapped her swollen cheek and bit her tongue, the pain bringing in the adrenaline she needed to stay awake.

Another minute of pure hell and the contraction subsided. Maybe the boy had had enough of loafing inside and wanted to come out. Iris felt a teardrop escaping her good eye, warm and pure, dissolving grime on its way.

It could be hours, or days, since Iris had made this corner her delivery ward. Contractions came and went, each spaced out between four to five minutes. She didn't force herself to push. Her mother had given birth to two of Iris's older brothers at home. Apparently, the midwife had always advised her to resist the urge to push, and only when the urge was unbearable did you push and everything happened naturally. Your body knew what to do as evolution had been doing it for thousands of years and ingrained the techniques in every woman's DNA.

After experiencing every second of what felt like a thousand contractions, she sensed the crowning. She reached in between her thighs and felt around. Her heart fastened when her fingertips found a foreign body there, yet so intertwined. The slimy, hairy protrusion gave her the kind of hope she didn't know she had in her. She just knew that the next few contractions were more important than anything in her life.

Her hands, which were first trembling, were now as controlled as a veteran surgeon's. Steadfast purpose infused her with the power of concentration and calm. When she couldn't resist the urge to push, she gave in to the feeling and the baby's head slid out into her cupped hands. On the next contraction, the boy's shoulders wedged out. She held the baby and gave one final push as the placenta and the remainder of his body were ejected. It didn't hurt that much anymore.

Iris closed her eye and a flood of relief and euphoria washed over her, giving her goosebumps.

Finally, she pulled the baby out from under her. His body was covered in fluid, his face pale and bloody. The most striking feature about him was his eyes: they were sparkling blue.

And composed.

So it didn't surprise Iris that he did not cry. Instead, he wrapped his tiny fingers around his mom's thumb.

Wild energy burst inside her and she shot up to her feet with one goal in mind: comfort the baby from the cold—he would have been cocooning in the warmth of his mommy until now.

Carrying the boy, she limped over to an empty cardboard box. In one quick motion, she yanked the bubble wrap out, upending the box. This new invention would provide the necessary warmth and protection for the newborn, but would not scrape his tender, wet skin.

She wrapped the sheet around the little bundle of joy, leaving only his head out. Lacking the means to snip the cord, she carried the baby to the street, determined to find some help. As she crossed the glass window, she glanced at her face in it. Even though it was purple from fighting the impossible battle alone, it flashed with pride, and a victorious smile hid at the corner of her lips.

The smog assaulted her as soon as she stepped into the world outside. Rubble was strewn across the tarmac, and the opposite building, Leroy's furniture shop, was now just a charcoal monstrosity. On her left, a gang of rowdy misfits were hurling stones at the shop next door, the second-floor windows of which were spewing fire, and a column of black smoke raged over it, hiding the sun and sky. To her right, a group of infantrymen shot at a bunch of rioters. In spite of hating them to the core, she hoped they were shot with rubber bullets, not lead.

She looked around and then glimpsed back at her dead husband and the obliterated shop. Clenching her teeth, she sniffled and stopped herself from crying. But it was not the isolation that brought tears to her eye. As soon as she had delivered successfully, all by herself no less, her courage had quadrupled. If she was able to give birth alone, then she could fight the devil himself.

No, what pricked her eye was the smell of tear gas, burning tires, and gunpowder. Utter chaos hung thick in the air, and her gritty newborn was breathing it all in. In a flash, Iris had an epiphany. She knew what to name her tough blue-eyed angel, a name that would never let her forget what kind of hell they had both survived this day.

Iris gently brought the baby's face close to her lips. "You and I are gonna brave this big bad world together." She kissed his soft cheek and whispered, "Ryatt."

Chapter 2

September 18, 1977. 03:27 P.M.

Iris watched Ryatt heaving himself out of the pool, his broad and chiseled shoulders gleaming in the afternoon sun. He took off after another boy, screaming, "Nick!" As the jubilant child rounded the corner, his left leg glided sideways, threatening him with a headfirst plunge into the turquoise water, making Iris skip a heartbeat. But he recovered effortlessly, giggled, and resumed the chase.

"Y'all don't be running now!" shouted Loraine, Nick's mom, who sat beside Iris. Loraine wore a leopard skin coat over a pink tank top. It hovered a few inches above the hem of vivid blue bell bottom pants which were squeezing the doughy postpartum belly that she never really cared to tame. Iris had on a well-ironed beige shirt dress. Indifference to trendy clothes wasn't the only thing distinguishing Iris from her friend. While Loraine slouched on a poolside chair, Iris sat with her back straight, her clasped hands resting together in front on her lap. Her ramrod posture was however a stark contrast to the kind smile that always reached her eyes, one real and one glass.

As the boys sprinted the last stretch and halted before their moms, they shook water off their bodies like wet puppies. Iris took out a towel from the bag and dried the panting Ryatt off. Loraine did the same to Nick, who was a year older than Ryatt but smaller.

Ryatt and Nick were having a serious dialogue about who superseded who, Batman or Superman, as they all ambled to the parking lot. Iris sauntered to her decrepit Plymouth, while Loraine got into the shiny Chevrolet that belonged to her drug-dealing soulmate.

Iris pinched her key and twisted it in the ignition, and the car coughed before jerking to a stop. Grunting, Iris leaned out of the window. "Mind giving me a boost?"

"Not this again," Loraine replied and proffered a contrived exasperation. "You have to change that old piece of shit, darling."

"I know, I know, I will." Iris pressed the clutch and put the car in gear as she pulled her head back into the car. "As soon as I buy insurance."

Loraine shook her head in what Iris assumed was pity but could easily pass for disdain as she drove the Chevrolet forward. Iris didn't wince when the front bumper of the Chevrolet scraped against the rear of the Plymouth's; she never did after the second time. She got used to the minutiae of being poor.

Iris had opened a new business with the money her late mom had borrowed from a local loan shark. She was behind in paying her dues, knowing full well this was not something she should let grow. But what else could she do other than work her back off? Iris had already sold everything in her house, even the bed and the couch, to keep pace with the speeding interest rate that only the Mafia could justify. They didn't even own a fridge as she had sold it last month along with her husband's old rifle that he had loved so dearly.

Loraine pushed her for several yards and then braked while the Plymouth continued to roll over the tarmac smoothly, until Iris released the clutch. The car jolted and skidded before roaring back to life. With the wet sniffle of a geriatric, of course. As she drove onwards, she put an arm out and waved to Loraine who honked an adieu in return.

Iris cruised down the M-3, colloquially known as Gratiot Avenue. The radio was playing The Beatles, her favorite band, and Ryatt hummed along. Seemed like he was having a hard time leaving his eyes be, squeezing the eyelids shut and opening them rather than blinking effortlessly. Must be the chlorine.

Then the DJ talked at length about a new space probe the Carter administration had pelted through the skies. Named Voyager 1, it had been launched into the unending void a couple of weeks earlier.

Iris shook her head, definitely not in pity but in disdain. She loathed technology. Gone were the days where you could just lie back and enjoy a nice book on a quiet Sunday afternoon without the prattling of a radio or a TV. Nostalgia was not the only reason why she hated technology though; her justification was more practical. Because of technology, people in Detroit were losing their jobs. Motor city didn't need the manpower it did back in the 1920s. The war and the Great Depression had only made it worse, what with the factories abandoning the city for the suburbs. Combine that with the climbing crime rate and a slowly growing drug problem, you got what the papers not-so-colorfully named 'White Exodus'.

But Iris couldn't leave the inner city. It was all she knew. Though it transmuted into a place that was gaining notoriety for violence, Iris would never give up on it. Home was not something you could forsake, even though it was sick. You tried your best to heal it. Her love didn't germinate so much from loyalty but more from her natural tendency to remedy the ailing. Motherly care, although not a totally altruistic one; this was not the world she wanted her survivor son to live in. Ryatt didn't rescue his mommy and fight his way out of her womb to come to this disgusting place. She promised herself that she would do everything in her tenuous power to make their community a better place to live in.

Ryatt finished humming the song and, out of the blue, he said, "Love you, Mommy." He always said it without a prompt, looking elsewhere, not at Iris. As if it was an incontrovertible fact that he stated just because. And her heart burst in love every time.

"Aw, I love you too, my angel." She rubbed his soft curls.

"Mom, look! A McDonald's!" Ryatt pointed at one of those new drive throughs.

"You're hungry?"

"No, but I wanna go." Ryatt clasped his hands and begged. "Please, Mommy."

Well, there was no denying a request put like that. What the heck, she decided she'd splurge, albeit slightly perplexed by his newfound interest. Ryatt used to love Burger Chef's Funmeal before Wendy's introduced drive-throughs and McDonald's followed suit. Now they were sprouting up like mushrooms, and Ryatt never missed their Golden Arches. How soon had he outgrown the chintzy toys that came with the Funmeals! Or maybe he hadn't. Something about getting fast food while sitting in a vehicle made kids forgo the excitement of going inside for a little toy.

Iris stopped the car in front of a window, and a teenager with a perpetually bored face jotted down their order, which was just an ice cream. Ryatt leaned out, paid for it, and collected the cold treat, never stopping to smile until the conclusion of business, even though his gum-chewing interlocutor offered nothing more than the obligatory greetings. Iris, who didn't turn off the engine due to her recent reminder of the condition of her car, shifted into the first gear, drove around, and resumed the journey.

The distant gray buildings were silhouetted against the sinking red orb behind them radiating in the sky. She glanced at her boy, and like always, the glance turned into a stare, not for the peculiar way he ate ice creams—he never licked or sucked but just bit the thing off and swallowed it like a starving wolf coming across a meal in the Siberian Tundra—but because of his oceanic eyes. There was something mesmerizing about them, deep and mysterious, and they always transfixed Iris. The color couldn't befit anyone better. Combined with Ryatt's caramel skin, they gave him such a wise look, as if he had got it all together already. A man with a plan. Cool as a cucumber. A survivor who came knocking down into the world, a world that was going up in smoke and spiraling into utter chaos.

As they got closer to home, Ryatt was rubbing his eyes vigorously, which were starting to look reddish. The Plymouth trundled to a stop in front of her store, and they both got down.

"Mom, my eyes feel funny," Ryatt said and wiped them with his knuckles.

"It's the chemicals, sweetie." Iris held his hands gently and pulled them loose. "You go rest now. If they feel funny after an hour, we will go to the doctor."

She unlocked the front door, which was thankfully not jimmied, and Ryatt ran towards the back that led to their bedrooms. She went inside and positioned herself behind the billing counter, looking out at passing cars.

A black Alfa Romeo stopped in front of the shop, blocking her view, and a short chubby young man alighted from the front. First thing anyone would notice about him was his white-blond hair and bushy eyebrows. Pulling his loose pants up, he walked to the backdoor and opened it. A man, taller than six feet and heavier than two hundred pounds, stepped down. He wore a hat that drooped to the side of his face, and he carried a white walking stick, which he didn't need. He was healthy as a mule, his muscles built like a wrestler who let his body go.

He came into the shop and smiled at Iris, the uncanny expression of a viper. "Bugsy." He tipped his head at the chubby man. "He's my cousin from Naples. They call him Roman. How about that?"

Iris's face crumpled. "Sorry, do I know you?"

"My name's Bugsy but people call me Mr. Hat. I'm the capo of the Detroit Alliance. Maybe you've heard of us?"

Iris had, from papers and hearsay. They were the zenith of evil when it came to Detroit. Murder, rape, extortion, drug and human trafficking, even pornography, nothing was beneath them when it came to debauchery.

Iris nodded.

"Your mother borrowed $5,000 from my boss before deciding to catch cancer and die."

Indignant, words tumbled out of her mouth. "I already told the kid—"

"*Kid* she says." Bugsy looked at Roman and laughed, before turning his attention back to Iris, without the smile, however snake-like it had been. "My *collection agent* has murdered two people so far, but the poor bastard's fallen for you. He just can't bring himself to carve you up like he's ordered to."

Frowning, Iris said, "C-carve me—"

"So, you are the woman who gave birth alone during the riots? The Strong Thing?"

"Yes," Iris managed to say, hating the fame the papers had brought her. When she had carried Ryatt that dark afternoon, with the cord still connecting them, she found a group of firefighters around the corner. They had used a wireless and called in an EMT who carefully severed the tube. A man was lying on a stretcher inside the EMT and when he heard how she managed to deliver the baby by herself, he introduced himself as a news reporter. He went on ahead and published her story and also printed her picture. The article's title read, 'The Strong Thing'.

"You're Italian, aren't you?" Bugsy asked and gave her body a once-over. "Those robust shoulders and feisty look on your face, these American women don't got those. They're all weaklings."

Iris didn't know how to respond to that. If his mom had sent him to school, he would have learned about Amelia Earhart, Jane Addams, or the one in Detroit, Rosa Parks.

"I've seen you out on the streets," Bugsy continued, "in Vito's butchery, in Carrera's vegetable shop, and I think to myself, you're the most beautiful bitch in the neighborhood. How come you married a nigger?"

Iris's eyes widened, and she clenched her teeth. "Watch your language."

"Can you believe this bitch?" Bugsy turned to Roman who shrugged.

"I said mind your—"

"Close the door!" Bugsy barked.

Before Iris could react or shout for help, Roman locked the front door. Bugsy pulled a knife out, the light gleaming on the metal's edge menacingly.

Roman circled the counter, but Iris didn't back up; she stood her ground. Then he came around and grabbed her arms from behind. Bugsy inched closer and touched her neck. His rough hand travelled down and squeezed her right breast, making her gag in repulsion, and he groped his way to her stomach.

Licking his lips, he said, "You lost touch with how the world outside works. Let me give you a reality check." He made a fist and punched her in the gut. Iris's surroundings darkened and everything spun. Roman let her go and she fell down at Bugsy's feet.

"You don't teach me how to talk, *bitch*." He nudged her head with his boot. "Not when you owe me, you got it?"

She just wouldn't talk to this racist animal.

Bugsy mashed her hand with the heel of his boot, and grated it against the floor. In spite of a yelp originating within her, she shut her mouth in time to contain it. Never give the animal the satisfaction.

"I'm asking you a question. Say you got it."

Iris pursed her lips, deciding not to be intimidated by this two-bit thug. When he lifted the boot, Iris held her dust covered hand. Skin had been scraped off and the tissue within slowly turned from white to pink before finally settling on red.

Bugsy sighed. "Looks like we're gonna have to teach this bitch some manners. Open the door."

Roman obliged and kept watch while Bugsy doubled over, tugged her upper arm and pulled her to her feet. He put the knife's tip on her back, inches above her hip, and whispered into her ear, "Make a sound, this goes in." He pressed his face onto the side of hers and bit her cheek along with her hair. "Damn, you smell good."

Roman opened the car door, and Bugsy said, "Let's go."

Even though she knew no one would cross these criminals, Iris wanted to scream for help. But then she remembered Ryatt. These unpredictably violent gangsters would not hesitate to hurt anyone, even a child. So she complied.

As Bugsy manhandled Iris out of the shop, she turned and looked back.

Though she was confident that she would never cry, that she would never let the corruption of this city get to her, she heard a loud sniffle.

And then she saw Ryatt's tiny head peeking from the back wall. He was terrified and frozen to the spot. Tears dripped down from his big eyes. Eyes that were now redder than that evening's sun.

Chapter 3

September 19, 1977. 06:45 A.M.

The van that transported Iris back to her shop jerked to a sudden halt. She heard the door beside her glide open and a cold morning wind flooded inside. The hood they'd put over her head was yanked off and she was pushed out of the vehicle, making her land on all fours. As the shock of hitting the pavement passed through her, the burning throb below her hips became more apparent. However, she had no time to process the disgusting things Bugsy and his men had done to her in the name of *teaching her a lesson*. Her baby had spent the whole night alone, starved and petrified, and that was what mattered the most. She scrambled to her feet and propelled herself at the entrance, throwing the front door open.

Ryatt was at the same place where she had last seen him, but in a different position.

He lay motionless on the floor!

Iris's motherly instinct took over. As she sprinted towards him, the rug caught her foot, causing her to stumble. Straight away, she got up and rushed to her child again.

She scooped him off the floor as tears cascaded down her cheeks. "Ryatt? Oh my God, Sweetie?"

Ryatt's eyes were swollen, and some kind of viscous fluid ran along the sides of his face in thin rivulets. It appeared too thick and gelatinous to be tears.

"Baby?" She stroked his right cheek, and his eyes fluttered open. "Are you alright?"

And she almost fainted when she saw his eyes. They were plump red, bordering on bloody, causing her heart to pause for a few moments before accelerating at its fullest speed.

"M-mommy?" Ryatt spoke but his eyes did not look at Iris, focusing on something over her head.

She held his chin and angled it gently so that he faced her. "Look at me, baby. I'm right here in front of you."

"Mommy…" Still not looking at her, Ryatt cried, "I can't see no more, Mommy!"

A ghastly chill froze her spine and traversed her back. "What do you mean you can't see?"

"I don't know." He sniffled as his small fingers wiped his nose. "Everything is just so black and glowing-like."

Iris lifted Ryatt up, maneuvered him onto her hip, and swiped the keys off the counter and hurried to the car.

* * *

In under ten minutes, Iris skidded her car to a stop before the Children's Hospital of Michigan. Maybe her Plymouth understood the urgency and decided not to make her day any worse.

She whisked the boy onto her arms and hastened inside. After telling the orderlies what had happened, they propped him on a wheelchair and rushed him to the Ophthalmology department in the East wing.

Though it was an ultra emergency for her, they put her in a queue of around twenty people, all with little kids in their hands.

And every child had swollen eyes, except Ryatt's were the worst of them all.

Iris craned her neck and found Loraine waiting at the front of the line. She almost peeled away from the queue, wishing to join Loraine, cutting everyone in front of her off. But her heart didn't consent. After all, these were all mothers and fathers feeling desperate for their children, even for a longer time than Iris. So she unwillingly decided to wait.

Loraine went in and came out. And a nurse led them towards a room in the far end of the corridor.

It was almost one hundred years before the line became the shortest and Iris was let into the office.

The doctor, a black senior with an air of authority, smiled apologetically. "I'm sorry for the hold-up. As you could see, the contamination has affected so many children."

"C-contamination?" Iris gave Ryatt's hand a gentle squeeze. "What contamination?"

"The children's swimming pool you took him to yesterday is contaminated with Acanthamoeba. And the long queue outside? They all took their boys or girls to the same pool."

"But the water was chlorinated. I smelled it myself."

"Doesn't matter. There are a few pathogens that can survive the chlorine. But no worries," the doctor said with a cheerful smile. "A few eye drops and proper rest, he will recover in no time."

"Thanks a lot, doctor." Iris placed a hand on her chest and chuckled. "I almost gave myself a heart attack when he said he couldn't see."

The doctor's eyes narrowed and his smile shrank. "What do you mean he can't see?"

He took a pen torch and skirted the table in one quick motion. He examined Ryatt's eyes, his expression turning grave with each passing second. "When did you take him to the pool?"

"Noon, yesterday." Iris scratched the nervous tick at the back of her neck.

"*Yesterday?*" the doctor asked in vehemence. "And you thought it wise to wait until his eyesight was completely gone to bring him to the hospital?"

No, she screamed inside.

If only the kind doctor knew what had happened; that Bugsy had kidnapped her, and the unspeakable things he and his goons had done all night. The relief she felt a minute ago turned into a dark hole that drained every bit of hope.

Ryatt gripped her hand tighter. "Mommy. It's starting to hurt."

The doctor switched off the light, the expression in his face still that of a very disappointed father.

"Acanthamoeba keratitis," the doctor said as he went to his table and picked up a pen and a pad. "It is a fairly curable condition if treated promptly, usually when the first symptoms appear. But delaying the treatment this long, you practically made your son blind."

A thousand knives pierced Iris's heart. Her voice was barely a whisper when she heard herself say, "H-he is going to be alright?"

The doctor gave Iris a resigned look. "Unfortunately, his vision is gone forever."

Iris clasped her hands together, praying. "There is no cure?"

The doctor shook his head. "The only way he will regain sight is by transplant. But the wait is long. It could be years before we get a pair."

As Iris's world stunned, the doctor filled a prescription and rang a bell on his table. A nurse came into the office. Casting one last disgusted look at Iris, he turned to the nurse. "Give this boy the same medication you gave to the other boy, Nick."

As Iris followed the nurse and Ryatt to a room at the end of the corridor, she spotted Loraine in the doorway. She was with a man in a tank top who had his head shaved and his body covered in tattoos. The drug-dealing soulmate.

Inside, she found Nick, Loraine's boy, almost done with the bandages. Something about it just didn't feel right.

Such a small head didn't really belong in all that white wrapping.

Loraine shooed her husband away before waddling to Iris and hugging her.

When she let go, Iris asked, "How did Nick get… so sick? Weren't you with him last night?"

"I was working, and my asshole husband was drunk out of his mind. Doesn't even remember Nick trying to wake him up when his eyes hurt. So I returned home and found the boy sitting beside the couch, sobbing."

Iris emitted a guttural sigh and teared up again as if Nick were her own child.

"Oh dear." Loraine gripped Iris by the shoulders. "We're gonna sue the owner of that pool."

Iris couldn't speak. She didn't want to sue anyone or get a billion dollars. All she needed was to reverse the damage done to her baby.

"I just want him to be okay again. To be able to see."

Loraine grabbed Iris's arm and pulled her to the side. "There's a way."

"What do you mean?" Iris asked, her voice a decibel louder as a sliver of hope lightened her being.

A nurse, who was wiping Ryatt's eyes with a cotton ball, looked up at them but resumed her work.

In a low voice, Loraine said, "My asshole husband has connections, you know?"

Iris did. He was a jailbird. But what did that have to do with anything? "I don't understand," she said.

"He just told me about an Oriental who can, for a price, fly in 'organ donors' from the East. They sell whatever body parts us lucky and relatively rich Americans need." Loraine looked into the room and lowered her voice further, bringing it down to a whisper. "We are going to buy a pair of eyes for Nick."

"What about the donor? Won't he go blind?"

"What? No. How good is money if they don't have eyes. No, sugar, we will buy from two different donors."

Iris couldn't accept to do something like that. On top of sounding illegal, her moral compass was too darn perfect to guide her anywhere but towards what was right. But Iris had no intention of waiting years for a legal donor in the US and let Ryatt miss his childhood. She loved her son so much that it hurt her. She would do anything for him. She would even…

Wait! That's it!

"Loraine." Iris took hold of her friend's shoulders. "Does your husband know any unlicensed doctors?"

"He should. Why?"

"I…" Iris dabbed at the corner of her left eye and looked away. "I want to give my own eye to Ryatt."

"What?" Loraine wriggled out of Iris's grip and took a step back. "That's crazy, woman!"

Iris glanced inside the room and shushed her friend.

"No, it is not. If someone on the other side of the planet is willing to give their eyes for money, then it really shouldn't surprise you that I am willing to do the same for love."

"But Iris" – Loraine's voice shook – "you will be blind."

Iris smiled calmly, and tears of hope escaped. She never felt so confident about something. In fact, this would be the most perfect decision she had ever made in her life.

"You only have one eye," Loraine said.

"And I am sure Ryatt will use it for the growth of our community and to help people. Because he is a good boy. Always has been such a good boy." Iris looked at her son. So handsome. So very calm. He was a good boy. A very good boy indeed.

"And he will always remain a good boy."

Chapter 4

May 18, 1981. 05:41 P.M.

Ryatt sat at the back of a police cruiser, steel restraints digging into his wrists. Call it some sort of intervention—divine or otherwise—or good old fluke: the donut-munchers were really fat. One was an obese black woman who took a good full minute to get out of and into the passenger seat, and one a bald white man with neck bearing enough folds to remind Ryatt of Michelin Man.

While Ryatt's eye studied them, his hands fiddled with the back of his NBA jersey. It was a ubiquitous navy-blue color, with *Detroit 16* printed in front, popular among the teens of his disintegrating metropolis; not that they loved Bob Lanier, the star player in Detroit Pistons, but the loose clothing could conceal anything, from knives and blackjacks to snubbies, and if worn correctly, even hide a sawn-off. Right now for Ryatt, it covered a white T-shirt, not as nefarious a reason but worn for a criminal purpose nonetheless.

Ryatt lifted both shirts. Hooked to the seam of his jeans, where a belt went, was a paperclip. When frisked, the pudgy hooves of the pig groped over it twice but missed it completely as it was clipped to the inside. Horizontally.

Ryatt's fingertips held the curve of the clip and tugged at it. But the smooth metal slipped under his damp skin. He grabbed hold of the cloth and wiped his hands dry before going back to the clip to perform the same maneuver again.

And voilà! This time he successfully plucked it loose.

Getting a solid grip on it, he straightened one end out. Careful not to move his upper body, he inserted the tip into the keyhole. Then he pressed the clip down on the restraint's flat surface, before pulling it out. The newly formed L-shaped edge was going to be his free ticket. Well, not exactly an L, it was bent probably at a 60-70 degree.

As Ryatt scanned for any unwarranted movement in front of him, drawing air in became tough. His eardrums felt as if someone had pumped air into his mouth and ballooned his head, making it light. This must be the high his boys were talking about.

As the adrenaline swooshed through his veins, there were a few things going through his mind. Namely failure, which was always a possibility regardless of the hours he'd been practicing with paperclips and handcuffs. There was always a chance that the makeshift key might get twisted beyond repair.

He pinched the edge of the clip where the bend started and jammed it into the keyhole again. He turned it to the left and then to the right; up and then down; finally clockwise and then anticlockwise.

"You feeling okay back there?" the She-Hulk asked, making him halt his actions.

"Wha—" Ryatt cleared his throat. "What do you mean?"

He made a conscious effort to regulate his voice, which edged on quavering; he shouldn't cave. Ryatt learned from his mom never to fear anything. It clouded your judgement, made you stupid, and got you in trouble.

"You feel good about selling drugs?" the lady cop asked.

"I don't feel good about getting caught," Ryatt answered and let out an inconspicuous sigh of relief. The pigs hadn't picked up on what he was up to, so he resumed his work. He needed to keep the chatter going, so that they wouldn't hear the metallic ticks as he continued operating.

"How old are you?" she asked.

"Fourteen, come summer."

The lady shook her head. "Shame on you children."

Children? Ryatt almost rolled his eyes. He was caught red-handed, selling crack to a detective in a sting operation. Did *children* do that?

Whatever. Ryatt couldn't end up in juvenile. His mom was home alone, thinking he stayed back after school playing football, his long-dead passion. Dead because when his coach had informed Ryatt that he needed to buy shoes, Iris had sold her mother's pearl necklace, the one she loved so much, and given him the money. But when the coach said Ryatt must also buy costly protective gear, he had thrown the towel in.

That's when Ryatt was schooled in yet another lesson for poor people: like decent clothes, shoes, and tasty food, ambition needed funding, too. Mad skills and natural talent weren't enough in Ryatt's world. The next day, he had given the money to the pawn shop guy who had bought the necklace from Iris. But the cocksucker had swindled an extra $20 out of Ryatt. *Interest*, he had said. Ryatt, biting down the anger, paid him and reclaimed the necklace and returned it to his mom.

However, the same night he and his two trusted lieutenants threw seven Molotovs inside the shop, converting the building into a dark skeleton of its former self.

"What do your parents do, son?" Michelin Man spoke this time.

There was a fatherly quality and care to his voice, and Ryatt took an instant liking towards him. He imagined this guy would be a cordial but stern dad, a responsible husband who probably owned a nice three-bedroom house in the suburbs which stayed free of crime, drugs, and vandals. No sirens, no gunshots, and no loud arguments like Ryatt's neighborhood. Oh how desperately he wanted to rescue Iris from that disgusting place which festered with vermin.

"They dead," Ryatt said. First rule of the streets, according to him anyways, was that no one should know anything about you. Except your very best buddies, everyone was an enemy, everyone a snitch.

"I'm sorry for that, I truly am," Michelin said, his sympathetic eyes locked at Ryatt's in the rearview mirror. "But crime is no way to live your life, boy. Trust me on this: money can't buy you happiness."

"You don't know what you talking about." Ryatt scoffed and smirked, his voice carrying a mix of anger and sadness. He didn't really need to have a heart to heart with this guy, but what he began doing to stall the pigs was quickly turning into a conversation he'd rather do without.

Ryatt chased the thoughts away, turning his attention once again to the job at hand. The tumbler clicked and the first cuff unlocked.

Yes! Fuck yes!

Like fear, he didn't allow excitement to go to his head. Calming down, he reminded himself he still had one more cuff to do, or undo rather, but not a lot of time. The precinct was just around the corner.

"I don't?" Michelin asked. "I've seen kids like you, good kids with a lot of potential gunned down in alleys and gutters, and left to die like dogs."

"If they have brains the size of dogs, then they deserve to die like dogs," Ryatt retorted.

The pig smirked. "Too tough for your age, you know that? Say, is this your first time?"

"Yup," Ryatt said truthfully. First time getting arrested that was. However, he had committed his very first act of crime when he was eleven. During recess at the playground, he threatened a nameless Asian kid with a sharp stone into handing over his batman lunchbox. That's when Ryatt discovered the gratification of taking things that didn't belong to him. The pleasure was double-fold when you yanked it right out of the possessor's hand. It brought some kind of much-needed justice to the world. The grotesque gap between the rich and the desperate slightly filled every time the latter robbed the former. In a way, people with things to spare were fat gazelles, and the poor and needy, a pack of hyenas. No matter what the law said or ordered—or like in Ryatt's case now, tried to reason with—nature happened. No one had the power to stop nature. Not the police, not the government, and certainly not God. If he did, why so much inequality in the world?

"There's hope for you, kid," Michelin said.

"How come?" Ryatt said, cursing inside. They had turned onto the street where the precinct was. He had one minute. The most important one minute of his life.

"The arresting detective said you didn't even try to run. Must mean you're feeling guilty for selling dope, don't it?"

Um… no. Ryatt didn't run because the odds were stacked against him. The pig that caught Ryatt was also black, but a lot leaner than these two. He had at least a foot on Ryatt, and his sinuous forearms and neck, and broad chest and long legs insinuated that, like Ryatt, he was also an athlete. Or he had been at some point in his life not so long ago. Running meant Ryatt would have easily been caught, adding 'resisting arrest' to his charge sheet, which didn't bother him as much as another problem: they would have taken better care of chaining Ryatt and kept a closer eye on him.

So Ryatt bid his time. And when he saw that the police cruiser the detective pig had called in was driven by two fat pigs, he had almost laughed in happiness. He knew, one way or another, he wouldn't see the inside of a jail cell that day.

"I am sorry, sir," Ryatt said, mainly to distract the pigs from the noise that the desperate paperclip was making inside the other cuff. It was not coming undone, and Ryatt believed that he'd bent the tip out of shape and got it stuck.

Then his stupidity dawned on him.

Ryatt could do a lot better by also employing his eye, couldn't he? Cursing himself, he slowly brought his hands around his stomach, not letting the movement reach his upper arms, which were visible in the rearview mirror.

"It's alright, son," Michelin said. "The judge's a good lady. She'd probably let you off with a warning, if you tell us just one thing."

"What?" Ryatt asked, almost too hastily. He should hurry.

"Who supplied you with drugs?"

Yeah, right. That would be the fastest way to meet your maker, but also the ugliest. If Ryatt pointed his finger up the food chain, he'd most certainly be made an example of. Either Michelin didn't have any brain cells or he didn't care about Ryatt. Both irked him because he liked the man.

As Ryatt watched the pigs, he rested his hands on his lap. He shook the paper clip free and tried to straighten the twisted mess on its end, but the result was it became too flimsy. Even if he made another L-shape with the same end, it wouldn't be firm enough to work.

Hold on a sec…

Out of the blue, an idea popped up.

He quickly whipped out the other end of the paperclip and inserted it into the keyhole, starting the process all over again.

But they had already entered the precinct's parking lot, now reversing between two other cruisers. Ryatt looked around. On the wall behind them, he found something peculiar. A vivid graffiti of the American Flag but with forty-five stars missing. He also found two pigs standing akimbo at the doorway, one of them lean and young.

Shit.

Michelin got down and walked to the rear while the lady cop began her one-minute struggle to get out, jerking the cruiser while at it. Just as Michelin opened the back door, the other cuff came loose. Ryatt put his hands behind and bundled the chains and the cuffs together into a steely lump.

"Come on out, kid." Michelin extended his arm. "I pray this is the last time I see you here in this godforsaken place."

"Oh, that I can promise you, sir." Ryatt put his legs out. One of his shoes had a hole, exposing his toe. He slightly leaned forward and balanced the weight on his calves, accumulating the tension like a depressed spring. "This'll be the very last time you'll see me here."

The lady pig now successfully dislodged herself from the car. As Michelin tried to grab Ryatt's arms, he jumped forward like a rattlesnake, head-butting the pig in the nose.

"Son of a…" Michelin's hands shot up to his face as he stumbled back. Ryatt took aim and pelted the handcuffs at the woman pig's face. It caught her square on the bridge of the nose, and she held her face, too, and doubled over. Ryatt slid across the hood of the other cruiser and took off like a bat out of hell.

Unsurprisingly, he heard someone shout, "Hey, stop." It was followed by the thundering and disheartening sound of shoes on tarmac.

So the chase began.

Since Ryatt could see only through his left eye, he tended to choose escape routes on that side. As he reached the entrance, another cruiser drove into the parking lot, blocking his way. It braked when the driver saw Ryatt, who climbed onto the hood and ran over the top of the car, leaping the strobe lights, finally sliding down the back windshield.

As Ryatt sprinted and built up to his full speed, he glanced back. To his dismay, the young pig had performed the same trick on the cruiser and continued to chase Ryatt. And worse still, the cruiser had reversed and turned on its sirens.

Shit! Shit! Sh— wait a minute!

The end of the street merged into a main road, and Ryatt decided to improvise. He threw his body forward, swinging his arms, and put himself into it. As he reached the busy road, he took a left. Police cruisers would never chase him in on-coming traffic.

Ryatt ran a good two-hundred meters, and the sound of sirens was slowly taken over by one of screeching tires and angry horns. He took a road not unlike the one the precinct was located in. This street was familiar to Ryatt. He zoomed past 'Love Juice', a pulp store his seniors bought porn magazines from. Beside it stood a VHS shop where Iris used to take Ryatt to buy cartoons. Not anymore, and not because Ryatt was older—he still preferred animated creatures over real people—but they didn't own a TV or a video cassette player anymore. Only childhood nostalgia remained.

Ryatt glanced over his shoulder to find the pig was still running after him. He needed to do something. And quick. He scampered into a seedy alley that led into a shadier part of the neighborhood. Sure enough, he heard the unmistakable click clack of a pair of boots echoing behind him.

Ryatt rounded the corner, and his eye quickly scanned the vicinity. Like he expected, several small groups of rowdies stood haphazardly on the street. Ryatt narrowed his options by picking three groups with at least one guy or girl wearing the same jersey as his. He selected a gaggle loafing at the corner of an intersection as two among that group wore the same jersey. He decided on this group because a few of them were of a similar height to himself.

He knew for a fact that almost all of them would have weed or crack, and at least one would be carrying.

Ryatt risked one last look behind. The cop hadn't come out of the alley yet, but he would shoot out of it any second now.

Ryatt faced the gang again. As he darted towards them, he crossed his arms and grabbed the hem of his jersey.

When the gang saw the fastly approaching Ryatt, their faces expressed confusion and anxiety. Ryatt ran *through* them, shouting, "Pigs!"

The rule of thumb in the streets was, in scenarios like these, everyone must take off in a different direction. Like how a triangle of colored balls scurry because of one white ball.

In the resulting jostling and clamor, Ryatt pulled the jersey over his head and dropped it on the curb. When he neared a parked hippie van, he crouched and hid behind it. The pig had exited the alley and stood on the road, scratching under his chin. Then he pointed in a totally different direction, not even close to where Ryatt was hiding, and shouted, "You there! Stop!" and resumed running.

Now that Ryatt had defeated one enemy, his nemesis within showed up: acid reflux. Ryatt's hand shot towards his mouth and cupped it. From his jeans pocket, he pulled out a lollipop with a yellow wrapper. He quickly removed the cover and put it in his mouth; seconds later, the heartburn subsided.

Acidity troubled Ryatt only after he had a meal, or whenever he performed activities that rattled his body, disturbing his stomach, or when he did something that pumped adrenaline into his bloodstream and raised his heartbeat. Given that he was a thug, who loved food, who ran a lot, and who also committed petty crimes for a living, he always kept a few lollipops handy.

Ryatt took a deep breath and wiped the sweat off his forehead on his sleeves. Just another day on the grind. Sighing, he went to pick up his jersey before walking home.

Chapter 5

May 18, 1981. 07:06 P.M.

Leg muscles burning, Ryatt traipsed along the remaining three-and-a-half-mile detour to his home. As his mind stopped thinking about his little stunt, it settled back into default mode.

Envy.

Ryatt had only three pairs of jeans, all peppered with tiny holes. He did not even have money to spare for a barber. So his shoulder length straggly dreadlocks weren't the outcome of trend but inability.

He crossed another main road and cut through the city center, which was lined with a gazillion stores. Out of habit, he window-shopped items he craved to own. Nothing for himself, though. Long-term poverty had that effect on you. It numbed your desires and expectations. Gone were the days when Ryatt stood outside a shop or a restaurant and fantasized about eating tasty food or donning trendy clothes. Now all he imagined was to buy a TV or a washing machine or a refrigerator; he wanted to make his mom's life better.

Rich folks didn't really think about the cost of things before buying them, but people on the less fortunate side of the spectrum always did. A dirt-poor kid like Ryatt had developed a nasty quirk of attaching price tags to anything he wanted, just to remind himself he couldn't afford it. When you saw a cheap pair of jeans or shoes, which in all probability could be knock-offs, and accepted the fact that you couldn't even afford that shit, it kind of showed you your place in the world.

Like all desperate people, Ryatt didn't compare himself to others. Nope. He was a man, and no responsible man acted selfish. He thought about other kids' moms and compared Iris with them. While middle-class moms wore silk shirts, jewels, and perfumes, Iris didn't own such fashionable apparels. Simple and functional, she had always been lower than them. Seeing his mom like that, which only became worse when she acted like nothing was wrong, agonized Ryatt. It pierced what was left of his heart and killed him.

He exited the city center, and eventually the neighborhoods transformed from good to bad and finally to worse. He let the painful change of scenery daunt him as he entered the ghetto. The buildings became shorter and shorter, the shiny glass façades replaced with cardboards, Nissans and Toyotas turned into lowriders blasting bass. The volume of trash strewn about on the streets and potholes increased, dumpsters overflowed, and strays prowled for pickings. Denizens changed too, becoming louder and more obnoxious, scantily dressed in vivid colors.

And the smell was just awful. Most people might not know, but poverty has a unique stench and low-income hoods reeked of it. An amalgamated odor of sweat, cheap rum, cigarettes, rotten meat, spoiled cabbage, and urine, both human and animal.

One could get used to it, like rats habituated to sewers, but Ryatt had long ago promised himself he would never become acclimated to poverty. He just hated it when people said we should be happy with what we are given and live in gratitude.

Well, fuck youse.

Evolution didn't function like that. Greed, the *want more* attitude, was what mutated us from some gooey multicellular organism at the bottom of the ocean to a species smart enough to photograph a ringed planet one and a half billion kilometers away from the Earth. If we had been complacent, satisfied with what we had, we wouldn't have crawled out of the darkest pits of ancient waters. So greed was good, not a sin, and even if it were, then Ryatt would gleefully compete to be the greatest sinner.

Twenty-seven minutes of revalidating his beliefs and justifying his perspective of the world later, Ryatt ambled towards a fence at the end of a cul-de-sac. It separated the tarmac from a vacant lot on the other side, which the homeless, junkies, and other garden variety bottom feeders occupied. The concrete platform of the lot was broken, and the rugged edges jutted up, greenery sprouting from the maws.

Across the lot was the back of a one-story building – the Durants' home/business. It nestled between a poultry and an auto parts shop, where a transmission tower stood supporting dangerously low hanging power cables.

Ryatt slipped through the narrow opening in the fence, went and sat beside one of the hobos. The streetwise guy, though inebriated, sensed Ryatt's presence, and left. Ryatt pulled his thighs up to his chest and hugged his legs, mimicking an antsy druggie.

Chin on his knees, he meticulously observed every little thing around him for fifteen minutes. Only when he was sure that he wasn't being followed did he get up and wipe the back of his jeans. Better that no one knew where he resided.

As Ryatt crept up to the building, he spotted an old guy with half a bottle of rum in one hand, pissing against their wall. Ryatt shook his head. This was what his mom had to live with. He stepped over the broken section of the picket fence and trotted towards the tramp.

The ground was soggy, and patches of algae made it more slippery. A sewage pipe sandwiched between the chicken plant and the picket fence had been broken by a random drifter. Their backyard absorbed the putrid water, and sometimes the runoff stayed there for days, stinking the surroundings.

When Ryatt neared the pisser, he said, "Scram, pops."

The hobo turned and grimaced, displaying crooked yellow teeth and black gums. "Why?"

Calm as ever, Ryatt answered, "It ain't a toilet."

The old man let go of his dick—the stream of his business going wayward, some spilling on his own pants—and gave Ryatt the finger. "Oh fuck you, mother—"

Ryatt's threadbare sneakers drove into the old man's boney hips. His head whiplashed, and his body jerked to the side as he lost balance and fell into the runoff. But even in this moment of disorientation, the old man took care of the booze, his dirty fingers holding the neck of the bottle firmly as it stood upright on the ground. Priorities. However, the old man didn't move. Perhaps the shock or the lack of energy contributed to the asshole's urge to play possum.

Ryatt wasn't bothered by guilt. Poverty costs souls. Only the purest and strongest came out of it as better people, like his mom. But Ryatt was no angel.

"Stop acting like you dead," Ryatt said. "I'm going inside, and you better not be here when I come back because I'm bringing a shooter with me."

Ryatt pulled a pair of keys from the jeans pocket and unlocked the back door but didn't push. Instead he took in a deep breath and surveyed the vicinity. The reek of chicken meat, motor oil, sewage, and human waste, and the sight of graffitied lot, broken walls, and damned vagrants made him angry. This slum was what a devil's anus must look like and only rectal worms thrived here.

And my mom ain't a worm.

Understanding that he was a helpless man, unable to save his mom, brought a dose of electricity underneath his skin, giving him goosebumps. Ryatt's purpose in life had never been clearer: get rich or die trying.

Fighting back the tears, he opened the door and stepped inside. He peeked out through a yellow tinted window. The old man pushed himself to his feet, rubbed his face on the muddied coat, and moved on, the pain and indignation of Ryatt's kick apparently already forgotten. Homeless, they disgusted Ryatt. But if he was honest with himself, he and his mom were just a few months away from losing the roof over their heads. Random bullying from strangers would then become an unavoidable part of their lives, too.

No. Death was kinder than the streets. Ryatt would rather kill his mom and himself.

Iris and Ryatt called that building their home as long as he could remember. But there was no radio, no couch, no oven, no nothing. This was a house without anything that made it a home. A husk mocking Ryatt of his impotence.

Releasing a sigh of self-loathing, he looked at the ceiling and resisted the tears once again. His feet dragged him to a small counter camouflaging as a kitchen. A lone dining stool sat there.

A narrow corridor connected the kitchen to the rest of the house that made up their shop. Two doors flanked the corridor. Left and right. Together they formed *bedrooms* though Ryatt didn't know if they could be called that since they didn't own a bed anymore. One room was a seven-by-four den with an old mattress that might as well be named a 'back-wrecker' and could easily pass for a torture device to extract information from Commie spies. And the other room had none, just a floor, a pillow, and a torn excuse of a blanket. Iris, being the wonderful mom that she was, always took the floor.

On the countertop, Ryatt found a dish covered by a plate. He didn't have to lift the china to know it was the sort of food the heathens and apostates would have been condemned to eat during the Inquisition: ramen. That goddamn ramen was going to be the end of him.

Taking it in one hand and grabbing a jug of water with the other, he made his way to the *bedroom*. He sat and dug into his meal. His hungry stomach sucked the thin noodles like a vacuum cleaner, even though his taste buds were light years away from being thrilled, but what could his mom do? She did the best she could with what she had. And in all fairness, it was Ryatt's duty to provide and stand up to be a man.

Some man, he thought, being chased around the city by pigs, forcing Ryatt to scram like a scared little roach.

"We have a bit of soy sauce!" Iris's voice sang from the front.

"I'm good, Ma," Ryatt shouted back. "Don't feel like it."

Actually, he did feel like it. Anything to cheat his jaded tongue that he was eating tasty food. But the thing was, Iris loved soy sauce, too. And when he was shoving ramen down his throat that morning, he noticed that the sauce would last only for another serving, if that.

"Okay," Iris said.

When Ryatt was done, like clockwork, his nemesis showed up. The contents of his stomach lurched up the esophagus. He needed a lollipop but his jeans pockets were empty.

Inadvertently cupping his mouth again, he dashed to the front of the shop. Ryatt inserted his hand in a jar that had a bunch of lollipops. He unwrapped one and sucked on it, and then felt the acids receding back to his stomach.

After taking three more, he returned the lollipop jar to the billing counter, beside a transparent box that had a picture of a dove. A fund his mom had created in Lawrence's name to educate the kids from their block and help them steer clear of drugs and debauchery. And it never filled as far as he knew.

"How's sales, Ma?" Ryatt asked.

"You know…" She put her head down and gave out a small smile, which was supposed to encourage him, but only made his eyes watery. Goddamn it. He quickly dabbed at the edges. He should never cry.

But apart from the lack of business, something else was not right. Though Iris was blind, she always tried to make eye contact when she spoke. Except when she was trying to hide something. Her eyes weren't teary, or her shoulders weren't slumped, the woman was made of the strongest stone. No apparent clues to suggest that she was battling inside, but Ryatt knew, just from the atmosphere, that she was disturbed. Which meant only one thing: Bugsy.

As usual, Iris digressed. "How's school?"

"Not bad," Ryatt lied without a stutter, because he expected this question, and massaged his wrists pensively. It was eight months since he had seen the school campus.

"Ma?" Ryatt's voice turned grave. "Did Bugsy visit here?"

"N—no," she said abruptly.

That moment's hesitation was all Ryatt needed for a confirmation. She was lying. Between them, this telltale sign inferred that one person was uncomfortable with the truth and the other should drop the subject.

Bugsy was a 'sottocapo', underboss in English, of a prominent Mafia family in their neighborhood. He had loaned Iris's mom, Ryatt's grandma, $5,000 to start a new business after their electronic shop had been plundered during the riots. Now Bugsy harassed Iris to pay back $20,000. Plus whatever interest these loan sharks saw fit to charge people who were desperate enough to borrow from them because the banks had abandoned them.

No one crossed Bugsy because he had two things that most peace-loving citizens didn't: gang and guns.

Word on the street was since Ryatt's mother was a beautiful Italian American woman and she married a black, not Bugsy, another Italian, he gave her shit whenever he could. Some even said he… assaulted Iris in the worst way one could defile a lady, and Ryatt couldn't bear hearing those words. Could be just rumors. *Should* be just rumors.

But his mom had never gone to the police, that's not how things worked here. Pigs didn't trouble guys like Bugsy. In this shitty economy, criminals' earnings surpassed the government's, and their kickbacks paid pigs a lot more than their salaries. Finally having their first black mayor was supposed to change everything. How wrong had they been. The only way out, Iris had said, was to pay the man up. And she had already settled an upwards of $10,000. Still that bastard was Shylocking what little Iris scrimped and saved. Not that he needed the money. It was a show of power.

Ryatt blamed Bugsy for everything wrong with his life. His mom was permanently blind, due to the botched surgery she had risked in order to give her eye to Ryatt, whose vision was destroyed because of Bugsy.

Maybe, just maybe, if there were no Bugsy in this world, Ryatt might have really been playing football right now.

In spite of Iris's colossal efforts, life treated them both like a really sticky gum under its shoe. It just wouldn't stop stomping and smearing them across the curb, tearing them apart bit by bit.

"I can cook you a snack." Iris changed the topic.

"Not hungry, Ma." Ryatt lied. He was a stray dog; he was always hungry. Since he spent most of his life in hunger, he just couldn't get enough of food. But he reckoned it was more psychological than real. "Save it for later."

"Okay." Iris extended her arm on the table. A sign she felt perturbed. And he knew what he had to do.

Ryatt held her hand. So soft, yet the strongest. He mouthed, "Love you, Ma." He didn't have the audacity to tell her he loved her when he was unable to emancipate his angel from this hell. It would sound like bullshit.

They stood there like that for a few seconds. It was her who let go first but not before giving a gentle squeeze. As if she understood he was dying inside.

"Alright. I am going to church." Ryatt headed towards the entrance.

"Sweetie?"

"Ma?" he stopped at the door.

"You seem so quiet lately," Iris said. "Are you doing okay? Is that why you're meeting with the pastor?"

"What's he gonna do if I ain't feeling okay?"

"Guide you towards the right place. Most times we don't know what we need, but yearn for what we want, and suffer."

"I am old enough to decide what I need, Ma. What *we* need."

"If you're wise enough to make decisions, then you should also be responsible enough not to make bad ones."

"I am responsible, Ma," Ryatt said.

"Negativity or positivity is like a plant. And time is water."

"Water?" Ryatt's asked, confused.

"Yes. The more you feed your plants, the stronger their roots get and the bigger they grow. But the catch is, you must be careful which plant you water."

"Sure, Ma," Ryatt said and pondered over it. Then he quietly left the building.

Too bad his mom didn't know that his plant had already become a monstrous banyan tree. And the schemes he conjured up, sitting under its shade, were the only respite in this scorching poverty.

* * *

Given all that was happening in his life, Ryatt surprisingly wasn't an atheist. In fact, he went to church regularly. He talked to God whenever he could. For instance, that morning Ryatt had looked at the sky and prayed.

For a meteor to strike his home.

It wouldn't even have to destroy the world because Ryatt was sure that so many of God's beloved children lived here. It's just that Ryatt and Iris weren't on that list. So even just a pocket-sized meteor capable of disintegrating their home would suffice.

All the pain had made Iris a better person. Like a fucking white swan. Poised and diligent. Beautiful and altruistic. But it turned Ryatt into what he was now: an angry beast who despised everything about the world. He could explode anytime now, lava seething out. But the same pressure made a diamond out of Iris. The more pain she accepted, the tougher she became but also kinder, her spine a little straighter, her gait more purposeful. Though they were made of the same material, one was a red-hot liquid that endangered people while the other was a glittering stone everyone adored.

Ryatt went into the well-lit church with a gaping void inside his center. He paced heavy-heartedly, fingers tracing the shiny wooden pews while his eye set firmly on the centerpiece. "You have high-ticket carpentry." He shrugged. "We have one piece of furniture. A dining stool."

Closing his fists, he tightened his arms and brought them forward, examining the meandering blood vessels. A chuckle escaped his thin lips. "Don't know if they are really veins and arteries, or just ramen, because thanks to you, I feel like it's all I'm eating. It's all I've ever eaten. Goddamn ramen."

His eyes prickled.

"You have some good air conditioning?" Ryatt sucked in his lower lip and nodded, the first drop escaping his bottomless tearducts. "We either sweat in the sweltering summer or shiver in the bitter cold."

Not really minding the torrents that began cascading down his cheeks, he sniffled.

"Smells good in here." Ryatt made a show of looking around. "Scented candles? Room fresheners?" He closed his eyes and shuddered. "We have ourselves the smell of chicken goo and hobo piss."

And then the penny dropped. He couldn't contain the flooding anguish anymore.

He collapsed on all fours and bawled, his misery forming little puddles on the clean floor. The tears dotted his path as he crawled to the altar, wailing. When he finally reached it, he grabbed the edge and pulled himself onto his knees. Angling his head sideways, he stared at the smudged image of the Savior hanging on the crucifix.

"If you really hate our guts so much, why don't you just end me and my mom right now?" He wiped his eyes. "Living ain't supposed to hurt this much, is it? I ain't asked to be born."

Ryatt felt dizzy, the pressure literally building up within his head and throbbing. For a few minutes, he was in a trance, devoid of motion, and everything around him stopped. No words were needed anymore. In fact he hated himself for opening up like that. God should understand him without all this drama. Like a mother knew her child was in pain even before the child had learned to articulate it.

A gunshot somewhere in the distance echoed inside and broke his stupor. Ryatt took a long quivery breath and shook his head in disdain. "Please stop torturing us. Enough is enough." He balanced his wet trembling palms on the landing and got up to his feet. But before he turned and walked away, he muttered, "Kill us already, you fucking coward."

Chapter 6

May 18, 1981. 08:56 P.M.

Ryatt headed to his stomping ground in Forest Park, a seedy neighborhood at the outskirts, five miles from his house. Not that there weren't any hangouts around 12th Street, but minority whites dominated them all, who in turn reported to Bugsy. Forest Park, though it had been influenced by Italian mobsters in the past, was not under their control anymore. Blacks ruled it, like they did most of the city. Bordered by Interstate 75 and the Detroit River, Forest Park was the remnant of an industrial town. Abandoned factories, deserted roads, and an absence of pigs combined, formed an ideal and snug retreat for many a scumbag.

Ryatt crossed the last drivable street and trod onto an unlit path, the bright full moon his only source of navigation. Potholes, made only more dangerous by lush undergrowth hiding them, were deep enough to upend even an SUV. It could easily pass for a haunted road, what with lack of traffic, thick tall trees flanking the jagged edges, and brick chimneys of old mills rubbernecking from the dark jungle.

Yawning, Ryatt trudged along. The vegetation around and under his shoes grew denser and denser, gradually merging into an imposing wall of bush that blocked the path. One might assume that nothing existed beyond it, except wilderness and wraiths. But if you waited and listened, you could hear faint music.

Covering his face with both hands, Ryatt shambled right into the thicket, the bristles scratching the back of his hand, ears, and neck. After thirty seconds of blindly pussyfooting through the bloodthirsty thorns, the flora became sparse, opening into an old basketball court. From where Ryatt stood, he could see and hear the beltway that stretched down to Ohio.

Across the ground was a building that had been white once, now washed pale yellow in the moonlight. Another automobile factory that couldn't survive the city, leaving behind a behemoth concrete structure that perched like a jaundiced ghost on the side of I-75.

It was the lair of the YBI, aka Young Boys Inc., the gang which Ryatt was not exactly a member of, but benefitted from nonetheless. He abhorred gangs. Not because they were violent or committed crimes—Ryatt had qualms with neither—but gangs meant connections that later became trails, which could lead the pigs, or most likely criminals, to his home.

Also for the same reason, he used the unique route through the bushes, not the main entrance to the building on its other side. Ryatt always came from the woods and disappeared into the woods, like some crazy survivalist, so that no one followed him. Paranoid, true, but that was how he managed to stay out of trouble this long.

As Ryatt neared the edifice, he eyed the offhand graffiti on the walls. He got so used to the vandal art of his city that it would surprise him only if he saw a plain wall. He went inside. The interior was spacious enough to house a private jet. Janky generators were lined up near the walls. A dozen bulbs lit up the space and loud beats rocked the floor. It was packed with people connected to the YBI. Members, benefactors, and like Ryatt, exploiters.

The YBI was like any other gang that plagued Detroit, except for one significant detail: The oldest active member of the YBI was seventeen. The gang was employed mainly by other gangs to commit major crimes without serious repercussions, as the YBI were tried as juveniles. However, it had also gained notoriety for unpredictable violence because the components were reckless, had no proper leadership, so no rules.

The person Ryatt needed to meet usually loafed on the other side of the party crowd. He squeezed his way past little islands of teenagers who were wearing frilly clothes and jumping to hip-hop. When he stepped on someone's toe, he blurted, "excuse me" and earned a smug look. He chided himself. You didn't proffer apologies here. You yelled, 'Move, motherfucker.'

At a dark corner, a boy was injecting something into a vessel on his ankle. He was black, his unnaturally straight hair dyed blond, with streaks of blue and red. His pierced nose, ears, and eyebrows all glinted with silver.

A *black* emo?

The kid looked like he had aimed for goth but landed on gay.

Ryatt stopped judging and concentrated on what he had set out to do. One quick look around, he found his supervisor, so to speak, who called himself Congo. Ryatt was sure that if Congo was asked to point that country on the world map, he would most probably touch somewhere on Antarctica.

Congo leaned back on the hood of a Mustang GTX he was not tall enough to drive, downing a beer he was not old enough to buy, fondling a hooker who was not safe enough to even provide him a BJ. Congo caught Ryatt's eyes and smiled. "Wanna join?"

Ryatt felt his face flush. "Hell, no. Something's happened."

Congo let go of the mature woman and came towards Ryatt, his welcoming smile shrinking. "Where's my money?"

"I was arrested today. The pigs got it," Ryatt said nonchalantly. No point in mincing words.

Congo frowned. "You pulling a fast one on me?"

"No. It's the truth."

"Then that ain't my problem, is it?"

"It kinda is."

"Yeah?" Congo's frown deepened. "How come?"

"I own nothing worthy you can take from me. So you have to learn a very important lesson today."

"Is that right?"

"Yup."

"What is it?"

"Count your losses and move on," Ryatt said.

"The music!" Congo's shout got everyone's attention and the song was cut off.

Congo rushed to his car. Diving into the passenger side window, he pulled out a sawn-off. He walked to Ryatt, casually slinging the gun. "Wisecrack now."

Ryatt found a smile stretching his lips.

"You laughing at me?" Congo lifted the gun and cocked it, the metallic click-clack echoing in the large arena. "Want some?"

A strange calm inside urged Ryatt to fear nothing, whispering him to *just* push it. "Sure, why not?"

Congo tilted his head slightly in confusion. "What's that? I thought you said—"

"Why not? Yup."

A pair of veins on Congo's forehead twitched. He screamed and pulled the trigger; debris and dust flew up from the ground. Everyone jerked, and a wave of clamor rose and subsided. But Ryatt neither flinched nor broke eye contact with the puerile brat.

Embarrassed, Congo brought the gun up to his face and took aim. Ryatt noticed the arm holding the gun shook as Congo wet his lips. Maybe it was all bark.

"Don't be shooting the floors. Let me help you." Ryatt moved forward, grabbed the hot barrel, and put the muzzle inches away from his right eye. "Now this is more like it."

"Don't, man. I'll really—"

"My ass, you'll really," Ryatt pushed. "I don't think you have the stones. Do it, you pus—"

A blurry figure whizzed towards Ryatt from the side. In a fleeting moment, it tackled him to the floor. They both landed hard, and Ryatt heard something grate inside his torso.

Short of breath, Ryatt grunted and wriggled out of the hold. The figure's steely arms loosened, and Ryatt looked at the man slowly getting up to his feet. He had the physique of a professional bodybuilder; his mere presence would rattle anyone. It was Thomas, one of Ryatt's lieutenants.

Thomas extended his arm and Ryatt took the help.

"I was handling it—"

"Just shut." Thomas put his finger on his lips. He then turned to Congo and promised him that he would take responsibility for Ryatt 'losing' his dope and Congo would get his money the next day.

Congo shrugged and looked at Ryatt. "We cool, bro?"

Ryatt spat down, his eye burning a hole through Congo who gave an icy smile before going back to the woman.

Someone yelled, "Cue the music," and the beats filled the room once again.

Thomas grabbed Ryatt's upper arm and led him away like an angry mom. "You suicidal?"

Was it that apparent? As his stomach churned from all the adrenaline-pumping activity and acidic bile rose up to his throat, Ryatt took out a lollipop and sucked at the candy.

Arm still in his grip, Thomas directed Ryatt to a flight of stairs at the back. That was their usual spot in the haunt. Ryatt's other lieutenant, Leo, was sitting on the third step. The smallest among the three, tiny actually, Leo was also the most vicious.

Leo was raised the way Ryatt had read most serial killers were raised. His mom, an addict who got pregnant by one of her Johns, used Leo as a punching bag to vent her bitterness at life. And drunk Johns, being drunk Johns, beat Leo around just for the hell of it. Most times, Leo was left free to wander the city, and one night, someone spotted the boy covered in bruises passed out in a ditch.

The foster parents weren't as indifferent; they did care. About the child support paychecks, that was. Out of which, not a penny went towards Leo's welfare, once again leaving him hungry and the butt of yet another cruel joke of the universe. Having had enough of the mean world, Leo set fire to the house. Legend had it that while the flames raged, Leo stood on the lawn, bathing in the orange glow and masturbating, while everyone inside screamed.

The legend might have some truth to it because Leo *was* into arson, so much so that he had actually burned down five houses on Devil's Night. It was a dare among the local hoods in Detroit during Halloween, which ended up killing people on many occasions. Leo was never caught for these things, but he was caught for torching a Ferrari, and they sent him to juvie for six months.

Leo suffered with a condition where patches of his hair fell out. These random bald spots gave him a disturbing look. Combine that with the fact that Leo giggled in a high-pitched voice frequently, straight from his throat, like he had some weird Tourette's syndrome, they practically made him a hyena. People generally treated him like a leper, but when Ryatt met him, he just knew he'd found his first real friend, because Ryatt *felt* like a leper.

Leo also reinforced Ryatt's belief: when God gave, he gave everything to one person. Looks, money, women. But when he fucked someone up, he beat him to the road, hammered him until there was no molecule of him left.

Ryatt said, "Sorry, guys."

"No sweat, Lolly," Leo said but Thomas still looked disappointed.

The basis of Young Boys Inc. was no one knew anything about anyone, except their street names. This was their survival method. So Leo was 'Badger,' because he was as fearless as honey badgers that fought even apex predators like lions and king cobras; Thomas was 'Buddha,' because he was always composed; and Ryatt was, unsurprisingly, 'Lolly'.

However, the rules didn't apply to them because they were friends from childhood. Still, they didn't use their real names at hangouts.

"What up, Buddha?" Ryatt asked. "You gonna be like that the whole night?"

Irked, Thomas asked, "Why did you pull that crazy shit? Don't tell me it's nothing." Thomas pointed his forefinger at Ryatt. "I can see it in your face. You're looking for trouble."

"It's Bugsy, man!" Ryatt's voice rose and earned looks of interest from a group near them.

Thomas shushed him. "You know we can't do nothing about him, except pay him off."

"I know but I just want to… I just want to rip his arms and legs apart. He's making my mom sad. Really sad, you feel?"

"I'm sorry to hear that," Thomas said. "But he's untouchable. He has something that we don't got—"

"Gang and guns, I know. I know." Ryatt waved him off. "You told me that already."

Leo got up and lifted his shirt, a .21 revolver shining in his waistband. "We have guns and we have each other. What we waiting for?"

Thomas scowled at Leo. "Don't go filling his head with that sorta stuff, fool." He turned to Ryatt. "Give it time. You need to become a big player to even think about icing someone like Mr. Hat. And you ain't ready for the big leagues yet."

Ryatt sighed and looked around. The walls were all painted: *YBI, Young Forever, Boys Better Than Men.* He spotted a new one today, a neon-green eyesore. It read, *Incorporashan.* Ryatt shook his head. Maybe if the genius behind the graffiti had known what 'Inc.' stood for, or even how to spell, he wouldn't be in a place like this.

Well, that wasn't true, was it? Ryatt knew how to spell it and here he was, amidst idiots and affiliating with gangsters and drug dealers. Loathing every second of it, he reminded himself that he needed to ascend, and he sure as hell couldn't do it here, not in this stupid club.

"What if I am?" Ryatt asked.

"Huh?" Thomas frowned.

"I mean, what if I am ready for the big leagues?"

"No, trust me, *you are not.*"

Ryatt gave it a few seconds of thought. "So what if I ain't? We're always pushed into situations that we aren't ready for or experienced enough to handle. But we struggle, fuck it up a few times, and eventually get a grip on it. Isn't *that* how you grow in *anything*?"

"Damn, that's deep. You learn that in school?"

Ryatt stared at Thomas. "No disrespect, Buddha, but I'm done with small-time shit."

"Yeah, me too!" Leo said. "We gonna hit the liquor stores now."

"What are you? My little bitch?" Ryatt asked with a lopsided grin. He pulled Leo close and rubbed his head, making him cackle.

"Fucking jackasses." Thomas shook his head. "Tell me which liquor shop ain't got a shotgun these days."

Ryatt let go of Leo, who laughed maniacally and wiped snot off his upper lip. Sometimes Ryatt wondered if everything was alright up there in Leo's head. He wouldn't put his money on it.

He turned to Thomas. "Don't care. I ain't dealing no more. That's not me."

Thomas said, "This is literally the first day of your job."

"And apparently, I suck at it. I just sold an ounce to a pig and got picked."

"So why can't we go back to boosting wheels off freight cars? Or mugging workers from the sweatshops?" Thomas asked.

"Nah, man. Not enough profit."

Leo said, "What you got in mind?"

Ryatt took a deep breath. He had been wondering about his career options for a few months now, and he had picked the one he thought was the most lucrative. The scariest thought had never been getting caught and going to jail, but rather that Iris would discover that he was a criminal. Since he had been taking that risk for years, it didn't matter whatever the crime was.

"Tell us," Thomas said.

"Robbery."

"Robbery? Like street robbery?"

"No punk ass chain snatching shit," Ryatt shook his head, "no mugging either. Actual robbery."

"Like 'Mad Dog Killers' style?" Leo asked in surprise.

Hayward Brown, whom their asshole police commissioner had dubbed 'Mad Dog Killer' was sort of a folk hero for the black community, especially black thugs. However, Ryatt didn't wish to be anything like Brown.

"Um… not exactly. Brown was a goddamn hero."

"What's wrong with being a hero?"

"Everyone knew Brown and his two minions, known right from juvenile. That was the cause of their downfall. But no one knows us. And *that* is going to be our greatest advantage."

"So we ain't ripping off drug dealers or their dens?"

"Hell no! None of Brown's vigilante bullshit. Real life ain't Shaft. That's another thing that got Brown killed, remember? We aren't militants with afros."

"Son, then whose money exactly are we robbing?"

Ryatt bit his nail, looking down. "The bank's."

Neither spoke, and before Thomas had enough time to raise an objection, Leo said, "We really going big league, uh?"

Ryatt nodded.

Leo shrugged. "Count me in. It's either get rich or die trying, right?" He lifted his fist. Ryatt, instead of bumping it, looked at Thomas.

"We can't do it without you, Buddha."

Thomas frowned. "Long as we ain't killing nobody."

Ryatt answered, "Yeah, sure, no."

Thomas eyed Ryatt for a few seconds. Then he said, "Fuck it. Not like we got a lot to lose." He put his fist on Leo's.

"I disagree," Ryatt said, the truth in the next sentence sent a jolt of pain through his heart and made his eyes water. "We got absolutely *nothing* to lose."

Then he bumped their fists.

Chapter 7

July 26, 1981. 01:21. P.M.

Robbery was tough to pull off if you wanted to do it right. The problem wasn't so much picking a bloated target that would make it worthwhile but the subsequent reconnaissance and hatching of a foolproof plan. It was as time-consuming as it was rewarding. *It should be.* They literally couldn't afford to go wrong.

Ryatt had done his homework to the best of his abilities and had chosen a dry canal as a point to ambush the cash van. The water way was one hundred meters wide and a bridge ran over it twenty feet above, its shade providing him and Leo an oasis from the broiling sun.

Used by skateboarders in the evenings, and drug dealers and hobos post dusk, it was deserted in the afternoon.

Ryatt crossed himself and mumbled; as he opened his eyes, he found Leo watching him with interest. "Are you… are you praying?"

"Praying is for weak asses." Ryatt touched the bulge on his hip for the umpteenth time.

"So why are you doing this?" Leo pantomimed crossing, then cackled.

"We're breaking out of this financial prison that God's put us in. A miscarriage of justice is finally gonna be righted, and I'm ordering that asshole to stay out of our way."

As Leo laughed again, the first whistle signaled them to get ready.

Ryatt nudged Leo who then jogged towards the canal wall and clambered up the slope, to his position.

As soon as Leo disappeared from sight, Ryatt squatted and inserted two fingers in his mouth and touched the back of his throat. He gagged instinctively, doubled over, and heaved.

Nothing came but contrived burps.

Since this morning, he had been feeling mildly sick due to the small doses of adrenaline regularly mixing in his bloodstream. The ardor from their little scheme had agitated his system. He had swallowed his fingers twice, hoping to barf the goddamn ramen out. Better now than later, but no luck.

Shaking his head in disappointment, Ryatt returned to his own post under the overpass, in the triangular space between the bridge and the side of the canal, which brimmed with weeds.

Once safely tucked between the plants, he ran his fingertips over the waistband yet again and made sure the .22 was still there. His hand then travelled into his pocket and pulled out a black bandana. Printed on it in bright white was a half skull, lower and upper jaw bones, and teeth glaring in gold. Ryatt tied it across his face and lay on the slope. He let his eyelids close and began taking in breaths. He needed all the oxygen he could pump into his lungs to calm himself down.

Unlike the first three attempts, Thomas didn't chicken out this time. For all that hulking body, he was not courageous when it came to doing something that required exceptional balls. Ryatt had convinced Thomas by assigning him the easiest part of the job: to operate the stolen backhoe and the getaway.

Seconds ticked past; the time for the cash van to enter the bridge neared, and Ryatt's insides churned more. His mom had run out of lollipops at the shop, so he asked Thomas to get some from somewhere else, which he had, but the thick-bodied, light-brained fool had forgotten to give them to Ryatt before plodding off to take his position.

The second whistle pierced the afternoon air.

It was time.

Ryatt could picture what was happening at the intersection above him as the plan played out.

Thomas would be waiting on the road perpendicular to the bridge, to T-bone their target. Probably revving the shit out of the backhoe, nervously gripping the steering wheel and unclasping it. His eyes fixed on the signal like a hungry hawk watching a rat hole.

Leo would be at the corner of the street the backhoe was idling. The brink van would come from their left and drive onwards to their right, if they let it pass the bridge, that was, which they had planned not to.

A long blaring honk reverberated in the hot atmosphere, and seconds later, heavy-duty tires screeched to a sudden stop.

As the van neared the intersection, Leo had jaywalked. The driver skipped a heartbeat, his eyes widening in horror as he was about to run over a small kid. Thanks to Leo's stature, which Ryatt hadn't forgotten and optimally factored in on his plan, he was never thought of as the fifteen-year-old that he was. Then the distressed driver stood on the brake, skidding the van to a halt.

That was Thomas's cue.

The backhoe lingered a good one hundred meters from the intersection, its front aimed at the van's right side. To the left was the guardrail of the bridge crossing the canal, under which Ryatt lay in wait.

Ryatt heard people yell at the driver and Leo, which eventually became panicked shouting and unrest, as they all scurried away, because Thomas had just put the backhoe in gear and accelerated it to its top speed, the metal jaw slicing through the shimmering heat distortion of the blacktop. The security guard sitting beside the driver saw the clamoring crowd quickly disperse, pointing at something. He then turned and noticed the unsettling scene outside his window that made him shit a little in his pants. A backhoe racing towards their van, its gaping metallic maw pointed at their flimsy door, at *him*, its lower teeth gleaming menacingly in the sunlight.

The guard's brain fumbled and tried to take the next course of action, wanting to apprise the driver of the situation. The driver who was busy scolding Leo. However, his mind and body had been paralyzed in fear; his legs wouldn't move, neither would his arms. He stunned the moment he spotted the raging backhoe descending upon them, blowing black smoke angrily through the exhaust on its head. A monstrous hellhound sprinting towards them, its claws pummeling the ground.

The last thing the guard saw was the equally terrified face of a teenager.

And then the beast bit its prey.

The entire weight of the ten-thousand-pound construction vehicle, concentrated on its impermeable cast-iron front-loader, smashed on the van's side, scooping it off the road and tossing it *through* the guardrail.

As soon as Ryatt heard the crash, he shot up to his feet. Rebar and debris rained down before him.

Then profound silence.

A flash of deceiving quietness as the van took the plunge was broken by an explosive sound of the durable steel box hitting the concrete, its top slamming on the ground. The gravity crushed the van and shattered its glasses. Upturned, its bent wheels rotated like an inept bug uselessly peddling its legs in a vain attempt to escape its predicament.

Not wasting a jiffy, Ryatt quickly ran to the van, drawing the .22 from his hip.

"Whoo!" Leo screamed from the broken section of the bridge. A group of onlookers gathered beside Leo, who pulled his gun out and shot at the sky, clearing the crowd. Then, without giving it a second thought, he jumped down and landed on the van's underside. He got off and pulled a spare kerchief hanging from Ryatt's back pocket that he tied across his face.

Ryatt and Leo turned their attention to the van as the front door was pushed open. They could hear men moaning inside the driver cabin.

"Move it!" Thomas tossed a thirty-six-inch bolt cutter and Ryatt caught it. Then he and Leo jogged towards the back of the van. However the tool became redundant because there was no lock in the door but a small box with numbers.

Leo studied it, with growing confusion. "The fuck is this? A telephone?"

Thomas craned his head from the guardrail above and shouted, "No, you dipshit. It's a Yale lock."

"What's a whale lock?" Leo scratched the back of his head.

"It's not a whale. It's a—forget it."

"Whatever. Just tell us how to open the fucking door."

"You can't. You need to know the numbers."

"What numbers? Can you come…"

Ryatt left them to it and rushed to the front. One of the security guards had crawled out successfully, and the other man was on his partner's tail. They both stopped moving when they saw Ryatt. The older security guy was black, and the young one was white.

The radio could be heard from the driver's cabin, the DJ talking at length.

Leo came up front. "Hey, motherfucker," he said to the old black guy, the one who was already out in the open. "What's the number combination for the door?"

"Did you just say 'number combination?'" the guard laughed. "You sure you know what you're doing?"

It pissed Ryatt off. The way this man spoke down to them. The way they all spoke down to them. The whole world looked down at them, didn't it? Little black street urchins wearing torn jeans and not by choice? Even if they had guns, they were treated poorly. Ryatt should teach this old fuck a lesson. No more—

His stomach finally exploded, the flood of puke drenching the skull kerchief.

Ryatt turned away from the van. Then he yanked the soggy cloth off of his face, threw it in the weeds, and panted.

"You okay in there?" Leo asked, holding the gun on the security guards.

"I'm fine, I'm fine." Ryatt rubbed his mouth on his shoulder. "Don't let them move, not even a pinky." Ryatt looked up at Thomas. "Lollipop."

"Oh shit." Thomas fumbled in his pocket, brought out the candy and threw it to Ryatt. He unwrapped it as if he had just been bitten by a snake and it was his antidote.

When the burn in his chest eased up, he let himself be embarrassed. The rush of committing a crime in broad daylight was just too much for him. But his will was stronger than his fear. No successful man had let fear stop him. Emboldening his thumping heart, Ryatt removed the jersey and tied it across his face. He didn't wear anything underneath, so his body glistened with the sheen of sweat.

The humid afternoon air blew through Ryatt's dreadlocks, the heatwave cooling his sticky skin.

As he turned, the DJ had finally stopped talking and put on a song.

Buddy you're a boy make a big noise…

Ryatt inched closer to the old guy on the ground. "Pin code." His voice was surprisingly calm and authoritative as he stressed those words. Poverty, lack of means and opportunities, God, and even his own body, they had all been throwing so many hurdles in his path and staving off his victory for too long a time. No more. Right then, he knew he was crossing an important threshold into a point of no return. He was not gonna be bullied by this world anymore, no.

He was gonna be the bully.

The old man regarded Ryatt. "A little vermin sucking on a piece of candy ain't gonna rob us," he spat. "Fuck you!"

We will, we will rock you…

"Pin," Ryatt repeated through his clenched teeth. "Code."

"Oh… that supposed to scare me?" He put his hands up in mock fear. "Why don't you run home to your momma, you little—"

The old security guard was unable to finish as a bullet hit him square on his forehead. Mouth hanging open, his head arched back violently and hit the ground with a thud. The shock froze his face, his pupils locked on the blazing afternoon sun, the eyelids not rushing to protect the eyes.

"What the fuck?!" Thomas's voice roared behind him, but Ryatt didn't break eye contact with the security guy's head. He was curious as to why there was no spatter.

Ryatt put his foot on the dead man's chest. With the tip of the shoe—the toe still poking out of the hole—he pushed the guard's chin to a side. The bullet didn't travel *through* his skull but slid across the top, tearing the scalp and knocking him out. The bastard was still alive. Fucking small calibers.

Ryatt hated half-assing anything. To finish the job proper, he lifted his gun and took aim.

"Lolly! No!" Thomas warned.

Ryatt looked up at him and smiled underneath his makeshift mask, but Thomas wouldn't know because it didn't reach his eyes.

Ryatt sang along, *"Buddy, you're a young man, hard man shouting in the street gonna take on the world someday…"*

Then Ryatt pulled the trigger. The firm recoil travelled through his palm, forearm, and upwards. Like a powerful guardian of some kind patting his shoulder, comforting him when everything was utterly painful. It gave him hope, and *oh God* did it feel good for somebody who had been deprived of it their whole life!

Just to experience that ephemeral feeling of hope and strength, a fleeting sense of control and serenity—not out of sadism or anger—Ryatt squeezed the trigger twelve more times, synching it with the drum chorus of 'We Will Rock You' but the gun had become empty on the fifth squeeze.

Ryatt winked at Thomas whose jaw dropped; he peeled his eyes off his appalled friend and regarded his work. Though the security guard's head was dotted with half a dozen holes, it did not explode, nor did his brains leak out. However, Ryatt knew the man was dead, because one of the bullets had popped his right eye.

Not looking away, Ryatt stretched his arm in the direction where a small figure loomed at the peripheral vision. He beckoned Leo over and dropped the empty revolver to hang from his forefinger, smoke coiling upwards. Leo retrieved it from him and replaced it with his .21. Fully loaded. But Ryatt aimed at nothing, the muzzle pointed loosely at the ground.

Ryatt, whose attention didn't yet leave the dead body under his foot, spoke in a smooth tone, addressing the remaining security guard. "You want to live?"

There was a movement at the corner of his eye. The man must have nodded.

"Then answer the question this brave idiot failed to, but remember," Ryatt finally looked at the shivering man, and lifted a finger, as if preaching the very meaning of existence to a devout, "don't be a hero. Heroes end up with a lot of lead in their tiny brains."

"B—but..." Tears streamed down the guard's face, choking him and drowning the words. "I—I just got married. Baby's due..."

Ryatt understood the security guard's fear: it's the fear of life. Newlywed, a little bun in the oven. Maybe they already bought a comfy pink cradle, tunes playing as some cute toy spun over it. Husband and wife huddled close to the baby's crib, kissing each other, caressing the bulge and expecting to be overrun with euphoria when the little precious finally came into their lives.

What a picture-perfect image!

Ryatt didn't give two shits though. If he couldn't provide happiness to his mom, then no one should be happy. He wasn't born to see others live fulfilling lives while his own deluged in hobo piss and goddamn ramen.

Ryatt said, "Give us the code, and I'll let you go."

"You... You are lying." The man wept.

Ryatt looked at the pathetic thing kneeling in front of him. Did people really love their lives so much? They would cry rivers to just live, meaning they had a lot to lose. A lot that gave them a reason to look forward to the next day. Ryatt couldn't relate.

"No, I ain't lying. So best believe when I say." Ryatt lifted the gun and thumbed the hammer back. "You got two seconds to answer me."

The guard put down his head and lifted his hands to protect his face. As if bones and muscle tissue would deflect the cold bullets. Ryatt's finger wrapped around the trigger.

Then the Whitey iterated. "Four, nine, seven, zero, five, three."

* * *

During the whole getaway, Thomas didn't stop giving Ryatt shit. "You killed an innocent old feller. We don't kill innocents."

Half naked, Ryatt sucked on his lollipop and looked out the window, not paying attention to the bitching.

Because fuck *innocents*.

Iris's husband had been beaten to death in front of her eyes while she was pregnant, and her shop raided, in that bloody riot. Which could have been easily prevented had the *innocents* showed some balls. There were literally hundreds of people for each rioter. Forget hundreds, if just three people had stood up against one criminal, that massacre could have been prevented. But they didn't. Instead they ran out of their neighborhoods, tails tucked between their legs. They ignored the evil happening right in front of their eyes.

Due to the inaction of these so-called innocent people, Ryatt's dad was murdered and his shop, their livelihood, was looted. Iris was forced to borrow money from a loan shark, and everything went to shit. Ryatt became a criminal to escape that life. The *innocents*, Ryatt just hated their guts and couldn't care less about spilling them on the streets.

The car stopped inside their hangout. Leo said he would later drive it far away and light it up. A few kids were getting high inside, but the place was otherwise empty. It generally was during daytime. The trio climbed down and Thomas shooed the junkies away.

Leo handed the cash bag to Ryatt. As he drew open the zipper, he thought that the key out of this miserable life was rather heavy.

Ryatt opened it and glanced at his friends. Wetting his lips, Thomas nodded and Leo twitched his neck. Ryatt upended the bag.

Wads of Benjamins and other lesser denominations fell in lumps.

Leo clucked and started doing a funky chicken dance around the mound. Thomas grabbed his temples and dropped onto his ass; a disbelieving chuckle escaped his mouth. Apparently, large volumes of cash cured guilt.

Ryatt wouldn't know because he did not feel a sliver of such feelings.

Chapter 8

December 17, 1981. 10:41 P.M.

More than four months had passed since the bridge, but every time Ryatt's eyelids rested, he saw the security guard's head mottled with red blots, the sunlight swallowed by his dilated pupils, his mouth contorted in disbelief. The vile memory murdered Ryatt's sleep.

Not that he worried about it. And he reckoned the image burned into his retina would soon dissipate. It should eventually go, right, when Ryatt replaced it with new images and fresher vile memories? His mind would then get used to the macabre and say 'meh' after a few times.

Now the security guard's dead face was supplanted by disco lights that flashed around him, accentuating the graffiti on the wall. Two Aux cables ran from the Delco cassette player in their ride's dashboard, to a pair of towering speakers that played Michael Jackson's Beat It.

The threesome chilled on their new Cadillac Eldorado, with its top down. Ryatt lay on the backseat. Thomas and Leo had chipped in and bought the car from their share. Ryatt, being the responsible son that he was, did not squander the money on anything fancy.

He did spend a little on an extravagant birthday cake. With candles, festoons, balloons, the whole set-up. It was the best birthday party, maybe because it was the first one he'd ever had. Not only did he buy himself some new clothes and sneakers, he also bought his mom dresses and jewelry. Robbing was the best decision Ryatt had taken in his life. If something made you feel *this* good, then it couldn't be wrong, could it?

Out of the $51,900 netted from the van, Lolly took $20,000 and tossed the remainder to Thomas and Leo. They didn't raise any dispute over the uneven split because it was all Lolly, the idea, the plot, and the murder, everything. If it weren't for his radical measures, they would have gotten nothing; so the duo acted grateful for what they received.

One of the toughest things Ryatt had to do following the robbery was lie to his mom. He told himself *not* to hesitate or stutter when tackling her questions, and he had built up a story that he could reiterate even if someone woke him up in the middle of the night and asked him to. The premise of the story went like this: a school in Toronto had offered Ryatt a football scholarship, and they would pay him $2,000 every month if he played for them. On top of giving Ryatt a decent excuse for the money, it also provided him a reason for his absence. Given his new profession, he decided to stay with Leo and Thomas, and visit Iris once a month. Though she was reluctant and heartbroken, they had agreed it was for the best, but for totally different reasons.

Then Iris got the money and, just like Ryatt predicted, made the first call to Bugsy. In total, he'd lent $5,000 and collected an upwards of $20,000 in return. A robbery, she had said, making Ryatt wince. Anyway, she was happy that they didn't have to deal with Bugsy anymore. Ryatt had planned to move her to a new place next month, then buy the household items he had been longing to own.

Ryatt wanted to pay Bugsy in installments, so as not to bring attention to themselves. If Iris had settled the whole amount at once, a street-savvy fucker like Bugsy would know something didn't add up. A little imagination, a few tips from the underworld grapevines, and Bugsy would have made the connection between the robbery and Iris's sudden riches. In fact, many kids in their hangout idolized Badger and Buddha because the idiots had bragged about the robbery to other YBI members when drunk. But no one knew anything about them except their street names. Till now, Bugsy had no clue that Ryatt was Iris's kid, so everything was as it should be.

Best if Ryatt stayed mysterious, though he was becoming increasingly infamous in their little part of town. The robbery had been a sensation for some time, and *Lolly* would be remiss if he didn't enjoy the notoriety. But unlike Leo and Thomas, he didn't allow beginner's success to get to his head. Ambushing a cash van was nothing compared to his ambitions for the future, so he did what he had to do in order to exploit his full potential.

He trained his body and mind.

Ryatt's thumb, forefinger, palm, and wrist ached almost always because he practiced his draw and precision five hours a day, for more than three months. He did okay, but he was far from becoming the most proficient shooter that he aimed to be.

If Ryatt kept training, he would achieve speed and accuracy, better than that of any gun-toting individual on the planet. As the fastest and the sharpest gunslinger he would literally be the one guy in the entire world no one fucked with. Each and every person would kneel and yield, but only after seeing Ryatt's determination to kill.

And that's what Ryatt would do. Flaunt his skills—shoot first, intimidate everyone in the vicinity with shock and terror, then watch them turn into putty in his hands. Hadn't Ryatt got what he wanted only after killing someone, having wasted so much time appealing to the better senses of man? Ryatt had decided it wouldn't be like that anymore. It would be fast, effective, and streamlined. For his method to work, the targets must be incapacitated within seconds, either by bullets or fear. So 'fast draw', as the gun magazines named it, was the most important skill he could master.

Ryatt put the tip of his thumb in his mouth and nibbled on the skin. It didn't exactly callus but slightly hardened. Maybe Ryatt should switch to pistols soon and forsake his SW Model 63 22LR.

While Leo and Thomas had been partying, chilling, and fucking, Ryatt was dreaming. Ryatt didn't smoke, drink, or even have a girlfriend. He was a teetotaler. His only pleasure came from robbing, the guarantee that he and his mom would never suffer again.

That's what he was thinking about now. The trio needed to graduate in order to make a proper income. Twenty grand was a lot for many, but for someone who didn't have anything at all, from a small TV to a big house with a pool and beautiful garden in the back, twenty grand was a pittance and grossly insufficient.

As Ryatt thought about their next hit, the music stopped, and a minor ruckus ensued. Ryatt rolled his eyes. Probably more small-timers trying to measure their dick sizes by kicking each other's face in.

But when Ryatt sat up and looked over the windshield, he found that was not the case.

An Alfa Romeo had rolled onto the floor, parting the crowd. The car's passenger was young, probably in his early thirties, but demanded supreme respect from the mafias, both Italian and Black. He was the untouchable Thomas talked about the other day.

"Mr. Hat," Thomas said, his voice grave.

Ryatt didn't need to be told who that was. Only one person he knew of travelled in that not-very-inconspicuous Cosa Nostra vehicle. An insufferable sense of dread wrapped around his heart the moment he saw it. The same car that had dragged his mom away that evening, leaving the parasites to fester upon his eyesight, slowly turning him blind.

Bugsy didn't pay attention to the fact the car had come to a stop because he was sitting in the back, two girls smooching him from both sides. They eventually licked their way down his chest and their heads disappeared under the window.

The front doors flew open and two white guys alighted. One was slim and tattooed. He wore a tank top, which for some reason, they called a wife beater; the other had on a shiny purple shirt, a gold chain, white-blond hair, and thick eyebrows; his body shook like a Jell-O blob as he waddled. Must be stuffing in pounds of cheesecakes but avoiding the gym like a plague.

Wifebeater was clearly a street soldier but Cheesecake was from the upper echelons.

Ryatt had been waiting for a chance like this to hit Bugsy; he cast a look at Thomas who gave a subtle shake of the head. Goddamn it, he was correct. Bugsy, before driving into a black hangout, would have intimated the leaders in this part of the city. Maybe paid them, too. If something happened to Bugsy, right then and there, the whole gang of black hoods would descend on them. They wouldn't like to hurt one of their own, but it's how it worked. Mutual respect, they said.

There was also a possibility that the Alfa Romeo could be bulletproofed. Ryatt's pathetic .22 would hardly make a scratch, and by the time Ryatt shot enough rounds to penetrate it, Bugsy would have climbed to the front and driven away.

As hard a fact as it was to digest, it was not the right time. Ryatt pulled a lollipop from his pocket and sucked on it.

That obsequious runt, Congo, jogged toward Cheesecake, his shoulders slouched in subservience. He whispered something to Cheesecake, and they turned towards their Caddy.

Ryatt's fingertip brushed against the gun at his hip. He might not have the fastest draw in the world, but in the last three months, he'd shot thousands of rounds in target practice. Spending time and dough to learn this requisite ability was a lifetime investment. No criminal that Ryatt knew exercised this skill. So he didn't fear gangsters, because by the time they fumbled with their guns, cocked it, and took aim, Ryatt would have emptied his cylinder and made every bullet count.

As the Italians made their way towards them, Congo shouted, "Party's over."

Almost all the YBI vacated the space, and Congo had to intimidate a few drunk hecklers into leaving. The congregation waited until the floor was empty; then Congo addressed Thomas, "Buddha. You know who these gentlemen are, right?"

"Sure." Thomas got down from the car. So did the other two.

Wifebeater smirked at Ryatt. "Are you sucking on a lollipop?" Then he spotted the holster on Ryatt's hip and burst out laughing. "What the fuck is that? You kids playing cowboys and Indians?"

Someone giggled. Not Congo or Cheesecake or even Bugsy. It was Leo. Thomas gave him a look, ordering him to put his fucking ticks on a leash.

Leo knew why Ryatt wore the holster. He was the person Ryatt really opened up to about life, about his mom, about guns, though Ryatt always wondered if the psychopath ever felt the same brotherhood.

"You think I'm funny?" Wifebeater asked Leo, who, not breaking his character, giggled again.

"Cut it out," Thomas warned but Leo didn't pay attention to him.

Wifebeater looked Leo up and down as his eyes shrank. Seemed like he couldn't figure out if the tiny black boy was alright in the head.

Wifebeater turned his attention back to Ryatt.

"Seriously, kid. You watch too many Westerns. Do you always show off your little gun like that?"

Nope. Ryatt only carried his gun to places where it was absolutely necessary. Like here at the hangout, or if he went to rob. Not always. Only gangsters needed to do that, as they never knew from where and when an enemy might jump out on them.

Wifebeater was still going at it, preaching. Ryatt was tempted to yawn.

"... I mean what kind of a criminal carries a gun in a fucking holster?"

Um... the smart kind?

Because it was a thousand times faster to draw a weapon from the holster than to scrabble at the insides of your jacket. Or if the situation demanded, shoot it from the hip. Fast draw was so effective that they taught it in the military. But Ryatt didn't wish to share his wisdom with a shallow-minded two-bit gangster like Wifebeater. So he kept quiet. Maybe a perfect moment would present itself for Ryatt to display his skill, prove its necessity, and earn their respect.

"I'm talking to you." Wifebeater produced a silver-plated pistol from behind him. "Answer me, you bastard."

And there it was. The perfect moment.

Ryatt drew his *little* gun and shot the pistol out of Wifebeater's hand.

Along with his thumb.

Less than half a second, Ryatt timed and shifted the candy in his mouth. Not bad, but he had a long, long way to go to become the best. Some legendary gunslingers clocked at less than a tenth of a second. To shoot two targets.

No one finished processing what their eyes had just seen. Everyone froze, except Leo who sprinted towards Wifebeater's pistol on the floor and retrieved it. However, Thomas and their guests were dumbstruck. Even Bugsy stopped and looked up.

Wifebeater doubled over and clutched his hand, screaming at the top of his lungs and mixing profanities in-between.

"I apologize," Cheesecake spoke in a thick Italian accent. "My associate has very bad manners."

"*You* apologize?" the boorish man with a missing digit yelled. "That runt shot me! That dirty—"

"Shut the hell up!" Cheesecake ordered. "That potty mouth of yours has already cost you a finger. You sure you wanna run it again and bust a ball? Just… just go to the car and wait, will you?"

Having been lessoned in humility, Wifebeater walked away, but not before giving Ryatt the stare.

Cheesecake walked closer to them, extending his arm. "I'm Roman."

"I'm American," Ryatt said but didn't offer his hand in return, which still had the gun in it.

Roman eyed the revolver and lifted his hand. "No need for violence. What I meant was, my name is Roman. Weird, uh?" He let out a laugh, which had no substance to it.

"I agree," Thomas tried to sound cool but bit his tongue and said, "I mean, uh… the violence part. Not the weird-name part."

Roman didn't acknowledge Thomas. Instead of responding, he regarded the bloody mangled finger on the floor.

Leo watched Roman's discomfort and giggled again, with a lot of throat. This time it was Ryatt who looked at him and shook his head. Leo covered his snicker and nodded.

"That's impressive and ferocious." Roman turned and gave Bugsy a wave-off, signaling him everything was fine. The boss once again leaned back on his seat and closed his eyes, while red and blond heads went back to work.

Congo said, "I told you, Mr. Rome. These boys ain't nothing but trouble. With the capital T. No respect, no rules, and no control. Another bunch of Mad Dogs in the making if you ask me."

"I didn't."

"Huh? What?" Congo looked confusedly at Roman.

"I didn't ask for your opinion," Roman said, then fixed Ryatt with an intense stare. "I've heard about you guys, and you three have the exact wild streak we've been shopping for."

"Is that right?" Ryatt asked.

"Uh-huh." Roman nodded. "I need a job done, so who do I talk to?"

Leo said, "That would be Mr. Lolly."

Roman eyed the white straw poking out of Ryatt's mouth. "And I bet you're him."

Ryatt shrugged.

"Straight to business." Roman clapped and rubbed his pudgy hands. "You heard of MacSharp?"

"Yeah. The new weapons factory in Livernois Avenue?"

"That's the one."

"What about it?"

"You know what are some of the most lucrative robberies? Booze distillers, chemical manufacturers, and automobile factories. But nothing beats the good old guns and bullets."

Ryatt, in spite of knowing that it was not very respectful, laughed. "Man, you nuts or something? How we gonna hit a weapons factory? Don't they have like a private army protecting them?"

"Not the factory. You're hitting their truck."

Ryatt frowned as cogs in various parts of his brain projected different scenarios. The foremost question it raised was, "What do you need us for?"

"Heard you are the best of the best when it comes to truck jobs. We need your expertise."

That was far from the truth because Ryatt's mind had spat the answer. Their *expertise* wasn't what the Detroit Alliance needed. It was their expendability.

Shaking his head, Ryatt holstered his gun. "We did one job and that's that. So our *expertise* can't be the only reason."

"Alright, you got me, Mr. Lolly." Roman sighed and lifted his hands. "The truth is, all our guys are known to the cops. We need someone new."

Wrong again. Roman was a good actor. He pretended to give credibility to 'Mr. Lolly' trying to feed Ryatt's ego. He wanted Ryatt to believe he was both smart and needed. The *real* truth was, they needed Ryatt because he was disposable. No one gave a shit about three poor black kids who'd gone missing. That thought angered him.

However Ryatt decided he would play this game along, hoping to manipulate it to his advantage.

"Okay. Count me in. But what about the recon?" Ryatt acted all innocent, but he knew how Italians operated. There must be a snitch working undercover in the factory.

"We have a routine to infiltrate businesses like these," Roman answered, confirming Ryatt's suspicion. "Our guy has burrowed himself deep in the logistics side of MacSharp." Roman's eyes beamed. "We have a date and route."

Ryatt matched the excitement in Roman's eyes. "All we need to do now is just hijack the truck?"

"You got it." Roman dared to reach out and grab hold of Ryatt's shoulder. "And when you do, you will be well rewarded." A warm smile stretched Roman's lips.

Ryatt mirrored the dubious expression and crushed the candy with his teeth. "Then we're in business."

Chapter 9

December 24, 1981. 11:11. P.M.

Ryatt stood near the opening of a dead-end alley, safely tucked away from streetlights. Roman had dropped them off two minutes ago and given them masks. Bugsy's gift, apparently.

Ryatt had received a green zombie design, a prosthetic wear big enough to cover his head and neck. Only thirty seconds had passed since he wore the mask but he disliked it already. It was stuffy, the breathing holes were disproportionate, and the most irritating thing was the rank of rubber, which was not doing wonders for Ryatt's upper intestines; the acid and half-digested mash of the dinner he ate earlier was pushing up his esophagus. If some improvisation wasn't done, history would repeat itself.

Fuck it. Ryatt removed the mask and inserted his hand into the opening. Grabbing hold of the lips from inside, he bit the soft rubber.

"Goddamn heathens." A woman's voice filled the alley.

Ryatt stopped his work dand turned back. No one. *Where did—*

Then he looked up. An old woman was observing him with disinterest from her balcony, a cigarette dangling between her fingers.

"That new crack shit," the old woman said. "It's making y'all boys a bunch of looneys."

Ryatt frowned. "What you talking about, Grandma?"

"The hell are you kissing that demon, boy?"

Kissing? What the fu—oh…

Ryatt couldn't help but smile. "I ain't kissing it, Grandma. I'm just putting a hole through it."

"Hole? What for?"

"Because this mask had been too nosey." Ryatt pulled his gun from the holster and pointed it at the head with ghostly hair. "Now you mind your goddamn business or I will put one through yours."

The old woman's eyes widened, but not as much as Ryatt would have liked. She was mildly anxious at best.

"That cute trinket supposed to scare me? Boy, let me tell you. When I served in the ANC, I was stationed in France during the Battle of Normandy. I treated the most horrible wounds. Wounds from tanks, bombshells, and .50s. Your little toy ain't shit."

"American Nurse Corp?" Ryatt put the *toy* back in, blushing. He wasn't gonna shoot her anyway. Thought he would scare her away, but apparently, she had survived tougher terrains. He could relate. You didn't threaten someone like that; you either killed them or moved on.

"You know what ANC is?" the old woman asked.

"I used to read a lot, ma'am."

"You can put alphabets together?"

"The best in school, in a different life."

"In a different life, he says," she scoffed. "You must be what? Fifteen? You don't have a different life, boy. You barely have one. Barely half!" She took a drag and spoke, smoke ejecting out in angry puffs. "What a good boy like you doing in an alley like this, fiddling with a mask and a gun?"

"Good question, ma'am." A bout of goosebumps ran across Ryatt's skin, his nostrils prickled, and eyes welled. "But you're asking it to the wrong person. Ask it to the big man above. I've been asking it for as long as I can remember."

"Oh then it's gonna be a long wait, dear." The old woman pinched the smoldering orange with her fingertips, making Ryatt wince. "When I saw what I've seen in the battlefields, I stopped going to church. I mean, what kind of a god lets a mean little man with a funny little mustache tear such a hideous scar in human history?"

"An indifferent god?" Ryatt said.

The old woman chuckled. "You're bright, boy. I hope you know what business you've got yourself into."

"I do, ma'am."

"And the most important question you gotta ask yourself is," the old woman stood straight. "Am I making my momma proud?"

That caught Ryatt's tongue. Before he could contrive an answer, she disappeared into the house, shutting the window.

Ryatt looked down at the disfigured face in his hand. "No," he whispered.

Taking in a huge breath, he tossed the candy into his mouth, wore the mask over it, and inserted the straw through the small nip he had just made on the mask's mouth.

"What's that about?" a voice enquired from the alley across the road.

"Tell you later."

"Okay."

Leo and Ryatt lay in wait on a lonely stretch in Livernois Avenue which was deserted at this time of night. The thirty-mile road used to be 'Avenue of Fashion', inundated with small businesses that sold clothing, shoes, and ornaments. Since the advent of malls, the Avenue began disintegrating, leaving behind empty retail shops as its legacy. By the mid-seventies, it was known as an obscure dark road where bad things often happened.

A high-pitched horn in the distance pierced the chilly night. Ryatt darted a look out of the alley. On his right was a railroad crossing. The bells rang, lights flashed, and the arms lowered.

Ryatt turned left. Their quarry usually drove through Tyler Street and merged with Livernois Avenue at the crossroads, twenty yards from where Ryatt and Leo had holed up.

Shit. The truck was always punctual, but today, of all days, it was late. Roman said valuable merchandise would be transported only once every semester; today was one such occasion. What if MacSharp took extra precautions by sending along a convoy? Ryatt and Leo could try to take them out, but if the timing wasn't right, there was nothing anybody could do.

The train's horn blared when it slowed and passed the crossing. As it choo-chooed away, the vibration reached Ryatt's feet and its rhythmic pounding on the road brought to his mind the hooves of horses.

The truck should turn into Livernois Avenue within the next minute if the plan was to work smoothly.

And it didn't.

Ryatt grabbed the mask; no use in wearing it now.

As he exited the alley, harsh light blinded him momentarily and then bounced off the crossbuck beside him. He looked left, opposite the crossbuck, and found that a pair of headlamps had turned onto the road.

The vehicle was a hybrid of a truck and a van, similar to a cash truck. Except there was no cash inside but costly weapons.

Heart pumping with glee and a sudden gush of blood, he scampered back into the alley and donned the mask once again.

With a glance, he could see that the last compartment of the train had crossed and the metal wheels rolled along into blackness. A deafening silence filled the atmosphere.

Shit, shit, shit.

Ryatt pressed his back against the damp wall. Once the truck passed him, it slowed for the speed bump ahead at the level crossing. Ryatt crouched and jogged towards it. But Leo, being the rabid dog that he was, took off before it passed him. The driver spotted a masked kid running towards the truck, and his mind worked at lightning speed. He swerved left and slammed Leo. The metal body swiped him square in the face, knocking him out cold. Ryatt yelped when the rear wheel missed Leo's tiny noggin by inches.

The bells and lights were switched off at the crossing, and the steel poles slowly ascended.

Fuck it.

Ryatt stood straight and broke into a sprint. And the truck accelerated before the gates were even halfway up. The driver must have seen Ryatt, another kid wearing a mask, in the side mirror.

The arms lifted just enough and the truck wedged itself into that space; its top scraped against the metal and sparks flew. In a matter of seconds, Ryatt reached the truck; at the same time, it also freed itself and gained speed.

Now or never.

Ryatt dived and grabbed the safety screen on the passenger side door. One of his feet landed on the running board, while the other missed it, dragging on the road below. Ryatt quickly pulled himself up and latched onto the truck. But he almost let go when he looked inside. The security guard had just removed a pistol from his holster. Luckily, when the guard tried to take aim at Ryatt from his confined space, the side panels didn't permit it. So he shifted the gun to his left.

Too late.

Ryatt already shot three bullets into the window. The first one punctured the glass, got deflected, and lodged itself in the top board. It was in no way wasted because the second and third passed through the crater the first had created, and hence did not ricochet. They pierced the man's temple and neck, and his chin slouched onto his chest. The meatbag was fastened to the upholstery by the seat belt, giving Ryatt an unhinged view of the pale driver, who on seeing Ryatt screamed, "Oh my god! You killed Ben."

Duh.

"Pull over," Ryatt shouted. "I will kill you too if you don't."

"You little…" The driver tried to shake Ryatt off by zigzagging on the road, tires screeching. The oncoming traffic staggered, some careened over into the ditch.

"Goddamn it." Now they would call the pigs. Ryatt put the gun back in its holster and grabbed the safety screen atop the windshield.

The driver was swerving left to right and vice versa, as vigorously as he could. Ryatt put a foot over the hood and, heaving himself across, pulled himself over it. Now that he was in the front, the driver scrunched and hid his head between his knees. In that position, it was impossible to operate the steering wheel. The truck climbed the curb and hit an alley, bursting open an innocent dumpster loafing there, yawning.

Ryatt was catapulted and landed on the garbage the dumpster had puked. Not wasting time inspecting himself, he sprang up to his feet and pointed the gun at the window.

The driver raised his arms. "Please—"

"Out," Ryatt ordered.

Having exhausted all his options, the driver obeyed. Arms up in the air, he got down and looked around the mess. Apart from the reek strewn about, the dumpster had also squirted old grease in a wide arc.

What a mess!

Though Ryatt wasn't hurt, he felt agitated. Iris, Leo, and Thomas were all Ryatt had. What if the truck wheel ran over Leo's small head? The head Ryatt slapped and rubbed so many times? It would have been burst open, the brain spilling—

No. He wouldn't allow himself to think anymore. An uncontrollable anger burned inside his stomach.

Ryatt stared at the driver, his vision smudgy. The driver must have sensed the hatred because he put his arms down, turned around, and sprinted.

Poor asshole never had a chance.

Ryatt got off the remaining shots. Three bullets were buried in the back of the driver's head, millimeters apart from each other. The driver half lurched, half stumbled, then face-planted. His arms hung loosely on his sides as he slid across the greasy tarmac.

Ryatt got in the truck, reversed from the alley, and drove towards the level crossing. The dead man blobbing on Ryatt's side had no exit wound. If it weren't for the unbridled way his head bounced, he would easily pass for a sleeping guy.

"Your friend shouldn't have hit Leo." Ryatt leaned across, pulled the door handle, and unlatched the seatbelt. "If he hadn't, he would be alive now. Not dead on the roadside." Ryatt could push the man out with his hand but he was raging inside, so he lifted his leg from the accelerator and placed it on the man's arm. "Like you."

He then kicked the dead body, twisting his hip in the process, and the truck jerked. Ryatt put his foot back on the pedal and got the truck back under control. In the side mirror, he saw the limp body rolling twice before coming to a halt, sprawled out in the middle of the road.

The door hung open. To shut it close, Ryatt swerved the truck violently, not caring about the 18-wheeler on the other side. It honked in panic and they both avoided a collision by microseconds. Ryatt, having blown the steam off, smiled and sighed.

Then he heard the sirens.

Oh shit!

He floored it and within a mile, the railroad crossing came into view. Ryatt had to pinch himself to believe it. Had he been only a minute away? When he was hanging from the truck, it felt like they were driving forever. Must be the adrenaline distorting the sense of time.

Leo was squatting on the sidewalk, still wearing his red demon mask. The truck stopped beside him and Leo climbed in, saying, "I knew you wouldn't need me to finish the job."

Ryatt shook his head. "Not true. I had to do double the work."

"And double the acrobatics." Leo cackled.

Ryatt gave out a dry laugh and rubbed Leo's head, over the mask.

They drove to a predestined road two and a half miles away from the hotspot. A semi-trailer was parked at the curb, carrying a 40-foot container. Seeing Ryatt, its back was opened up and a ramp was placed on it. A big old monster lolling its tongue out.

Ryatt drove straight into the mouth and Thomas quickly shuttered the backdoor. As Leo and Ryatt finally removed their masks, the semi moved and, minutes later, climbed the old highway of I-96, locally known as Jeffries Freeway.

Leo opened the door and slipped on the wet blood on the running boards. He lifted his foot up, saw the red smear under the sole, and cackled.

"You gonna open it up?" Ryatt asked.

Leo nodded and switched on a generator at the corner. Then he tugged a jackhammer connected to it and went to work on the weapons truck.

The battering noise was too much for Ryatt, nauseating him. He used the internal door that connected the trailer to the driver's cabin.

Thomas's fingers clasping the steering wheel were visibly tight.

"What's up with you?" Ryatt slapped Thomas's stiff shoulder and sat on the passenger seat.

Thomas took one hand off the wheel, and his trembling finger pointed outside the window.

The side mirror showed an army of police cruisers racing through the traffic. Ryatt shook his head and tsk-tsked. "Have some faith, will you?"

Ryatt nodded at the first cruiser that overtook their semi and kept on driving. In the next few moments, half a dozen police vehicles whizzed past them, none of which gave the semi a second glance.

Chapter 10

December 25, 1981. 12:04 A.M.

Thomas reversed the semi into a building not unlike their hangout. Rubble was strewn across the floor, and graffiti adorned the walls. No one occupied it, except a few hobos whom Leo chased away, running towards them wearing a red demon mask and shooting at the sky, cackling as they stumbled over each other and screeched in horror to save their meaningless existence.

Leo had breached open the truck with the jackhammer, and they found caches of weapons inside. Ryatt hadn't been happier on Christmas mornings. He spent quite some time with the contents, until he remembered they had work to do.

He sauntered to the Caddy they had stashed in a corner and opened the door.

Twenty minutes later, Ryatt entered Oak Park and rolled the car to a stop in front of a payphone booth on Parklawn Street. He fished out a ten-cent coin, fed it into the slot, and dialed.

The call was answered on the second ring.

"It's done."

Silence.

"Hello?"

Roman said, "Drop the trailer at the boathouse like we've planned. My guys are waiting there."

"Change of plans," Ryatt said.

"What change?" Roman asked. Ryatt could practically see those bushy brows suffocating the bridge of his nose.

"I want to meet Mr. Hat."

"What? Why?"

"I… the other day, I shot your guy's finger off. Now I understand how stupid it was of me to do that."

"All's forgiven."

"Yeah, no, pardon my skepticism but I find it hard to believe. There ain't no guarantee you'll let me leave the boathouse vertically."

Roman laughed in a condescending tone. "Nothing like that will happen. Come on down."

"You can't expect me to just believe your word and hand over the truck."

Roman took a breath and sighed. "What do you want then?"

"To meet Mr. Hat," Ryatt said, making it sound like he respected Bugsy a lot and he wanted to be in Detroit Alliance's good graces.

"Alright. Fine, take note," Roman iterated the address to Bugsy's mansion. Ryatt smirked, not jotting it down; he was already on its street corner.

Thirty minutes later, Ryatt stopped the Caddy at the front gate and pressed the intercom to announce his presence.

Roman came outside and got in the backseat. "Nice ride. Yours?"

"Ours."

The mansion was at least 20,000 square feet with a pool and tennis court. Was this the same person who had harassed a poor blind woman for unpaid interests on $5,000?

Roman directed Ryatt to a garage, where the Alfa Romeo was parked.

They both got down and walked to the front door.

"Where are your friends?" Roman asked.

"With the truck."

"And where is the truck?"

"Here."

"Here?"

"An hour later, it's here, if you do everything like I… um… request you to do."

Roman pointedly looked down at Ryatt's holster. In a blink of an eye, Ryatt swiped the gun out. Roman's laid-back brain was late by a second when it decided to react. Eyes bulging, he fumbled to reach his back. All this time, Ryatt could have killed him ten times over if he had wanted to.

Ryatt shook his head. "No, Mr. Roman." He grabbed Roman's doughy wrist and placed the revolver on his palm. "I'm handing you my gun. I understand you can't let me carry it when I meet Mr. Hat."

Roman held his chest and let out a chortle. "You cheeky little fuck." He jabbed Ryatt on the arm playfully. "You almost gave me a heart attack."

Roman pocketed the SW. "Put your arms out on your sides."

Ryatt did, and he was given a complete pat down.

"Satisfied?"

"Uh-huh." Roman nodded. Then he took out a key and worked on the door lock like a burglar. His behavior piqued Ryatt's interest, he seemed too fastidious as he inserted the key into the doorknob and turned it. Like it would jump and rip his face if he moved any faster.

Fascinated, Ryatt took a closer look. The lock had a slim slit for a keyhole like other locks, but unlike them, it had a hollow above the slit.

"What's that hole?" Ryatt asked.

"If someone tries to tamper with the door without a key…" Roman slowly pushed it open and beckoned Ryatt to step in. On the other side of the doorknob was a sizable revolver, attached to some peculiar homemade contraption. The hollow facing outside was its muzzle.

"Boom." Roman laughed. "Every door to the property has one."

"Why don't you fix it two feet higher and kill the intruder altogether?"

"Nah, it doesn't work like that. We know because we've tried. It depends on the asshole's height. If he is too tall, the bullet hits his shoulder and he runs away. Too short, and it completely misses him."

"So the midsection: it presents a wider target than the head, hence lesser probability of failure."

"Correct. Also, we don't want to kill him. Not that quickly anyway."

"You have to 'interrogate' the poor fuck," Ryatt said. "Then publicly make an example out of him, to deter other potential hitmen."

Roman smiled, which didn't reach his eyes. So they *had* interrogated people here, maybe in the basement. Drilling the eyeball or nail-gunning testicles to a chair? Ryatt had heard stories about Bugsy. None of them portrayed him as merciful.

Roman led Ryatt inside through a lengthy hallway. A tall Christmas tree was perched in front of the largest TV Ryatt had ever seen. An indoor fountain gurgled water; its drizzle carried pleasant coolness and not so pleasant chlorine. Bronze statues of men with ancient weapons stood guard around the walls.

"Enough staring." Roman waved his arm towards a flight of stairs at the far side of the living room.

Ryatt climbed the steps, and when he reached the landing, Roman said, "Take a left."

Ryatt did and came across another series of bronze statues flanking the corridor, this time not of medieval warriors. They were of Kamasutra postures.

"Nice, uh?" Roman winked.

No. Bugsy was a sex fiend. The fact angered Ryatt when he thought about this filthy animal abducting his mom.

Roman opened a mammoth teak door to the right, and in they went.

Bugsy sat at a mahogany desk, and two chairs were placed across from him. Numerous framed photographs hung on the walls: Bugsy fishing, hiking, running, swimming, kayaking.

In most of the photos, he wore his ridiculous hat that drooped to the side of his face. A fucking Al-Capone-wannabe.

On a showcase behind Bugsy, a phonograph played some opera music; it was that soprano shit where women sang high-pitch numbers and broke glasses.

Roman sat in one of the chairs but neither offered a seat to Ryatt.

"So, kid, why you wanted to see me?" Bugsy took out a cigar from a green velvet box on the table. "Just leave the truck to us, get paid, and crawl back to your hole, eh?"

"There's no guarantee you'll let us live after we give you the truck."

"What the fuck are you babbling about?" Bugsy snipped the cigar's tip and lit it with a match. His words distorted as he spoke with the cigar in his mouth. "We ain't gonna whack you. You'd already be fish food if we wanted to."

"I'm sorry, Mr. Hat, but I can't take that risk. I can't bring it here."

"So we pay now and expect you to give us a call with the location of the truck?"

"That's not—"

"We tread with little to no trust when we do business with negroes." Bugsy glimpsed at Roman who laughed and slapped his left knee.

"I know you can't pay upfront." Ryatt swallowed and tried to wet his mouth that had suddenly become dry. It was no time for indignation. "How about you and Mr. Roman come with me?"

"What if you take us to a quiet street and rob us? I mean, we'll hunt you down and skin you alive after, but you get the idea."

"If we were stupid enough to steal from you, we would have crossed into Canada by now, along with the truck. Why am I here, unarmed, talking to you?"

"I don't know, you tell me."

Ryatt let out an exasperated breath. "Know what? You take me to any other place except the boathouse, but it should be on neither of our turfs. A no man's land where you can't hurt me and I can't hurt you."

"Boy, you can't hurt me anywhere."

"Yes, sir, I know. I completely agree." Ryatt placed a hand over his heart. "I was just trying to make a point. When we reach the neutral territory, I'll ask one of my team members to drive the truck there."

Bugsy studied Ryatt with eyes that were just a pair of slits.

Ryatt continued, "Don't even have to bring the cash with you. Come and check your stuff. If you're satisfied, call one of your guys and tell him to deliver the money to my other team member, who will be in a totally different location. In fact they will go wherever you tell them to. Your choice."

Bugsy looked at Roman. "You smell a trap?"

"We don't have enmity with the blacks, so it makes no sense for them to instigate a war they know they can't win." Roman shrugged. "Plus we ain't taking the money with us. And he agrees to bring the truck anywhere we tell him to; he is riding around with us all the while. If this is a trap, it's pretty shitty."

"I wanna do business with you, Mr. Hat." Ryatt leaned on the smooth shiny wood with his arms. "I swear, this ain't no trap."

"Take your damn mitts off my table."

Ryatt did and stepped back, hands up in the air.

Bugsy regarded Ryatt, the black beads scrutinizing his blue ones. "Fuck it. Let's go."

They exited the same way they got in and walked to the Alfa Romeo. But not thanks to fate, it had a flat.

"We can use my car," Ryatt offered.

Roman sat in the passenger seat while Bugsy commandeered the entire back row.

For the first few minutes, Roman and Bugsy discussed where to transact business. They still wandered around in Bugsy's turf.

Ryatt said, "Rome?" He was more than aware that this was the first time he addressed Roman by his first name, something that would surely rub him up the wrong way.

"Rome?" Roman stopped his chatter with Bugsy and stared at Ryatt. "What happened to Mr. Roman—"

Ryatt's arm sprang out; a tight slap from the back of his right hand impeded Roman's words, his paws shooting up to tend to his face.

"What the—" Bugsy lurched from the backseat but froze midway. His face slowly drained all anger and became pale as all the movements in his body stopped.

Roman lifted his fist to punch Ryatt, who calmly said, "Ask your boss if it's really a good idea to do that."

Temples twisting in fury, Roman looked back. "Mr. Hat?"

Bugsy replied with a subtle shake of the head.

"If you so much as breathe fast, see how close my hand is to the horn." Ryatt's palm hovered over the center of the steering wheel for a moment before receding back to its circumference. "I'll honk thrice."

Roman's features displayed a kaleidoscope of confusion. "You'll *honk*?"

"That's the signal for him to pull the trigger."

Roman looked even more flustered than before. "Him? Whose *him*?"

Bugsy finally broke out of his trance and answered, "I have a gun pressing against my spinal cord. And it's mighty fucking big." His voice failed him at the last word.

Roman's face slowly showed recognition. "That little psycho bastard is with us, isn't he?"

Ryatt couldn't help giggling. And Leo, from inside the trunk, cackled in return. "Yup. We cut out the backboard and put it together in a way that it's easy to remove from the trunk."

Roman shook his head. "You unbelievable punks."

"Whatever." Ryatt smirked. "Throw your gun out and hand me my baby back. I miss her." Ryatt pressed a button on his side and Roman's window rolled down. "Did you see that?!" His voice betrayed excitement. "I can lower your glass from here. Also look at the speedometer. It's digital! Everything's digital! What a time to live in!"

Roman didn't move.

Ryatt let go of the wheel and traced the horn with a finger.

"Do it, goddamn it," Bugsy barked.

Roman pulled out his gun and chucked it out the window. Then he returned Ryatt's revolver to him.

Ryatt roamed around the city, making sure no one followed them.

For some time, Roman didn't open his mouth. Until he got bored that was. "So that weasel punctured our car?"

"Look who decided to stop pouting." Ryatt rubbed Roman's blond hair, which was oily. "And, yes. We built a small set-up inside the trunk, so *Weasel* let himself out and slashed your tire."

"But why?" Bugsy asked. "Why go through all this trouble?"

"Survival," Ryatt said.

"What?"

Ryatt did not answer.

"What do you mean survival?" Bugsy asked.

Ryatt rolled his eyes. Looked like the asshole would not shut up without an explanation, so he gave him one. "Once we deliver the MacSharp truck to you, you'd kill us three and dump us in Lake Michigan. Following tradition, probably slice open our torsos, so as not to let the gas build up inside and balloon us up to the water's surface. Maybe tie cinder blocks to our feet, just in case. The world would never find our bodies as they're slowly absorbed into the lakebed, eaten by bottom feeders and time."

"Is he for real?" Roman scoffed and turned to his boss.

"We didn't plan to kill you," Bugsy said between his clenched teeth, as if that really was the truth.

A little more frustration in his voice, Ryatt would have believed him. "Then why did you need us to do the job? You have every kind of low life working for you, including robbers."

"Cause like I said, all our guys are known to the cops. We needed fresh meat."

"Then why make us wear full masks? You'd have a better chance at the pigs not suspecting you if the witnesses said it was black kids who robbed the van."

"That's too obvious a diversion, kid. Remember, me and my guys met you at your little recreational club the other day? At least one snitch must have seen it. So when the cops link the robbery to black kids, who do you think the snitches will point their fingers at?"

Ryatt had to admit, he didn't think this deeply.

Bugsy shook his head. "You don't understand all this yet. You're not even shaving, and you're playing at a man's game." From his facial expression, Ryatt could see that Bugsy was trying his best to stop himself from jumping up and throttling him. "We. Did. Not. Plan. To. Kill. You."

"Then you got nothing to worry about. We'll finish the transaction and off you go."

Bugsy bit his lower lip. "Paranoid little shit."

Chapter 11

December 25, 1981. 01:57 A.M

Ryatt parked the Caddy between the MacSharp truck and the semi, all of them around ten meters apart from each other. Thomas jogged to the car, his eyes widening at the sight of their guests. "You gotta be…"

"No, it's happening," Ryatt said.

"You kidnapped the one person you don't wanna fuck with in Detroit? What the hell?!" Thomas grabbed the hair on his sides. Leo cackled but Ryatt's face was stern.

"Not now, Buddha. I ain't ready for your bitching. I literally had a trashy day." Ryatt put his arm out. "Give me the Eagle."

Thomas looked at Bugsy apologetically. Then he ambled to the truck and returned with the gun, which he passed to Ryatt.

Ryatt grabbed it and got down. "Clear."

The trunk lid flew up, and Leo stepped out with a shotgun. He was sweating profusely, his T-shirt smudged with dust and oil.

Finally, Bugsy relaxed and without waiting for instructions, stepped out of the car. So did Roman.

Ryatt had nothing to fear though. The pistol in his hand, 'Desert Eagle' the inscription on it read, was a strong backup. As he tapped its hefty barrel against his palm, he got reminded that this gun was not easy to maneuver like the SW. So he brought down his confidence level a notch. "Desert Eagle is heavy. Almost thrice my gun," Ryatt spoke to Thomas. "Need some training."

"What's a Desert Eagle?" Roman asked.

Funny. Ryatt would have thought that Bugsy and Roman didn't have secrets between them.

"An impressive pistol that's not going to hit the markets for a few years," Bugsy answered.

"A prototype," Thomas said.

"Yes. MacSharp has been stealing designs from Magnum."

"So they can't report the hijacking," Ryatt thought out loud.

"No, they can't. That's the whole point. Listen here, kid," Bugsy said. "Don't make this any worse for yourself than you already have. Give us the weapon crates, get your damn money, and we'll pretend this whole thing never happened."

"What if I wanna?" Ryatt asked.

"What?" Bugsy screwed his face.

"I said what if I wanna make this worse?"

"I don't get—"

In one casual but flickering movement, Ryatt shot Roman.

On his left knee.

The bones splintered open and a bloody mist sprayed back. Ryatt could visualize the kneecap exploding by the velocity of .44. For all intents and purposes, Roman's chunky leg was severed. Such was the raw power of this pistol, Ryatt had learned when he first opened the crates and tested it out. The recoil was the worst, but Ryatt was born for taming guns like this. In fact, he kind of liked the kick. What he didn't like though was the sound. It deafened him for a minute every time he fired the damn pistol. He ought to do something about it.

"Santa Maria…" Roman muttered as his knee buckled under him. He tilted sideways and crashed on the ground like a soaked log.

Bugsy gawked at Roman in horror, then turned to Ryatt, his eyes spewing venom before his mouth did. "What the fuck?!"

As he stepped forward, Leo rammed the butt of the shotgun at the back of his head. Bugsy fell. To make sure he stayed down, Leo repeated the strike. Still Bugsy slowly tried to get up, disoriented.

"I can't smack any harder," Leo whined.

"Not like that you can't," Ryatt said. "Grab the barrel and hold it like a mallet at a game of high striker." Ryatt showed him how by doing it empty-handed. "Then whack him in the head. But be sure there's no round in the chamber."

Leo emptied the gun and lifted it over his head.

"Stop it." Thomas got fidgety. "Please, Lolly."

Leo watched them both like mice peeking out of a hole, unsure.

As Ryatt held his chin and put up a show of pondering, Leo cackled and brought down the stock on Bugsy, who finally went to sleep.

* * *

"What the fuck?" Bugsy asked when he came to and found that he couldn't move. He was fastened to the metal bedding of the semi, wrists and ankles tied to the corners of the container with nylon ropes. The underboss of a

Mafia family sprawled on the floor like an X, butt naked, taught Ryatt an important lesson: never be brash.

"Why?" Bugsy asked. "I told you we ain't planning to kill you."

"You really weren't?" Ryatt scratched his chin.

"No!" Spittle shot out of Bugsy's mouth.

Hm. Maybe they weren't. Ryatt was indeed becoming paranoid. Good. That meant he would take better care of himself and stay vigilant.

Ryatt said, "Don't make no difference." He walked out of Bugsy's field of vision. From a corner, he grabbed a device and dragged it towards Bugsy. As it was heavily grating against the metal floor, their hostage anxiously tried to get a glimpse of it.

Bugsy's eyes almost popped out of their sockets when he saw what Ryatt was tugging. His fingers scrabbled blindly before catching hold of Ryatt's pant leg. "No, no, no, no, no—"

Ryatt yanked it away. "Take your damn mitts off my leg."

He lifted the jackhammer and put the chisel near Bugsy's head, which landed with a loud clank. "Say Hi to Jack."

Bugsy shook like a fish caught in a net, thumping on the floor.

"Badger. Grab the fucker."

Leo cackled and wrestled Bugsy's left arm down. He was comically small compared to Bugsy, but as he put his entire weight on one forearm—pinning it down with his hands and knees—it was highly secure.

"Please, please, please, just listen to me for one second…" Bugsy's desperate words tumbled out like an unrestrained flash flood.

Ryatt hauled the tool and placed it on Bugsy's left shoulder. On its touch, he tried to jerk aside, but to no avail. The rusty tip wedged itself between the sockets, scratching off his white skin and smearing it with dark tar particles from its previous job.

"Oops. Almost forgot." Ryatt took out a lollipop from his jeans and put it in his mouth. "Can't forget this."

Bugsy shouted. "No! Why?!"

Bugsy would never know why this was happening. Just like how Ryatt would never dare to find what exactly Bugsy did to his mom, and if the rumors on the streets had any truth to them.

"Why?" Ryatt smiled while also shedding tears. "The axe forgets; but the tree remembers."

Three pairs of arms and shoulders stiffened in anticipation of Jack's force, when Ryatt took a deep breath and pressed the switch.

Nothing happened.

Ryatt frowned and lifted its cable to check it was connected to the generator. It was.

He asked Thomas, "What's wrong with this piece of sh—"

A whimper interrupted him. Ryatt looked down and found Bugsy crying in a low-pitched voice.

"Pipe down."

But Bugsy didn't. He shook uncontrollably.

"I said shut your fucking yap." Ryatt put his sneaker on Bugsy's mouth and shushed the sniveling pig, then he looked up at Thomas. "Hey. It ain't working?"

"The generator," Thomas said without turning. He was sitting at the entrance, keeping watch. How did he know what the problem was without even looking at anything?

"What about it? Jack's connected to the generator."

"Start the damn thing first, fool."

"Oh," Ryatt felt his cheeks getting hot. "Come in and turn it on, Buddha. We all got our hands full."

Thomas did as he was told, trying his hardest to not look at the threesome.

"What you mad at me for?" Ryatt scratched the back of his head.

Jack slipped from Ryatt's one-handed grip and plummeted towards Bugsy's petrified face. But Ryatt grabbed it at the last moment and apologized. A little damage was however done. The chisel had gouged a patch of Bugsy's skin and it was bleeding. "Sorry. My bad. Totally new to this whole torture thing."

When the generator started, Bugsy said, "Pi—pi fauri—"

"Here we go!" Ryatt pressed the button, and Jack's metal tip drilled into Bugsy's shoulder. He writhed as if he had been electrocuted. The blood spritzing out of the pounded meat, along with the smell of exhaust fumes, merged together and formed a hypnotizing odor. It didn't take Jack more than a minute to pierce through the body and batter the steel floor beneath.

When Ryatt let up, he was exhausted. Though they weren't trying to amputate the limb but just pulverize the bones underneath, operating Jack even for a short while was an exacting task.

"… disembowel you, you cocksucking son of a whore." Bugsy screamed.

Ryatt grinned, having gained a sudden burst of motivation. He told Leo, "The leg."

"Wh— no, no!"

Leo grabbed the leg and Ryatt went to work. As Jack speared its way between Bugsy's hip and femur, his threats slowly turned into driveling beggary.

Jack seamlessly shattered the bones, like they were potato chips. The only complaint Ryatt had with Jack was that its motor was extremely noisy. The ear-splitting sound overlapped the wailing of Bugsy, and Ryatt had to strain hard to even pick out bits and pieces of it.

When Ryatt was done, he stopped the machine and wiped the sweat from his brow.

Leo released Bugsy's thigh, and the leg moved like jelly, independent from the torso.

In spite of his eardrums being numb, Ryatt heard Thomas coughing and heaving. He looked up in time to see his burly friend hurry to a bush, which he eventually decorated with puke. Ryatt didn't feel disgusted because his hatred for Bugsy superseded his revulsion. But what about Leo? He acted cool, just another day in the job. Ryatt didn't know, didn't want to know, what made Leo this strong. Or broken.

"Done?" Leo asked.

Ryatt examined the partially destroyed man on the floor. Bugsy's face didn't yet show the same level of agony Ryatt had seen in Iris's face whenever he visited her. "Nope. Only halfway done."

Bugsy muttered something. Could be English or Italian. It came out as air and thin sprinkles of saliva. But when Jack started the penetration once again, some mysterious entity infused Bugsy with the energy to communicate in the language understood by every human on the planet: the guttural cry.

However, to Ryatt's chagrin, Bugsy made no noise when the duo went to work on the last limb. Bugsy took the pummeling without any resistance whatsoever. Flogging a dead horse. In this case, hammering.

When they finished, Leo looked up and regarded Ryatt's face.

"What you staring at?" Ryatt panted. "You think it's a beautiful moment to declare your love for me?"

"Fuck you, I ain't no homo." Leo cackled.

Ryatt closed his eyes and sniffed. The unmistakable rank of defecation floated in the air. "This asshole shat himself?"

Leo shrugged. "Guess so. Didn't hear it in all this racket."

"Ew, bail." Ryatt let go of Jack's handle, and the 60-pound machine fell atop Bugsy who didn't even react.

As they jumped down and made their way to the exit, Ryatt spotted Roman crawling towards the container.

"Hey Cheesecake!" Ryatt called him. "Now I know what you meant when you said *shitty trap*."

Leo and Ryatt burst out laughing while Roman cried and muttered something. Then he resumed his crawling, his leg brushing along a red streak on his trail.

"Cocksure douchebags," Ryatt said.

"Yeah," Leo agreed.

Outside, Thomas was making divots on the damp earth with his boot, looking pale and nauseous.

"You okay in there?" Ryatt asked.

Thomas gave Ryatt an are-you-kidding-me look. "Detroit's too hot now. Cops and gangsters are both after us."

Ryatt nodded. "We go nomadic."

"How? All we know is our city."

"We don't have to know. Just watch, learn, plan, kill, rob, and jump to the next place." Ryatt pointed his chin at the weapons truck. "We have the means."

"Means?" Thomas frowned.

"Yes." Ryatt pulled the Desert Eagle and caressed its robust barrel. "Let's go find ourselves some profitable ends."

Chapter 12

November 24, 1994. 12:21 P.M.

The aroma of turkey permeated Ryatt's dreams. Nothing beat spending the cold Detroit morning in a Jacuzzi and napping afterwards, then waking up to the delectable smell of lunch. Especially on Thanksgiving.

Ryatt began making his bed. An imaginary price tag at its corner read $7,050. The exclusive mattress, the pillows, the duvet, all came from Duxiana, a company of luxury bed engineers based in Sweden.

He'd bought them with his share of the profits from a bank robbery they'd performed in Minneapolis.

Thanks to Ryatt's regime of reckless violence, precise execution and meticulous planning, they had never failed once. Shoot first, talk later.

At the Minneapolis job, Ryatt, as soon as he burst through the front door, shot a customer waiting in the queue to withdraw money. A bullet to the back of the head splattered his brain across the cashier's window. The terror-stricken cashier was then transformed to putty in Ryatt's hand. Just the way he liked them.

That day they earned $38,000.

Satisfied that he had made the bed without a crease, he shambled to the switchboard and turned off the AC. While he did, the hand-knotted Persian rug caressed his bare feet and tickled between his toes. He stopped and let the hedonistic pleasure travel up. Goosebumps blanketed his legs and hardened his morning wood into steel.

The rug carried a price tag of $2,850 and was bought with the money he had earned from a job in San Francisco. The one where Ryatt had been forced to improvise. When they had bolted in through the entrance, to their dismay, they found the bank to be void of customers. No one to threaten the cashier with.

Quick-witted and wild as ever, Ryatt acted upon the first idea that popped up in his head as a solution. He wedged his bag into the gap and began peppering the cashier's safety window. Each shot cracked the see-through material. The eventual white blots on the "bulletproof" glass enlarged every third second; the cashier jerked involuntarily and could have possibly peed a little every fourth second. Her green eyes widened in horror when they espied that the slugs actually penetrated the glass at last and dropped on the other side. She quickly shut her ears and wailed at Ryatt to stop shooting.

They only netted $10,200 that day, but the laughs Ryatt had, which lasted the 200 miles to Reno, were priceless. The stupid cashier hadn't known that even though the bullets had penetrated the glass, they were as harmless as a foam ball from a Nerf gun. The glass was more "lethal energy absorbing" than "bulletproof". This misnomer had helped Ryatt on more than one occasion.

Ryatt never returned empty-handed from a job. He understood that if you could get inside the head of the cashier successfully, you had practically won the game. He would pick out a cashier who was middle-aged. The young ones tried to be heroes, and old-timers didn't care enough about their lives to feel threatened. It was the people in-between, with various commitments hanging over their heads, who had the most to lose and would hold their lives most dear, at least for the sake of their dependents.

Ryatt dragged his feet along the Persian rug, to a closet on the left, which he had aptly named 'dirty closet'. On the far-right wall stood another closet, a walk-in one he called 'clean closet'. It was three times as spacious as the dirty one. It contained clothes, sneakers, ties, watches, and boots, boasting the costliest price tag in the bedroom: $47,970.

A proud smile escaped his lips. Ryatt had outdone himself.

Ryatt followed just three simple rules for his phenomenal success in his profession:

> *1) Show the cashiers murder, hence proving your shooting skills and determination.*
>
> *2) Get close, even if a glass is separating you both. This intimidated them as no normal person would look at a criminal that closely, especially a bank robber whose pistol had just torn away half the face of some innocent customer.*
>
> *3) Never let them think. Keep doing something that unnerves them. Shout or shoot. As fate would have it,*

On one memorable occasion, a cashier in Staten Island just refused to knuckle under, even after Ryatt had demonstrated his shooting skills and determination. As soon as he dashed through the entrance, he had killed a security guard before the cashier's eyes. He was an old black man with a lot of grit. This was where Ryatt had learned not to try to intimidate the elderly. Anyways, so when nothing worked, when the old man was visibly contemplating pressing the red button under his table, or maybe dropping a dye pack along with the cash, Ryatt stared through the white shattered glass, and warned, "No clowning and no tricks. And I will keep shooting until you give me what I want."

But this time, he hadn't aimed at the cashier's window. He pointed backwards at the gaggle of hostages. Not breaking eye contact with the old man, he shot at random angles. Leo cackled every time a bullet was ejected from the muzzle. As Ryatt squeezed the trigger, the old man's demeanor changed. His half-closed, laid-back, you-don't-shock-a-New-Yorker-with-violence eyes became big and glassy like a fiend high on meth.

On Ryatt's seventh shot, someone in the back screamed. A lady. The old man clasped his hands in front of his chest. Should be a big wound. Good. Some random citizen was hurt, and the resolute cashier would now think it was his fault. His adamance was to be blamed, the people would complain.

Ryatt ejected the mag, pocketed it, and clipped on a new one.

"Round two." Ryatt lifted the gun again.

"No!" the old man finally yielded.

He opened a steel door behind him, and a minute later, handed Ryatt a full bag.

When Ryatt turned to leave the booth, the old man called, "Stop!"

Ryatt did.

"Look around you," the old man said, his voice shaky. "Look at the chaos you've caused."

Ryatt did, curiously. Thomas guarded his post, the front door, wearing his blue demon mask. Leo besieged the hostages. The security guard lay on the floor, missing a quarter of his head and leaking red. A woman crumpled in fetal position and held her torso, blood seeping between her fingers.

The scene really was chaotic. But so what? Wasn't chaos the natural order of how everything ended? The old man needed a lesson in entropy.

"God's watching you," the old man said.

That made Ryatt turn back. Hiding beneath his zombie mask, he stared at the old man. "Is he now, Gramps?"

"You bet," the old man said with so much conviction that Ryatt actually believed it.

"Good. Then I hope that voyeur sees this." Ryatt lifted his gloved hand and pointed a middle finger at the bullet-pocked ceiling.

And that was how he had pulled his biggest robbery to date. $98,000.

In order to live this good a life, Ryatt had done sixteen jobs, killed seventeen people, and robbed around $1,250,000, including his first two robberies in '81.

As he reached above the dirty closet, his Giza cotton shirt lifted over the hem of his underwear. Manicured fingers found a key that he used to open its door.

Displayed on the back wall was his threadbare NBA jersey, at the bottom lay his old shoes that suffered at least a pair of holes each. Literally rags to riches, Ryatt thought.

The Desert Eagle, locked and loaded, and dozens of boxes of .44 rounds rested on the shelf to his left. Under it hung the gun with which he broke into this business. SW model 63 22LR. A special little guy.

On his right was the tool he simply couldn't put a price tag on. Yet it was the most invaluable thing he owned. A jackhammer with blackish brown stains on the tip of its chisel.

Ryatt sat on his haunches, lifted the board on the floor, and recovered a bunch of magazines that had pictures of naked women on top. He understood his mom couldn't see, but he considered it utterly disrespectful to have them lying around.

He selected the one which had two girls, one black and one white, hugging each other erotically, their breasts pressing against each other like water balloons. This would do. With porno in one hand, he picked a rose-flavored lubricant and got up. He hadn't used spit since his teenage years. Why would he have shower sex like a hobo when he lived like a king?

Iris had tried to talk marriage to him, but he'd paid no heed. He didn't think he'd ever felt love. Except the love he had for his mom and his best friends. Maybe he was scared, not willing to pull another woman into his life.

And he didn't dare break the cherry with the help of a prostitute. A hypochondriac like him would never live peacefully after that. However, his partners had dragged him along to a brothel once.

Ryatt, in a room alone with the *service-girl*, begged her to lie to his friends that they did it.

Ryatt and the girl came out from the room. Leo and Thomas both looked at him expectantly, because they knew he had never had sex. It was the argument they had used to coerce him into a brothel in the first place.

"So?" Thomas asked.

"I-it was wonderful," Ryatt said, cursing himself. His friends very well knew he stammered whenever he lied.

Leo looked up at Thomas who shook his head disapprovingly. Leo burst out laughing. And the girl joined them too, massaging Ryatt's tense shoulders. "It's a'ight, lover boy. You good."

So yeah, Ryatt was the most wanted bank robber in the US, but also a twenty-seven-year-old virgin. A fact neither Thomas nor Leo failed to exploit.

Sighing, he took the sex kit to the bathroom, readying himself to waste yet another million sperms into the shower drain.

Chapter 13

November 24, 1994. 01:39 P.M.

Dabbing the towel on his shiny head, Ryatt unlocked the bathroom door and ambled to the clean closet. Leo, who had been losing hair in patches, had gone full bald a few years ago to conceal his condition. So Ryatt began shaving his beloved dreadlocks to support Leo. He had asked Thomas to do the same, but the narcissist was too proud of his looks to even consider it.

Clad in a Gucci button down and jeans, $990 and $2,990 respectively, Ryatt exited his second-floor bedroom and walked down. In the dining room reposed a Brazilian rosewood table, complete with a rotatable marble top and chairs. $18,280. Made illegal before a few years, Ryatt knew he just *had* to get it, no matter the extra cost. It was the table he had imagined to be in his dining room when he was just a poor boy, peering into furniture shop windows.

Sitting down, he looked at the sterling silverware. Each piece of cutlery had 925 inscribed under it, denoting its purity. The whole set was bought from Tiffany. $1,950. The money came from a job done in Baton Rouge.

"Be right there, sweetie," Iris said as she transferred hot gravy to a vessel.

"No hurry, Ma. Need a hand?"

"Yes."

"Sure, Ma," Ryatt said, pushing himself up. "What you want me to do?"

"Finish everything I've cooked for you."

Ryatt, half-standing, chuckled and sat back down. "My favorite kind of work."

"Alright." Iris sat at the head of the table and clasped her hands in front. "Just a moment, please." Her lips mumbled a prayer. She knew Ryatt had an aversion to everything God related so she didn't impose.

Yawning noiselessly, Ryatt looked around. His eye settled on a framed photograph on the far wall in the hall. Iris and he were sitting on the steps of a church in the Vatican. Cross European tour, price tag $20,570.

Beside the photo was a framed certificate that had been presented to his mom by the mayor of Detroit for actively participating in cleaning up the city. The 'Lawrence Fund' jar had ballooned and become 'Lawrence Foundation', as Iris had pumped Ryatt's earnings into it. She reached out to young boys on the streets, rescued them from drugs and gangs, then got them enrolled in schools in other parts of the country where they could do well.

Ryatt pleaded with her to stop wasting the money. And she had, in an uncharacteristic snit, argued with Ryatt.

She had said, "What good is money?"

"Um... you buy houses, cars, good food, comfortable beds." Remembering Iris's wish of getting him married, he played dirty. "And also, girls love a successful man."

"You buy the most luxurious bed, but you *can only* sleep for the maximum of eight hours. You buy a whole farm of wheat, vegetables, and fruits, you *can only* eat what your tummy can hold. And do you really want to be with a person who is impressed by your success, rather than your personality? And even then, you impress one thousand girls with your money, the cars, and designer attire, but you *can only* have coitus for a limited time…"

Ryatt coughed and spluttered the milk he had been drinking.

"… money isn't going to buy you happiness. If money is synonymous with contentment, why do so many rich and famous people kill themselves?"

"I don't know, Ma. It's really hard to earn. If I'd known you were gonna blow off all the dough, I'd have stopped working long ago and lived off what I've saved."

"No son of mine is going to retire young and slack. That's irresponsible. God has given you certain abilities to become successful. Even if you are not going to make use of it for yourself, you owe it to the people down on their luck."

Ryatt had almost rolled his eyes, but stopped as if his mom could see it. He never treated her like a blind person. His heart would never accept it. Poor Iris was better off without the knowledge that it wasn't God that gave Ryatt the abilities he used to become rich. It was his ex-employee downstairs.

"After a certain amount," Iris continued, "money is just a unit in the bank. Meaningless digits. Do you want to spend your life adding zeros behind that digit, just stacking on void after void, paradoxically hoping for fulfillment? Or do you want to make a change?"

Ryatt liked to go with the first option, but he knew better than to tell his mom that.

"But Ma…"

"Will you not listen to your mom?" Iris had said.

She had never asked him this question before. Ryatt felt guilty for talking back. He just loved his mom too much to even have this silly conversation. So what if she wanted to spend it all on children on the verge of becoming criminals? Fine.

"Let's dig in," Iris said, crossing herself.

"Finally." Ryatt regarded the contents on the table. A 16-pound turkey, stuffing both traditional and Cajun, mashed potatoes and gravy, green bean Casserole, ham, cranberries, and of course, pumpkin pie. $45.20. This money came from a job in Chicago they did last week. Just one dead.

Killing people and living a good life from the profits didn't bother Ryatt in the least. He was a man and a man's primary objective was what it had always been: to provide. Ever since men dwelled in caves, they put themselves in constant danger, slaughtering their way to the top of the food chain.

As Iris carved the turkey, Ryatt watched the fork being inserted into the glistening meat and his mind jumped to Bugsy. The last he heard, Bugsy was still alive. The new title the Detroit Alliance bestowed upon him was *Don* but on the street, he was known as Mr. Scarecrow, not Mr. Hat.

Because doctors had to amputate his arms near the shoulders and legs near his hip.

Befitting but funny monikers aside, he was still the head of the Detroit Alliance. With that came a lot of power and resources, most of which Bugsy diverted to one task: to identify *Lolly*. But as Ryatt had hid himself pretty well, both before and after the incident, no one was able to find him or his friends.

Thomas had once asked Ryatt why he used the zombie mask Bugsy gave him. Ryatt answered, "So that he knows the same kid who made him a cripple is now the greatest bank robber in North America. It'll piss him off beyond imagination."

Ryatt shoved the first forkful into his mouth and thought about how Bugsy would have to pay someone to feed him his Thanksgiving meal. Not just that, he needed assistance for everything else too. That image warmed his heart, and a smile found its way to his lips. Like Iris said, maybe money wasn't everything.

"How's your team doing?" Iris asked.

"Good, Ma. They're getting ready for the Christmas season." Ryatt didn't stutter when lying because he knew she always brought up his *work* whenever he was home. So he had prepared himself for her questions pertaining to that.

Ryatt had told her that he did not participate in the field anymore. He was now an assistant manager. People talked about football players, coaches, even managers, but not about assistant managers.

"I heard that your team made good headway in the tournaments," Iris said.

"Yes, Ma. But I'm planning to change teams," Ryatt said. If the team became too famous, then Ryatt ran the risk of being found out.

"Why? They give you good benefits."

"We just lost an important match," Ryatt lied again, feeling guilty because she would now try her absolute best to do her motherly bit.

"Failure is like a cement and every success is like a brick."

"Cement and bricks?"

"Even if you have more than enough bricks to build a house, without the lessons that failure would have otherwise taught you, the wall will inevitably collapse in the long run and crush you. Dead under the weight of your own success. All you need to do is look at these teenage pop stars and millionaires and their meltdowns. They haven't had the chance to become strong enough to handle success. Failure gives you character. It burns you, melts you, and molds you into a strong person who is able to handle the eventual, colossal success. Failure pressurizes you for a long time, but in the end, it makes you the best version of yourself."

Ryatt felt guilty even more. She was bestowing her wisdom upon someone who would never use it.

He said in a tired tone, "Thanks, Ma. But I don't wanna talk about work," acting as if he was stressed and forlorn.

Iris said, "You're not gonna find a solution to your problem ducking or pouting. Nothing good comes out of sadness and self-pity. A happy brain is a fertile brain. But sure, let's digress if it's spoiling your holidays."

They both talked about her. She told him that the 'Lawrence Foundation' was attracting donors from around the city. This fall, she was expecting to send at least three boys to college. And her shop, which she still ran in the same neighborhood from the same disgusting building that used to be their home, did well. That neighborhood was notorious for crime, but she said that no one even thought about robbing Iris. Ryatt knew that because she was sort of like a beacon for unfortunate people living there.

When they finished eating, Iris collected the vessels and went to the kitchen. She didn't accept Ryatt's offer to lend her a hand. Not like Iris needed help. Actually, she could take better care of herself. Her sense of place was far better than inborn blind people.

He followed her in. As he watched her load the silverware into the dishwasher, his brain attached price tags to all the items inside their kitchen.

Out of the blue, she said, "That Leo is trouble."

"I know, Ma. Won't be friends with him no more," Ryatt said. One of the oldest but most meaningless lies he had been telling her. And Iris knew it was a lie. But what could Ryatt do? He neither had the courage to challenge his mom nor the heart to abandon Leo.

"He is driving his stupid car," she said, "playing that hackneyed Grandmaster Flash 'The Message'. And he will be here... right about now."

Lolly looked through the window, and surely, there was a white Hummer slowly coming to a stop. He closed his eyes and tried to listen to the trippy music, and after a few seconds, he could only hear bits of it.

How did she even...

When he opened his eyes, they were misty. Though not a role model, his mom had always been his hero. And now with this super-hearing ability, she became a superhero.

She said, "Come here."

As he scrunched his tall frame, she held his shoulders and regarded his face, as if she could see him. Up close, Ryatt noticed her hair had started graying, the wrinkles on her face more prominent, but she looked stronger than ever. Ryatt had wondered if his mom was like The Terminator. She sure acted like she had an indestructible endoskeleton.

"I know they've been your friends for years," she said. "But past attachment is not a reason to prevent you from disowning something that becomes toxic to you. Or to society."

Ryatt nodded, and strangely, that always seemed to be enough for his mom. She gave a squeeze and let go.

He climbed back up the stairs and packed his things before exiting the house and sauntering across to the Hummer.

In the reflection of the Hummer's dark tinted windows, his new house bore the biggest price tag of them all: $254,000.

Chapter 14

November 24, 1994. 03:27 P.M.

Ryatt had been caught red-handed in Charleston nine years ago, when boosting a Subaru. It was Thomas's duty to ready cars for their jobs, but that morning he felt under the weather. So Ryatt, who'd never broken into cars, tried his luck. He was a robber after all. How tough could stealing a car be?

Turned out it was a completely different animal, requiring fineness and stealth, with a sprinkle of cowardice, none of which Ryatt possessed.

Seconds after he slid the slim jim in, blue and red flashed behind him. He tried to yank the tool out, but it was jammed. He pulled the hoodie over his head and started walking away hastily, leaving the shiny metal arching awkwardly from the car's window slit.

Then the siren blared and Ryatt took off.

However, there were no meandering alleyways Ryatt could have used to escape. Plain fields spanned as far as his eye could see. While handcuffed in the backseat, he refrained from employing the paperclip, because the pigs who had arrested him were young. And they seemed like the sort who the media labelled 'trigger happy'.

Ryatt's fingerprints had been lifted from the slim jim. The judge screamed *two years* before banging the gavel, jailing a newly turned eighteen-year-old.

For attempted theft!

It hadn't surprised Ryatt, though. West Virginia wasn't famous for its equality. Didn't they still have Jim Crow here? Their constitution supporting the segregation of colored and white children in schools? In the fucking nineties?

Ryatt had first met Jake at the yard. A thirty-something jailbird, Jake belonged to a different wing. But as the prison complex contained only one exercise ground, inmates had to share.

To pass time, they began chattering. Ryatt told Jake how he was arrested when he tried to steal a car. Except this, he never blurted anything out, about who he really was and what he had done. Jake said that if Ryatt ever needed stolen cars, he could contact him.

A New Yorker, born and bred, Jake had been in the carjacking business for as long as he could remember. He said even his father was a car thief, and he used to sell cars to Roy Demeo himself. Ryatt didn't know if he should be impressed, but he was relieved that he wouldn't have to rely on Thomas's pudgy fingers again to procure getaway vehicles.

Jake's acquaintanceship proved convenient. Their agreement worked like this: from where and how Jake got the cars wasn't something Ryatt cared about. What Ryatt did with the cars was no business of Jake's.

Their partnership worked well, benefiting both parties for seven years. Even the Ford Ryatt used on the Chicago job came from Jake.

So when Ryatt's gang needed a new set of wheels for their next job, they went over to meet Jake.

Leo took the I-80, which led them eastward. It had been three hours since they picked up Ryatt, and the sun had called it an early day. The highway scooted past him; bright headlamps on the other side flickered constantly on Ryatt's face, giving him a migraine.

Worried that he might get a seizure, Ryatt turned away from the window and looked at the time.

His Rolex ran slower by an hour, unchanged since his return from Chicago. He nimbly wound the hands on the dial to display EST.

Thomas lowered the volume of the stereo, looking in the rearview mirror, at Ryatt.

"Now we got enough money to retire in style. Why don't we call it off?"

Ryatt said, "No, I don't have enough."

Thomas frowned. "You don't?"

Ryatt shook his head.

"I ain't no fool to believe that."

"You calling me a liar?" It was Ryatt's turn to frown.

"I'm calling you greedy."

Ryatt stared into the mirror, trying his best to get angry, to look offended.

But he couldn't.

Who was Ryatt kidding? Thomas was correct.

Ryatt cleared his throat. "We… I—"

Thomas lifted a hand, cutting him off. "Just promise me one thing."

"What?"

"Call it quits before you get any of us hurt."

"Promise," Ryatt said and yawned. "I had a full-course meal." He lay down and stretched on the backseat. "Gonna rest for a few moments."

* * *

"Wake up." Ryatt felt two pairs of hands roughhousing him. "We're here."

Wiping the drool off his cheek, Ryatt sat straight. Both his partners were looking at him; Thomas's face curled in uncertainty.

"What's up?" Ryatt asked.

Leo nodded at the window.

Ryatt peered outside. They'd parked across from Jake's chop shop, which he used as a front. But something seemed wrong with the picture. A car stood haphazardly at the entrance. Like someone skidded it to a halt urgently.

The car was a Crown Vic.

"What's a pig doing here?" Ryatt asked.

"We don't know," Thomas said. "I saw it angrily pull up and an angrier man tromped inside."

"It's him!" Leo said. "But Thomas ain't believing me."

"Whose him?" Ryatt asked.

"You remember Staten Island?" Thomas asked and rolled his eyes.

How could Ryatt ever forget that? Not just due to the tough elderly cashier, but this was also where Ryatt's old nickname began following him. The cashier had informed the press in an interview that the robber had been sucking on a lollipop.

The presumptuous editor of the newspaper had printed *Lollipop Man*, and the TV and radio downsized the epithet to a catchier *Lolly*.

"I remember." Ryatt pinched the bridge of his nose. "What about it?"

Leo jumped in. "The NYPD held a press conference with the police captain... what's his name—"

"Raymond Hughes," Thomas said.

"Yeah. You remember the detective standing behind Hughes? He looked like he is always sad."

"Yes, I think I do," Ryatt said.

"That's him," Leo exclaimed. "I have his name right here." Leo pointed at his throat. "But I just couldn't spit it out." He grabbed his head. "Something like a Hunter... no... Runner?"

"No way. He looked different back then," Thomas said, not paying attention to Leo's agony.

"Nah, it's him!" Leo let go of his head. "He grew a beard now, but it's him alright."

"He is *still* investigating our case?" Ryatt asked, surprised.

"If it really is him—"

"It is!"

"Let's ask Jake," Ryatt said.

Leo smashed the dashboard.

"What now, asshole?" Thomas shouted.

"I got it!" Leo beamed. "The detective's name."

Ryatt and Thomas looked at the little man expectantly.

"It's Chase," Leo said in a poor James Bond imitation. "Joshua Chase."

* * *

Ryatt cooked up a plan. Leo and he would interrogate Jake while Thomas followed the Crown Vic and tried to learn more about the pig.

They got down and walked to a bus stop opposite. At this time of night, no one was there, except a bum sleeping on the seats.

Ten minutes later, Jake's front door flew open. The angry pig stormed out, piled into the pig cart, and zoomed off.

And the Hummer followed.

Leo and Ryatt waited a few more minutes, deciding on a keyword, if things were to turn sour. Then they went in.

Jake sat behind a small desk that carried a bowl of popcorn and an ashtray overflowing with cigarette butts. Dark smoke rose from it. Yet Jake had another cigarette between his lips already. Ryatt knew Jake wasn't a chain smoker.

Jake's pale face turned paler when he spotted Ryatt and Leo. But he quickly masked the shock and pushed himself up. "My man."

He opened his arms. Ryatt hugged him, Leo following suit.

Pleasantries out of the way, Ryatt sat across from Jake, while Leo perched on Jake's side of the table, facing him. They'd cut Jake's only escape route, just in case.

"Your next car's ready. It's outside." Jake tried to get up, but Leo shoved him back into the chair.

"What's this?" he asked, his breathing labored.

"I've seen that pig before," Leo said.

"It—it's not about you, guys." Jake's Adam's apple bobbed once.

Ryatt knew then and there that Jake would fuck them over. Liars always did.

"Turkey," Ryatt uttered the keyword.

Leo, giggling, pulled out a pistol and pointed at Jake.

"No, man." Jake lifted his hands. "I said nothing to him."

"What'd he ask?" Ryatt said. "And no more lying."

Jake squeezed his eyes shut. "About that car I sold you, man..."

"The black Firebird?" Ryatt asked. It was the car they used on the Staten Island job.

"No," Jake said.

"What do you mean, no?" Ryatt was confused. "Then about what car?"

"This guy, he is like a genius or something, I tell you. He was asking about the Mustang."

Ryatt skipped a heartbeat. Why would a detective serving at Staten Island enquire about the car Ryatt had used in a different robbery, a robbery they'd pulled off in Chicago last week?

Ryatt knew the FBI used his lollipop habit and ballistics to connect the crimes. But they wouldn't have any inclination to share the information with a pig from a different state.

"Why would he ask about the Mustang?"

"I don't know. H-he's got a list of all the cars I ever sold to you."

"What the— How?" Ryatt felt something he hadn't experienced in a long time. Helplessness.

"I really have no clue."

A stone had clogged Ryatt's throat. All these years, no one had come this close.

"What'd you tell him?" Ryatt asked, though he could imagine what had transpired here. The angry way the pig stomped out of the shop meant Jake had resisted. But the pig must have threatened Jake to his core. That's why he looked pretty shook up. The pig's ego would never allow him to accept defeat. He would try his best to lock Jake up, by kindling some old dirt. Or he could just get a warrant and turn this chop shop upside down. Jake certainly had many things to hide.

So Jake would weigh his options, and arrive at a conclusion: either work with the pig, help him arrest Ryatt, and earn some neat reward on the side; or don't rat, gain nothing, possibly lose the shop, and go to prison.

Jake didn't know this yet, but eventually he would betray Ryatt. Jake, as if he had read Ryatt's thoughts, eyed the doorway.

"Can't you see there's nowhere to run?" Leo nudged Jake's head with his gun. "Don't make this harder on yourself."

Ryatt told Leo, "Don't shoot. The noise will attract people. We have no car."

Jake's eyes started spilling tears. "Please, man. I— we just had a baby."

Ryatt chose to hear nothing. In his mind, Jake was already a dead man. So he got up and switched on the TV above, fixed on the wall. Rerun of The Simpsons was airing. Nice. He grabbed the popcorn bowl and sat back.

They all waited as the clock ticked. Jake was whimpering like a hurt dog, crying rivers and drenching his sleeves. He sometimes bent and held Ryatt's hand and begged him to let him go.

But Ryatt and Leo were busily watching the episode, Lisa On Ice, passing the popcorn between them.

Finally, when the Hummer honked outside, Jake almost jumped out of his skin. Ryatt shot up to his feet and retrieved a baggie from his front pocket. It had various sizes of earplugs; each pair blocked different intensities of sound waves. Ryatt looked around. The place was tiny and crammed, so he selected two big plugs and wedged them into his canals.

Once he was satisfied with the numbness the plugs had brought, he pulled out the Desert Eagle. While Jake's bawling was being muffled by the plugs, Ryatt lifted the gun, his forefinger wrapping around the trigger—

"Hold on, hold on, hold on." Leo put his hand in front of the muzzle, giving Ryatt a heart attack.

"What?!" Ryatt asked, easing the grip on the trigger.

"Give me a minute. Wanna see how this ends." Leo nodded towards the TV.

Ryatt sighed and blew out air. He stood like that, right arm extended with a pistol in its extremity, aiming at a pathetic excuse of a man clasping his hands, weeping. As seconds passed, the pistol became heavier. Ryatt gave up and transferred the weight elsewhere, putting the barrel on his shoulder.

Leo's arms stretched with the popcorn bowl and Ryatt scooped the last handful. It took them a good five minutes before the credits finally rolled in, the chirpy music filling the office.

Thank fucking God.

Ryatt's shoulder cramped when he brought down the weapon. Wincing, he took aim once again.

Leo placed the empty bowl on the table and plugged his ears with his forefingers.

Jake lifted his arms, his palms facing the muzzle of the Desert Eagle. "Please—"

The bullet penetrated Jake's hands, then his nose, and ripped the brain stem along the way, before exiting through the back of his neck. A goop of viscera ejected and splattered on the wall, then blood squirted.

Leo and Ryatt made a speedy escape, climbed into the car which rocketed forward even before the doors were completely shut.

"What the hell?!" Thomas asked. "You killed Jake?"

"That pig killed Jake," Ryatt replied and explained everything to Thomas. "Heard something about wrong place wrong time?"

"Yeah?"

"Well, we were in the right place at the right time. We wouldn't have known about any of this if we came, say like ten minutes later." Ryatt paused. "What's the take here?"

"What?" Thomas said.

"Something is giving us a chance. We're never gonna make a blunder like this again."

"I agree," Thomas said.

"Meaning, no more involving second parties."

Thomas sighed. "So it's me back to stealing cars."

"We're safe that way."

"*Safe?*" Thomas scoffed. "This detective looks desperate and acts desperate. Those obsessive types are always a problem, Ry. What're we gonna do about it?"

"What we always do with our problems." Ryatt traced his finger along the barrel of the gun, its tip still warm. "We deal with it."

Chapter 15

November 25, 1994. 02:14 A.M.

The Hummer parked across from a two-story building in Staten Island. The house had once been painted, and the wood underneath was chipped on more than a dozen spots. The lawn could use a mow, the roof a few shingles.

A lush tree guarding the front partially blocked the streetlamp, so the right side of the property was dark. However, a lone rectangular light fell onto the shadow of the tree. A window. They had also discovered tendrils on that portion, which was going to be Ryatt's key into the house. The pig's Crown Vic standing on the gravel driveway had two flats, thanks to Leo's army knife.

Ryatt pocketed a lollipop and opened the door.

"I'm gonna slip in through the upstairs window on the right-side wall. When I'm in, I'll whistle. Then you," Ryatt pointed at Leo, "come through the front. Thomas will start the Hummer and keep it ready."

"What if someone else is also in there?" Thomas asked.

"Collateral." Ryatt exited the car and pressed the door shut noiselessly.

As he crossed the road, he scanned the vicinity and found that the street was quiet. Not missing the opportunity, he crouched and snuck under the tree's shadow. Like he'd guessed, the rectangular light falling onto the side came from the window on the second floor.

However, Ryatt spotted another window on the lower level that they hadn't detected in their hasty recon. He quickly dashed from the safety of the shadows and dived below the opening. No light emanated from within, but he picked up voices.

A loud argument.

He craned his head a few centimeters and peeped into the window. It appeared to be a storeroom. Its door hung open and Ryatt could see the well-lit living room on the other side.

The man whom Ryatt knew as Detective Joshua Chase was sitting on a couch. Elbows on his thighs, his head hung low and shoulders slumped.

In front of the detective was a svelte woman, marching right to left and vice versa as she yelled, "... what kind of a man misses the Thanksgiving dinner with his in-laws to go after some bank robber?"

Ryatt felt naughty and pleased. They were talking about him, while he was tucked in the darkness beyond their window, eavesdropping.

"I'm sorry," the pig said.

"Sorry?" the woman's voice rose a notch. "This is how it has been for months. I can't..." She sighed. "I don't think I even love you anymore."

"Come on." The pig looked up and grabbed the woman's elbow. "Don't say that."

She yanked out of his clasp. "Now that I think about it, I don't even know how I ever loved your pathetic ass."

Ryatt winced.

"What should I do? Just tell me. I'm ready to give you anything you want."

"A goddamn divorce." She spat.

The pig stared at his wife, his lips quivering. Finally he put his head down and muttered, "Fine."

"Look at me when I'm speaking to you, not at your fucking shoes." The woman swung her hand, and the slap landed with a heavy thwack.

Ryatt winced again. True, he was here to end the man, but he couldn't help but feel a little sorry for him. However, the pig sat without any movement whatsoever. As if he had not been hit on his ear by his wife.

"React, goddamn it!" the woman shouted. But her voice wasn't domineering anymore. It sounded grainy, as if she was on the verge of crying.

It looked like the pig picked up on that, too. He heaved himself to his feet and walked towards the woman.

"Don't you dare come near… don't you touch me, you piece of…"

The pig wrapped his arms around the woman. She tried to push him away, but she really wasn't putting any muscle into it. Then she broke into a cry.

"I love you," the pig said. "I'm so sorry for hurting you."

The woman, now bawling like a kid, clasped his collar. "Please leave this job."

The pig eased up, took her by the shoulders, and looked into her eyes. "I really think it's best if you leave me."

The cry became hysterical as she once again buried her face into his chest. The pig caressed her head as she let it all out. Two full minutes had gone by, before the woman calmed.

She cupped his hands in hers and kissed it. "Do you think you can make this world a better place all by yourself?"

"I… I don't," the pig said, his voice trembling. "But I can't stand idly by when bad people make this world worse for everyone else."

Ryatt frowned and something clicked in his mind. His mouth dried and heart raced.

"Pl-please…" she implored.

"I am sorry."

Face twisting in rage and vehemence, the woman swatted his hands and lifted her arm once again. But she didn't hit. A few moments passed, and she dropped her hand, as if it weighed a ton. "There are some leftovers on the table," she said and walked away. Ryatt had to rise a little and lean left to see her.

The pig… no, the detective followed her as she trudged to a room. She stopped at the threshold, one of her arms holding the door frame, barricading entry. Should be their bedroom.

The detective opened his mouth, but closed it before saying anything. He repeated the action two more times, like an amnesiac goldfish.

The woman sighed. "I packed already. I'm leaving in the morning." With the back of her wrist, she smeared the tears cascading down her cheeks without consent. "I-I'm sorry. I just… I just can't."

Still shaking, she closed the door ever so slightly. Joshua lingered, watching the door. Then he wiped his face on his shoulder and sniffled.

Silently witnessing all this, Ryatt couldn't breathe or swallow easily.

Ryatt never had a problem killing because he didn't believe good people existed. Any person who didn't try to stop evil deeds happening before their eyes was bad, weren't they?

Except his mom, every single one of them was as selfish as they came, including himself.

Even pigs did their duties, got paid, and didn't give a shit about good and evil. But this Joshua, his demeanor, his voice, it all suggested that he was dying inside. He was going way out of his way to sacrifice his marriage, hence his life and happiness, to catch Ryatt.

To stop evil.

With difficulty, Ryatt digested a truth that had dawned on him a while ago: Joshua was like Iris. They both belonged to the unlucky clique of angels God had forgotten to collect when he abandoned the world usurped by demons.

"Hello?" a voice called from above, jolting him.

Heart pounding, Ryatt looked up.

A small head was protruding out of the window on the second floor, the eyes on it peering at him. The boy waved and Ryatt returned the gesture.

"A-a-are you hungry, M-mister?" the boy asked and brandished half a cookie with the other hand. "Want s-s-some?"

"Don't mind if I do." Ryatt grinned and looked around. The streets were still quiet. He grabbed hold of the tendrils and climbed up.

The boy's room was small. Painted in periwinkle blue, it had no posters or drawings. Books were strewn across the floor but no toys or video games or TV.

The boy was sitting down, his legs tucked under him. He stretched his arm towards Ryatt, holding the cookie he had been eating. But the cookie slipped from his fingers. Seemed like the little one had difficulty with movements.

The boy picked up the cookie and gave it to Ryatt again, who accepted the generous offer and tossed the whole thing in his mouth. It was coconut flavored, laced with butter and cashew.

What was the boy doing up at this time? The ruckus downstairs would have woken him up. The half-asleep child treated himself to a cookie, evidently quenching the sugar crave you get when randomly woken up in the middle of the night.

Snaking a hand into his jacket, Ryatt knelt down in front of the boy and watched his big brown eyes. He pulled out a lollipop and gave it to the boy who accepted it hesitantly.

"I could be called a villain." Ryatt shrugged as if that was not his problem, but a universal fact that everyone just had to deal with. "But even I love superheroes. You know who my favorite is?"

The boy shook his head, absent-mindedly toying with the lollipop.

"My mom." Ryatt smiled. "You know who yours should be, handsome?"

The boy smiled shyly and shook his head again, picking his nose.

"Your dad." Ryatt gave the boy's bony shoulders a gentle squeeze. "He's a goddamn hero."

Ryatt put his head down, ashamed for having planned to kill Joshua and deprive this world of yet another good person.

Then he lifted his head. "You never forget that, you hear?"

The boy nodded and began unwrapping the candy cover.

Ryatt got up and slogged to the window. As he swung a leg over the ledge, he halted and turned to look at the boy one last time. He gave Ryatt a beautiful smile that filled his heart with pure joy. The child must also be an angel. An angel that would inevitably rise above and make this world a better place. Like his mom. Like Detective Chase.

Ryatt just had to ask. "What's your name, tiger?"

"G-G-Ga..." The boy closed his eyes and tilted his chin up, as he struggled to construct the word. Then he said, in the feeblest of voices, "Gabriel."

Part II: Joshua

Chapter 16

November 24, 1994. 11:13 A.M.

The piano played in the background a crude, repetitive tune, as he shuffled along in a queue, waiting to deposit cash. The music was temporarily overlapped by commotion.

The ground in front of him caved in. From the smoldering hole, three entities clambered up. Red, blue, and pale green faced demons.

While the red and blue disappeared somewhere, the green masked demon snarled at him. Then it pulled out a huge gun with its claw, blood dripping from the muzzle.

Two loud explosions!

Stunned, he looked back. A woman sprawled on the floor, her pinkish red entrails drooped from a grisly laceration in her stomach, onto the shiny marble.

Wait... two explosions?

He looked down. A red dot appeared on his chest and slowly stretched into a wide blot. Sudden darkness sucked his mind. He unfurled his fingers. Let the coldness consume him.

But...

Why is that goddamn piano still playing its goddamn jingle?

* * *

Joshua awoke with a start, springing up so fast that his forehead banged on something hard. Cupping the hurt, he lay back again, grunting.

Promising retribution to his injured noggin, he opened his eyes. To his chagrin, he found the upper half of his body stuck underneath the bed.

The tune from the nightmare blared again, giving him another start. Was he not in reality yet? Where did that sound—

His new cell phone!

He rolled out and shot up to his feet. Now there was a stunt his alcoholic ass shouldn't have pulled. Always sorrier than safe, he gritted his teeth through the comeuppance. The mother of all headaches exploded within his cranium. The edges of his vision darkened while the center flickered with a bright blur. Nausea followed almost immediately, his hand covering his dry mouth.

But nothing came. False alarm. Or it could be true, but just a bit sooner.

He lumbered to the other side of the room, where his table stood. On its top vibrated a Nokia Cityman 300, playing that monotonous tune, its LCD display glowing in the semi dark room.

He picked it up and pressed the green receiver button.

"That's fast enough," the voice on the other end said, generous with sarcasm. "Let me guess. Another all-nighter?"

"I'm close, Ray." Joshua rummaged through the stuff on the table and lifted a wild newspaper. Hiding under it was a Skoal tin. Joshua loved dipping tobacco, but his wife's aversion to him squirting brown liquid every tenth second made him switch. Now he used snus. No spit. No bulge. Certainly no smoke. Just all the cancerous goodness of tobacco.

"You gotta let go, man," Raymond said, his voice tired. "It's not our responsibility now."

"I'll take you to the victims' families. Can you tell them that?"

Silence.

"Thought so. What's your problem anyway? I'm working my shift and do this in my spare time. Why do you care?"

Joshua twisted the cap open, plucked out two pouches, and fixed them between his gums and cheeks. A rush of energy coursed through his veins and hammered the hangover back into the nothingness from where it came.

"I care because you drink a lot, you only eat once a day, if that, and your marriage is practically in the coffin. All that's left to do is bury it."

It was Joshua's turn to be quiet. He didn't remember getting back home last night. But seeing that he had been sleeping on the floor and his wife hadn't woken him up when she left for work, Raymond was correct. His marriage was as good as dead.

It hadn't always been like this, not until that fateful day.

A year ago, Joshua was called to a crime scene which would change his life forever. A cold-blooded animal, whom the media would eventually christen as Lolly, shot two people at a bank in Staten Island before robbing it. One security guard was DOA and one woman died in the hospital later.

Witnessing the havoc, Joshua knew right then it was his duty to stop this madman.

But Lolly turned out to be one of the most elusive bank robbers in the US, having robbed fourteen banks in as many counties. His crimes were linked by three distinguishable things: the mask, the use of .44 caliber, and his blatant hobby of sucking a lollipop while gunning people down.

"You're not gonna answer?"

Joshua offered more silence.

"Ugh. Fine. How's it going?" Raymond asked. "Are you any closer?"

"I don't know, you tell me," Joshua muttered, then yelled into the phone. "We are gonna get the fucker tonight!"

"Wait," Raymond said, his sentence paused doubtfully. "We're going to get Lolly, *the* Lolly, tonight?"

"His identity, I mean. Once we know who the asshole beneath that mask is, then it's only a matter of time."

"But how?"

"Unrelenting detective work, that's how," Joshua said and proceeded to explain.

After Lolly's gang robbed the bank in Staten Island and hightailed it, they dumped the getaway vehicle in New Jersey, probably switching to another set of wheels. The abandoned car was a 90s Firebird. The FBI tracked it and found that it had been stolen in Memphis.

And they dropped that line of inquiry.

In the months that followed, the FBI tried to trace the bullets and the money, but nothing worked. Joshua insisted they looked into the car angle deeper. But the FBI refused, stating that it was a dead end. In fact, they had a list of cars that Lolly's gang had used and abandoned, since they first achieved prominence in 1982. All the cars on that list were stolen but the cases were unsolved. All dead ends, they had concluded.

Joshua disagreed.

He had spent a lot of time with the list and was rewarded for his fortitude.

He had noticed that the cars Lolly's gang used before 1987 were beat cars. Cars that even a novice, or particularly a novice, would steal. No resale value. But from the second half of 1987, the cars employed in the robberies became sedans with good torque and control, which had a lot of resale value. Types of cars professional thieves would steal.

In March 1987, Lolly's gang used a Ford Escort. But in November they used a BMW, the latest model released that year. How did they graduate from using soccer mom

SUVs to high performance vehicles in a matter of months? Joshua hadn't found an answer for that.

Until he put together the other pieces.

The leader of their gang, Lolly, was not present in three robberies they had committed from 1985 to 1987. Only the other two, the red and blue-masked demons, operated during this time. A criminal doesn't take hiatus this long *voluntarily*. They got killed, either by cops or their partners, or they got arrested. Lolly was back in 1987 and resumed his work, meaning it was the latter.

"Okay, so you think he was in prison from 1985 to 1987?" Raymond asked.

"Yes. And if we have his latent print recovered from either the casings or the slugs, we could search for it in NCIC."

"But we don't," Raymond said. "They always wipe their cartridges clean and wear gloves when they fill their clips."

"Unfortunately, yes."

"Forgetting wishful thinking, returning to topic," Raymond sternly said. "Lolly comes out after serving his sentence. His gang, who was using shitty vehicles in their jobs until then, starts to use top end cars? Could be Lolly made a new friend. Prison contact?"

"Bingo!" Joshua chirped.

"A professional carjacker."

"Yes." Joshua walked out of the room, to the kitchen. "From 1987 till last week, a robbery in Chicago, they used a total of nine getaway vehicles. I visited the places where these cars were stolen and conducted my own investigations."

"By yourself?"

"The FBI didn't think I had a lead and refused to help me."

"So all the annual leave you made me approve for your 'marriage counseling' was just me getting my anus bigger, uh?"

Joshua laughed. "I wouldn't put it in so many words, but yeah."

"Let me remind you to whoop your ass when you come to the precinct," Raymond grumbled. "Anyway, tell me, did you solve those cases?"

"Not officially. I got no evidence."

"But you found out who stole those cars?"

"I did. With the help of our brothers in blue." As Joshua approached the fridge to get some water, he spotted a note stuck on its door. "Excuse me," he said into the phone and read the note.

His wife's attractive cursive reminded him that her parents would be joining them for Thanksgiving dinner, and he should not forget it.

After filling his stomach with half a pitcher of cool water, he ambled to the couch in the living room and plunked himself on it.

"Hello?"

"Still here," Raymond said.

"Alright. Sorry about that." Joshua burped. "So those nine cars were stolen from different cities, by various unrelated professional carjackers, controlled by various unrelated auto theft rings. Nine cars, nine rings. But the respective PDs had info on them."

"They gave you the names of the gang leaders?"

"And I spoke to them."

"And they told you to fuck off."

"They told me to fuck off, yes."

"But you didn't."

"But I didn't, no. Instead I spoke to the snitches and low-level assholes who needed a quick buck. I mean, I'm not asking them to testify or anything. I just needed a name, a common denominator, who bought nine cars from these nine rings."

"But why? Why can't the gangs sell the cars themselves? Why do they need him? What's linking them all?"

"Greed. That's the link."

"I don't get it."

"These nine cars were stolen from three states: Tennessee, Missouri, and Kentucky."

Raymond didn't speak for a few seconds, possibly his brain recovering from the sudden apparent change of conversation. "That supposed to mean something?"

"They're landlocked."

"I am still lost."

"You remember the time when the Mafia used to *export* cars to Arab countries."

"Oh…" Raymond said. "From Jersey and New York?"

"Yes. The Auto Theft gangs in these three landlocked states stand to make a lot of money if they sell it to a middleman who later exports the stolen cars to foreign lands."

"They are reasonable discoveries. Where did it all lead you to?"

"Every scum I spoke to—snitches, gang members, thieves—repeated only one name. And according to the criminal records of the leaders of these nine rings, under the Known Acquaintances sub-divisions, the same name was repeated again."

"The middleman. The common denominator."

"Uh-huh."

"Who is it?"

"Jake Caridi. A chop shop runner."

"Let me guess. He also exports scraps?"

Joshua chuckled. "He exports scraps to the Eastern hemisphere."

"I don't think any of this is coincidence, but are you sure it's him who supplies the wheels to Lolly?"

"I am because he was serving a three-year sentence in the eighties. Care to guess when?"

"Any period that includes 85-87?"

"Right you are. The same timeframe when I believe Lolly was in prison."

"It all makes sense in a strange way. My mind is now just one soup of random information." Raymond whistled. "You did a lot of work. Alone."

"It's worth it. Numerous family members of the victims can finally get closure and see that justice gets done."

"Definitely worth it, if everything goes to plan," Raymond said. "When are you visiting Jake?"

"Gonna have to do some backgrounds."

"Like what? His cellmates?"

"Already did. Jake had three bunkmates during his stretch in West Virginia, but none of them is Lolly. They are all white."

"Shit."

"As you know, apart from the witnesses swearing by the conjecture that the robbers spoke with a slight Ebonics dialect, the surviving cashiers reported they saw through the eyeholes in the mask and Lolly was black. With blue eyes."

"That's correct. Then what else are you checking for?"

"Don't know but I need to find some dirt on Jake. Then threaten him and make him believe that he has to give up the name of his friend who's been buying cars from him."

"Those Mafia types don't rat much."

"Italians are only interested in killing a snitch and stuffing a canary down his throat if it affects other Italians."

"What are you gonna threaten him with?"

"Jake recently had a baby. I'm gonna tell him that I will have my friend in Child Protective Services take the baby away, what with Jake having a mile-long rap sheet and all."

"You won't do it." Raymond chuckled.

"I won't. It's a bluff. I'm gonna act all desperate and angry and—"

"Act?"

"I'm gonna give him what will seem like an ultimatum. Give up his friend or his child."

"What if he calls Lolly and warns him—"

"Looking forward to that."

"What? Why?"

"Already tapped his phone. He makes a call, we don't just have Lolly's identity, but also his address."

"The FBI tapped his phone?"

Joshua murmured, "I didn't say FBI."

"Be louder. I can't hear you."

"I stopped sharing info with the feds when they made me solve their biggest case all by myself, spending my own money for gas, motels, food, and snitches."

"No one asked you to," Raymond remarked. "Don't change the topic. How did you tap Jake's phone? I don't remember a warrant coming by me."

"Who said anything about a warrant?"

Raymond laughed again. "I'm your captain, you know?"

"Well, *Captain Asswipe*, my work is to protect innocent people. I don't care how I go about doing it. As long as I save someone from getting practically decapitated by Lolly's elephant gun, nothing I do is wrong or unethical."

Raymond sighed. "I must ask. To get this one lead, which might turn out to be nothing, you solved nine carjacking cases in three different states? On your own time and expenses?"

"Uh-huh."

There was nothing but silence on the other line.

Did Raymond just hang up?

Joshua looked at the phone. The call timer was still running. "Hello? Captain Ass—"

"You're a ram," Raymond said.

That gave Joshua a pause. "Ram? The Hindu deity?"

"No. Ram as in goat."

"Why am I a goddamn ram?"

"Rita and I went to Bali last year for our holidays."

"Yeah, I know. My missus never lets me forget how romantic you two are."

Raymond laughed. "Apart from the coastline, we also toured parts of the Indonesian countryside. In a village, we watched two rams fighting. They just bash their heads, walk back a few yards, then run and bash their heads again. Blood drips down the thick skulls of these vindictive bastards, and they still go at it. Even when they are hurt, even when they *know* they will probably die from a gaping wound in the head."

"Wait… are you telling me that if I don't let go, I'm gonna die with a gaping wound in my head?"

"All I'm saying is that you just don't know when to give up."

"Thank you."

"That's not a compliment."

This time, Raymond did hang up.

Chapter 17

November 25, 1994. 02:30. A.M.

Joshua stared at their bedroom door, which his wife had closed after her. The slap still tingled his cheek, but the subsequent hug had more than compensated for it. His wife emanated a unique scent. A mix of rosewater and sandalwood. The smell of purity. Must be how heaven smelt.

Amidst this pleasant sensation, his heart imploded in agony. It could very probably be the last time he would be allowed within close enough proximity to his wife to inhale her angelic waft.

The separation, although painful and humiliating, was not shocking in the least. It had been a long time in the pipeline, and wholly attributable to Joshua's negligence. He was designed like that, he presumed. Manufacturing defect, so to speak, having been programmed to give more importance to the overwhelming responsibility he felt towards the homicide victims than to the love towards his wife. The murdered themselves didn't bother Joshua much but the ones left behind, their families, did.

Not their fault though. Even imagining losing someone dear to a violent crime disquieted Joshua.

One night your mom or dad, husband or wife, son or daughter didn't come home. You called them, but they didn't answer. You began to fidget. You made apologetic late-night calls to their friends and colleagues, but no one knew anything. The jitters morphed into dreadful foreboding. You felt in your stomach—not in the heart because these sick premonitions originated only in stomachs—that something was wrong. The next morning your phone rang, and you picked it up on the second ring. The caller began with 'I am sorry' followed by empty words that had 'incident' in them. Then they told you that someone had yanked your loved one away from your life at the snap of their fingers.

No last words, no amendments, no goodbyes.

But this was the easy part. The hard part came after the burial.

Everywhere you looked, you saw the murdered; their place on the couch or at the dining table; when you got a whiff of their favorite food, listened to their favorite band, changed through their favorite TV channels.

It wasn't fair. Not fair at all. You were just a regular Joe going about your regular Joe business. You were a *good* regular Joe. You didn't even deserve the paper cut you got in the office the other day, let alone seeing your loved one on a gurney, missing a quarter of their head.

And during one of your late-night crying fits, you gnashed your teeth and promised them you would make the son of a bitch pay. But what could you do? You were, after all, just a languished *regular* Joe. Life rarely mimicked TV. You didn't don a latex T-shirt with a skull printed on it, pack a bag full of guns, and chase the killer. No. You chased the people responsible for catching the killer.

People like Joshua.

You developed a despondent relationship with detectives. Helpless, it had become your duty that whenever you found free time, you called them. You were now a steadfast believer of the adage involving squeaky wheels and grease. In your eyes, they weren't detectives anymore. Not cops, but some divine entities. Powerful authorities, the only friends capable of bringing some sort of peace to you. And Joshua was usually the type of friend who delivered.

But not tonight.

Jake was dead, and the lead Joshua had been working on for ten months was now lost forever. The fact that he *almost* unmasked Lolly made him wanna puke.

An unbridled anger urged him to kick the door down and explain all this to his wife. He wanted to yell that she was being unfair and shake some sense into her. But he couldn't. She had no obligation to put up with the aftermath of his gloomy crusades.

So he did what his body had been wanting to do ever since he saw Jake's exploded brain an hour ago: hang his head.

A minute later, he sniffled and rubbed his face on his shoulder. Picking up a bottle of Jim Beam, he dropped into the recliner in front of the TV. He took a huge swig; the alcohol burned its way down to his empty intestines. Though the light from the paltry infomercial flickered through his watery eyes, the images his brain saw were something utterly different—they were of Jake's crime scene.

Who killed him? One of his criminal friends, criminal enemies, criminal customers, or hell, even his criminal wife? Too many criminals surrounded Jake's life, but Joshua had already arrived at a supposition, considering the hole the size of an apple in Jake's head.

Lolly.

Ballistics would later confirm or deny his hypothesis, but Joshua trusted his intuition for now.

That murdering bastard had cursed New York again with his riotous presence. The mere thought that he and Lolly were possibly sharing the same few square miles, but that he was unable to do anything about it, demoralized him. It seemed as if some greater evil protected Lolly, which begged the imminent question: where the fuck was Joshua's greater good? Most likely cowering in some church or temple, leaving Joshua to pick after its battle.

He downed another long gulp, uninhibitedly. Not that he needed any excuses lately. These days, his waking hours were those murky gaps between morning hangovers and midnight blackouts. Not a moment of clarity there.

The presenter on the infomercial, a semi-naked girl, was now advertising a magic pill that cured baldness. Why she had to expose her cleavage and tan stomach a good three inches below her navel to sell something that men bought to restore some of their youthful confidence was beyond Joshua.

Deflated, he wrapped his fingers around the bottleneck and pushed himself up with the other arm.

But his palm slid over the armrest. The cheap rye spurted out of the bottle and spilled on the back of his hand, the chilly liquid evaporating in an instant. Shaking his head at the disappointment he had become, he placed the bottle on the floor and heaved his body up again.

Carefully navigating his way across the room, he reached the stairs and climbed the steps. His son had probably woken up due to the ruckus he and his wife had caused and might need tucking in.

As Joshua reached the landing, he thought he heard someone talking behind his son's door. Weird. The boy had no imaginary friends.

He knocked and waited a few seconds, before entering.

The little guy had problems with his motor skills, due to his condition. So instead of standing, he was hanging onto the ledge of the window, waving. Joshua rushed to his side and peeked out.

A white Hummer parked across the street, on seeing Joshua, sped off. Its screeching tires must have woken half the neighborhood.

Hadn't Joshua seen it somewhere before?

Squeezing his eyes shut, Joshua sifted through the drenched cabinets of his inebriated memory.

Where did I—

Outside Jake's auto shop!

"Gabe!" Joshua turned the boy towards him. On seeing Gabriel's face, everything spun out of control, and the alcohol in his bloodstream was not the reason.

The boy was sucking a lollipop.

Joshua darted out of the room and stomped down the stairs, taking three steps at a time. As he bolted through the front door to his car, adrenaline thumped in his ears.

But before he got inside, he observed that the vehicle sank lower on one side. Two tires on the left were slashed.

Undeterred, Joshua took off after the Hummer which was just a pair of receding taillights in the fog. He didn't care that he was barefoot. He sprinted towards it at full speed. But for all the acceleration, he felt like he was suspended in space, like trying to punch or run in a dream.

They gained a lead on him, gradually dissolving into the distance. Inside he screamed, "No." Joshua stretched his arm out, grabbing at the spot where the Hummer had disappeared.

The lack of stamina caught up with him all at once. His eyesight blurred, making it physically impossible for him to continue running. A lamppost provided him a shoulder. He held its sides, not allowing the tears of anger escape. Tried to close his eyes and collect his breath and his thoughts.

Having had Lolly within spitting distance, for the *second time* the same night, broke Joshua's heart into pieces. Under his nose. So close. Just meters away. In front of his home. *In his son's room.*

Frustrated, he shook the lamppost, punching and kicking it. Not feeling the pain of hitting the metal. Not hearing the sound.

"Stop it, asshole!" a voice carrying an unmistakable bravado warned.

Joshua opened his wet eyes and turned around. A young fat cop was holding a pistol on him with quaking arms, a cruiser parked beside him. The flashing blue and red gave Joshua a new surge of nausea. The officer must have assumed that Joshua was one of those crack junkies that terrorized the city these days with their capricious vandalism and violence. Drug epidemic, the popular news had dubbed it. So the uniform must have called it in and pulled over. Joshua couldn't blame the poor kid though. To any passing person, a hyperventilating guy grappling with a lamppost wouldn't look friendly. Or sane.

"Which precinct?" Joshua asked.

The bald-headed cop's ruddy face twisted in bewilderment. "D-detective Chase?"

"Yeah, the one and only," Joshua said. "Is that you, Ivansky?"

"Yes, sir." Officer Ivansky lowered the gun. "What happened here?"

"Call the dispatch and request them to issue an APB on a white Hummer. I want every road exiting the city cordoned off. Also, ask them to contact the FBI and tell them that Lolly is in New York City and if they coordinate with staties and us, we might catch him."

Officer Ivansky looked stupefied.

"What?!" Joshua barked. "Did you get everything I've just said?"

"Y-yes sir," he said, his hands slipped as he fumbled to holster the gun.

"Goddamn it, Ivansky. Don't shoot yourself in the dick."

Ivansky nodded, his blubbery jowls vibrated as he did, and piled into his cruiser. Notwithstanding the flash of guilt for browbeating the young cop, Joshua's plastered mind warned him that it was futile. Lolly was an animal, but a really paranoid and farsighted one. He had backups for backups that were Plan Bs.

Enervated, Joshua faced the truth squarely: he had missed his chance. And the three masked demons had retreated to whichever hellhole they'd crawled out of.

Chapter 18

June 10, 2001. 02:12. P.M.

Although Joshua had sworn to abstinence six years ago, to care for Gabe as a single parent and help with his speech impediment, he missed alcohol every day. Sleep had become his coping mechanism against the nibbling desire.

And now Joshua was irritable because he had been woken up from his nap by his newbie partner.

"I'm one hundred percent sure…" Peter placed his palms on Joshua's desk and leaned forward, his tie askew and hair ruffled.

Peter Lamb had been working in Gang Unit before their new captain had tagged him with Bernadette, a veteran in the homicide squad. The duo's first case was a bank robbery committed in Staten Island on April 30th of that year. The perpetrator murdered one person and robbed $98,000; coincidentally the same amount Lolly had robbed from a different bank in the same neighborhood in 1993. The FBI screamed Lolly, the media screamed Lolly, and even the cops did, like Bernadette and Peter. Though Joshua knew better, the investigating team considered his input trifling, so he shrugged and watched them chase their own tails.

Bernadette availed maternity leave the previous month, and the captain had partnered the tyro with Joshua.

"It *is* Lolly," Peter implored.

"No, it's not." Joshua stretched his arms over his head and groaned.

"There are too many similarities between them. Can't you see it, Chase?"

"That's the thing, rookie, I can't see any pattern. I don't suffer from pareidolia."

"It's the same technique, for fuck's sake," Peter said.

"What same technique?"

Peter eyed Joshua with abhorrence.

"Robbers generally don't think about shooting people, at least not before making a demand. But Lolly always kills someone as soon as his gang enters the bank, to exert dominance and gain absolute control. Only then does he rob the money. *This* modus operandi is similar to what I have now."

"Could be a copycat or a really twisted fan. You know these infamous criminal types have a weird following, confused wannabes attracted by their tinsel world. John

Dillinger, Bonnie and Clyde, Jesse James…" Joshua stifled a yawn. "You get the idea. What you have, it isn't Lolly."

"What makes you so sure?" Peter asked, irritation creeping into his voice.

"The perp in your case is a loner. And Lolly hunts in a pack."

"But I read your reports. You mentioned that Lolly's gang committed at least three robberies from 1985 till mid-1987 without Lolly himself. So they don't shy away from breaking the pattern."

"In your case, the witnesses say the perp was lanky and highly-strung, both of which Lolly isn't. Sounds more like a teenager than a man. Not to mention that *your* robber used a totally different type of mask and gun."

"No. *My* robber also used a .44 round," Peter nettled, unwilling to let go. "Just like Lolly does."

"Sit." Joshua sighed and motioned Peter to a seat opposite. "It'll take a while but I'm gonna share with you certain info that most people don't know about the Lolly investigation. It's only because you are as restless as a fucking half-puppy that got its first boner."

Peter sat, a smile twitching at the corner of his lips. "Okay. I'm all ears."

"You know what rifling is?" Joshua inserted his hand into his pocket and pulled the Skoal tin out. He didn't need much energy to explain something he knew inside out; one pouch would do.

"Rifling?"

Joshua said, "Yes. It's a spiral groove, like candy cane, carved inside the gun's barrel. It helps the bullets spin as they're ejected from the chamber and stabilizes their flight path. Like how a moving top or a bike doesn't fall while the stationary ones do. Angular momentum. Same principle here. The spin increases the bullet's accuracy."

"I flunked in physics." Peter gave an apologetic smile.

"That's not very important." Joshua shrugged. "What is though, is the factor that determines the spin of bullets: the barrel's *twist rate.*"

"What's that?"

"Simply put, it's the number of inches a bullet travels to complete one rotation after it leaves the muzzle." Joshua paused, giving his rapt partner's brain a moment to catch up. "For example, a barrel with a 1:10" twist rate spins the bullet in such a way that it rotates once for every ten inches it travels."

Peter pinched the bridge of his nose. "The lower the inch count, the higher the spin?"

Joshua clapped and pointed a finger at Peter. "You're smart. Barrels with lower twist rates spit more accurate bullets. You know what striations are?"

"Um… the markings left on the cartridges where the firearms marred them?"

"Exactly. For our case, we will just need to talk about striations made by the grooves in the barrel. This marking on the bullet is actually a mirror image of the rifling. A reverse blueprint, if you will. By examining the bullet, you can conclude the twist rate of the barrel. Combine that with the type of bullet and its grain, you can find what gun was used."

"I think I get it."

"Here is where the problem lies. We shot every pistol that uses .44 into the water tank but no recovered slug has the same striations as the ones from Lolly's gun."

"Have you checked them all?"

"I have. I even researched improvised firearms."

Peter blinked in confusion. "What are they?"

"Homemade guns. Any asshole with a lathe, a milling machine, and mediocre skills to operate the apparatus can do it, which is totally legal in this God-blessed country but as illegal as Satan in other developed nations."

"Do you think Lolly uses homemade guns?"

Joshua said, "I don't. Most homemade guns use smooth bores for barrels."

"No grooves, meaning no striations."

"Yes. But the slugs obtained from his crime scenes all have rifling striations."

"If he is using bored barrels, then it must have come from some brand, right?"

"That's where I'm stagnated," Joshua said. "The striations on Lolly's .44 bullets reveal that he uses a gun with a barrel that creates a 1:21″ twist rate."

"Um… so?"

"There is no gun in the *world* with that combination."

"Oh…" Peter said. "He must be like a ballistic genius, uh?"

Joshua laughed. "Not likely."

"Why not? He has been doing this for what, nineteen years? And we don't even know what weapon he uses. His gun is peculiar, yet we are unable to trace it."

"I think he sucks at ballistics precisely for that reason. For using that broken gun."

"B-broken?" Peter said. "What do you mean?"

"We need to go back to the spin of the bullets. Higher twist rate means the accuracy is compromised. Lolly is using a 1:21″ which—"

"See. There." Peter's forefinger jabbed the table. "What type of criminal knows all this? I still think he is a genius."

"Let me finish. Lolly knew his gun lacked accuracy, probably when he was practicing. That's why *all* his victims were shot within fifteen yards or closer. Shoot someone farther than that, the bullet misses the target, according to our ballistic scientists," Joshua said. "And get this, he never missed in his career. Not once."

"Oh." Peter scratched under his chin.

"But this accuracy problem has a simple fix. Care to guess?"

Peter pressed his knuckles against his pursed lips, head low. Then he lit up. "It's the barrel that spins the bullets, right?"

"Right."

"So… he can easily solve it by switching to a barrel that has a lower twist rate?"

"Yes!" Joshua clapped again. "And also, he could've made the gun more powerful with a barrel that supports .50 AE cartridges."

"But he didn't do any of that," Peter said, more to himself.

"He is an expert in shooting an imperfect gun, and dare I say, I even admire the determination that went into mastering a broken gun, but an expert in ballistic? No, sir, that he isn't."

"Okay. I don't think this new robbery in Staten Island is Lolly," Peter finally admitted.

"But you could have learned it even before knowing all this."

"How?"

"You tell me how. If you're going to be my partner, I need you to be able to think. Not be a dead weight, dragging behind me, slowing me down."

Peter frowned. "Lolly never visits the same place twice. Since he'd already hit Staten Island in '93…?"

"That's something even a civilian could figure out from the MO. Dig deeper."

"Clue?" Peter hesitantly asked.

Joshua pointed at a box on the back shelf. Peter walked to it, picked it up, and returned to the table. With one careless movement, Joshua upended the box and a bunch of crime scene photographs spilled out.

Peter observed the 8x10s, his fingers drumming the desk absently. "Lolly always shoots people on his left, and the other robber, the one wearing the red mask, kills people on the right." He looked up, eyes beaming with excitement. "Lolly never attacks on the right!"

"Could it be that he is left-handed?" Joshua smirked.

"No… multiple witnesses have reported he is a rightie."

"Why would a right-handed man prefer targets on his left? Maybe he is missing something that makes it harder for him to take the right side? Or rather, some kind of coordination?"

Peter squeezed his head, as if the strength his thumbs applied on his temples was directly proportional to the speed at which the answer escaped his brain. "Got it!" Peter said. "Hand-eye coordination."

"What about it?" Joshua watched Peter expectantly.

"Lolly could be blind in the right eye. That's why he needs someone else to cover that side. Even though all it takes is a slight twist of the head and a few microseconds, those seemingly little things can mean life or death when robbing a bank. The robbery I have now, the perp shot the victim on his right. So it probably isn't Lolly."

Joshua nodded. Peter was indeed smart. But he had one last test. "Why can't it be that the red-masked robber, who always picks the right, is blind in the left?"

"Because at the three robberies between 1985 and 1987, he shot people on both left and right."

"We have a winner. Yay…" Joshua yawned again. The energy the snus gave him had reached its limit.

Peter smiled and shook his head.

"What's funny? I'm not a goof-off. I just exercise my jaws a lot."

"Sure you do, but it's not that. You're a pro when it comes to Lolly, aren't you?"

Joshua chuckled drily. He was a *pro* because he had worked hard and made sacrifices personally. Whenever news about Lolly broke, Joshua travelled to the city where the crime had happened. Then he would go through forensics and conduct parallel investigations.

Nothing would jump out, though.

The reports were all the same. Masked gunmen blasted through the entrance, locked it, shot either the customers or the security guards, and threatened the cashier into filling their rucksacks. By displaying sheer violence and determination, they always managed to terrorize the cashiers and prevent them from sneaking dye packs with real wads or pressing the alarm buttons under their desks.

"I wouldn't call myself a pro."

"Then how do you know so much about Lolly?"

"I can't give up. And apparently, it is a bad thing."

"I agree. You could have let go. With your experience, you might have become a lieutenant or captain by now."

Joshua smiled, thinking about his ex-captain and friend Raymond. That bureaucrat had climbed two more rungs in the ladder and become Inspector, while Joshua, who joined the academy the same day as him, was still a detective.

"The next level contains too much desk and too little policing."

"Isn't that good?"

"Not for me. I believe it's better to die on the field than sitting around, broadening my ass."

Peter pondered over that for a few moments. "Perhaps I should follow that belief, too."

"Copy me if you want to get divorced," Joshua muttered under his breath.

"What's that?" Peter tilted his head.

"Nothing. I just said welcome to the team."

Chapter 19

March 15, 2019. 06:52 P.M.

Coke in hand, Joshua was sitting in front of the TV, watching the news, dry eyelids peeled back. Fingers scrabbling in the almost-empty bowl of nachos, Peter slouched at the other end of the same couch, head adhered to the same TV. A quarter century of chasing the most wanted criminal in the country, Joshua had never seen footage of Lolly.

Now he's gonna!

There was no CCTV recording in the robbery he had investigated in 1993. And the FBI weren't candid with their subsequent cases. Now a TV network, Daily Herald, DH as known colloquially, was going to broadcast it to the world.

"It's just mind boggling, what the media can get away with these days," Peter said.

Joshua didn't know if it was distaste or thankfulness in Peter's tone. A higher up in DH, one Ashley Stuart, had called Joshua a few days ago and asked if he would participate in a live telecast and *share insights* about Lolly.

Insight? He was an unholy animal that murdered people for green cotton-linen! There was nothing philosophical or poetic about it. Plain old noxious stew of greed, envy, and selfishness at play.

Joshua had declined, not so politely, but now he regretted calling her a *Ms. Ashley Stooge*, even though it was accurate—the girl hadn't told him they possessed a freaking video of Lolly! Joshua would have agreed not just to give an interview, but also one of his balls if they'd so demanded, provided that they showed him the video. But everything turned out well, he guessed, for his useless ball at least. Now the DH was going to show the video anyway.

The anchor on the TV droned on about something drab, not yet bringing up Lolly's news that they had made the whole country wait for.

And they cut to commercials.

"Goddamn it!" Peter muted the TV and placed the remote beside him on the cushion. Then he upended the nachos bowl into his mouth.

Of course the DH was not going to play their prized video clip before the final advertisement, saving the best for last. The mongrels would prolong the suspense, create hype until they made sure they got the attention of as many viewers as they could.

Joshua placed the half empty bottle of Coke on the table, sighed, and rubbed his temples between his fingertips. Years of melancholy flooded his mind.

Joshua had voluntarily retired from the NYPD as he was unable to concentrate on any cases except Lolly's. An unfocused homicide detective translated to murderers walking free. So he quit the force in 2002. To pay bills, he took odd jobs like consulting security, investigating thefts, surveying adulterers, performing backgrounds on job applicants, and what have you. Not a full-blown PI exactly, but a part time one. There was not a ton of evidence to go on in Lolly's case anyway.

Lolly's gang had robbed a bank in North Dakota in 2008, and poof, they were gone. No one had heard from them ever since.

Joshua initially thought that Lolly's two partners might have killed him and expropriated the business, but no bank robbery across the contiguous United States after 2008 fit their pattern. Joshua knew. He had been going through all the national criminal databases with the help of Raymond, who was now the commissioner of the NYPD. Lolly's gang had truly stopped their trade.

Everyone breathed a sigh of relief, including Joshua. He kind of felt bummed as his life's work was gonna be for nothing. But hey! At least they weren't murdering anyone.

Until they showed up again last month.

A bank robbery in Bristol, Connecticut, left one dead and one gravely injured. The newspaper and media were all over it because one of the robbers was sucking a lollipop when he did the deed.

Since they might have a new case now, Joshua called the FBI. They were stingy with video evidence but liberal in giving other information. Well, not *they*. Just one person had helped Joshua. The same person who had been his *snitch* for years: Nigel Harris.

He was a member of the fourth or fifth special task force the FBI had created in 2003 to apprehend Lolly. Joshua and Nigel had developed a bond of sorts over the years, but it slowly severed after Lolly disappeared. Joshua hadn't spoken with him in a decade.

When Joshua heard about Bristol, he rang Nigel who confirmed that Lolly had truly returned. And he had promised he would call back with more information.

Joshua had waited without sleeping that night. But when Nigel had said *call back*, he hadn't mentioned it might take him twenty-one days and thirteen hours. However when he did get the call, it was worth the wait.

As soon as Joshua answered the phone, the tired sounding FBI agent had said, sans any greetings, "We know what gun Lolly uses."

Joshua's fingers gripped his cell phone.

"A Desert Eagle."

"That's impossible," Joshua said almost immediately. A part of him, the one which knew everything about the case back and forth, took over, and he was in autopilot. "Desert Eagles create 1:18″ twist rate for .44 but the bullets we recovered from Lolly's victims bore 1:21″, which I'd like to point out, doesn't come from any gun that uses a .44. And wasn't Desert Eagle released only in 1983? But the very first robbery Lolly committed was in 1982?"

"How are you even sane? Why do you know all these facts off the top of your head?"

"Tobacco, for the first question. Because catching Lolly is the reason I live and knowing these things is half the battle, for the second."

"Fair enough," Nigel said. "It's the same old 1:21″ twist rate alright. But the magic was in the casing."

"What did you find?"

"The combination of firing pin impression, breech mark, and ejector striations is unique to only one gun in circulation. Desert Eagle."

"But you guys always had the casings. Why didn't you figure it out sooner?"

"Because we didn't have the technological advancement to do so ten years ago."

"I don't understand. You're telling me we got the tech to track Lolly around the same time he breaks his ten-year hiatus? Isn't that convenient!"

"No, we got the tech a few years back. But as Lolly was inactive for so long, we'd forgotten about him."

"That's irresponsible."

"You know how many cold cases we have?"

"I know 40% of the murders go unsolved. Upwards of two hundred K, maybe?"

"More than 250,000 cold cases from 1980, the time Lolly started contributing to it."

"Wow. That's a lot. But what does that have to do with new forensic gadgets?"

"Understatement of the year." Nigel inhaled noisily. "It's impossible to analyze all the tiny bits of evidence every time we have a little technical advancement in forensics. I believe Moore's law doesn't apply only to processors and computers. Even other technologies, like our comparison microscope used in examining bullets—aka the best friend of Forensic Ballistic Examiners—has evolved exponentially in the last decade."

"You lost me somewhere in the middle."

"You can't expect us to examine all the forensic evidence from every single unsolved case whenever we have new technology, can you? Forget resources, the number of times you would need to work on even one unsolved case is monumental."

"But Lolly is not some random murderer. He is number one in the FBI's top ten."

"Who was dormant for more than a decade. You thought we had a team full of bodies, actively looking for Lolly?"

"I didn't," Joshua admitted. "Would have been nice though."

Nigel grunted. "I don't have time for this. Our boss works us twice as hard since Lolly came back."

"Same man?"

"Yeah. Fucking Gregg." Nigel sighed deeply. "So can we get back to the topic, please?"

"Sorry," Joshua said. "Lolly's first bank robbery was in 1982, and the Desert Eagle was not available then. How the hell did Lolly procure some gun before it was released onto the market?"

"Fuck if I know. This is all the information I have at this point. When I know something, you'll know something."

Joshua blew out air.

"Sorry, Josh. You want more gold, you're gonna have to dig further."

Dig was what Joshua did. And oh boy, did he find a goldmine!

"Say, what have you planned for your retirement?" Joshua asked Peter as he brought the lukewarm Coke to his lips.

"Nothing as of yet. Maybe fix the wobbly couch leg, paint the house, plant some roses in the garden. Maybe have a warm glass of milk, tuck myself in, and swallow a bullet?"

Joshua almost choked on the Coke. He wiped his nose and jabbed Peter on the shoulder. "How about a tour?"

"Where?"

"Detroit."

"Anything's better than tasting the lead," Peter said. "Lolly's in Detroit?"

"Could be. Not sure." Joshua hesitated. "It's just three days since I started working on it."

"No problem. Tell me what you've got so far."

"Nah. I need a lot of questions answered, details to collect. I'll tell you on our way over there."

"Suit yourself. Should keep us occupied until we drive—"

"Shhh!"

Peter nudged Joshua's leg with his shoe. "Don't shush me, ass—"

"It's on!" Joshua's frantic fingers pointed at the TV. "Turn it up."

"Oh shit!" Peter retrieved the remote that his right ass cheek was smothering and increased the volume.

Joshua grabbed his Skoal tin from the table. His eyes didn't leave the TV, while his hands opened the tin, plucked two pouches from within and tossed them into his mouth.

The commentator, after advising viewer discretion, announced that the video was five minutes long.

Three robbers entered the bank, which was almost empty at the early hours. They wore black T-shirts, black bomber jackets, and camo pants. Two of them ran in different directions just as soon as the swing doors closed behind their backs. The remaining one, a stocky, blue-masked demon, locked the only entrance to the bank with a device that looked like a thin wheel clamp. Then he grabbed an assault rifle strapped on his back and manned the door.

Lolly wore his famed pale green zombie mask. In his right hand, he carried a shiny silver-plated pistol with a longish barrel. A white lollipop stick poked out from the zombie's mouth hole.

Lolly cannonballed toward the space between the cashier's table and a confused-looking security guard. Once he was close to him, he shot the guard in the face.

Joshua shuddered. No matter how many dead bodies he had seen, it hadn't desensitized him. He bit his teeth and uttered a small prayer. He asked forgiveness from the security guard and his family. If only Joshua had caught Lolly. Seeing that savage son of a bitch on the TV made the blood in Joshua's veins boil.

Lolly, however, didn't give a shit that he had just killed someone. He didn't even slow his sprint, but angled himself toward the cashier's table and slid over the marble floor. Without waiting to check if the preemptive strike had made a kill, Lolly leaped over the counter.

His movements were precise, aggressive, and slick, like a quarterback with a football in his hands. In just four seconds, even before the blue demon locked the entrance, Lolly killed a man, made a sharp turn, and jumped over a tall table.

Lolly pulled one of the dumbstruck cashiers up as if he were a ragdoll, and held the gun to his temple. The hostage repeated a set of instructions whispered into his ear. Linda, the second cashier, put her hands up. Another dumbstruck but unharmed security guard and every one of the bank's five morning customers lay on their stomachs and placed their interlaced fingers at the back of their heads.

A red demon, which dashed in a different direction when the front door closed, went out of the camera's focus, to the right. A few seconds later, he reemerged with a black pistol in his hand.

From the victims' accounts, the red demon had barged into the bank manager's office and buried two bullets between his ribs. The cops said it was a brutal but effective tactic. The manager was the only one who wasn't in the lobby, and he could have called for help when the robbers were busy.

The red demon jogged toward the sleeping security guy and took the machine gun he'd kept over his head. Then he headed toward Lolly. When he reached the counter, he unstrapped the bags from his body and threw them at Linda. The bags hit her chest and fell at her feet.

Linda put her hands down, doubled over, and brought up the bags. She started filling them, wiping her cheeks at irregular intervals.

When Linda finished filling the bags and handed them over, Lolly kicked his hostage's right buttock hard. Linda's frenzied attempt to catch her colleague from hitting the floor would have been comical if it weren't for the blood spreading under the head of the dead security guard.

Then they beelined towards the entrance, all three disappeared, and the video mercifully came to an end.

Chapter 20

April 6, 2019. 8:01 A.M.

The swelling river snaked between a series of hills, before flowing right and disappearing along the woods. The road they were on looked feeble and thin, running through majestic mountains and forests. Like a floating noodle on a green ocean.

Joshua opened the glovebox and took out the Skoal tin. Just as he finished burying two in his mouth, an impatient douche honked behind, forcing him to drive onwards. The congestion moved at a snail's pace and the toll booth was a good three minutes away. What's the rush then? Why not look outside at the scenery nature had been chiseling for millions of years? The fortitude of a river that eroded its way through titanic rock was inspiring.

Having no choice but to watch the arid I-80, his mind disassociated.

"Boring," Peter voiced Joshua's thought.

He grunted in return.

"Now would be an optimal time to say why Detroit."

"Couldn't agree more," Joshua replied and started filling his partner in.

After Nigel told him about the Desert Eagle, Joshua talked with Magnum and eventually with the Detroit PD. He gathered a trove of knowledge, the chief among it was that Lolly could be using one of the first models of Desert Eagle Magnum had experimented with. That explained the abnormal 1:21″ twist rate. It was a functioning piece, but not the perfect handgun they released in 1983.

"Where did Lolly get a gun like that?" Peter asked, his wrinkled eyelids barely containing the same puppy-like curiosity they did eighteen years ago.

Joshua whistled. "You might wanna strap yourself. It's one hell of a story."

He proceeded to explain: in 1981, the then new company, Magnum Research Inc., filed a lawsuit against MacSharp, its competition. A prototype Magnum had been developing in their Michigan facility, apparently the most powerful pistol in the world at that time, had gone missing.

"The Desert Eagle?"

"Yes," Joshua confirmed. "Their corporate security conducted an investigation. Turned out one of the employees in their research team was a double agent working for MacSharp. But Magnum couldn't prove anything."

"How did Lolly get the Eagle from MacSharp?" Peter said.

"A few months after the theft at Magnum, two of MacSharp's employees were found dead on a seedy road on Livernois Avenue. A driver and a security guard who delivered trucks. But the company said that no truck left their Detroit facility that night."

"Maybe they didn't."

"But the witnesses on Livernois Avenue reported they saw a truck, resembling the same models MacSharp employed for transportation. It was driving dangerously, and get this: someone was clinging to its passenger side door."

"A hijack," Peter said.

Joshua affirmed with a nod. "The arms on a level crossing nearby had some paint scraped. Same type of paint used on MacSharp's trucks. But they denied everything, and the case went nowhere."

"What will a burglar do if a scorpion stings him at a house he's broken into?"

"Keep his goddamn mouth shut." Joshua chuckled. "Another important detail is, like how MacSharp had a snitch in Magnum, someone had a snitch in MacSharp."

"Who?" Peter frowned.

"A crime family named Detroit Alliance. The homicide detectives investigating the double murder on Livernois Avenue looked into the history of all the employees in the MacSharp facility where the driver and the security guard had worked."

"Go on." Peter's frown relaxed a bit.

"A guy in the logistics department was a relative of a known repeat offender, who'd been a soldier for the Detroit Alliance."

"Seems like the DPD gave a lot of time to you. He's a retiree, too?"

"No, he's a captain. Who hates Lolly as much as I do."

"Hm."

They paid the toll and continued driving. Peter was looking outside but his thoughts weren't with nature. He was thinking about something else.

"What's up?" Joshua asked.

"It doesn't fit." Peter turned towards Joshua. "You can't just assume that the hijacked truck transported the prototype Desert Eagle. It could be anything."

Joshua laughed. "I knew you'd try your damn best to find holes in my theories."

Peter lifted an eyebrow. "Would you prefer it any other way?"

"No."

"Then plug the hole."

"So a Caddy drops a bloody guy in front of the ER on Christmas in 1981. The poor bastard drags his way inside and admits himself. He said a rowdy gang mistook him for someone else and shot him in the knee. A victim of a *drive-by*, he'd claimed. The doctors treated the poor bastard and bagged the bullet for the detectives." Joshua gave Peter a knowing smile.

"Forty-four?" Peter asked. "From the broken Desert Eagle?"

"The one and only."

"But that's even earlier than 1982, before Lolly's first recorded robbery."

"Exactly. Could be Lolly's very first shot."

"First shot?"

"MacSharp truck was hijacked at midnight on December 24, 1981. And the Desert Eagle was used to shoot someone a few hours later."

"So why was the bullet not in any records? If it were, we could have made this connection a long time ago."

"National databases were used to log evidence only from most notorious cases, not *drive-bys* with no fatalities. How many cases did our own NYPD fail to record in the

ViCAP? And computers weren't that popular among cops in '81." Joshua squeezed Peter's shoulder. "Come on, man. You're asking all the wrong questions."

Peter thought for a whole minute. "Alright, who was the *poor bastard* that got shot?"

Joshua glanced at Peter and smirked. "A right-hand man to the Don of the Detroit Alliance. The snitch who was siphoning information from MacSharp was suspected of working for him. So I'm fairly sure that the hijacked truck contained the prototype."

"Wow." Peter shook his head. "That's the final part in a very convoluted puzzle."

"Wrong." Joshua's gaze intensified. "It's just the beginning."

They stopped at a fast-food van in Williamsport, and each downed a cup of chicken rice. When done with the late lunch, Peter got behind the wheel and drove. Joshua rolled the window up, then leaned on it and closed his eyes.

* * *

He felt a strange sense of sickness in his stomach. A black bile. He discerned he was stuck in a lucid dream, but he couldn't get up. As he writhed and struggled in the timeless ether of his mind, he felt the car's movement slow. As if the road suddenly turned into tar and the air into oil. So much resistance. And something soft touched his chest, pushing him back.

No, Joshua thought, it was not pushing him back. It was him who was moving forward and the hand was trying to stop him from going further.

As he tore the last shackle of sleep paralysis and pulled himself out, he gasped and sucked in air greedily.

Peter passed a bottle, and Joshua thankfully gulped the water. He hadn't realized how parched he was until then.

Peter did not show any sign that he'd seen Joshua awaken in trepidation. He knew about Joshua's perpetual bouts with night terrors.

Wait.

Was it already night? The dark sky said as much.

Then Joshua's eyes lowered.

They were still on the highway, but he could see their destination. The city glowed on the horizon, the skyscrapers and factories protruding from the Earth. They looked to be floating on the sea of blackness.

No, not floating. More like the arthritic fingers of a desperate captain as he went down with his sinking ship.

"Where to now?" Peter asked.

"Calabria." Joshua programmed the location in the dashboard GPS. "It's a bar in Gratiot Avenue."

"Who's there?" Peter asked.

Joshua lay back and closed his eyes. "The poor bastard."

Chapter 21

April 6, 2019. 08:17. P.M.

"I don't know no Roman," the barkeeper behind the table said as he wiped a beer glass with a cloth.

"Tell him it's about Lolly," Peter said.

The barkeeper paused cleaning but quickly resumed. "I don't know no Lolly."

Peter snapped, "It's the asshole who shot your boss when you were just a slow-witted sperm in your dad's nutsack."

The barkeeper eyed Peter with a hint of mischief. Though he was too young to have been around in 1981, he might have heard stories from the criminal grapevines before but now he was a part of it.

Smirking, he placed the glass on the table and went over to the corner. He picked up a wireless from under the table and mumbled something in it.

Joshua looked around the bar. The lighting was dim, the music was tacky, and cigarette smoke coiled upward from almost all the tables. But the customers looked neither like the complaining type nor like they would go to the authorities for help. And there was not a single woman in the bar. Its clientele was purely men, purely suspicious, and lastly, purely quiet. However, the silence came only after Joshua and Peter had stepped into the establishment a minute ago.

The barkeeper returned the wireless to its place and tilted his head towards a door at the back.

"It's not me," Joshua said. "The smell's coming from you."

"What smell?"

"Smell of pork. Why else would the barkeeper be so wary of us?"

"Oh, screw you."

As they skirted the table, Joshua inserted his hand into his jacket. The bartender's eyes widened, and he reached behind his back.

"Whoa!" Joshua lifted his hands and showed him the Skoal tin. "It's just tobacco, hoss. Slow down before you shoot your toe off."

He opened the tin and tossed two pouches in his mouth. When he offered it to the barkeeper, he murmured something and led them through the door, closing it behind. The music abated suddenly, worrying Joshua. If the sound didn't seep in through the reinforced door, then it didn't seep out either.

The inside was entirely different. No smoke, no dark setting, and no blue-collar atmosphere. The left wall shelved costly wines and liquor. On the front was a medium sized desk carrying a PC. The idea of the Mafia using computers for data storage amused Joshua. The civilian part of him fathomed the practicality while the detective side appreciated the fact that nothing entered into the system could ever truly be deleted, not unless you obliterated the hard drives.

There was a kitchenette in the right wall, and the pleasant smell of cheese wafted from it. Not mozzarella. Something else. Something with a strong flavor. He had eaten it with meatballs or crispy chicken at authentic Italian restaurants back home. Parmesan, he guessed.

A fat person, with a crutch extending from his left elbow, was whistling as he waddled along the counter, cluttering cookware and china. He took a pair of tongs from the utensil holder and picked a huge brick of lasagna from the rectangular glass dish. He laid it on a white plate on the counter, where already a few scoops of garlic-prosciutto Brussels sprouts were strewn. He added two dollops of butter atop, letting it melt by the heat of the food.

Joshua found himself salivating. Roman must be one hell of a gastronome. He waved the bartender over and motioned at his mound of fat-adder. "Put it on the desk."

Then he turned, licking the tips of the tong and tossing it into the dishwasher.

Roman must be in his seventies. He blobbed like he ate bacon for food and drank beer for water. Joshua's attention crossed Roman's colossal midsection and slipped to his left leg. The pant, though loose, couldn't entirely hide the wreckage beneath. The knee arched back and formed a hideously zigzagged joint. Seeing it without cringing was a feat.

"What the fuck you staring at?" Roman turned and walked towards his desk.

Joshua hadn't realized Roman was talking to him until Peter nudged him. He was transfixed by the deformity. Could really one bullet destroy a leg like that? Joshua had seen firsthand the detrimental prowess of Lolly's anti-aircraft gun, but usually the wounds were in the head. Now to see it in a different body part induced morbid curiosity in him.

Peter walked behind Roman and Joshua followed him.

He tried his best not to look at the back of Roman's knee, which accentuated the damage as he walked. He tried and failed. Even though the crutch supported most of Roman's weight, his left leg folded back unnaturally in the middle and something blunt protruded as it did. A shiver ran up Joshua's spine, forcing him to look away.

With the barkeeper's help, Roman maneuvered his ass onto the chair.

Joshua began. "I'm sorry. I didn't mean to—"

"What you know about Lolly?" Roman asked as he shoved a spoonful of food into his face hole.

"Everything there is to know about him," Peter said.

"*Everything about him*, uh?" His words distorted as he spoke. "Where's he now? What's his name?"

Peter bit his lower lip and snapped his fingers. "Except those."

Roman glowered at them, giving each at least a two-second stare. "Are you here to ruin my dinner, which by extension means, your faces. Who're you, clowns?"

"I'm Joshua Chase. I used to be an NYPD detective."

"Detective Chase?" Roman frowned. "Why does that name ring a bell?"

"It's my son. He caught a serial killer back home and became a national sensation."

"Oh yeah, that's correct. Mr. Bunny, right? Crazy shit, that. He must be really smart, your son—" Roman paused mid-chew and stared at a blank space on the desk. Apparently, he couldn't think when his mouth was at work. Explained why he ate so much without fearing diabetes or ticker failure.

"Can you help us?"

Roman broke out of his trance. "How?"

"Talk to us about a truck hijacking in nineteen—"

"Not this again." Roman dropped the spoon and leaned back on his chair.

"We just need some basic details," Joshua said.

"What makes you think I'll tell you even if I know? I ain't no fucking turncoat."

"Just tell us who hijacked the truck?" Peter said. "We're not asking you to testify."

"Testify?" Roman smiled but it didn't reach his eyes. "Get the fuck out of here, you two!"

* * *

Both climbed into the car, Joshua taking the wheel.

"Well, that was a farce," Peter said.

"I expected as much. Tried the easy way, but predictably, it didn't pan out." Joshua eased the Audi into the traffic.

As they exited the dingy neighborhood, Joshua felt dreadful. Something was wrong.

He angled the rearview and found a black SUV driving behind them. While most other vehicles behind them either changed direction or overtook them, the SUV maintained a steady pace and interval.

But a few minutes later, when Joshua pulled the car over in front of a shoddy hotel in downtown, the SUV drove past without slowing or speeding.

Joshua sighed, chiding his brain. Why would anyone tail him? His overactive amygdala was crying wolf. Tired, having travelled for a long time, his head vibrated constantly. And the bar full of criminals had given him the jitters. He needed a stiff meal, a hot bath, and bed.

Joshua got down from the car and opened the back door. A notebook that he had placed on the seat when they started their journey lay down on the floor.

Cursing that he had to bend, he retrieved the notebook and dusted it off.

They went in and booked two rooms. As the receptionist filled the forms, Peter pointedly looked at the notebook. "You're gonna make me ask?"

"This is the culmination of all my work relating to Lolly. Years of investigation, stripped of drama and bullshit, leaving only the cold, useful facts. I've been writing it since '93."

"Why?"

"I don't…" Joshua searched for the right way to explain without sounding emotional. "This is my life's work right here. I want someone to pick up where I left off, you know, if I die before solving the case. Or worse. If anything happened to—"

"Nothing will happen to us."

"*If!*" Joshua pinched Peter's ear and shouted in it. "If, Grampa. Remember that word, you senile dildo? *If?*"

"Leave me alone, asshole." Peter jerked away.

The receptionist tried her best not to look up at them as she pushed the forms forward. "Please sign here, gentlemen."

As Peter signed, Joshua said, "If we fail, I want my son to carry on my legacy. One Chase or the other, we're gonna bring this motherfucker down."

The receptionist passed each a key, still avoiding eye contact.

* * *

Joshua was vaguely aware of his consciousness returning. His eyelids were heavy and grainy, brushing against his eyes. His lumbar region stung, and he reckoned his body was covered in sticky sweat. The room was cool, but the temperature under the blanket was stifling.

A creak made him open his eyes. The noise didn't seem to have come from his bed. Aggravated by the lack of comfort, he threw the blanket away and kicked it down.

And his heart froze in terror.

A form, resembling a three-headed hellhound, stood in front of him, snarling, its red teeth sharp and rugged. Unable to grasp the image his retina was feeding him, he rubbed his eyes. The sight returned along with the reasoning, and the Cerberus transformed into clothes hanging from the wall hooks.

Releasing a huge breath, he looked around the dark room. A shadow under the door moved ever so slightly, and the wood creaked again.

"Peter?" Joshua called out.

The movement halted and the shadow disappeared. As if it had never been there.

Bemused and wondering if he had dreamed the whole thing, he fell back onto the damp pillows and dozed off.

Chapter 22

April 07, 2019. 3:21. P.M.

Joshua had slept until late afternoon. Grumbling why aged bodies took longer to recuperate, he shambled to the bathroom. He took a Spartan shower and dressed up before rapping on the adjacent door.

Thirty minutes later, Peter and Joshua were cruising on the main road, their destination being the DPD.

Driving through downtown without hectic traffic made Detroit look weird. At this time, the city center back home would be replete with exhaust fumes and road rage. Maybe he got so acclimated to the hurly-burlies of NYC all day every day that his cognition was biased.

His head wasn't in the right place, groggy from the fiasco the previous night.

"You came to my room?" Joshua said, momentarily looking at Peter.

"I did, around eleven this morning, but you were snoring like an elephant. So I left."

"No, before that."

"I didn't." Peter regarded Joshua, with worry on his face. "You don't look so good. Didn't you sleep well?"

The mere mention of sleep made Joshua yawn. "Tossing and turning the whole damn night, I feel restless."

Peter said, "It's evolution, you see. Can't help it."

"Evolution?"

"Tell me, when is someone in danger?"

Joshua sensed it was a rhetorical question, so he bit. "When?"

"When sleeping and shitting. Your reflexes slacken, which by definition means your guard's down. So the reptilian brain overcompensates by constantly being alert. That's why tourists feel like they miss their own toilets and beds, when in reality, they miss the secure familiarity they experience in the inviolable habitat of their own toilets and beds."

"Hm." He mulled over his friend's point. Or Joshua was really being stalked.

The view outside transformed from city to ghetto. The change was painfully obvious—buildings turned from marvelous edifices to skeletal geriatrics.

Joshua couldn't stop looking in the rearview. Call it paranoia, not hallucination, but he always found a leery vehicle lurking ten to twenty meters behind. A motorcycle this time, not an SUV.

Even with all the distraction, they reached the precinct safely in under twenty minutes.

While pulling over into the parking lot, Joshua noticed a rusty tandem bike chained to a horizontal pole on a brick wall in front of them. Drawn above it was some old graffiti. Joshua squinted and tried to fill the missing sections and make out the shape. Then the design jumped on him.

It was the American flag, but with only five stars.

* * *

The precinct was in no way different than his 122nd. In fact, it was not unlike any other office place. Except three things: guns on the hips of residents, tattooed guests cuffed to benches, and offhand use of bigotry slurs, which would lead to your termination of employment in any other setting.

The cops themselves were mostly black, about 80% of them. Back in Staten Island, the cops were mostly white. However, Detroit had a ratio of 80:20 black to white, while Staten Island's ratio was the same inversely.

Anyhow, the cop they met, the one who had been helping Joshua, was white. Captain Wheeler ushered them into his office.

After the pleasantries and obligatory lame jokes were out of the way, Joshua began by confessing that he felt like he was being followed. It surprised Peter as much as it did Wheeler.

"Why would anyone follow you?"

Smiling apologetically at Peter, Joshua said, "We talked to Roman."

Wheeler tsk-tsked. "Now why would you pull Maverick shit like that?"

Peter said, "So what? He's just a regular scum. We thought he'd spill some beans."

"He is a capo regime. You know that capos are made men and made men take a certain oath?"

Omertà. An oath of silence, which most carried to their graves. Joshua hadn't thought of that before. The Mafia thing seemed so old to him even though he grew up in New York.

"If they're tailing you, losing them is impossible," Wheeler said. "With Instagram and Facebook Live, they don't tail with just one vehicle. They do it as a gang."

"That's pretty advanced of them."

"Yes, they've been known to use high-tech gadgets, hack phones, and emails, too."

"Or maybe he's just losing it." Peter grabbed Joshua's shoulder. "Roman refused to help. Cool. But why follow us?"

"Good question," Wheeler said, and they both looked at Joshua for the answer.

Joshua deflated. "Fine. I'm being a worrywart. Let's get down to business."

"What'd you need, Chase?" Wheeler asked. "I thought I gave you all the intel I had. About the truck hijacking, about Detroit Alliance."

"Yeah, I've been thinking." Joshua leaned on the table. "Before I linked the MacSharp truck hijacking to Lolly, we thought his first ever recorded crime was in 1982."

"Yeah."

"Now that we know he began sooner, maybe we could find something before that."

"Before 1981?"

"Yeah. Crimes related to theft or robbery, with Lolly's signature unfettered violence."

As Wheeler's fingers drummed the desk, the lines on his forehead deepened. "That timeline falls under the period of John Nichols."

Peter shrunk his eyes. "Are we supposed to know him?"

"Not if you aren't an old, black Detroiter or an old-timer cop. Uncle John, as Mr. Nichols was affectionately called, was famous because he'd gestated STRESS when he was the commissioner of the DPD."

Peter asked, "Stress? Stress for who?"

Wheeler laughed. "No. It's an acronym." He pronounced each letter separately, as if Peter couldn't spell the word. "Abbreviation for *Stop The Robberies, Enjoy Safe Streets*."

Joshua said, "Yeah, I think I've heard about it. A controversial decoy unit within the Detroit PD, right?"

"Correct. Back during those desperate times, there was no subtlety in crime. The voracious street urchins robbed people in broad daylights, in front of witnesses."

"That's ballsy of them," Peter said.

"Uh-huh." Wheeler nodded. "Those hellions put the kids who call themselves *gangstas* these days to shame. None of these hoodlum-wannabes with low-hip jeans and YOLO caps. No. What the kids in old Detroit had was desperation. And zero fear. That's what kindled so much will and courage in their little rotten hearts, it was unworldly."

Peter said, "So that's why this STRESS was created?"

"Correct. Officers would disguise themselves as oldsters, drunks, Johns, or hippies. When the evil sons of bitches decide to rob the officer... well, that's where the *controversial* part comes in."

Peter said, "Because the cops were trigger-happy?"

Wheeler burst chuckled. "That's putting it mildly. When STRESS was active, they were responsible for more than 90% of death by the police. Most of the *criminals* they shot down didn't even have a gun. And in a few publicly embarrassing incidents, officers were found guilty of planting weapons on the victims they'd killed."

Peter said, "Wow. That sounds a lot like TV."

"I hear you. But remember that reality—history specifically—is far more violent and animated than any movie or show ever created."

"I've heard about a few dirty cops taking bribes, or even doing some favors for the Five Families, but not something as blatant as this."

"The STRESS officers weren't dirty per se, not at least in the normal sense."

Peter scoffed. "Except they were murderers with a license to kill minorities."

"I agree." Wheeler lifted his hands. "Old time Detroit, particularly the seventies and eighties, was the golden age of crime."

Peter lifted his eyebrows. "That bad?"

"Cowboys and Indians, real-like."

"Were you in STRESS?"

"Good god, no. But I was still in the force. Wanna know about my first day as a cop?" Wheeler's face turned as if he'd tasted something sour. "I chased a scrawny kid for two miles on foot. The idiots who'd brought him in didn't frisk properly. So he unlocks the cuffs *while back in the police cruiser*. When they open the door, he smashes their faces in and runs out like a bat out of hell. And since these two were obese, I had to take off after the kid."

"You catch him?"

"Nah."

"Too fast?"

"Also too smart." Wheeler looked up and sighed, as if he still regretted failing to catch that boy. "But that day was still a lot better than others. I'm telling you all this so you'll get the gist of how prevalent crime was back then."

Joshua asked, "There's no use researching all the violent property crimes from that time period?"

"Too voluminous you wouldn't even know where to begin." Wheeler shook his head. "And people didn't trust us back then. Chances are, we might have had as many unreported crimes as the reported ones."

"Fuck," Peter said.

"I second that, brother," Wheeler said.

As Joshua thought, he took out his Skoal tin and utilized two packs to accelerate his brain. "How about your snitch from the Detroit Alliance? Is it possible for us to meet him?"

"Can be arranged, but why?"

"The mole in MacSharp's logistics department was working for the Detroit Alliance. Without his information, no one would have known that the Desert Eagle was being transported that night. If we find out who hijacked MacSharp's truck on behalf of the Alliance, we unmask Lolly."

"You're correct." Wheeler clasped his hands on the table. "If anyone can shed light on this, it would be the snitch. He used to be an enforcer."

"*Used to?* What happened? Has he gone straight?"

"Ha-ha." Wheeler didn't try to hide the duplicity of the laughter. "Far from it. He's in the big house for attempted murder." Wheeler brought his voice down and murmured. "Could have been murder if the bastard were able to shoot straight." Then he laughed at his own inside joke, while Peter and Joshua exchanged awkward glances.

"Let's go then?"

Wheeler checked his watch. "The visiting hours are over for today. I'll schedule a meeting for tomorrow."

"What do we do in the meantime?"

"Take a load off, guys. Enjoy our fine city's nightlife. Just don't forget to bring your sidearm."

Joshua said, "R-really?"

"Detroit isn't as bad as they make it out to be." Wheeler waved him off and laughed. "I'm kidding." Then he stopped abruptly, staring icily. "Or am I?"

* * *

Joshua couldn't sleep that night. It had been almost two hours since he'd switched off the lights and started minding the door, with his revolver on his lap. No phone or TV. He needed his vision to be perfect.

And then he noticed it. Not under the door, but much closer. The window beside the bed. It became darker in the middle. Although the glass was frosted, he could tell from the light outside.

Joshua crept to it, regulating his breathing. The person outside couldn't see his silhouette—not even a night lamp was lit in his room. When Joshua was near the window, he gripped the handle of his gun. Taking one last breath, he pushed it out.

The frame rattled, but didn't budge a millimeter in the way of opening.

And the shadow outside had disappeared.

Joshua switched on the lights and searched the window. A pair of hooks secured the frame to the windowsill. Cursing himself for not having checked that before, he pulled the hooks from their eyes and climbed onto the fire escape.

He aimed the gun at the stairs running down, then at the alley. He rotated and pointed at the bare walls of the opposite building and the street below. Everywhere was dark and empty.

Only the stink of garbage assaulted him.

Placing a hand on his thumping heart, Joshua felt angry with himself. Was he really losing it?

He locked the window and checked the latches in the front door. Then he lay on the bed and closed his eyes, gun laid on the pillow beside him.

Once the fervor of adrenaline from anger and fear had subsided, his mind gave way to reasoning.

What if he hadn't imagined it and someone was indeed trying to break into his room? As a guy who'd solved homicides for a living, Joshua knew that one hundred percent of the time, a stranger never broke into your room in the middle of the night bearing merry thoughts. He might have something else on his mind that began with the letter M, but *merry* was not it.

Chapter 23

April 08, 2019. 11:21. A.M.

Joshua's phone woke him up. It was Wheeler confirming that the meeting was on. After he hung up, Joshua lay back and groaned. He had been watching the door and the window the whole night, unaware of when he had dozed off.

Just a few more winks.

But he needed to talk to the snitch.

An hour later, Peter and sleep-deprived Joshua left the hotel, and fifteen minutes later, they turned onto Mound Road where Detroit Detention Center was located. They pulled over into the visitors parking lot and walked inside the concrete behemoth.

A stern hulk of an officer, cocooned within bulletproof glass, instructed them to drop their cell phones and belts on a tray jutting out from the booth. Joshua also had to surrender his Skoal tin. When he drew his gun out, the officer's eyes almost popped out.

"We used to be cops." Joshua placed his .38 Ruger Service Six on the tray. The revolver, which Joshua never fired on duty, had been replaced by semi automatics since 1993 in the NYPD. But as any old cop, he had grown quite fond of the one thing that had been literally by his side as he patrolled the shady streets of the Bronx, silently assuring his safety. The wooden handle that had absorbed his sweat was warmer and more comforting than any cold steel.

Peter dropped his flashy SIG-Sauer P226 on the tray, the one that succeeded the Ruger, which in turn was replaced by flashier Glocks and upgraded Sigs.

They informed the officer that they were visiting a man named Joey Marco.

"Ten minutes," the officer said.

"No, you don't understand," Peter said. "This is regarding a high-profile—"

"Ten minutes for civilians," the officer said, louder this time.

Just as Peter went to argue, Joshua put a hand on his shoulder. "It's their dominion."

Emasculated, they followed a blue line on the wall that read *Visitors*. The labyrinthine corridors led to a musty hall that smelled of stale cigarettes, sweat, and the sewers. The floor was laden with rat droppings and cockroach eggs that looked like brown Tic-Tacs. Oscillating fans mounted on the walls provided a transitory respite every five seconds.

A barrier separated the prisoners and the visitors. The bottom half of it was concrete, the top half made of reinforced glass. The barrier was divided into a dozen neat partitions vertically, and a single chair was placed in front of each.

They chose the middle, the only spot to receive two drafts of air from two different fans. Peter took the seat, and Joshua pulled himself a chair from beside.

As they waited, a lean guy in orange prison garb was ushered in through a metal door on the other side.

"Ten minutes," the guard shouted and stood with his back against the wall, while the prisoner made his way towards them.

His hair was closely cropped; his face could do with fewer scars. For a guy over seventy, his ramrod physique and black hair were begrudgingly absurd.

"I know why you're here. Wheeler told me," Joey said as he sat, his hoarse voice a few decibels lower when it filtered through the holes on the glass. "Lolly."

Both nodded in unification.

"Now the country fears him, but back then, he was just a little runt," Joey put his hand out, slightly over his shoulder, "about yay big."

"Go on."

"Not so fast." Joey grinned and scratched his cheek. Joshua noticed that he missed his right thumb. Joey caught him staring and quickly drew his hand down. "Show me your wallets."

Clueless, they looked at each other but obeyed the scum, brandishing the leather front to back over the glass.

"No, you idiots. How much you got? Put it over there."

They emptied the wallets above the ledge and all three counted. Two hundred dollars and a bit of loose change.

"Nice," Joey stretched the E. "Transfer it to my JPay."

Joshua's fatigued mind took a moment to understand what was happening. Joey was mugging their $200—while in prison, in front of the authorities—by making them deposit it in his commissary account.

Peter said, "But we have just ten minutes."

Picking his teeth with his nail, Joey said, "Then chop-chop!"

Joshua glanced at Peter sideways.

"Oh, come on," Peter whined, but got up, holding his hip. "Hope you rot in hell."

Then he made a show of looking around. "Oh! You're already there."

"Whatever."

Peter's footfalls disappeared along the corridor.

"Okay, now that you've bilked us out of our cash, play your part."

"It's payment. I ain't no shyster. My lawyer is."

"Using the prison library, uh?" Joshua smirked. "Let's not waste time."

Joey said, "My cousin was hired by MacSharp, a weapons factory that had opened near Livernois. Back then we had several people working in various plants who kicked up information to us—"

"I'm sorry. I neither have the time nor the inclination to learn the mechanics of the Mafia. You may have noticed, it's not the dominant force it used to be back then. Bigger and meaner evil overtook it. Heard of cartels? How about Isis? Just tell me anything you know about Lolly."

Joey sneered, but spoke nonetheless. "So… we got information from our guy in MacSharp about a shipment. But our soldiers were all known to the system. Though my cousin was sure it wouldn't get reported if we ambushed it, we didn't want to take that risk. Robbing a weapon carrier could generate a lot of heat."

"So you outsourced the job."

Joey nodded. "Roman had just become a capo, and he wanted to prove his worth to the family."

"He became innovative."

Joey chuckled. "He put a word out that he needed some lowlifes skilled in robbery but not known to the cops." Joey's face stiffened. "That's when we heard about a scrawny black kid who had a rep as some kinda batshit daredevil."

"Wait! Lolly was renowned in the underworld even before he hijacked the MacSharp truck?" Joshua hadn't doubted that Lolly must have committed some sort of crime prior to MacSharp, but didn't think he would be infamous in Loserville.

"We chose him to rob MacSharp *because he was already famous.*"

Famous. Joshua rolled his eyes. "For what?"

"Another truck job." Joey leaned forward, his eyes beaming. "They T-boned a freaking backhoe into an armored cash van and threw it down a bridge…" Joey went on about what Lolly did that day.

"When was this again?" Joshua didn't need a pen. His desperate mind was sucking in new facts like the vacuum of the space.

"We met Lolly's gang in December of '81. This robbery would've taken place some three to six months before that."

"Alright. Tell me about your meeting with Lolly."

Joey massaged the stump of his missing digit. "We made a really simple deal with the little Satan. Bring the MacSharp truck and get paid."

"But you guys planned to kill them," Joshua spoke out his suspicion. "Lolly shot Roman and possibly you and escaped?"

"We didn't plan to kill them!" Joey implored and told him what happened.

By the end, Joshua was appalled. He hadn't imagined the story to be this sadistic. The deeper he went, the darker it got, giving him the chills.

"I don't understand the need for torture. It doesn't fit Lolly's pattern. Did your Don do something to Lolly before you guys met him?"

"If we remembered every bad deed we did our brains would go like this." With his left hand, Joey made an action of explosion beside his temple.

Good point.

"You haven't figured it out? No suspects?" Joshua asked.

"We had a lot of enemies. But the guys—no the kids—who did us in were blacks. Our Don always kept them at distance, both in friendliness and enmity. Still he rounded up the bosses of all the black neighborhoods in Detroit. He got their permission and put out an offer, which is still valid."

"What offer?"

"Time!" the officer behind Joey said.

"Bring Lolly's blue-eyed head, you get two million."

"How many for alive?"

Joey stood up, with a lopsided grin. "I'm a finger shorter to show you."

* * *

Joshua resigned to sit at the passenger side of the car. His brain worked double time, computing the latest data, while his eyes studied the mirrors.

They drove on the 8 Mile Road, made famous by Eminem. It did seem like it separated the poor inner city from the wealthy suburbs.

They turned onto Livernois Avenue, and a mile ahead was an overpass the GPS called the Michigan highway. Joshua asked Peter to take this route because Lolly had killed two people there almost four decades ago. The sparse road allowed them to cruise at a leisurely pace of twenty miles per hour.

In the side mirror, Joshua noticed something. A beat SUV, driving two cars behind, took a sudden turn and accelerated.

As the SUV gained on them, the driver's face behind the windscreen became visible.

The guy was wearing a balaclava.

The SUV was *almost* flanking them. Another man in a balaclava, sitting in the second row, was aiming a shiny pistol with both hands. A Desert Eagle, not an Uzi or similar types the drive-by shooters preferred. Both men were black. It hadn't crossed Joshua's mind until now. Could... could it be Lolly who was after Joshua?

The guy took a shot at the car, the bullet bouncing off the metal. For a split second, the deafening boom whelmed the sounds of the busy road. Joshua watched the recoil fold the shooter's elbows and his forearms hit the rim of the window, making him scream in pain.

Grabbing the hair at the back of Peter's head, Joshua ducked and yanked the gear stick. The car teetered to a stop, and the SUV flew past; but it skidded around in front of them.

Blood pounding in the ears, Joshua sat up straight.

"Holy panties!" Peter finally understood what was happening. As he shifted the car into gear, Joshua noted the gunman holding his ears. Since the shooter was on the left side of the SUV, Peter swerved the car right and floored it.

The Audi zoomed ahead at incredible speed. Joshua turned around. The shooter got down from the SUV and aimed at their car. But he twisted his face away from the gun. Like he was as afraid of the cannon-gun's trigger as they were of its bullet.

However, he managed to confront his fear. Twice.

Both shots missed them. Not surprising. Closing his eyes shut and turning away from the target had proven to have adverse effects on accuracy.

Peter climbed onto the ramp that merged with the highway. Good thinking. Interstate meant more room for speed, which their could-have-been killers' SUV lacked.

As the g-force pulled them back, the glorious Audi unleashed the full might of its fleeing capacity.

Chapter 24

April 8, 2019. 06:03. P.M.

"You guys got your car back?" Wheeler asked as he filled some paperwork on the desk.

"Uh-huh," Peter said.

Joshua said, "May I borrow your PC and access the crime records?"

Wheeler dropped the pen and stared flatly. "You're kidding me?"

"No, why?"

Wheeler frowned. "Two masked men just tried to murder you in broad daylight."

Joshua counted with his fingers. "The report's filed, the slug's recovered from the car, we've given our statements, the detectives are out there collecting CCTV recordings. What else is there?"

"Your mental health!" Wheeler said.

Joshua glanced at Peter who shrugged impassively.

"Don't you guys feel shaken?" Wheeler asked.

Peter said, "I've been shot at more than a dozen times when I was in Gang Squad. It's no biggie, as long as you don't compel me to visit a shrink."

Wheeler looked at Joshua. "And you, Chase?"

"I admit, I've never been in a gunfight before." Joshua lifted his hands. "And I was scared shitless even as we drove into the precinct. But then I remembered my choices. Either tuck my tail and run away. Or stay in Detroit and finish what I came here to do, what I started doing twenty-six years ago. When I simplify it like this, it's easy for me to put my foot down and deny myself the chance to feel scared. Maybe later in the night, but not now, when I've got stuff to do."

"Is that norm— You know what? Never mind." Wheeler stood up, pulled his chair out, and motioned at the monitor. "Here. Use it all you want. It's already logged into the police servers." He walked around the table and took Joshua by the shoulders. "I'm not supposed to, but I am because: A) You guys are old detectives and B) I'll do anything I can to help catch that bastard." Wheeler let go. "I'll get us some coffee."

Joshua sat behind the desk, while Peter leaned on the wall beside Joshua.

Michigan's crime database wasn't unlike the NYPD's. With Peter's help, Joshua sifted through the files from

1981 and found the armored cash van robbery Joey had told them about.

On July 26, 1981, a group of three boys bulldozed a van, killed a man, and robbed $51,900. An upwards of $150,000 by today's value.

"Hey! You're going too fast," Peter said, as Joshua scrolled to the next page.

"Let me read first," Joshua said. He knew he was an asshole sometimes.

"Cocksucker," Peter mumbled and pulled his phone out.

Joshua read through the reports and discovered something peculiar. Lolly had apparently puked before he shot the security guard. It didn't make sense. Normally, murderers never vomited before committing the mortal sin.

After the nasty episode, Lolly's friend had given him a lollipop, and he became better.

When Joshua scrolled to the next page, his heart paused for an instant before fluttering like a butterfly. A pleasant tickle originated within his being and sent a mild electricity across his skin, blanketing it with goosebumps. His vision blurred and an uncontrollable smile spread across his face. Years of toil, agony, and sacrifice had finally paid off!

"A-are you crying?" Peter asked.

Joshua, unable to control himself, hugged Peter's waist and yelped.

"Let go, goddamn it." Peter wrestled away.

Wheeler, standing in the doorway with two mugs, was staring at the duo. "Um... I thought you guys were partners. Didn't know it was that kind."

"What the—" Peter looked at Joshua and then at Wheeler. "Good grief! This hideous psycho isn't my lover."

"Then why's he all emotional-like, like you just proposed to him?"

"Beats me." Peter turned towards Joshua and smacked him on the back of his head. "What's gotten into you?"

Joshua rubbed where Peter had hit him. Then he beckoned Wheeler over, who skirted the desk and handed each a cup, and tilted the monitor.

Squinting at the tiny words, Wheeler asked, "What is it?"

"D," Joshua dabbed at the corner of his eyes, "fucking NA."

"Get outta…" Peter said and read the report with newfound enthusiasm.

A bandana soaked in Lolly's puke was recovered from a bush in the crime scene. As there was no statute of limitations on murder, the DPD had stored it safely. All they had to do was derive the genetic profile from it. No tests were done on the stained cloth because the DNA Identification Act was only passed in 1994, thirteen years after Lolly barfed his intestines out under the bridge he'd just broken.

* * *

As they drove back to the hotel, a FedEx building flickered past. So did a wild impulse. Quickly turning on the indicator, Joshua stopped the car. He took his notebook from the glovebox and began writing on it.

"What are you doing?" Peter asked.

"We had a close call today."

"Amen to that."

"So I'm updating the notes and gonna send them to Gabe." Joshua emitted a tiny smile. "Just in case."

Peter pursed his lips but didn't say anything. Joshua hadn't been paranoid. His fears had proven to be valid.

"Okay. I see a Mickey D's across. Let me grab us some food." Peter exited and jaywalked to the shop.

Once Joshua had completed his notes, he went inside the FedEx and mailed the notebook to New York City.

After Peter returned to the car with mouthwatering goodies, Joshua resumed driving. Eyes mirror-hopping, he found no vehicle following them.

* * *

Joshua tried to sleep, but he couldn't. Light on the window, footsteps outside, shadows underneath the door, everything unsettled him. Oh, and what a splendid time for his brain to vividly reminisce the near-death experience he'd had just hours ago!

A close brush with the Reaper's scythe had put things in perspective. Joshua wasn't safe in Detroit, but he couldn't go back home, not when he'd made such a tremendous leap in the case.

Though his will power surpassed his fear, it couldn't mask the nefarious truth. There were people itching to kill him. They had tried once—possibly three times—and failed. If they were the kind to learn from mistakes, they would eventually succeed.

Joshua desperately needed something to calm his nerves. And then, amidst the cluster of dark thoughts, a bright light shone through. An epiphany.

Gabe doesn't need you.

His mind was correct. Joshua had stopped drinking to nurture his son. Now that the boy was a full-grown man, Joshua shouldn't be this cruel to himself anymore.

Yeah. You shouldn't.

"Yeah," Joshua whispered. "I shouldn't."

* * *

"What was I saying?" Peter said, his words slurred. It's alright. A lightweight wasn't in a kinder place than in the presence of an alcoholic. Plus they were in Joshua's room. As a responsible drinker—an experienced drunk mostly—Joshua had given his car key to the receptionist, ordering him not to return it until morning. They had enough liquor and fast food to last for two days.

180

Peter stretched on the bed and turned onto his stomach as he droned on, "… my ex-wife always told me you were a bad influence."

"I don't blame her," Joshua said. That was true. He'd woken up Peter and explained his desperation to him. Then he dragged him out.

"We can pretend we're celebrating… didn't we find something today?"

"We did."

"Just figured something out," Peter said.

"What is it?"

"You know, when you delete a message on your phone, it pops up an option, asking if you want to 'Delete it for Everyone', and if you select it, the receiver can't see the message?"

"Yeah?" Joshua asked, thinking, *no more heavy stuff for you.*

"It's a good tool, that option. I mean, someone gets real angry and types a page long venom and sends it. Then they sleep and wake up the next morning, feeling like a total douche, regretting they sent it. With this tool, you can delete the hate before the damage is done."

"You just figured this out?" Joshua asked.

"Nah, I figured something else. You remember the time when random assholes tossed a matchstick into mailboxes? I don't think it's meaningless vandalism anymore. It could be the old school way of 'Delete it for everyone'." Peter laughed and pulled a pillow under his face.

Smiling, Joshua poured the fourth round in his glass.

His long-lost comrade, Jim Beam, filled his heart with blissful warmth. Joshua took a sip and held it in his mouth, twirling and sloshing it around, before swallowing. The aroma, the taste, the texture, it all felt just like yesterday. If Joshua were smaller—or the glass bigger—he would have plunged his head into the brown ambrosia. And sucked the goodness in with all his holes and pores, like a sponge.

People might judge him for his love of Jim, but those people hadn't been shot at with a gun that could make baseball-sized holes *through* their bodies. So fuck them.

"Petey," Joshua called. "French fries."

Peter said something, but the pillow had muffled the sound.

Joshua got up and turned Peter. "The fries. Where are they?"

Even without anything obstructing his face hole, Peter's words were unintelligible.

Joshua thought for a moment. He could let Peter sleep. But where's the fun in drinking if your buddy was just gonna lay on his crotch?

"Oh, no you don't." Joshua hauled Peter to a sitting position and shook him. "The night's still young."

Peter's eyes opened asymmetrically as he got his bearings. He needed a push. Joshua opened the Skoal tin and placed two pouches in his palm.

"What's…"

"A little boost." Joshua showed him how to use them, and Peter followed suit.

Thankfully, the nicotine visibly brought some sobriety in his friend.

"Bad influence, indeed," Joshua muttered and handed Peter a Miller Lite, before pouring himself the fifth round.

Chapter 25

April 10, 2019. 05:17. P.M.

A strong urge to throw up awoke Joshua. Covering his mouth, he half-blindly rushed to the bathroom.

But no draw.

Dizzy and nauseated, he stood straight. Chapped lips, dry throat, and foggy vision. How irksome.

And how... nostalgic. It reminded him of the spontaneity of his younger years.

Also Joshua low-key welcomed these discomforts. It felt good—kind of dirty—to spoil oneself after decades of stoical abstinence. Anyway, as he splashed tap water onto his face, he promised he would quit drinking when he went back to New York. Jim had already claimed one angel from Joshua's life, his wife, and he was not ready to lose another, his son.

But here in Detroit, the drinking neither affected him nor his job. He and Peter were waiting for lab results. Lolly's kerchief had been tagged as high priority. However it would still take at least three days for processing it. Though DNA was considered as admissible evidence from the second half of the 1980s, the National Level CODIS was only implemented in 1998. That had given Lolly ample time to have learned and taken precautions against leaving his genetic fingerprint.

But no harm in trying, right? If the DNA didn't match any criminal record from the past, it might match some case in the future. Anyone sharing Lolly's genes, like his son or daughter, might get arrested.

Since the lab was taking its time, he and Peter were bored.

Yesterday had been fairly uneventful. The morning after their little party, Joshua had woken up, whizzed, and slept again, until noon. Later that evening, he had charged his dead phone and checked it. The browser had shown him the sort of porn he would never dare watch sober. What kind of demented fuck was he?

Wincing, he had closed the browser and opened the call log. Only one entry was there. Gabriel. Holding his head, he'd tried to recall the conversation. He had told him that he'd mailed the notebook. But nothing else popped out. Embarrassed, Joshua had put off speaking to him.

Then he and Peter had met the security guard who survived Lolly's bridge robbery. He'd said he still remembered that day in minute detail. Particularly, the visceral memories of three kids with kerchiefs tied across their faces. Two *bastards*, one with dreadlocks and the other with bald spots, robbed while the third stood guard on the bridge. Except for the firsthand account of the survivor, there had been nothing to garner from the meeting.

Both had returned to the room and started partying again, the binge stretching into morning. This time, Joshua had the mind to give the phone along with the car key to the receptionist. He hadn't known that cell phones were as deadly to possess when sloshed.

Joshua had been awake for five minutes, and he was getting ready for an important task. Peter had suggested something crazy when he was liquored up, and unlike most drunken ideas, this one looked promising even when sober.

They were meeting another survivor today.

Joshua came out of the bathroom and tossed four pouches of Skoal into his mouth before picking up the towel and going back again.

The hot bath and the sudden nicotine rush should have curbed some of the hangover. But it didn't. Feeling fresh and clean—only on the outside—he waddled to Peter's room.

His friend looked a lot better than Joshua. He had only consumed a few lite beers and held his own pretty well last night, unlike the one before.

Twenty-five minutes later, he braked in front of a pair of intimidating mechanical steel gates. They were as tall as the palm trees surrounding the property's peripheral wall. Joshua got down from the car and pressed the buzzer.

"Hello. This is Joshua Chase from New York. I'd like to see Mister…"

Goddamn it.

What was his last name? Unable to recall it, he settled for, "Mr. Don."

A few seconds later, the gates parted automatically.

The Audi cruised along a tree-lined driveway, which was longer than Joshua's street back in Staten Island. As they drove onwards, lush branches receded, and a grand mansion came into view.

Peter whistled. "Christ on toast!"

Joshua didn't share his partner's awe. Criminals might live a life of luxury while good people barely had enough to get by, but it wasn't about lavishness. No matter how rich a person was, inner peace could not be bought. Particularly by a guy like the one they were visiting, who'd exchanged his soul for ephemeral worldly pleasures.

Most of the evil men Joshua had known and put away didn't die peacefully. In that way, he thought, the ending was only the beginning. To some eternal destination. Paradise or damnation.

Joshua's wild ruminations halted when he saw three men standing under a canopy. Peter stopped near them and they both got out of the car.

"Let me park it for you." One man held his hand out.

A valet?

"It's alright. Show us where."

He shook his head. "We don't let strangers into our garage."

Weird rule.

Peter handed the key, and two of them drove away with the car.

The remaining man, a kid really, in beige shirt and chinos frisked them. Then he opened the largest teak door Joshua had ever seen and took them in.

After crossing a smoke-filled lobby and spacious hall, they climbed the stairs at the end. A length of rail ran along the lower portion of the wall, and a stairlift chair rested on the landing, cobwebs drifting between its armrests.

The kid led them through a corridor flanked by a dozen niches in the walls and each lighted recess exhibited a carnal figurine. Then the kid turned right into a room; they followed.

As soon as Joshua entered, he was assaulted by the reek of cocaine, liquor, and barbecued chicken.

The first thing that caught Joshua's attention was Bugsy's prosthetic arms. They sprouted from underneath the sleeves and hung limply. Bugsy was wearing an orange T-shirt and sitting back on his chair, behind a mahogany table.

Could it even be called sitting?

Joey had said that Bugsy's legs had been amputated at the hip. How was it possible to *sit* without thighs? Were prosthetic legs competent substitutes? Joshua didn't know, except for the fact that Bugsy's weight was supported by his stumps. Propped on a chair like a half mannequin.

Joshua had imagined that immobility might have rounded Bugsy's physique. But it was not the case. Bugsy was prism-like. From his hairless head, jowls, and neck to flabby chest, every visible muscle sagged, giving his body the appearance of a melting candle or soft serve.

But the most disturbing of all was not the plastic arms or the drooping torso. It was his skin. It was oily and had a yellow sheen to it. Like he suffered from caustic jaundice. How long had it been since he'd been out in the sunlight? The stairlift appeared as if it wasn't being used anymore.

Questions. So many questions.

How did Bugsy shit, pee, eat, or bathe? How did he scratch an itch on the nose? What if a mosquito or a bug bit him? Even to wipe off snot from a sneeze, he needed assistance. How cruelly embarrassing!

No one deserved this kind of hell. Until now, Lolly seemed logical. A robber, just another hungry animal hunting for food. But now he appeared scary. A psychopath maiming a fellow man.

And enjoying it. Why else would he do it four times?

This was not an animal. It was much more dangerous. It was human.

Bugsy, though a rotten soggy potato, controlled the Detroit Mafia. That should count for something, right? Joshua told himself it did, so the languid *Don* would appear somewhat less pathetic.

"Thanks for seeing—"

"Ah…" Bugsy grunted.

Peter looked at the kid who shook his head.

Bugsy acted weird. Biting his lower lip and rolling his eyes into his skull, before moaning loudly and arching his head back. As if he was having an erotic heart attack.

A few seconds later, Bugsy's wheelchair rolled back a little. How did he move it without help?

And then a naked young Asian girl emerged from beneath his table. She crawled out on all fours, before standing to her full height, which was under five feet. She wiped the corner of her mouth and sashayed her way out, winking at Peter.

"Thirty-seven seconds. Longest this year." Bugsy smirked at the kid. "Pay her double."

As the kid nodded, Bugsy pointed his chin at a pair of chairs opposite him. Joshua pulled one back and sat, folding his legs below the rung. He'd much rather not stretch his feet under the table, where the girl had just been.

Bugsy caught Joshua squirming. "I don't bite, you know."

Joshua, wanting to avoid eye contact, looked around, at the photos on the walls. They portrayed a burly man trekking, swimming, kayaking, and doing other arduous but gratifying physical activities.

Bugsy said, "That was me. Strong, handsome, and I lasted way more than thirty-seven seconds."

"I... I feel horrible, I'm sorry," Joshua blurted. And meant it. "Why do you think Lolly... um... did this to you?"

"That's what's been driving me nuts all these years," Bugsy shouted, spittle shot in angry wisps. "I don't fucking have a clue who the fuck he is and what his fucking beef with me is."

Joshua was at a loss of words.

Panting, Bugsy slowly gained composure. "I'm desperately clinging to this useless body just to know the *why*. And then skin him alive, of course."

Peter said, "Tell us what you know. Even if it's illegal. Any information you give can help us catch him."

"Illegal..." Bugsy laughed.

Joshua said, "I've been after Lolly for twenty-six years. I could probably be the only person who knows a lot about him."

"I know who you are, Chase. I also know about your family."

Joshua blinked deliberately. "M-my family?"

For the first time since their visit, Bugsy appeared menacing. His dark lips stretched into a bone-chilling grin, displaying two rows of yellow teeth. As if he knew a secret about Joshua that no one else did. "Thanks to you, I finally have a chance at Lolly."

Joshua said, "You do?"

"Yes. With your help."

"What do you want me to do?"

"You'll know that in time." Bugsy nodded to himself, then yelled, "Now fuck off, fuck off, fuck off!"

"What?" Joshua was dumbstruck. Why would he throw a tantrum like that? Perhaps his body wasn't the only thing that was melting. Maybe his psyche had, too.

The kid walked towards them, and they both stood up. Joshua almost crossed the door's threshold, the kid practically jostling them out.

"Goddamn it," Bugsy cursed aloud.

"What?!" Joshua asked, holding the door frame, hoping to get something, anything, from the arrogant whale.

Bugsy shook his head in vehemence. "That whore forgot to do the zipper."

* * *

They had called it quits with the alcohol. Peter said enough was enough, and they weren't college kids. He didn't want to drink three nights continuously. Although Joshua was against the decision, he didn't like to drink alone. That was the first gear in the fast lane to become an alcoholic.

For the last two nights, he had slept harmoniously because he'd blacked out.

Now the fear returned. With a vengeance. And Bugsy's disfigured body flashed before his eyes whenever he closed them.

Carrying his revolver, Joshua plodded to a couch. He switched the TV on and let his brain rest out of exhaustion whenever it could. Short fitful bouts were all he could manage.

He slipped in and out of reality, until the sunlight glowed through the window, and he heard traffic outside.

A message from Wheeler vibrated his phone on the coffee table. He read it quickly and resumed staring at the TV.

An hour or three later, Peter knocked on the door and let himself in with a spare key.

"Been up the whole night?" he said.

"Don't know," Joshua said, tepidly. "Can't remember."

Gun in hand, he pushed himself to his feet. But his hips cramped halfway, and he sat back, cursing. After placing the loaded weapon on the table, he twisted his torso, left to right and vice versa.

A warm hand touched his shoulder and gave a gentle squeeze.

Joshua looked up at Peter.

"Don't let your enemies wreck your mind," Peter said with a small smile. "They can get your body, but your mind should always belong to you."

"Whatever." Joshua sighed and got up. "Let's go."

"Where?"

"Wheeler texted me the address of a regular who knew Lolly when he was a kid."

"What's his name?"

"Marcus Thomson," Joshua said. "Street name, Congo."

* * *

Joshua watched the side mirror as Peter exited the city through Michigan Highway. He was observing a black sedan coming up behind them. It flashed the headlamps and overtook his car.

The driver didn't don a ski mask or carry a big ass gun. The person behind the wheel was a redheaded white girl, in professional attire. She smiled at him warmly, before driving ahead and pulling over at a gas station. Joshua read *Physician* under her plate.

Hating himself for being timid, he forced his mind to concentrate on something else. The green woods on the roadside might do some good.

"Put your gun away."

"It makes me feel safe," Joshua said.

"Oh please," Peter said. "This isn't Die Hard, and you aren't John McClane."

Joshua laughed. "Fine."

As he reached the glovebox, the car swayed.

"What?" Joshua asked.

"I don't know. Something wrong with the car." Peter parked up and got out while Joshua stayed inside the vehicle.

For now, he would hold on to the weapon, he'd decided. Because a silver truck was approaching them from the opposite lane. He could feel his heart beginning to race as sweat escaped through his skin. He was uneasy until the truck sped past them.

Sighing, he reminded himself to stop being unreasonably jumpy.

"We got a flat," Peter said, looking at the front left tire.

"Shit." Joshua placed the gun on his crotch, pulled out his Skoal tin, and used two pouches. Then he grabbed the gun.

The black sedan, driven by the doctor girl, slowed as it reached them. And again, Joshua tensed.

When it crossed the Audi, Joshua craned his neck and scanned inside her car. It was empty, except a few stuffed toys jammed near the back windscreen.

Damn. I'm losing it.

The girl pulled over in front.

She got out, so did Joshua, the gun hidden behind his back. Waving, she walked towards them. Joshua returned the gesture with his free hand. As he did, he scanned her head to toe. She was wearing a pantsuit, and it had no bulge of a weapon. At least on her front side.

Shut it. She's just a good Samaritan.

"Got a flat?"

"Yes, ma'am," Peter said.

"Two at the same time?" the girl said. "That's super weird."

"What?" Joshua asked.

He hadn't noticed until then, but the girl was correct. The front *right* tire was flat as well. What were the odds?

Very fucking slim.

The dull uneasiness at the pit of his stomach upgraded into full-fledged paranoia pounding his heart. He sat on his haunches and took a closer look at the tire. Some kind of metal protruded from the dusty rubber, fueling the paranoia.

Pocketing the gun, he jogged to the trunk and rummaged through the tools. No pincers but he recovered a pair of pliers from it. Then he returned to the tire and yanked the metal out.

Seeing the shiny item pinched between the pliers, his fears were validated.

It was a caltrop, colloquially known as *ninja road star*. Basically, it was a metallic object with strong nails on all sides. Didn't matter at what angle it rested on the road, one spike always pointed skywards.

A device of ambush.

Breathing fast, Joshua stood and surveyed the vicinity. Nothing seemed out of the ordinary.

Except the girl, chatting with Peter.

He quickly slid over the hood and grabbed her upper arm.

"Ow," she yelped.

"Are you crazy?!" Peter said.

"Shut up, both of you," Joshua said and frisked her.

"What the hell?" she yelled, but too shocked to move as Joshua's desperate hands groped for a weapon.

But they didn't find any.

"I'm extremely sorry." He took a step back, confused.

"*Sorry?*" The girl tied her arms across her chest.

"Give me a sec." Joshua took a long meticulous look around. Still nothing suspicious. The road was free, not a single vehicle in sight.

But how long would it be that way? Gunshots might pierce the atmosphere any second now and rob the beautiful girl of her future. Life full of unexplored opportunities and unachieved dreams lost because she helped two pensioners stranded on a highway. They should hurry, and for that, he needed to calm the indignant girl first. So he played the guilt-trip card. "Please forgive the old man."

Tongue nudging at her cheek, the girl stared at him. "Fine," she said. "I'll let it pass as a senior moment."

Peter laughed. "Damn right."

A smile crept to the girl's face.

"We're in danger," Joshua said. "We need to change the tires as soon as possible."

"D-danger?" The girl glanced back at her car and took an unconscious step back. "I-I don't wanna get in trouble, Mister."

"We really need your help because we have two flats."

"But I don't know how to change wheels. And I can't give you my spare. It won't fit your car."

"No, ma'am," Peter said. "We have two spares, but only one Jack. Give us yours, and we'll drop it at your workplace later."

"M-my workplace?" The girl was possibly regretting her choice to help strangers.

"It's too risky for you to be here right now." Joshua showed her the caltrop. "People who dropped it will come any minute. I'll pay for the Jack if you want."

The girl bit her upper lip. "It's alright, you don't have to pay me." She hastened to her car; apparently the gravity of the situation had finally sunk in. Her little voice trembled as she spoke. "But my Jack's a bit heavy."

"No problem." Joshua waved Peter over. "We can both carry it."

Once they positioned themselves over the trunk, she clicked the remote and the lid popped open. From inside, two men pointed shotguns in their faces.

Chapter 26

April 12, 2019. 9:02 P.M.

The sound of snoring brought some sense of normalcy whenever Joshua drifted into reality. He'd deduced they were held in Calabria's back office. The smell of cheese betrayed the location, although his head was covered with burlap. The bag, a gift from the people who'd abducted them on the highway, had not been removed even once.

It could be a few hours or a day or two since he was dragged to this place and fastened to a wooden chair. The zip ties were cinching his wrists, cutting off the blood flow. He couldn't feel his hands anymore, except a tingling sensation of coldness. Not to say he wasn't in pain. His lower back stung as if a shiv was jammed into his vertebrae, knees gnashed and throbbed at the slightest movements. The soreness on his ass had started burning, like the skin was abraded, making him scared of shifting even an inch. Being forced to sit for an extended period of time should be in the top ten torture methods, he'd guessed.

The snoring abruptly stopped, worrying him.

"P-petey?"

"Oh, we're still stuck." Peter cleared his throat. "Thought it was a dream."

"Are you okay?"

Peter said, his voice grainy, "If having your head wrapped in a cloth and limbs tied to a chair, potentially to be gunned down is okay, then yeah, I'm A-Okay."

Joshua said, "I'm really sorry, man. If it weren't for—"

"Spare me the crap," Peter said. "You didn't drag me into this. I wanted to come."

"But you have a remarkable service record. Good pension."

"So what? You think I'd rather spend my days watching the news and sitcoms?"

Joshua nodded as if Peter could see. "Beats having a sack over your head."

"Someone taught me it's better to die in the field than sitting around, broadening your ass."

While Joshua smiled, his eyes prickled. His best friend remembered something he had told him almost two decades ago. He felt blessed for having Peter by his side, at this moment of his life.

"Thank—"

Metallic grating paused Joshua. A key opening the door. That *soundproof* door. Alright. End of the road.

Joshua wanted to get something out of his system quickly. He said, "You're a good friend."

"I know," Peter said. "Wish I could say the same, but honestly, you were a douchebag to me mostly."

Just as the snide comment began to hurt, Peter said jovially, "I'm kidding. You're a great friend. And the most tenacious guy ever."

"You're talking like it's a good thing," Joshua said. "Look where it's got us."

Both burst out laughing.

The door was opened, then shut. Two pairs of shoes approached them, and amidst strong footfalls, a less-than-capable leg was dragging a foot behind.

"This is not funny, knuckleheads!" Roman said.

"That's because you haven't heard the joke," Peter said.

When Roman first talked to them hours ago, he was surprised that they knew about the location. But after Joshua said it was the cheese stench that gave it away, Roman had acted embarrassed, mincing words and sounding insecure. Must be self-conscious of his weight.

"Say, who's the redhead?" Peter asked.

"A high-ticket hooker," Roman said. "We didn't pay her though."

"You killed the girl?"

"We don't leave witnesses," Roman said. "Neat trick, uh? Hiding in the trunk to ambush? We learned it from Lolly, and thanks to that, we finally caught you slimy assholes."

"Now that you did, what's next?"

"What do you think?" Roman said. "We're gonna shoot you and kill you dead."

"*Shoot you and kill you dead?*" Peter mocked. "Get your bad-guy script right. It sucks balls. Not man balls. I mean huge swollen gonads of an elephant."

"Levi," Roman said in a stern voice and someone pulled the slide of a gun, chambering a round. "Give it here."

Joshua heard Roman's foot scuffing along the floor, moving closer, finally halting behind them. A few seconds later, he said, "Try being a clown now. I dare you."

"Anything for you, pumpkin," Peter said. "So a fat Italian with a tiny pecker walks into a bar—"

The explosion froze everything for a microsecond. The thunderous bang ruptured Joshua's eardrums and vibrated through his sternum, stopping his heart momentarily. But he recovered from the shock and called Peter's name out, his voice muffled, like he was underwater. No answer.

It just couldn't…

His partner. His *friend*. Who followed him everywhere. Like a puppy. Warm tears cascaded down Joshua's cheeks.

It just…

An eighteen-year bond was severed in half a second, by a piece of lead.

His mouth parted in a disbelieving shock, drool escaping from one corner, as he gasped and sucked in air.

It…

Somewhere deep within, an animal screamed, "No!"

As the world span out of control, gravity acted strangely. Joshua fell off a cliff, a precipitous drop, but he never hit anything. While he battled insufferable agony, his breathing became labored. He shook the chair, rattling it on the floor.

The bag was yanked off, and the light hurt his eyes. Joshua smeared his wet face across his shoulder.

To the right, he spotted Peter. His head slumped forward. It was covered with a burlap sack, just like Joshua's.

Except it had two holes in it.

Blood dribbled from the front hole and poured between Peter's thighs, making an eerie dripping sound as it hit the floor. And smoke coiled upwards from the one in the back.

As vertigo returned, and the animal inside him howled again, the bag was pulled over his head.

When wailing in agony, he realized something. Peter had remembered what Joshua had told him so many years ago and lived by it, hadn't he? Then *shouldn't* Joshua value what his late friend had advised him recently?

Never let your enemy wreck your mind.

Peter wouldn't forgive Joshua if he cried before his enemies. They might take your body, but your mind always belongs to you, he'd said.

Trembling, Joshua sat straight and took a few deep breaths. He calmed himself and made peace with the inevitable.

He didn't have a say in his birth, so why should he have one at his death?

As he relinquished the want of control, a smile appeared on his lips, which transformed into a laughter.

"What's wrong with you two?" Roman asked in irritation. "You guys on drugs or something? Why aren't you scared?"

"We all gotta go sometime. And I'm ready to meet the maker." Joshua tilted his head, angling it towards where he supposed Roman stood. "The question is, are you?"

Roman didn't speak for a few seconds. Then he said, "Nothing personal, man. Our boss is old and desperate. He's willing to do anything to get Lolly."

"Then why kill us? We were after him, too."

"No offence, but you've been searching for him over a quarter century with no results. Now that we know who you are, who your family is, we thought of a better way to use you."

Family? Didn't Bugsy say the same thing? What were these assholes planning to do?

Then Joshua put it all together. "You don't mean…"

From that loud bang, Joshua was willing to bet that Peter was killed by a Desert Eagle. And Roman would use the same gun on Joshua as well. Now he understood why the drive-by shooters employed a Desert Eagle—an unusual gun for their line of work—and why they hadn't covered their faces fully, showing CCTVs their ethnicity.

Bugsy wanted the world to think that it was Lolly who killed Joshua.

No… not the world.

He wanted just *one* person to think that. Because that specific person was practically the best detective in the US. Joshua had to agree with his captors there. If anyone could catch Lolly, it was them. By murdering Joshua, they were setting the smartest of good against the coldest of evil.

"Gabriel," Joshua muttered. "My boy."

"Thanks for saving me the time of having to explain. I hate basic villain's monologuing," Roman said. "Is it true that Gabriel caught a serial killer in under a week?"

"Uh-huh." Joshua nodded. "And uncovered the identity of another, also *under a week*."

"So he's the better hunter? The smarter Chase?"

Joshua smiled proudly. "Yup, that I can't deny."

"Our boss's plan is perfect then," Roman said. "I'm calling your son from your phone right now."

Roman put it on speaker. The automated voice said that the person they were trying to reach was speaking to someone else and asked to either wait or call again later.

"Alright," Roman said. Then Joshua heard something pelted at the wall. Probably his cell phone. "He'll call you back, but you'll never be reachable ever again." Roman giggled at his own tasteless pun. "When he learns you're dead, he'll come running to Detroit with one thought in mind: find Lolly."

Joshua chuckled and shook his head. "But like any *basic* villain, you missed a teeny-tiny detail in your convoluted scheme."

"Yeah? What's that?"

"Gabe is one vindictive bastard," Joshua said. "You, Bugsy, Lolly, and his two friends, none of you are going to escape this alive if you pull my boy into this."

"Oh…" Roman mocked and put what Joshua assumed was the muzzle under his eye. "I'm so scared."

"You should be because he *will* come to Detroit." Joshua smirked. "And you can bet your sweet ass that when he does, he *will* bring holy hell down upon you evil motherfuckers."

Then Joshua heard an explosion, which stretched into an echo disappearing into the distant void. Suddenly it was all cozy and bright.

Just before everything stopped being relevant, he thought he smelled his wife's angelic whiff. Rosewater with a hint of sandalwood. Right then, he knew he was heading to a better place. A smile found its way to the last thread of his consciousness.

Peace... at last.

Part III: Gabriel

Chapter 27

May 10, 2019. 06:15 A.M.

The Camaro's headlights raced over the blacktop, its steering wheel rumbling under Gabriel's grip. A sign board overhead read *Welcome to Detroit*. Clenching his teeth, he floored the accelerator, and the beast's engine roared, propelling the muscled machine forward.

The red orb rose in the rearview mirror, and the freeway slowly turned into glistening gold. The sunlight stretched along the road and illuminated the distant city before him, removing darkness from every nook and cranny.

William Lamb, Peter Lamb's son, was lying on the backseat while his crutch rode shotgun. His hackneyed curiosity and energy were absent. Neither felt like talking, the murders of their dads still fresh in their minds.

Gabriel had been worried ever since Joshua drunk dialed him because he sounded paranoid. He called again on April 12, but Gabriel was talking to someone at that time. From that point onwards, any call made to Joshua's number went straight to voicemail.

Thankfully his FBI friend, Conor Lyons, offered to help. He detected the source of Joshua's call, and also found that Peter's cell phone was last active around Lake Erie. Using this location as a reference, Conor searched the NamUs—the National Missing and Unidentified Persons System—with Peter's and Joshua's descriptions.

He found them in the database and their case files.

An anonymous call made to the DPD reported that two men with burlap bags over their heads were dumped at the bank of Lake Erie. The cops were unable to find IDs or phones near the crime scene. Lowlifes stealing stuff from dead bodies wasn't new. Due to these scavengers, the investigation was delayed.

It had been six days since the news shattered Gabriel. Taking care of the funeral and other related services took only two days. The remaining four were spent with the FBI.

Conor was promoted as Special Agent in Charge of a new department under the FBI's NCAVC. It was named Bureau's International Serial Killer Investigation Treaty, BISKIT for short. The exclusive role and responsibility of this department was to hunt serial killers internationally, if the respective country asked for the FBI's help.

Conor implored Gabriel to join BISKIT, and he accepted under one condition. He should be allowed to go after Joshua's killer and the most wanted bank robber in the US: Lolly. Cleaning another's house while your own stank was unreasonable.

Gabriel aced the exams and physicals. His experience in catching two serial killers and working as a homicide detective for more than a decade were highlighted in his resume. Commendation letters from the commissioner of the NYPD, New York City's District Attorney and Mayor, did wonders in boosting Gabriel up as a distinguished candidate.

And only yesterday, they knighted him. It was unusually fast because Conor coerced the Assistant Director of the

FBI, saying they needed to get Lolly while the trail was still hot.

"Take a left, Detect— um… Agent Chase," Bill said.

Gabriel hadn't stopped paying attention to the dashboard GPS, but he understood Bill's need to chip in.

Glancing at the side mirror, Gabriel pushed the turn signal and twisted the wheel. The car swerved, its tail almost swiping a lamp post.

Their destination was a hundred meters ahead, which he covered in under five seconds, skidding Bill's car to a halt.

Gabriel stared at the building across. It had an unlit neon sign on top reading 'Calabria'. It was closed.

Gabriel stepped down with the crutch, before carefully helping his friend climb out. Bill's femur, cracked by a cannibalistic psychopath they caught last month, hadn't had enough time to heal. But Bill wouldn't stay home.

They had selected a hotel opposite Calabria for their stay, and Gabriel had picked his room carefully on their website.

While inside, he nodded at the receptionist. "Reservations for Chase and Lamb."

Consulting her PC, she said, "That'd be 203 and 204." From the board hanging on the back wall, she unhooked two keys and handed them over.

As they waited for the elevator, Gabriel's mind jumped to the case.

Joshua had been shot with a Desert Eagle, the type of gun Lolly used. But to be one hundred percent sure, additional tests were needed. The FBI had made a request to the DPD, and the recovered slugs were now on their way to Quantico. But it would take time. Time that Gabriel's burgeoning desire for vengeance couldn't afford.

The bell chimed, derailing his train of thought; they got in and rode the elevator. When it stopped at the second floor, Gabriel and Bill went to their respective rooms in silence.

Chapter 28

May 10, 2019. 07:11 A.M.

Cold water from the shower caressed Gabriel's body. One particular horrible image repeatedly flashed behind his eyelids: Joshua on a gurney with a grisly hole in his face.

Rage that had been simmering inside since he saw that photo seeped out. As his fingers curled into fists, tears of wrath flowed down his neck, their warmth a stark distinction from the cold water. Gabriel tried to stop crying, cupping his mouth with both hands. It was extremely difficult to tame the agony pulsating at the threshold of his throat.

Gabriel never had anyone except Joshua. He had not been just a dad, but also a role-model, a mentor. More than all, a mom. Gabriel couldn't believe that Joshua was not here anymore.

It was unfair. To have lived a life of community service, dedicating his time to people who were wronged and in need of justice, only to be gunned down and discarded like garbage, left to the mercy of fish and flies.

Thinking this, *picturing* this, another fit of rage exploded within.

This time, Gabriel's strong hands couldn't contain the misery.

He squatted and plunged his head inside a bucket. The raw pain shot from the pit of his stomach and ousted into cold water.

Half a minute had gone by before he stopped bawling and resurfaced. But he quickly drew air in and dived again, not caring about his voice box bursting or some vein in his brain rupturing.

When he eventually ran out of air, he opened his eyes and looked through the water. As the tears made their presence known by warmly touching his skin, he pledged, again, that no one involved in his dad's death would live. Lolly's gang for pulling the trigger, the Detroit Alliance for enabling them years ago.

Gabriel tied a fluffy towel around his waist. Turning the doorknob, he half expected to see hotel staff or Bill waiting for him, probably rattled by the animalistic screeches.

But the room was empty.

His improvised muffler of a bucket of water had apparently worked. He sat on the bed's edge and went over his plan, letting the draft of air from the ceiling fan dry his skin.

How'd you kill two groups of violent murderers? Pit them against each other, of course. And it wouldn't be a problem because Lolly's gang and the Detroit Alliance hated each other, Joshua had written.

Adequately dry, Gabriel got off the bed and dressed in his usual attire. A white shirt, jeans, and a brown jacket. Then he dragged a chair to a window overlooking the street.

Calabria was now open, and people were going in. Twenty minutes later, a black Land Rover arrived. The number plate read 80085, prompting Gabriel to roll his eyes. Two tough-looking guys, twins with ponytails, got out and went inside the bar. By observing the crowd thus far, he had surmised that the bar attracted only the types whose faces would be picture perfect for mugshots.

Another fifteen minutes later, a white Chrysler pulled over. A fat man in a loose-fitting Miami shirt and looser chinos clambered down, followed by a bodyguard. The fatso had a crutch and the unmistakable white-blond hair his dad mentioned in the notebook.

Gabriel left his post and exited the room hastily. Time to make the first move.

Gabriel crossed the street, jogging towards the bar's entrance. When he reached it, the bodyguard tried to stop him. Bad move.

In the blink of an eye, he grabbed the man's arm, turned him around, and folded it. If Gabriel applied more force, it would pop out of the socket.

The bodyguard shouted, "Ah! My arm!"

"No shit, Sherlock," Gabriel said, then addressed the big man. "We need to talk."

"Who are you?" Roman asked, his eyes just a pair of slits.

"I'm Gabriel Chase." He glowered at Roman. "And I've come too far to take no for an answer."

Something in Roman's face changed, and he did an *almost* inconspicuous double take.

"Alright, fine," Roman said.

Gabriel pushed the bodyguard at the front door who threw it open and stumbled in. After fumbling behind his back, he pulled out a tiny pistol. A bit too late. Gabriel already had his Glock drawn, aiming at his center of mass.

Roman barked something in Italian, making the bodyguard retreat with a sour expression.

As Roman waddled inside, Gabriel followed closely. He plodded around to the back of the bar counter, and the barkeeper skulked to obscurity.

"So?" Roman said. "What can I do for you?"

Gabriel holstered his gun, but neither buckled the strap nor turned off the safety. "Tell me what you know about Lolly and my dad, Joshua Chase."

Roman scratched his temple. "Sorry, never heard of them."

He was one of the worst liars Gabriel had encountered in his career.

"I can prove otherwise," Gabriel said nonchalantly.

Roman pointed at the CCTV behind with his thumb lazily. "It doesn't work. The ones outside don't either. Unfortunately, they are all broken."

"No need," Gabriel said. "We traced my dad's movement from his cell phone."

Cockiness gone, Roman licked his dry lips.

With a mocking smile, Gabriel continued, "He was around your bar when he made his last call to me."

Roman's Adam apple bobbed. "You've got no right to come here and question me. You're no DPD."

Gabriel nodded in agreement. "You're correct about the second part. I'm not the Detroit PD." From his jeans, he pulled his new ID out and brandished it. "But you're wrong about the first. I have the right to ask questions where-ever-the-fuck I want."

Roman stared at the shiny shield, as if it were a snake getting ready to spring out and bite him. "You… uh, you're with the FBI?"

"Nothing escapes your eyes, does it?" Gabriel put it back. The Mafia and the Feds never got along well, and it always ended badly for the former. Maybe Roman hadn't expected Gabriel to be a Fed.

After a few long moments of thinking, Roman said, "Your father told me you were NYPD."

"So you *do* know my dad?" Gabriel asked.

"He said nothing about no FBI."

"He—" Gabriel began but his voice failed him; he cleared his throat and tried again. "He didn't tell you because he was shot in the face before he knew."

"I'm sorry to hear that, I really am. Your father seemed like a really great man," Roman said. "We all need to catch Lolly before he does any more damage."

"Couldn't agree more," Gabriel said. "First tell me what my dad was doing here."

Roman lifted his hands. "Fine, fine. He asked me about a truck robbery that my associates *might* have had a part on." And Roman explained about the Livernois hijacking and what Lolly did to their Don. Which Gabriel already knew from the notebook.

When Roman was finished, Gabriel leaned over the table, and whispered, "Give me your card. I'm sure we can work something out."

Roman gawked at Gabriel who winked in return.

He let out a breath and laughed, muttering something. It was evident that he was relieved. Then he said, "I got no card." He wrote his number on a piece of paper and slid it across the table. "We want Lolly."

"Why?"

"Just like to meet our old friend is all." Roman shrugged.

Gabriel pocketed the paper and stood straight. "Is that wise, though?"

"Huh?" Roman frowned.

"I mean, the last time you and your boss met with Lolly, it didn't end well for either of you, did it?"

Roman's face reddened, either in embarrassment or anger. He said, "You just bring him to us, and we'll make sure you never need to work for money ever again."

Gabriel also knew about the humongous bounty Bugsy put on Lolly. It was twenty times higher than the government's reward.

"Alright, fine. I'll bring your *old friend* here," Gabriel said, smirking. "But don't you know what they say? 'Be careful what you wish for.'"

Not waiting for an answer, he turned back and walked out of the bar.

Chapter 29

May 10, 2019. 10:43 A.M.

While returning from Calabria, Gabriel placed his ear on Bill's door. No TV, no crying fits. Just the strong vibration of fatigued sleep.

Unwilling to wake him up, Gabriel went to his room. He pulled out his rucksack and rummaged through it. Gabriel's NYPD shield shone from inside. He had requested his old captain that he held onto it until he caught Lolly and the good captain allowed him to. Gabriel retrieved Joshua's dog-eared notebook and sat back on the bed.

Its cover was the picture of a snow-peak mountain. The binding must have come loose at some point, which Joshua had tried to fix by stitching with twine. The ill-advised DIY had bound the papers together a little too tight for comfort.

Gabriel was hit by Joshua's scribblings. Every time he opened the notebook, the lines, the indentation, the scratches, the side notes, they all hurt Gabriel. As his fingers traced over the words, he thought, *why couldn't your old ass just play Yahtzee or watch reality TV?*

He chortled but felt the corner of his eye prick.

No!

Weeping should only be done in the bathroom or at nighttime. Now he had work to do.

Sniffling, Gabriel skimmed through page one. It contained details of the robbery which the FBI had thought was Lolly's first until Joshua discovered the 1981 cash van ambush on the bridge.

However, this page had info pertaining to the 1982 case—the bank Lolly's gang robbed, the amount of money they bagged, the car they used, where they discarded it, and what possible routes they might have taken afterwards.

There was also a list of evidence—shoe prints, casings, slugs, GSR, glove prints, the whole nine yards.

Also included were the victims' names and their kin; the witnesses and their addresses; the investigating officers' names and pager/phone numbers.

Each robbery filled a page, sometimes two. But as the years passed, the number of pages increased, as new criminal investigative techniques came into practice. Still, Lolly beat them all, apparently keeping abreast with the technological advancements in forensics.

As Gabriel reached the middle, something rustled: a wrinkled yellow lollipop wrapper, stapled to a paper. Bright red letters on it read 'Zesty'.

Whenever Gabriel saw this, *touched* this, a strong sense of déjà vu assaulted him.

No, not déjà vu. The vibe was between déjà vu and an actual memory. Akin to the sensation you got when you couldn't remember a word or a name, but you felt it hanging at the edge of your memory, just millimeters away from your grasp.

For this reason, Zesty's wrapper always mystified him, ever since he first came across it when he perused the notebook back in NYC. Under the wrapper, his dad had written: 'Lolly's lollipop cover: 1994 Thanksgiving'. No mention of where he had acquired such a significant piece of evidence from. Or why he'd kept it to himself.

Joshua's findings about the candy were written on the next page.

Zesty belonged to a confectionery company named CORBY & HEISZ. This particular lollipop was manufactured only in two different factories—one in

Oregon, the other in Maryland—but distributed to 2,036 shops across the country.

The notes ended, not having arrived at a conclusion. It was unjust to expect more. This was back in 1994, when the PDs hadn't used computers to cross-examine monumental data.

Gabriel studied the wrapper. Again.

There was neither a manufacture nor an expiry date, and no ingredients list. The FDA wouldn't approve any brand to retail their products with such minimal information. But the words *not to be sold individually* were printed on the cover. So the likely scenario was that it came from a pack.

Gabriel pulled out his phone and opened the image he had already downloaded and looked at a thousand times.

It was Zesty's box and the ingredients list was printed on it. But the photo was not HD; hence he could not zoom in and see what they were. Google couldn't educate him on it either.

Gabriel moved on.

He thumbed through to the last page where Joshua had summarized all of Lolly's crimes:

1982 – 1994: 14 robberies, 21 murdered. Lolly - 14 and Red Mask - 7.

1994 – 2001: 8 robberies, 12 murdered. Lolly - 7 and Red Mask - 5.

2001 – 2008: 10 robberies, 15 murdered. Lolly - 9 and Red Mask - 6.

Note: Blue Mask never shot a gun. He manned the entrances, threatened hostages (he's physically the most intimidating of the three), and drove cars.

The shade of the ink was dissimilar in the next lines, meaning it was written a while after the other entries were made, with a different pen.

2019: 1 robbery, 1 murdered. Lolly - 1.

1981: 2 robberies, 3 murdered. Lolly - 3.

A knock on the door distracted him. "Agent Chase?"

"Come in," Gabriel said.

Bill tottered into the room, his crutch supporting a half of his weight.

"What are you doing?" he asked in an enervated tone.

Gabriel showed him the notebook.

"Please, tell me you got something," Bill said, his voice cracking.

"I do." Gabriel shot to his feet. "Let's go."

Chapter 30

May 10, 2019. 12:01 P.M.

The I-94 took them around Lake St. Clair, and twenty minutes later, they exited on Harper Avenue.

Gabriel was amazed by Downtown Detroit, a victim of selective reporting. The sensationalist media led many to think of the Motor City as some sort of crime-ridden, post-apocalyptic dystopia. But nothing could be farther from the truth. There were no prostitutes on curbs, flagging down cars; no sign-throwing thugs, flaunting pistols in their waistbands; no low-riders bouncing off the tarmac, blasting loud music.

Instead the sidewalks bustled with people rushing to work, coffees in hands and cell phones on cheeks.

As the Camaro entered East Lafayette Street, a ladder-like monolith passed by on Bill's side. Gabriel hunkered down and looked at it. The awe-inspiring structure was erected in front of a multi-storied headquarters of BCBS Michigan. On the right, an even bigger edifice greeted him. Greektown Casino.

But sign-throwing thugs, low-riders, and hookers didn't entirely disappear, did they?

Detroit had come a long way since it filed bankruptcy, Gabriel cynically thought, because the politicians had simply defeated one evil with another. Crime and poverty were *cured* by gentrification. It was the timeworn story with government representatives. Got a problem? Let us migrate it to some place out of sight, cover it with a blanket, and hope that it magically disappears. But in reality, the problems festered into meaner and uglier ones, which always resulted in the loss of precious human life.

"Is this our first break?"

"Could be," Gabriel said.

"Okay?" Bill lifted his brows.

"Remember the cash van ambush in 1981? That bastard was treating himself with a lollipop even back then. And he was still sucking on the damn thing as recently as 2019."

"At the Bristol robbery." Bill frowned. The thinking broke a little of his melancholy. Good. "Seems like he's used to it."

"Yes," Gabriel said. "As you know, my dad somehow got hold of his lollipop wrapper."

"We're gonna track Zesty?"

Gabriel nodded.

"How do we even know if Lolly's stuck to the same brand?"

"We don't but there is nothing else we can do right now, is there?" Gabriel said.

"No, I guess not," Bill said. "But you don't think he changed his preference?"

Gabriel shook his head.

"Why?"

"Let's analyze what kind of a man Lolly is."

Bill shrugged.

Gabriel said, "All his robberies were committed using only one method. Kill first, intimidate, then demand money. The reason behind his success is that he doesn't deviate from his routine. Even his gun, his attire, his mask, he's changed nothing."

"A man of habit."

Gabriel nodded again. "It's possible that he didn't switch brands."

"I agree. There could be a slim chance at Lolly here."

Gabriel looked at Bill, a glint in his eyes. "And a slim chance is all I need."

* * *

Gabriel turned onto Beaubien Street and crossed a restaurant named Niki's Pizza. The smell of fresh food bypassed Gabriel's hurting heart and crept down to his stomach, making it rumble.

He stopped in front of the location they'd programmed into the GPS. A small glass facade with a name board reading CORBY & HEISZ.

"Are you hungry?" Bill asked.

"Let's get it over with." Gabriel reversed the car and parked in front of the pizza joint. Then he helped Bill down.

Gabriel bought a square pizza with plain mozzarella cheese, and Bill got something called *Greek Pizza*. His face brightened as soon as he took a bite. He wolfed it down in a few minutes and ordered a second slice. In those fleeting seconds, Gabriel saw the glimpse of the old Bill. Curious, child-like, and full of wonder.

And it broke his heart.

For the millionth time, Gabriel promised himself that he would be the end of Lolly.

* * *

As they crossed the threshold into CORBY & HEISZ, a draft of cool air blew down on Gabriel and ruffled his hair. Both the lobby and reception were empty. There was a glass door on the left, but it required an access card to open. Beside the door, a beige couch was pushed up against the wall, a coffee table placed in front. Tabloids and newspapers were strewn above it. One headline read: *Lack of funding. Several libraries in Detroit at risk of closure.* The other screamed: *The first Kardashian BILLIONAIRE!*

As Gabriel considered sitting Bill down, a beep sounded and the door opened. A woman was laughing and chatting to someone behind the door, before closing it.

"Um… can I help you?" she asked, then walked to the reception desk and positioned herself behind it. Her laughter ceased and her expression turned grim.

Gabriel didn't blame her. He sported a two-inch thick unruly beard and rampant hair that flew out in all directions like Einstein's. Emma, his partner in the NYPD, had said that Gabriel looked like a recovering drug addict who was on the verge of slipping. It was true to an extent. Except his drug of choice was alcohol.

The receptionist's eyes travelled to Bill's face, then settled on his legs. And she relaxed a little. No criminal came on a crutch, she might have assumed. Most people were under the presumption that a wounded or handicapped man was harmless. This bias made them vulnerable, and killers capitalized on it. Just ask Bundy.

Gabriel showed her his badge. "We'd like to talk to someone from logistics."

"Sure," she said. "Let me call Dave."

She lifted the telephone and murmured in it.

A minute later, the glass door beeped again and a young man appeared. He wore glasses, carried an iPad, and dressed in what these corporate types called business casuals.

Dave greeted them, motioned to the couch, and helped Bill down before sitting.

Gabriel said, "I need something from your sales records. If you want a warrant, I can get one faxed here in ten minutes."

"Nah." Dave waved it off. "It's not like I'm gonna give you information about our ultra secretive project."

Gabriel frowned. "Huh?"

Dave lowered his voice. "We're disguising as a candy factory but actually building a lunar base for world domination."

Gabriel slowly shook his head, without offering even a twitch of a smile. He was not up for Dave's funnies.

"I-I'm…" Dave managed an embarrassed grin. "My stupid attempt at a joke. But I see it's a serious matter."

"Very."

"So… um, do I really not need a warrant before giving out information?"

That was the one question you never asked a cop who wanted to look into your house. So naturally Gabriel said, "No, you don't."

"Alrighty then. What do you need?" Dave unlocked his iPad.

"Tell us about Zesty."

Dave brought up a program on the tablet. "It used to be one of our bestselling lollipops but not anymore."

"Why's that?"

"I don't know, I'm not from marketing." Dave shrugged.

"How many shops still stock them? And look only in Detroit."

Dave swiped and typed and did his magic on his iPad, before he said, "Thirteen. Hope you aren't superstitious." He slid his glasses up his nose. "Let me guess. You need their details."

Gabriel nodded. "If you'd be so kind, thank you."

Dave touched the iPad and something chimed in the lobby, but not from the device in his hands.

When he turned to the receptionist, she said, "Yup. Got the email. Want me to print it?"

"Yes, please." Dave turned back to Gabriel. "Anything else?"

"Yes. The thirteen shops buying Zesty, that's this year, right?"

"Correct."

"Can you tell me how many shops regularly bought it back in 1981?"

Instead of responding, Dave gaped at Gabriel.

"What?"

"No. It's… it's so long ago. Our servers don't have that data. The earliest records I got for you are from the mid-2000s." Dave worked on his iPad. "In 2006, just over 400 shops in Detroit bought Zesty."

"How do I get older records, before that?"

"From physical logbooks, I guess?"

To the good ol' backbreaking police work then, Gabriel thought. "Okay. Point us to your archives."

"No, sir. They're at our HQ in Wyoming." Dave gave an apologetic smile. "I'm afraid this is the limit of my capacity to help you."

Well, that wasn't enough.

Inhaling a large volume of air, Gabriel closed his eyes and collected his thoughts.

No worries, he assuaged himself. It was still a win. Because an idea had just popped up in his mind.

Chapter 31

May 10, 2019. 02:37 P.M.

Back in the car, Gabriel called Conor.

Though his new FBI friend had promised Gabriel that he would do everything in his power to help him catch Lolly, Gabriel didn't believe that it was an altruistic gesture. As a new SAC, Conor was given the responsibility of BISKIT. Catching the most wanted bank robber in the US would bolster his position. True, it was not the BISKIT's job to investigate crimes that weren't international or serial killer related, but Gabriel refused to work on any case until he caught Lolly. So Conor went several extra miles in supporting Gabriel.

"Yes, Gabe?" he said.

"Zesty. It's the candy Lolly uses."

"Hold on," Conor said.

Gabriel heard papers rustling in the background, then Conor came online. "Come again."

"Zesty." Gabriel repeated and spelled it out for him.

"Okay, got it. What now?"

"I have a list of thirteen shops that sell Zesty in Detroit. Could you check their histories?"

"Let me boot my computer," Conor said, and the line went blank.

While Gabriel was pressing the warm phone against his face, Conor took almost three minutes to come back. "Sorry. Had to pee."

"Could have done without that trivia."

"I concur," Conor said. "I'm ready. The first shop's name and address, please?"

"Or I can give you their license numbers? To save us all the time."

"Much better. May I have the first number then?"

Bill passed the paper to Gabriel and he read it from there.

"Okay. The shop was opened in 1987 and registered—"

"Nope. Not it."

"I barely began," Conor said. "How can you know?"

"Lolly's first crime was in 1981. This shop didn't exist back then," Gabriel said and read the next license number.

This was not it either. Seemed like most candy shops that operated in 1981 hadn't survived until 2019. Paradoxical. Shouldn't businesses that sold sweets have thrived, given that diabetes and obesity had skyrocketed in the last few decades?

As the list decreased in number, Gabriel became hopeful. The fewer the shops, the sooner they could take the next step.

Whatever that was.

A steadfast hater of multitasking, Gabriel rarely worried about many problems simultaneously. He believed in solving one at a time, giving it his undivided attention and doing it cleanly, before moving onto the next.

At last, they ended up with only two shops which were open both in 1981 and 2019.

"Great. Thanks. I'm heading there now."

"Heading where?"

"Haven't decided that yet. Whichever is closer to me, I guess."

"Well…" Conor dragged on.

"What?"

"One of the shops, when it opened in 1963, was an electronic shop."

"What happened then?"

"I-I don't know. In 1968, they switched their products to pastry and candies. As their location remained unchanged, they have the same license number." Then Conor proceeded to fill in other tidbits about the shop and its address.

"Thanks." Gabriel turned on the ignition. "Bye now."

As he eased the car back onto the main road, Bill grabbed the paper. "Where are we headed?"

"Goodwill."

"Strange name for a candy shop."

Gabriel nodded and programmed Rosa Parks Blvd into the GPS, the street where Goodwill was located.

Bill studied the display and then looked at the paper. "You've entered the wrong address."

Gabriel shook his head. "It's correct. Conor told me that the shop was registered on '63 and its street name has since been changed."

"Oh? Did he say why?"

"Apparently, that place was the epicenter of the 1967 Detroit Riot. So they renamed it to hide history associated with it," Gabriel said. "Rosa Parks Blvd was previously known as 12th Street."

Chapter 32

May 10, 2019. 03:12 P.M.

Ten minutes later, Gabriel pulled over in front of Goodwill. The one-story building, sandwiched between a poultry and an automobile parts shop, was painted in the color of rainbows. No child in a hundred-yard radius would miss the vivid purveyor of sweets.

A bell jingled overhead when Gabriel held the door open for Bill before following him in.

Although he had just eaten, the smell of freshly baked cookies and cinnamon buns made him salivate. There's always room for desserts. He looked around at the shelves. Candy corn, tootsie rolls, cupcakes, jellybeans, gummy bears, chocolate truffles, and several hundred other goodies, small to big, all colorful, teleported Gabriel to his childhood.

And it was an uncomfortable place to be.

Joshua always let him stuff his pockets as much as he wanted whenever he took him to a candy shop. No limits. This world didn't have a sweeter dad—

Gabriel grabbed the bridle of his thoughts and halted them before they took pace and ran amok in his mind, ruining his mood. Crying in a candy store, he was not young enough for that shit.

An old lady behind the billing counter stood up. "Hello."

"Hi," Gabriel said, and Bill nodded at her.

"I said hello," she repeated in a stern voice.

"Hi, ma'am." Bill lifted his hand. "Sorry about that."

Trying not to be obvious, Gabriel studied her. She was old only on the outside—her hair was as white as milk, her skin wrinkled—but her bone structure and muscles looked strong. Neither did she stoop nor hold her hips when she stood to greet them. Though shorter than Gabriel, she somehow appeared taller, because of her ramrod posture.

He recognized her as one of those people that life just couldn't beat down, and in the end surrendered at their feet, whimpering like a dissatisfied dog.

The way she addressed them, something was off, but he couldn't put a finger on it.

"Nice shop you got here," Bill said.

"Thank you, dear. One of the oldest in the city," she said. "Are you just going to stand there or come inside and browse?"

"We're not here to shop, ma'am."

"Well, you can't rob me. All transactions here are done electronically." She laughed. "I'm just kidding."

"We're cops," Bill said, offering a little smile. "Do you get robbed a lot?"

"Not once," the old lady said. "I couldn't be in a safer place. Everyone knows me around here."

"Even the kids?" Gabriel asked. It was often the desperate kids that turned to the life of crime.

"Especially the kids; they love me." She pointed over her shoulder with her thumb.

Gabriel leaned towards his right and craned his head to see the back wall.

A plaque on the top of the wall read: "He who opens a school door, closes a prison - Victor Hugo."

Below the plaque, the entire lower part was dedicated to framed photographs.

And every single one of them had the old lady in it. She was either presenting a medal or a certificate to some kid.

Though kids changed from frame to frame, she remained as a constant in them.

Squinting, Gabriel examined the photographs. Something was definitely off about her. She smiled but it was as if she really wasn't looking at the camera.

Bill asked. "Were you a teacher or something?"

"I wish!" the old lady said. "They're the kids I've sponsored through school."

Gabriel quickly counted the photos. "All 34?"

"Yes." She took a breath and her chest inflated. "Most of them are doctors, bankers, and architects now. One kid even went to space and worked at the ISS." With her knuckle, she dabbed at the corner of her eye. "Before that, Mr. Astronaut was a purse snatcher."

Gabriel's eyes widened. She was rescuing kids from crime. It was the first time he'd felt something positive in days.

Bill asked, "Were they orphans?"

"Worse. They were from—and I'm talking verbatim here—the *hoods*. Older thugs use little kids to sell drugs, carjack, burgle, even rob and murder. These innocent boys were trained in exactly the kind of things that their privileged counterparts all over the world were warned to stay away from."

Gabriel asked, "Isn't it dangerous to approach them on the streets? How do you get hold of them?"

"Through word of mouth mostly. Once I locate a kid, I talk to his parents. Have an intervention-like meeting and then send him to a boarding school far from here."

"That's just... wow," Bill said, voicing Gabriel's thought.

"You know about crime a lot better than I do. But one thing I can be certain of is that," she lifted a finger, as if preaching, "only education cures crime." She paused to think. "Except maybe the white-collar variety."

"Couldn't agree more, ma'am," Gabriel said. He had digressed, but it was alright. Not every day one came across a paladin. "May I ask you something?"

"Shoot."

"You saved all those kids with the income from a candy store?"

"Heavens no! It's my son's money."

"But... private schools cost tens and thousands of dollars, if not more. Your son's okay with it?"

"He loves his mommy too much to say no." She smiled. "Anyway, we have enough. A spacious house, tasty food, a reliable car, and neat clothes. And what good is money if it's just sitting in a vault somewhere? We all live on this planet together. Best if we act like it."

Gabriel's lips stretched. It was the first time he smiled in days.

The old lady was either incredibly naïve, or had reached a level of wisdom that he couldn't fathom.

Gabriel said, "I-I would like to meet your son sometime. He seems like a great man."

"He is! Next month he'll be on leave; come then." She smiled proudly.

Gabriel couldn't imagine a strong and philanthropic mom like her raising anyone less than perfect.

The old lady clapped her hands in front of her. "Now my other children have started earning. Due to their generous contributions, my charity's expanding and saving more at-risk kids. You do one good, it splits and does two goods and so on."

Gabriel nodded. He had a similar idea of exponential growth about evil.

"Enough bragging," she said. "Now are you going to tell me why you're here?"

"I thought I would borrow your video recordings. But I see you don't have CCTV."

"Can't use it." The old lady shrugged. "Is there any other way I could help?"

While Gabriel processed what she had said, Bill asked, "Can you tell us about Zesty?"

"That's one of the few products we've been selling right from day one."

"1968?"

"That's correct." For such an advanced age, she doubled over seamlessly and pulled a Zesty box from under the counter. Her hand reached into it and pulled out a lollipop.

Gabriel got it from her outstretched arm. Seeing that candy, not just the wrapper, gave Gabriel another bout of déjà vu. *Feeling* that solid thing in his hand, its stick, kindled some deep-seated memory. He had definitely seen Zesty before. And eaten it, too. Because he could *almost* taste it in his palate and at the back of his throat. He reached towards the distant memory and grasped parts of it.

There was a… black man, talking about a superhero…

"Are you okay?" Bill asked.

Gabriel snapped into reality. "What?"

"For a second there, you looked like you'd lost your breath."

Gabriel shook off the feeling and placed the lollipop on the table. "May I see the box, ma'am?"

"Sure." She pushed the box to his side.

He picked it up and turned it around. And there it was, the ingredients list. Frowning, he read through them—black peppers, long peppers, ginger, honey, lemon, cumin seeds, sugar, black salt, rock salt, and sal ammoniac.

"Can you clarify something for me?"

"Yes," she said.

Gabriel iterated the ingredients that weren't sweet. "You don't see these in candies, do you?"

She said, "Zesty is not a candy, per se. It is a ginger-flavored digestive assistant that helps acid reflux and other indigestion problems."

"Then why aren't they widely available anymore?"

The old lady sighed. "In the late 2000s, a new chew tablet was introduced. It's not tangy and it tasted a lot better than the salty-spicy Zesty. So most people simply switched to it. However, a very few still prefer ginger candies."

"But why?"

"Could be placebo and the chew-tablets don't work? Or they could have been used to Zesty from a young age?"

"A man of habit," Bill said.

"Yes," she said. "As long as the symptoms of their condition are alleviated, it doesn't matter, does it?"

What she said clicked something in Gabriel's brain.

"Thanks a lot, ma'am. You've been most helpful," Gabriel said.

"My pleasure."

Gabriel turned around and opened the door for Bill, the bell tinkling again. Then he said, "We will be off now."

"Alright. You have a safe day now," she said, not looking at Gabriel who was still inside the shop, but at Bill who was exiting.

And then he understood what seemed off about her: the old lady was blind.

Chapter 33

May 10, 2019. 03:29 P.M.

As soon as Gabriel got into the car, he unlocked his phone and opened the browser. When the old lady had mentioned symptoms and conditions, it made him think about incurable diseases. At Lolly's first robbery, they left a security guard alive. In his eyewitness statement to the DPD, the guard had reported that one of the kids had patches of baldness.

Why would a *kid* have bald spots?

And the ever-mighty Google confirmed what Gabriel had suspected. A condition called Alopecia Areata caused hair to fall in patches. Continuous treatment from a dermatologist was advised.

That's it! He figured out how to possibly identify one of Lolly's partners. He explained his plan to Bill before calling Conor and putting it on speaker.

"It's Goodwill that's been selling Zesty for a long time," he said into the phone. "As per our findings, it's also the only shop that survived from 1981 till now. My gut tells me Lolly gets his Zestys from here."

"Then ask the person who runs the shop if they remember one of their regulars, a black guy with blue eyes.

That's something unique, and they would remember, right?"

"She's blind."

"Shit," Conor said. "What about CCTVs?"

Gabriel sighed. "She. Is. Blind."

"D'oh!" Conor quickly added. "So why do you need me now?"

As Gabriel took a deep breath, he heard Conor say, "Oh my god."

"What?" Gabriel asked.

"I know that gesture. Generally you ask me stuff that's hard to do. Like excavating dozens of dead bodies or performing thousands of DNA tests or the browsing history of a huge city, you know, typical Gabriel stuff…"

From the corner of his eyes, he saw Bill smiling. Probably nostalgic.

"… but when you take in a lot of air and prepare yourself to ask something, then it's damn near impossible for me to do. However, it would be *technically* possible. And I would have to work my ass off for a really long time to make it happen."

"Don't be dramatic." Gabriel drummed his fingers on the dashboard. "I just need access to the medical record archives of the Children's Hospital of Michigan."

Conor shouted, "See?! I told you. You're sliding it in as if it *ain't no thang*. But newsflash, mister! This is America. Medical records are more sacred to us than, I don't know, pfft, Jesus himself!"

"Are they now?"

"Hospitals are crazy about their HIPAA, you know that."

"But the records I'm requesting are from 1981 and earlier."

"And that is different how?"

Gabriel bit the tip of his lower lip. "The Health Insurance Portability and Accountability Act was implemented in 1996. So technically, those records aren't protected, right?"

"Oh… no, no, no. It's like saying that speed law doesn't apply to you because you bought your car before the law was implemented."

"Worst analogy ever."

"But you get what I'm saying. There's no way to circumvent HIPAA. A few years ago, a hospital down south ended up paying a multimillion-dollar lawsuit when they failed to follow HIPAA. And making the FBI bleed out millions of dollars just weeks after they promoted me will put a damper on my career, don't you think?"

"This is one real shot we have at Lolly, and I'm not going to let bureaucracy ruin it. I *will* break into the hospital if I have to." Gabriel glanced at Bill. "Won't be our first time committing a little evil to defeat a greater evil."

Another smile from Bill, if only a little. Nostalgic, again.

"Please don't do that," Conor implored. "You're too old for that maverick shit."

"This is very important." Gabriel explained about the bald spots, about Alopecia Areata and how one of Lolly's partners might have suffered from it.

Conor was quiet for a few seconds, then he said, "So I assume you want to go through all the medical records from that hospital?"

"Uh-huh. Mostly from the dermatology department."

"If you need just a few, then a local PD can help you with the warrant. Now to sift through thousands of records, you need a really powerful authorization from a really powerful person."

"Who?"

"US Department of Justice's Assistant Attorney General for the Criminal Division."

Gabriel felt good. AAG was the head honcho in the country when it came to criminal matters. Seeing that Lolly was the most wanted bank robber in the US, the AAG would authorize it, no fuss.

"Why're you still on the call?" Gabriel asked.

"Don't hold your breath. She isn't on my speed-dial. Give me time. I'll arrange everything and let you know." Conor hung up.

"So what do we do now?" Bill asked.

"Get Lolly's DNA."

* * *

Big golden teeth grimaced from within the plastic cover. Gabriel turned it over, and the back of the black cloth was smeared with dried puke. They had analyzed it and found that Lolly had ramen for breakfast that fateful afternoon thirty-eight years ago.

Lolly's DNA had been extracted from it and uploaded into CODIS.

Gabriel handed the evidence bag across the table to Captain Wheeler.

"They were good men. Great detectives. I'm sorry for your loss, Agent Chase." Then he looked at Bill. "Sorry for both your losses, I mean."

"Thanks, Captain," Gabriel said and Bill nodded.

"I should have known this was coming."

Gabriel frowned. "What do you mean?"

Wheeler frowned in return. "Because someone made an attempt on their lives?"

"What the?!" Gabriel leaned forward, and Bill sat up straight. "What are you talking about?"

"H-he didn't tell you?" he asked.

"No!"

Wheeler shook his head and told them the story about drive-by shooters trying to kill Joshua and Peter on Livernois Avenue, on April 8.

The same day his dad drunk dialed him. Now Gabriel understood why he had been out of it that day. He had never been shot at in his life. Traumatized but being too adamant for his own good, Joshua drank to let some steam off and calm his nerves. He had gone to Detroit with a purpose and he neither half-assed his work nor bailed in fear.

But the story didn't add up. It had a huge gaping hole in it.

In his notebook, Joshua wrote something that Gabriel researched and found to be true.

Lolly never missed.

Chapter 34

May 11, 2019. 05:01 A.M.

A series of impatient knocks on the door startled Gabriel out of his sleep.

That was not Bill.

He grabbed his Glock from the bedside table and crouched to the door. The peephole was dark. Had it always been like that?

Not willing to take a chance, he picked a shoe and put it over the fisheye. If the person on the other side was an adept criminal element, Gabriel's knockoff Adidas would be blown to smithereens.

But it wasn't.

He chucked the shoe and saw through the hole.

A chubby woman with blonde hair and in a pantsuit stood outside, her arms tied across her chest.

Since there was no axiom that soccer moms couldn't moonlight as hitwomen, he took cover behind the wall and asked, "Who is it?"

"Agent Chase?" the woman said. She had the voice tailor-made for oratorical jobs, like podcasts, motivational or unboxing videos. "This is Carla Brooks with the OCR."

"What's an OCR?"

"Office of Civil Rights, from the Department of Health and Human Services. Got a call from the Attorney General's office last night. And I would rather have this conversation with a human than a talking door."

Except Conor and Bill, no one knew about this new lead. So Gabriel pocketed his pistol and grabbed the doorknob. He invited Brooks in and directed her to the only chair in the room while he took a seat on the bed.

He said, "Waking me up this early means you have good news."

"I'm sorry, but I was told it's urgent. And yes, I do have good news." Brooks proceeded to explain. HHS and AAG of the Criminal Division came to an agreement. Lolly must be caught at any cost, but they couldn't bypass HIPAA by giving unsupervised access to protected health information.

So the HHS temporarily appointed a person from OCR, Carla Brooks, to supervise the operation and make sure nothing got lost. Meaning they would allow Gabriel and Bill to read all the medical records, but Brooks would act as a proctor.

Gabriel had to laugh because the billing services of almost every hospital in the US exported their *PHI*, aka medical records, to Eastern hemisphere call centers.

She took out an envelope and a pen from her suit and passed them to Gabriel. "Inside it is the agreement. You have to sign it before we let you near the medical records."

Gabriel never partook in pissing contests that sprouted from ego and misplaced sense of self-esteem. He would do anything to establish justice, even break the law, or in this case, give in to this inconsequential mandate.

He skipped to the last page of the agreement. It was approved by the Assistant Attorney General from the DOJ and Deputy Secretary of HHS.

When he signed it, Brooks said, "That's a bummer."

"What is?" he returned the documents and pen to her.

"That you signed it without any protest. I had a whole argument prepared on my drive here."

"It's alright." Gabriel stood up. "You give your presentation while I bathe and get ready."

* * *

Brooks rode shotgun and Bill sat in the back. She had got his signature too as soon as she met him. After that, no one spoke for around fifteen minutes. Then Bill broke the silence.

"I've been thinking, Agent Chase. About how Lolly's friend has this condition and that's helping us track him?"

"Yeah?"

"We can apply the same method with Lolly."

Interested, Gabriel asked, "How do you mean?"

"Like you did yesterday, I performed an internet search last night about the causes of indigestion and heartburn."

"Because the old lady said that Zesty is used to soothe acid reflux?"

"That's correct. The results were too many to be useful. And then I repeated the same search," Bill paused. "But this time for kids."

To Gabriel's surprise, Brooks chipped in. "Because that problem is fairly uncommon in a younger and brisker anatomy."

Gabriel glanced sideways.

"What?" Brooks asked. "I know. I'm a mom."

"That's correct," Bill said. "Kids don't suffer acid reflux as much as adults do. But Lolly was using Zesty in 1981, when he was a kid. He continued to use it until 2019. So I assume he suffers from some sort of chronic indigestion problem and he uses Zesty for the symptoms."

Gabriel pondered over the bridge robbery. Lolly had vomited *before* killing the security guard, not *after*. Maybe guilt and disgust with himself wasn't the reason Lolly puked. Maybe it was because of acid reflux, which only worsened when doing something that released a busload of adrenaline into the body. Like T-boning a fucking truck with a backhoe and pushing it off a bridge.

"Okay?" Gabriel said, proud of Bill. "What do you suggest we do now?"

"These problems with the esophagus are relevant to what the Internet calls *gastroenterology*. Since we're already on our way to the medical record archives of the Children's Hospital, it wouldn't hurt to sieve through that department, too."

Gabriel angled the rearview mirror and caught the eyes of the depressed but brilliant police officer. "Bill?"

"Yes, Agent Chase?"

"It's time you take up the detective exam."

Chapter 35

May 11, 2019. 06:37 A.M.

In the hospital, Brooks took them across a grand echoing lobby, straight to an elevator in the corner.

"You know this place?" Gabriel asked.

"Yes. Sometimes we conduct random drills to check if staff are following HIPAA compliance."

After entering the elevator, she pressed *-2*.

When the doors parted, they turned right and walked to a room at the end of the corridor. It had metal shelves like the ones in libraries. Also like a library, the place was hauntingly quiet.

Before they began, Brooks asked them for their cell phones, and papers and pens if they had any.

"Why?"

"Sorry guys. HIPAA."

They handed over their phones. "No paper or pen."

Gabriel looked around. The shelves were categorized by departments—pediatric neurology, cardiology, and other -ogies—and the rows were labelled with years.

"There must be thousands of records here," Gabriel said. "Is there an expiry on the warrant?"

Brooks shook her head. "You have all the time in the world."

Bill said, "Then we go through each and every single record, page by page, line by line. It's the only lead we have."

"I agree," Gabriel said. "But let's concentrate on records from the late seventies to the early eighties. That's when Lolly and his bald friend were kids. They might have started visiting adult hospitals later."

Bill nodded.

Gabriel turned to Brooks. "So where are we sitting?"

Brooks picked up a stack of files from the year 1975-1980 in dermatology. "Follow me."

Gabriel took a stack from the same section and obeyed her, Bill walking behind them. She led them to the end of the room, where a broken hospital bed without mattress and a bunch of wheelchairs were discarded.

Brooks placed the records on the bed and started towards the shelf. After unloading, Gabriel held Bill's shoulder and sat him down in a wheelchair. "Let me bring the files for you. What's that word again? Gastro...?"

"Gastro-enter-ology."

Gabriel nodded and went to work. He did not bother to keep count of how many trips he made after the 8th.

The bed eventually overflowed with files, and they had to use the floor.

By the time Brooks and Gabriel plunked down onto their respective wheelchairs, they were sweating profusely.

They had two piles of medical records. One from dermatology, the other from gastroenterology. The latter was twice as voluminous as the former.

Gabriel took the first file from the dermatology pile and started reading.

"Brooks." Bill motioned at his pile. "Mind giving me a hand?"

"Sure." Brooks picked a file and asked, "What am I looking for?"

"Any symptoms relating to indigestion," Bill said.

"Okay?" she said, her eyes glued to the medical record. "Symptoms like?"

"Vomiting, nausea, acidic taste, acid reflux, heartburn, lack of appetite, stomach pain. And they aren't exclusive. Ask yourself one question: will the symptom make me take antacid? If yes," Bill pointed at an empty wheelchair with his crutch, "put that file over there."

Gabriel felt proud. Again. Bill did his homework last night.

"Got it." Brooks closed the file and dropped it on the floor before taking the next.

* * *

Gabriel bought food and snacks as he'd finished first. His pile was easier. Not just because it was smaller; all he needed to do was scan for the words 'hair loss' or 'Alopecia Areata'. But as a lot of keywords were associated with indigestion, Bill's pile took a while to get through, even with Brooks's help. It was evening when the work was finally done.

In the end, Gabriel had isolated 102 kids that had *hair loss* in their medical records. Twenty-eight suffered from Alopecia Areata, nineteen among them were blacks. Bill and Brooks had picked around 780 kids, 630 of them blacks. So in total, they had narrowed down to 649 entries.

Brooks, the only one with access to a cell phone, had notated the names and dates of births from all the selected entries.

Gabriel regarded the 649 files. Bill's idea increased the number tremendously, but they were now twice as likely to succeed.

"What do we do now?" Brooks asked.

"We have a plan," Gabriel said.

"What plan?"

"Cross reference what we've collected so far with NCIC."

"What's that?" Brooks said.

"National Crime Information Center, a database created by the famous Edgar Hoover," Bill answered. "If you have a criminal record, you're in NCIC."

"How's that going to help?"

"From this 649, we'll look for anyone who served a sentence from 85-87," Bill said. "That's the time period Detective Chase, um… I mean Senior Detective Chase, hypothesized Lolly was in prison."

Brooks said, "How are you gonna check it against the NCIC? We have no computer here."

"Not us. The new SAC from the FBI."

Brooks shook her head. "Sorry, guys, no can do. We're strictly prohibited from sharing PHI. Can't send it anywhere."

"*Technically*, we aren't smuggling PHI." Gabriel came for Bill's rescue. "It's just names and DOBs. Call your boss and ask if you want."

Brooks actually called her supervisor and disappeared along the aisle. A few minutes later, she returned. "Okay, where do I send them?"

Gabriel gave her Conor's email ID.

* * *

It had been more than two hours since they sent the list to Conor. Gabriel and Brooks were putting the stacks back into the respective shelves while Bill was reading the files Brooks had isolated. Micromanager or a perfectionist, Gabriel didn't know. But a good detective. He had come a long way since the Mr. Bunny investigation.

When they were done and took their seats, Bill was gripping a file. Gabriel's stomach churned because Bill sat motionless. He was frowning deeply, his eyes welled. Knuckles white, his hands shook.

Brooks touched his shoulder. "Are you okay there, bud?"

He looked up at her, then at Gabriel. He was biting his quivering lower lip and a teardrop fell, bouncing off his cheek.

The frown slowly loosened, giving way to a smile. Not a lame half smile, but a full toothy grin.

And no words were needed.

"A-are you positive?" Gabriel asked, a chill traversing his spine.

Bill nodded, passing the open file to him.

A newspaper article from Detroit Free Press was pinned to a page. It had colored photos of two kids on the front.

One of the kids was black. With blue eyes. Gabriel read the name under it.

Ryatt Durant.

The world stopped moving, static electricity vibrating across his skin, bristling his hair.

The rush was unlike anything Gabriel had ever felt. The lungs seemed to consume more oxygen, the heart thumped and pumped blood faster, while his brain rewarded all the hard work by releasing a soup of euphoric chemicals.

While floating in bliss, he read the newspaper article. A swimming pool contamination blinded two kids and infected dozens more. *Keratitis,* they had written, caused by amoeba.

"What is it?" Brooks asked.

Gabriel stood up and handed the file to her. With a tearful smile, he walked over to Bill who sat straight and opened his arms. Gabriel hugged him, whispering, "We got the fucker."

He gave a final squeeze and let go.

Brooks asked, "Why do they have a newspaper section on a medical record?"

"The doctor was required to provide an expert witness in court," Gabriel said. "So he must have attached each file of the infected kid with the article to differentiate them. When the case was over, he returned the files to the respective departments."

"It says Durant is blind."

"Eye transplant. Conor will either confirm or deny our presumption shortly," Gabriel said. "What digestion problem does he have?"

Bill wiped his face with the heels of his hands. "Something called Dyspepsia. Symptoms include acid reflux, burning sensation, and nausea with or without vomiting. That's why he sucks onto Zesty, a ginger-extract candy."

Just then, Brooks's phone blared and she answered it.

"No— I switched off their phones— It's protocol— Please listen— What did you say? Oh screw you, pissant—" She tossed the phone to Gabriel. "It's for you. What a prick."

Gabriel said into the phone, "Conor?"

"You fucking did it again, Chase. There was only one person on that list who served a sentence from 85-87. You got the guy—"

"Ryatt Durant," Gabriel said.

Conor did not speak for a few moments. Then he said, "How did you— forget it. I can't decipher the way your brain works. Anyway I forwarded his address to you. He's unmarried and lives with his mom, Iris Durant."

Chapter 36

May 11, 2019. 10:49 P.M.

Iris Durant lived in Indian Village, an upscale part of Detroit. The streets were flanked by trees with lush low-hanging branches that sprinkled the blacktops with autumn leaves. The Camaro turned onto Burns Avenue, which really did seem like it was burning, due to the fiery orange leaves of the trees on the sidewalks. Houses had no fences or guard dogs. Old people walked briskly, holding colorful dumbbells.

Gabriel's phone rang. Conor. He put it on speaker for Bill's benefit.

"The CIRG finished the recon," Conor said.

The Critical Incident Response Group was the muscle of the FBI. Trained in tactical combat, they were called in for situations that might escalate into gunfights.

"What did they find?" Gabriel asked.

"One person in the house. The mother."

"I hope the CIRG isn't obvious."

"No. They used Range-R."

"Good," Gabriel said. Range-R radars were like x-ray vision for the law to see through walls. "You set up the cameras?"

"Will be up and running in an hour," Conor said. "Your ETA?"

"One minute." Gabriel turned onto Iroquois Street, where Iris's house was located.

"There's something you need to know," Conor said. "Out of the nineteen kids with Alopecia Areata, only one has a criminal record. Leopold Williams Jr, convicted for setting a Ferrari on fire and sent to juvenile for six months. He hasn't filed for expungement, so his records are accessible."

"Found anything linking him to Ryatt?" Gabriel asked.

"Yup. Leopold visited Ryatt forty-eight times when he served a two-year sentence for attempted theft in West Virginia."

"Alright. Keep digging." Gabriel stopped in front of a majestic two-story house. It was a detached property, surrounded by a three-foot hedge. Two dormers jutted from the slanting roof; the right-side wall had a balcony, and flower baskets with small pink flowers hanging from them. A chimney pot on the left side of the roof blew white smoke.

"Let me call you back." Gabriel hung up and exited the car, after which he helped Bill out.

They walked over rocky tiles, each framed with a square of grass. Bill grabbed Gabriel's forearm as they climbed the granite steps. The teak door was massive and robust; inscribed on its plaque was *213*. Gabriel lifted the brass door knocker and struck the wood thrice.

As the sound of locks being undone penetrated the silence, Gabriel scanned the place. The CIRG was indeed ultra stealthy. He couldn't find anything out of the ordinary.

When the door opened, Gabriel gaped, unable to form words. Or thoughts.

"Aw, crap," Bill muttered, looking at the old lady they met yesterday at Goodwill.

She chirpily said, "It's you two. The police boys!"

Gabriel did not have the mind to wonder about her sense of smell and memory.

"Iris Durant?"

"The one and only," she said.

Goddamn it!

"Sorry if we woke you up," Bill said, seemingly less appalled by the twist of fate. She didn't look like she had been sleeping, though. The book in her hand said as much.

"No. One of the perks of being old."

"Perks?"

"You don't waste a lot of time sleeping. You get to enjoy many waking hours." Iris laughed and tapped the hardcover. "This book always makes me appreciate life." She frowned. "Why is the other boy so quiet?"

It took a nudge from Bill to understand that she was talking to him. Gabriel cleared his throat. "Sorry, ma'am. It is just… it's been a tiring day."

"I'm so sorry," she said. "Where are my manners! Come in, please."

She let them inside, then closed the door behind. "This way." She went to a couch and waited for them to sit. Taking a seat, she placed the book on a glass-top coffee table before them. The book's title read *Tuesdays with Morrie.* Beside the book was a tray carrying a pot, cups, and saucers.

As if she saw what Gabriel was looking at, she asked. "Fancy some peppermint tea?"

"No, thanks. We just ate," Gabriel lied.

"Then you must have some." She poured out two cups, not spilling a drop. "It has both peppermint and spearmint, and a splash of ginger extract and honey. It's good for your stomach. My son loves it."

Gabriel took a cup, but Bill did not touch his. As he sipped the tea, he observed the walls around which displayed more of Iris's charity work. There was a black and white photo of young Iris in a wedding gown, arms hooked to a tall black man. They looked happy. Then his eyes moved to the next photo, a colored one. Iris and another black man in front of a church. He was athletic, his eyes the hue of a clear sky.

In spite of the warm liquid soothing his digestive track, Gabriel felt a vile bile rise up his throat. Was that murdering demon really born to this angel?

"Is that your son, ma'am?" Bill asked, his voice shaky.

"Me with a handsome man at a church?"

"Uh-huh."

"Yes. That's St. Peter's Basilica. My son took me to Europe in 1993."

Must be from the money Ryatt robbed in Staten Island. The robbery that pulled Joshua into this mess, ultimately ending with his head exploding inside a burlap sack.

Iris continued. "He explained the statues to me, their geometries and colors—"

"How do you know to imagine?" Bill asked, his voice a bit harsh.

"What do you mean?" Iris asked, frowning.

Gabriel shook his head but Bill asked the next question nonetheless. "I mean how do you know what is blue or white or red?"

"I wasn't born blind," Iris blurted.

Gabriel deflated while Bill continued the assault, "You were blinded forty-two years ago, when you gave your eye to Ryatt?"

Iris's mouth parted a little.

Bill proceeded to tell her what they had learned during their drive from the Children's Hospital. Conor researched the other kid who had gone blind with Ryatt, the one on the front page of the Detroit Free Press. His name was Nicholas Brown, aka Nick. Conor used his FBI magic and sent his phone number to Gabriel.

Nick had said that his mother, Loraine, never stopped talking about Iris because she was the purest soul ever. Unlike Nick, who got his corneas from some Chinese guys, Iris had said that it was wrong and gave her own sight to Ryatt. The corneal transplantation was botched, making her permanently blind.

And the mere thought that Lolly was her son, living with her, infuriated Gabriel. Though Iris didn't have vision, it was Lolly that made her blind, by doing what he did behind her back.

Iris listened to Bill with a stern face, and when he finished, she turned to Gabriel. "I don't know what your friend is talking about."

Gabriel said, "W-we aren't here to establish the law, ma'am. I actually think what you did is the noblest thing."

Iris's face softened. "Yes. Ryatt has *my* eye. It is *my* eye and *I* gave it to *my* son. Law has no business telling me not to. Imagine that you go blind and your parents have an option to give their eyes to you, they would do it without a thought."

"I agree," Gabriel said. Joshua really would.

"So why are you here?" she asked, her warm and hospitable demeanor eroded, thanks to Bill.

While Gabriel winced and got ready for the truth to break Iris, Bill said, "We're reaching out to people who might be witness to a carjacking."

Gabriel exhaled. He knew this scenario was something he needed to face one day or another, but he wished it was later rather than sooner.

"Carjacking?" Iris asked, as if she didn't buy into the story.

"It's really important that we talk to him, ma'am." Bill's tone became authoritative. "Tell us where your son is."

"I don't know. His job requires him to travel."

Bill let out a contemptuous chuckle. "It sure does."

"Don't you take that tone with me, young man!"

Gabriel, feeling like a kid watching his mom and older brother argue, jumped in. "Do you have Ryatt's phone number?"

"He is a busy man. I'd rather you didn't disturb him."

Bill's eyes fluttered to an old landline phone in a corner table. He pushed himself up and walked towards it.

Leaning his entire weight on his crutch, he opened the drawer under.

Was he searching for a phonebook? Why would a blind woman with such a remarkable memory need one?

Iris's face twisted in indignation, and her voice shook as she spoke. "Don't go snooping around the house of a kind person who let you in and served you tea. You've outstayed your welcome." She turned in Gabriel's direction. "Both of you."

Bill returned to the table, empty-handed. "But the—"

"I will give you Ryatt's phone number when you hand me a warrant. Make sure it is braille."

Gabriel said, "I apologize for the inconvenience, ma'am."

As they left, Bill stopped near her. "Sorry, Mrs. Durant," he said, his voice breaking.

Iris acknowledged with a curt nod but said nothing.

As the door closed behind them, Gabriel spotted a Land Rover passing through. Hadn't he seen that car somewhere? He squinted at the plate.

It read 80085.

Chapter 37

May 12, 2019. 12:31 A.M.

Gabriel was gazing at the ceiling fan, thinking about the Land Rover. How did they sniff their way to Durant's residence? The house where Lolly, the person the Detroit Alliance was searching for thirty-eight years, lived.

Ever since Gabriel had met Roman and publicized his presence at Calabria, he had been keeping an eye on the rearview mirror. No one had followed him, but now Gabriel was sure that he had a tail.

How?!

An avid fan of shooting and espionage video games, he arrived at a possible answer in a beat. He sat up straight and whispered, "No freaking way."

Pocketing his gun, he got off the bed. Then he ran down to the parking lot in the basement, taking two steps at a time. When he reached the Camaro, he dropped to the floor and rolled under the car.

Five minutes later, his hand groping above the right rear wheel, he found a plastic box the size of a Lego.

* * *

Bill lay on the bed, watching TV and eating Pringles, and Gabriel sat at its edge. An hour past midnight, a fifty-year-old lanky man carrying a briefcase knocked on his door. He introduced himself as Special Supervisory Agent Morgan from the Detroit field office. Gabriel wondered why the SSA would be personally involved, and Morgan said that Conor was a friend and he had requested him to help Gabriel in any way he could.

Morgan specialized in computers, both hardware and software. The *briefcase* was actually a device that resembled a laptop. It had a keyboard but also a myriad of slots and loose wires.

Gabriel passed the GPS transmitter he found under the Camaro to Morgan.

Inspecting the device, he asked, "You guys didn't switch it off, right? Your trackers would have known if you did."

"We didn't tamper with it."

Morgan took out a small Swiss army knife from his pocket and pried the case of the device open. A red and green wire ran through it; he plucked them out. Then he connected their copper tips to a pair of wires in the laptop and began typing.

When he stopped, the screen read *Initializing*, and a status bar appeared under it.

Ten minutes later, the bar was at 37% and Bill got bored and became inquisitive. He asked, "Now that we transferred it from the basement to our room two levels up, won't they smell that something's fishy? I read that these GPS things can calculate height, too."

"Nah… I'm sure your car is parked only a few dozen feet below, not more than hundred feet. Altimeters in GPSs are known to give off wrong readings, sometimes by 400 feet." Morgan regarded the plastic device. "This is cheap. Your trackers did not have altitude in their minds when they bought it."

"So, basically, what you're saying is," Bill took out a chip from the Pringles tube on his stomach and put it in his mouth, "they won't know? We're fine?"

"Yes. You are fine." Morgan sighed, evidently regretting having provided Bill with a comprehensive answer, when a few-word response would have been sufficient.

"What's happening in there?" Gabriel pointed at the laptop screen.

"Doubling back."

"I don't understand."

Morgan looked uncertain; Gabriel could see the cogs inside his brain going off. He was wondering if he should share his in-depth knowledge again. Apparently, he decided he would give them another chance. "Alright. You know how GPS receivers work, right? Trilateration?"

Gabriel said, "At any time of the day, you have at least three satellites hovering over your head. They always broadcast their locations in space in relation to Earth. The GPS receivers collect that data to compute *their* locations in relation to the satellites, and give us longitudes and latitudes."

"Correct." Morgan's face brightened. "Then the GPS chip sends the coordinates to some output device that's attached to it, generally an LCD."

"Like in cars."

"Yes. But since GPS trackers don't show the location to you on an LCD screen but to someone else, they constantly transmit information by cell phone towers, which is then saved on the cloud."

"Oh," Gabriel said. He almost didn't understand but when he pictured the process, he got it.

"Usually, there is a third-party company that stores the data from the GPS *trackers*. And this baby," Morgan touched the laptop, "can find out to which company the data is being transmitted. Once I zero in on that server, I can hack into it and trace who is constantly viewing your location."

Bill kept his face blank, while Morgan continued.

"… Ironically, whoever is tracking you *would have* used the Internet to connect to the cloud. And I'll phish their device's IP address or IMEI number from that server, and then their location."

"So, basically, what you're saying is," Bill took out another chip from the Pringles tube on his stomach and put it in his mouth, "we can track them because they are tracking us?"

"Yes." Morgan deflated, the animation his face had been reflecting when he talked about computer stuff evaporated.

The status bar was finally at 100%.

"We found the device that's accessing the data from the GPS tracker," Morgan said. "It's a cellphone."

"Who does it belong to?"

Morgan played his keyboard some more. Then he said, "Roman Marino."

Honestly, that didn't surprise Gabriel.

He walked over to the window and peeked outside. Calabria was closed.

"You have a location?" Gabriel asked as he returned to them.

"I do. Roman's GPS is turned on," Morgan said.

"Where is it?"

Morgan pointed at the zoomed in section of a map on his laptop. When he read the address, Gabriel skipped a heartbeat. He knew that place; he'd just been there, having mint tea.

Roman was in Iris's house.

Chapter 38

May 12, 2019. 12:31 A.M.

Iris was woken by a peculiar noise that didn't belong: a wet crunch, like someone breaking a tree branch. Pushing the blanket aside, she got off the bed. As soon as she left the comfort of her room, a cool breeze swept her gown and sent chills across her skin, giving her goosebumps.

The cold wind was blowing from the direction of her front door. Wondering if she had forgotten to lock it, she made her way towards the entrance.

When she reached the door, something poked under her foot, making her wince. She bent down and picked up the object. It felt like a tiny lump of wood.

Not sure from where it had chipped off, she closed the door. But she couldn't lock it. The place where the deadbolt used to be was now hollow.

"You're blind?" Someone laughed behind her. Then she heard a strong hum, like her son's trimmer, only louder. As the sound neared her, she got a whiff of something she hadn't smelled for a very long time.

"It's you," she said.

"It's you who?"

"Bugsy."

He chuckled. "I forgot how it feels to be called by my Christian name. No one dares to these days." The hum travelled to her right and Bugsy's voice came from there. He would be in a motorized wheelchair, she'd guessed. "But you can call me anything you want. Our experience has created a powerful bond, hasn't it?"

"Violating a woman isn't bonding. It's cowardice."

"But you still remember me."

"I can never forget that day. My son became blind because of you."

"Really?" Bugsy asked.

"That is a part of my life I'd prefer not to reminisce," she said. "Why did you break into my house?"

"Thirteen thousand six hundred and fifty-three," Bugsy said. "That's how many days I've been waiting for this moment."

"What moment?"

"Rome?" Bugsy called. "Bring it here."

Iris remembered who Rome was. That guy with white-blonde hair and bushy brows who had helped Bugsy abduct her.

"You know what Rome's got in his hands?" Bugsy asked. "A photo of you and someone with blue eyes that I've been thinking about every hour of those thirteen thousand six hundred and fifty-three days."

Ryatt?

An evil incarnate like Bugsy did not deserve to even see the shadow of an angel like her son.

Bugsy rolled closer to her. "Who is he?"

"M-my son, why?"

Her question was met with silence, so Iris asked again, "Why?"

"Did you say I made him blind?" Bugsy asked.

"You did, inadvertently."

"But somehow you got his sight again? Transplantation?"

Why were all these people suddenly questioning her about Ryatt's eyes? What had he done?

Bugsy tsk-tsked. "You should have let him stay blind."

"W-what?" Iris was confounded. "Why do you say horrible things like this?"

"I don't wanna beat around the bush. Your sonny boy is the most wanted bank robber in our country. Far surpassed me in evil and infamy, murdering dozens."

Iris had to repeat the words in her mind to make sense of them. The implication was preposterous; they were mistaken. She said, "I think you got the wrong address."

Bugsy giggled. "Oh, you poor bitch."

Iris stiffened. "Get out!"

"Let's make a deal. You know where your son is working, don't you? Call that organization, and if they say he is employed there, we'll pay for your door and leave. How about that?"

Iris thought it through. Finding that she no other option, she walked purposefully over to the phone and dialed Ryatt's football team.

But it said the number did not exist.

She frowned. From the drawer, she recovered her cellphone.

Unlocking it with her fingerprint, she said, "Ok Google." When the phone chimed, she put the mic near her mouth. "Floridan Crocs."

Once the results were loaded, the Text-To-Speech function began reading what was on the screen. As it iterated the phone number of Floridan Crocs, she memorized it. This was not the number Ryatt had given her.

Putting the uneasiness aside, she dialed Floridan Crocs from her landline.

The answering machine advised her to call between 10:00 a.m. and 5:00 p.m.

As she placed the receiver back, the hum of the wheelchair moved towards her.

Bugsy said, "Tell us where he is. We'll bring him here and you can ask him yourself."

"I'll never tell you anything about him."

"We'll see." As the wheelchair receded, Bugsy shouted. "Dry drown the broad!"

She jumped to dial 911, but two pairs of hands caught her arms and pulled her away. Grasping her wrists, they dragged her across the floor, to the kitchen.

They freed her left wrist, letting her hang by her right, her shoulder bone threatening to rip out of the socket. But she would never scream or cry or beg.

Silverware and cutlery fell from the dining table.

One of the two hands holding her right wrist grabbed her left. Then someone else got her ankles. She was lifted off the floor and dropped onto the hardwood.

Her ankles were clasped by a pair of strong hands, so were her wrists. The dining table tilted, sloping downwards, and they placed something under the legs to make it stay like that. Iris would have slid headfirst onto the floor if it weren't for the hands holding her feet.

As she reminded herself not to be afraid, a wet cloth was wrapped around her face.

"Last chance, Granny," the person pressing the cloth against her face said. "It's a CIA torture technique. Trust me, you won't be a fan."

When Iris lay motionless and unresponsive, he said, "Have it your way."

Her face was then doused with water. She reckoned that someone was pouring it over the cloth. At first, she didn't feel anything, except it was cold. But due to the decline of the table, the water flowed into her nose.

Her head jerked involuntarily when it was impossible to breathe. She struggled to remove the cloth, but she couldn't move even an inch. As seconds passed, water turned acidic, burning her nostrils and airway.

Writhing in agony, she reminded herself not to cry or scream. When she felt her consciousness slip, the cloth was yanked from her face. She gasped deeply, greedily sucking in air. Never before had she appreciated sweet, sweet oxygen so much.

"We have gallons more where that came from," Bugsy said. "Tell us where your little nigger is."

Iris turned her head to the direction of Bugsy's voice.

Shuddering uncontrollably, she said, "C-come closer."

The wheelchair rolled and stopped near her. "Yes?" Bugsy said, expectantly.

She lurched her head forward and spat forcefully.

"Goddamn it!" Bugsy's wheelchair rolled back. "Rome! Get it off! Get it off!"

A few moments of dubious silence. Then he barked, "Again!"

She instinctively flinched, and the wet cloth smothered her once more. As water was poured above the cloth, she lost control of her convulsing body. It was on autopilot now, evolution mistakenly making her believe that she was drowning, forcing her arms and legs to thrash about.

For some reason, she thought of the time she had to deliver Ryatt, unassisted, during what was practically a battlefield. This *dry-drowning* was painful, but not nearly as bad as giving birth alone. Not even close.

As she recalled that day, other thoughts scrambled. Everything spun out of angle. Her sinewy arms and legs became flaccid, and Iris entered into a world that was bright. The deprivation of oxygen did not seem so bad anymore. She ascended into the void, her body relaxed, and the last of her earthly afflictions vanished.

It is… peaceful…

The cloth was removed. The air, now an unwelcome guest, rushed to her lungs like hot steam, scalding its way down. A bout of coughs knocked the air out just as quickly.

"You changed your mind yet?" Bugsy asked.

Her throat had swollen from the violent coughs, so her voice would be very raspy if she spoke. But her answer did not require words.

She turned towards Bugsy and spat again, though it wasn't nearly as forceful as the first time. She heard the spit land on the table beside her.

"You fucking bitch!" Bugsy screamed again. "Once more!"

Smiling crookedly for egging him, she didn't even flinch when the wet cloth hugged her face. There were two things she was certain of. One, this was not the most overwhelming experience she ever had, because she was a single parent. Two, she would never let Bugsy near Ryatt.

The water came rushing into her nose. Though her limbs tried to splay, she did not do it willingly. And she visited that serene place between life and death once again.

When the cloth was removed, she neither coughed nor heaved.

It was getting old now. Definitely not a masochist, she was ready for this little game of theirs. Let them do it a thousand times; still they wouldn't be able to squeeze a word out of her.

"Boss," the man holding Iris said. "She'll die if we keep at it."

"Damn it," Bugsy sighed. "I didn't think we'd be able to crack her anyway. Couldn't do it the first time."

"We even broke wise guys who were ex-Marines by waterboarding," he said. "What's this grandma made of?"

"Grit of headstrong women," Bugsy said vehemently. "We're gonna have to figure out a different approach."

"Should we let her live?"

"I guess the Feds are watching the house. If she dies, it'll be a problem for us."

The hands around her wrists and ankles unclasped. She slid backwards and crashed down onto the floor.

"Do me a favor?" Bugsy said. "Just call that Florida cock or wherever your son said he was working."

The wheelchair rolled away from her, out of the kitchen, so did the scuffing of the shoes. When they left, the house was quiet. She shot up to her feet and marched out, dragging a wooden chair behind. Once she closed the front door, she wedged the backrest under the doorknob.

Sure that the entrance was as secure as it could be, she made her way to the bathroom. She toweled her hair and face dry, then plugged in the dryer and evaporated the dampness out of her hair.

Should she report the incident to the authorities? Then she would be required to live through the ordeal again, and tell them that Bugsy thought Ryatt was some bank robber. Which might make the police want to question Ryatt. Her son didn't need to see that side of life, no, thank you.

She went to the dresser and changed into a set of crisp fresh clothes. Sleep now a distant dream, she returned to the living room and sat on the couch, picking up *Tuesdays with Morrie.*

But before she touched the first word, she whispered, her voice raspy, "My son is not a murderer."

When saying that sentence out loud, the absurdity of it sank in. Ryatt never even used expletives, he attended church on Sundays, and donated hundreds of thousands to charities.

Really absurd.

Shaking her head, she began tracing the indentations on the paper with her fingertips.

However, calling Floridan Crocs in the morning wouldn't hurt, would it?

Chapter 39

May 12, 2019. 02:02 A.M.

Gabriel and Morgan watched the feed from the cameras the tactical team had installed around Iris's house. The black Land Rover and white Chrysler were parked up front. A Rolls Royce stood between them, which Gabriel assumed was Bugsy's. Morgan, the computer wizard, looked it up and confirmed his suspicion.

Gabriel called Conor. "We have the armed response unit around Iris's house?"

"Watching it like hawks."

"So you know that Bugsy and his men are inside the house?"

Conor did not speak.

"Mobilize them and save Iris," Gabriel said.

"Sorry," Conor said. "Bugsy's men will have weapons. If we try to save her, it might escalate into a gunfight and hit the news, tipping off Ryatt."

Gabriel did not care. He would not sacrifice Iris for his revenge. Just when he began to insist strongly, Morgan pointed at the video feed.

There was movement in front of Iris's house. Six men came out, one of them in a wheelchair. Then they got into the cars and left.

A few seconds later, Iris appeared at the door and Gabriel could breathe easily again. She closed it and went back inside.

Gabriel wanted to know if she was ok. He said into the phone, "They are gone. Can you send someone now?"

"Look, these men are holed up pretty good. It'll give away their positions," Conor said. "How about this? I'll instruct the local PD to check on her in the morning."

Satisfied, Gabriel began discussing the case. Conor was very careful because no one had an inkling where Ryatt was. Chances were, even Iris didn't know. And they couldn't get a warrant to search her house with what they had.

At Gabriel's suggestion Conor went through Ryatt's history, especially the records from the IRS. They found that whatever money Ryatt had robbed, he had deposited it in the Lawrence Foundation. Not all at once but in five or six installments. They knew it was the banks' money because the Lawrence Foundation saw sharp growth in anonymous donations, always a week after Ryatt robbed some bank.

The IRS did flag this account. But when they saw that Iris was really spending all the money on public welfare and not using the Foundation as a device to launder money, they cleared her.

Ryatt co-owned an electronic shop, Goodwill Electronix, and he paid taxes for what measly income he earned from it. Two other guys had shares in this shop. Leopold Williams Jr. and Thomas Brown, who Gabriel guessed was the third member of their gang.

One of the biggest puzzles Joshua couldn't crack was why Ryatt had taken a hiatus. This was revealed through his tax records.

Goodwill Electronix was opened at the end of 2008, after Ryatt's gang stopped robbing. But it was a really bad year to come into the retailing business. Many online markets were taking the world by storm, buying in bulk from factories and selling them at discount rates that physical retailers just couldn't keep up with.

Still, Ryatt and his friends managed to run the shop until 2018, when it finally began sinking.

Evidently lacking the skills to run a business, they turned back to the only lucrative job that they could do. Robbery.

Seeing how Goodwill Electronix might be the only other location where they could find Ryatt, Conor had suggested that they storm the place.

Gabriel refused, stating that they would observe it first, since they had no assurance that Ryatt was there.

Conor had a camera installed across the shop, and like Gabriel had said, only Thomas was in, not Ryatt or Leo.

Conor called it a night, Morgan left, and Bill had been sleeping for the last hour.

Gabriel dug into his rucksack and took out a phone, a burner he'd bought the day before, then he went to buy food for Brooks and Bill.

He typed *Goodwill Electronix - Howard Street* and sent it to Roman. A minute later, Roman texted back *Tnx. If this leads us to Lolly, you get reward.*

* * *

A few hours later, a call from Conor blared and woke up Gabriel.

"You won't fucking believe what happened."

I will.

Gabriel said, "What?"

"Thomas was abducted. The guy manning the camera before the shop just told me. I sent two plainclothes to investigate."

"Let me go," Gabriel said.

"Okay," Conor said. "Shit!"

Twenty minutes later, Gabriel braked in front of Goodwill Electronix. The shutter was down. A bloody streak trailed across the sidewalk, leading from inside the shop to the road.

An unmarked car was parked a few yards down the shop. A guy with a marine haircut behind the wheel greeted Gabriel with a nod. A small black kid was sitting beside him on the passenger seat.

As Gabriel got down from the Camaro and walked to the car, its window rolled down.

"Agent Chase?" Jarhead asked.

"Yup." Gabriel flashed his ID. "What happened here?"

"We got information that the shop owner was taken." Jarhead pointed at the shutter. "My partner is in there, analyzing the CCTV. We closed it because this little shit," Jarhead motioned at the black kid, "and his friends were stealing chargers and headphones from the shop when we came. Others escaped, but I caught him."

Gabriel peeked inside. The boy couldn't be more than thirteen. He was trying to look tough but his chest was heaving, forehead peppered with sweat. He was too young for prison. Juvenile didn't rehabilitate boys. It criminalized them. Gabriel had seen kids going inside, all innocent, but coming out with a vast expertise in the art of crime.

Gabriel's eyes shifted down. The boy's thin wrists were tied together with plastic wires, and a thick cable extended from it, which Jarhead held.

Gabriel pointedly looked at the degrading harness.

"We don't got no handcuffs." Jarhead shrugged. Then without a prompt, he leaned in and slapped the boy on his head. "I didn't know we were going to encounter these sticky-fingered sons of bitches when we came."

The boy stared at Jarhead, his eyes tearing up in humiliation. Oh brother, was he in for a surprise when they strip him naked and powder him on his first day in juvie!

"Mind if I talk to him?" Gabriel asked.

"Sure." Jarhead exited the car. "I'm going for a smoke."

Jarhead transferred the cable to Gabriel. He got it and climbed into the car.

Once the Jarhead was out of earshot, Gabriel asked, "What's your name?"

"LC," the boy said, his voice full of fake depth.

"LC?"

"Lil' Cessna."

Gabriel lifted his brows.

"Because I love planes." LC got defensive.

Gabriel shook his head. "What's your real name, kid?"

The boy did not open his mouth.

"Okay, LC. Do me a favor?"

"Man, I ain't snitching on my friends."

"Not on your friends, though you must ask yourself, are they really your friends?" Gabriel said. "Friends don't take you down a path that ends with you getting slapped around by strangers."

The boy didn't answer.

"Tell me what happened in the shop, before you guys ransacked it," Gabriel said.

LC gawked, unsure what to do.

Gabriel added, "I'll make it worth your while."

LC smiled and said that he and his friends were hanging out at an alley across the street when some guys arrived in a Land Rover and abducted the *Black Hulk Hogan*.

"The Land Rover had a funny number plate?" Gabriel asked.

"Yeah." LC giggled, his veneer of toughness gave way to his childhood naiveté.

Gabriel tugged at the cable. "Is this how you want to be treated the rest of your life? Like an animal?"

"Man, cut the crap. I'm ready for the slammer."

"You've been?"

"First time for everything."

"Then you aren't entirely gone. You think life is unfair to you and you gotta push back and take what you want? Take what doesn't belong to you?"

"You know how it feels to not have stuff?" LC said.

"I do. I also know poverty doesn't justify stealing."

"You don't know what you talking about." LC shook his head. "You haven't been through shit."

"Let's say your assumption is correct, and that I haven't been through shit. But I know someone who's been through shit. *Tough shit.* Shit that will make your shit look like a cake walk."

"Yeah?" LC sat straight, challenging Gabriel. "Like what?"

"His family was so poor that he was born on a dirt floor. He lost his mom at ten. Not rich enough to go to school, he taught himself to read, *after* working as a farmhand during his days. Say, you've been through this shit, working in hot sun from dawn till dusk and *then* study?"

LC's eyes fluttered and he looked down.

Gabriel continued. "He tried to be a politician, but it didn't work out. Tried to be a lawyer, and that didn't work out either. He tried his hand in business with a partner and guess what?"

LC said, "It ain't worked out?"

Gabriel nodded. "His partner drank to death and left him with a huge debt that he worked for 15 years to settle."

"Man, this ain't inspiring me. This fool born to be a loser."

Gabriel smiled drily. "He *was* a loser. Just like how you are right now. Everyone's a loser at some point in life. I was too, trust me. We all have to be losers before we become winners. Before we get our shit together."

"So this guy, he got his shit together?"

"He did. Went on to achieve many great things. He's kind of famous, actually."

"Why? What'd he do?"

Gabriel stifled a yawn. "Just freed slaves is all."

LC's eyes bulged. "Honest Abe was a loser?"

Gabriel nodded. "Every great man had to go through trials and tribulations. Poverty, failure, humiliation, betrayal, self-loathing, you name it."

"But why?"

"How else would you get the wisdom to be great? You go to the gym, you put your muscles through pain, and in the end, they become stronger. Likewise, being a loser puts your mind in extreme pain but it gives you the strength to handle the eventual success," Gabriel said. "Pain is good. It means you're blessed and gonna live a fulfilling life."

LC was at the loss of words.

Gabriel asked, "You don't lie, do you, LC? Only punk ass snitches lie, right?"

LC nodded. "Word."

"Then promise me something."

LC laughed. "You a fool? You believe in promises?"

Gabriel shrugged.

"Okay." LC wiped his nose and giggled. "First tell me what it is."

"You go to a candy store called Goodwill. It's in Rosa Parks Blvd. Tell the nice old lady there that you'd like to become a pilot."

LC stared at Gabriel. "What? You crazy? Why will I go tell a stranger something personal like that?"

"Just do it."

"If I do, I get to fly planes?" LC asked, his eyes wide, voice animated.

"Yes."

"She like a genie or something?"

"Just. Do. It."

"B-but how?" LC lifted and showed his tied-up hands.

Gabriel smiled. "Promise."

LC frowned, but said, "Alright, promise."

"Good." Gabriel let go of the cable, which dropped to the floor.

LC looked at it and then at Gabriel, his face slowly registering what was happening. Opening the door, he quickly got down.

As he made his way to the other side, he stopped mid-road and jogged back to the car.

He leaned into the window. "It's Benjamin."

Then he crouched and ran towards the alley mouth across the road. When he was there, he got out of the makeshift cuffs. He looked at Gabriel and smiled, before putting his arms out and running into it.

A few minutes later, Gabriel ambled to the shop and pulled the shutter up.

"Fuck! You scared the bejesus out of me," the woman behind the billing counter said. She was watching something on a PC.

Gabriel showed her his ID. "You found out what happened here?"

"Yes." She turned the monitor in Gabriel's direction and rewound the video back to a specific point.

A lone man was sitting at the counter, scrolling through his phone. He was tall and beefy, like a retired bodybuilder. He must be the Black Hulk Hogan that LC had mentioned, Thomas. A few seconds later, his focus shifted from the phone to the shop's entrance. Lifting his hands, he got up from the chair. Two guys in balaclava came through the door, pointing shotguns at Thomas. They had ponytails; the twins Gabriel had seen outside Calabria.

One of the guys lifted the stock and hit Thomas on the nose, whose hands tended to the hurt instinctively.

Grabbing Thomas's arms, they dragged him out over the table. When he was down, they stomped and beat him some more, turning his face into a bloody pulp. Then they pulled Thomas to his feet and shoved him out of the shop.

Gabriel scratched his nose, smirking behind his hand. Now to the next part of the plan.

And he needed the FBI for it.

Chapter 40

May 12, 2019. 09:48 A.M.

The Camaro headed northeast, and the Google lady told Gabriel to take the Trumbull Ave. After a few minutes, she advised to turn onto Detroit Ave. He crossed M-10 and, half a mile later, arrived at his destination: Patrick V. McNamara Federal Building.

He cleared security, parked the car, and entered the edifice. A colossal direction board on the front wall listed what offices occupied which floors. IRS, HUD, VA, and other assortment of abbreviations. He shuffled to a series of elevators, got into one, and pressed 26.

Another security station checked his ID and let him through a wide hallway, which opened into a spacious office. He asked a random passerby as to the whereabouts of the SSA and was pointed to a room at the far-right corner.

Gabriel thanked her and made his way there.

SSA Morgan slouched on his chair, watching his laptop and nursing a strawberry smoothie. Looking as miserable as Gabriel felt, his bloodshot eyes were partially closed and lips chapped. Neither had got more than one hour of sleep.

"Good morning," Gabriel said.

"Good?" Morgan scoffed and motioned Gabriel to a chair across his desk. "Conor said that Thomas was abducted. He's asked me to monitor the CCTV cameras surrounding Bugsy's mansion."

"Can't we storm his place?" Gabriel asked, hoping they couldn't.

"Not enough grounds for a warrant…"

Thank God.

"It's too late for Thomas anyway. They've had him for what? Two hours now? I think he broke. You can do a lot in that time, believe me."

Gabriel believed him. "Why do you say he broke?"

"Because I've got this," Morgan turned the laptop towards Gabriel, "from one of the cameras."

The video showed the street where Bugsy's mansion was situated. Its front gates parted and a number of GMCs drove out. Four in total. Morgan paused at the third SUV and pointed to a man behind the windshield. "This guy is Anastasia, a known hitman. In total, we counted twenty men in all four cars. Could be more."

"Must be Bugsy's entire squad," Gabriel said, thinking how to use this new development to his advantage. Ryatt never committed a robbery in Detroit, except the first two. Chances were, he was out of state and it might take a while for Bugsy's army to reach him. "You're tracking them?"

"Yes, they're about to leave Michigan."

"Ryatt should be out of state, most likely doing homework for his next job."

Morgan sucked the straw before saying, "Anyway, there's nothing happening here. Go have a coffee. You look tired. I'll call for you if something's up."

Gabriel nodded and pushed himself up. The lack of sleep was catching up with him. He needed some shut eye, at least a power nap, to even concentrate. As he followed directions and trotted to the cafeteria, he felt agents looking at him with interest. No one had facial hair, not even a stubble, and they were all groomed neatly.

Once in the cafeteria, he located a vacant table at the far end and walked over to it. The wooden chair was uncomfortable, but his brain needed no comfort to rest.

Folding his forearms on the table, he dropped his head above it and his eyes drooped automatically.

Gabriel was then struck with an idea. It was pure genius. Maybe when the brain traversed the slim layer between extreme exhaustion and oblivious sleep, some magic happened.

The idea was simple. Let Ryatt know that Bugsy had Thomas, and probably his location was compromised. It would smoke him out of whatever hole he'd burrowed himself in. And if Bugsy killed Thomas, which Gabriel thought was most likely, Ryatt would scream revenge and come running to Detroit.

But how would Gabriel let Ryatt know anything? Maybe he should build an enormous satellite loudspeaker and shout it to the world. Nah. There was a more practical way to do the shouting: media.

* * *

"Gabriel Chase…"
The Google lady called, waking him up. As his eyes opened, he found several trays of food around him and people chattering.

He sat straight, wiping the drool off of his beard. The speakers crackled and the robotic voice of a woman said, "Gabriel Chase, report to the SSA's office."

He stood up and waded through the bustling cafeteria. In under a minute, he was inside Morgan's office.

"I'm really sorry," Gabriel said. "I nodded off."

"It's alright. Come, take a look." Morgan patted the seat of an office chair next to him and Gabriel obliged.

Morgan's laptop displayed an aerial view of Bugsy's mansion. The Land Rover was parked at the pebbled path that connected the back door to a swimming pool. The imagery was too clean to be from satellite.

"Drone?"

"Drone," the SSA confirmed.

"Excellent—" Gabriel held the side of his stomach. "Damn. That chipotle isn't exactly breakfast food, is it?"

"Why would you even?" Morgan said. "Last left down the aisle."

Gabriel nodded and followed Morgan's directions. He went inside the bathroom and took a seat on the commode.

Listening for footsteps for a few seconds and finding none, he pulled the burner out from inside his jacket and called Roman. "So I see you've squeezed Lolly's location out of Thomas."

"We did, thanks to you."

"Thanks again to me, I'm helping your sorry ass for the second time. You left a witness when you took Thomas. The cops are going to storm Bugsy's house. You got 20 minutes, max."

Gabriel hung up and exited the cubicle. After splashing water over his face, he looked in the mirror. He felt Joshua standing over his shoulder, shaking his head in disapproval.

Back in Morgan's office, they resumed watching Bugsy's mansion with the drone.

Twelve minutes later, four guys came out the back, carrying two sacks. It was the twins, the barkeeper from Calabria, and one other guy Gabriel hadn't seen before. They tossed the sacks into the Land Rover's trunk space and began driving.

And the drone followed, controlled by Morgan's laptop.

When they climbed onto John C Lodge Freeway, nearing Southfield, Gabriel spotted a landfill and a lot of birds scavenging. He prayed that the drone did not get attacked by a rowdy bird. It didn't.

The SUV took an exit down on West Eleven Mile Road and, a minute later, turned onto a nameless, dead-end street that was flanked by rundown buildings. They halted near a swamp at the edge and opened the trunk.

All four got down. Two of them lifted the first sack and carried it to the marshland, while the other two kept watch.

Placing the sack down, they grabbed its bottom corners and upended it.

"Can we lower the drone?" Gabriel asked.

"If we do, it's possible for them to hear the rotors."

The two guys repeated the exercise for the other sack too, before getting into the car and driving back the way where they came from.

When the car left the vicinity, Morgan flew the drone down and zoomed in on the contents spilled at the swamp. They were like parts of a mannequin. Legs, arms, torso, and a head.

But mannequins weren't supposed to be bloody red, were they?

Chapter 41

May 12, 2019. 12:13 P.M.

A cup of coffee warmed Gabriel's cold fingers. He needed something to wash the bad taste clinging at the back of his throat. Morgan seemed equally flummoxed, resorting to milk instead.

Prying the attention from his nerves and conscience, Gabriel said, "Let's move to the next part of the plan."

"Which is?"

"Let Ryatt know that Thomas has been chopped into pieces by the Detroit Alliance, and that his location could be compromised."

"How do you communicate with him?"

"The news."

Morgan frowned as he took a sip of his milk. "Good idea. Let me handle it."

"I don't think the FBI should be involved. Might tip off Ryatt."

"No worries." Morgan emptied his cup. "We'll pass it as an anonymous tip."

"Excellent. Also, we must work on stopping that hitman whatshisname."

"What? Anastasia is leading us to Ryatt. Why would we want to stop him?"

"He's most probably been ordered to either capture or kill Ryatt, who himself is not a novice when it comes to guns. A massacre will ensue. And in this age of Facebook and Instagram Live, the gunfight *will* escalate into a national sensation. The FBI will be chastised if we did nothing when we knew it was going to happen. We may both lose our jobs."

"But... but if we intercept them, a shootout will ensue nonetheless."

"It's not the same as inaction," Gabriel said.

"Let me see what I can do." Morgan took out his phone. "But getting the SWAT ready will take some time."

"That's alright. But keep it under wraps. The news doesn't leak to the media," Gabriel said. Bugsy should not know that his men were arrested. Gabriel needed the Detroit Alliance to be down on their guard, because their *old friend* was coming to them.

* * *

At 10:47 p.m., they received a live feed from the strike team on I-80. Gabriel was told that either a body or helmet camera was worn by each SWAT agent.

They were positioned on Fred Schwengel Memorial Bridge, a mile-long bridge crossing the Mississippi River, connecting Iowa and Illinois.

Civilians were denied access to the bridge. The road was barricaded on Iowa, and when the four GMCs entered the bridge from Illinois, the local PD would cut the traffic behind them, boxing those SUVs on the bridge.

Morgan's laptop screen was divided into four neat squares, which displayed four agents waiting to ambush.

The first camera showed the interior of a truck the agent was sitting in. Well, it was not a *truck* truck. It was a ramming vehicle, waiting on the shoulder lane.

The first GMC appeared in the distance, cruising at a normal speed, and three other GMCs followed.

"Target on sight," the agent said and revved the accelerator.

The GMC was around two hundred yards when the agent's truck moved. He drove on the side road, gaining speed, until the target was close. Then he swerved and collided head on into the GMC.

One down.

Thirty seconds earlier, the second camera showed the inside of another truck, but not of the ramming variety. It was a Ford Interceptor, one of the fastest pursuit vehicles ever made. It was going after the fourth GMC, the last in the formation.

The agent pressed a button. From underneath the Interceptor, two metal claws unfolded. Between them were lines of yellow ribbons. The Grappler. Gabriel had never seen one in action, but he knew that no prey escaped its claws.

The agent accelerated, and when the claws were close to the GMC, the yellow ribbons tangled with its rear wheels, forcing them to stop their rotation. And the GMC skidded to a halt. It happened precisely at the same time as the first GMC was crushed.

Two of Bugsy's hit squads were taken down simultaneously.

Only two left.

The second and third GMC raced away, apparently understanding what was happening.

The third camera was worn by a lone agent lying in wait in the dark night, behind a switched-off streetlamp. When the GMC was within his reach, he deployed a spike strip. All four tires burst with satisfying pops.

The agent moved away from the streetlamp and laughed. "Is he for real?" he said and turned the camera towards the second GMC which was swaying along the road. The dumb asshole kept on driving, until he broke through the bridge and the car fell into the river below. The water splashed and the car floated upside down, carried by the stream.

"Holy shit!" Morgan said.

The third and final GMC drove across the median, to avoid the spike strip.

"Time to bring in the big gun." Morgan pressed a key and the feed from the fourth camera maximized, filling the screen.

It was a chopper.

The helmet-mounted camera moved at incredible speed and caught up with Anastasia's GMC.

"We got visual." The agent slid the door open and brought up a rifle. It was hefty, like a grenade launcher, but when the agent squeezed the trigger, it shot a pellet that attached itself to the car. It was called StarChase, a thin GPS device. Anastasia could now run all he wanted, but he could never hide, not unless he dumped the car and ran on foot. Which he couldn't do as they were on a tall bridge. Gabriel appreciated the tactfulness of the SWAT.

Then the agent lifted another rifle fit with a scope. A sniper. He took aim and shouted, "Pop goes the weasel."

The shot went off and the back tire of the GMC exploded.

It swerved, the trunk of the SUV lowered and grated against the tarmac before coming to a grinding halt.

Three men came bursting out with machine guns and shot at the helicopter.

"Sons of bitches," the agent said and closed the door. Gabriel could hear tinkles as the bullets struck the metal. The agent rummaged through his bag and selected a weapon. An M4 carbine this time. Sliding the door open, he returned fire and all three fell down in under five seconds.

Stupid gangsters. Why did they even try? SWAT agents were heavily trained pros and almost all of them served in the Army.

The agent did say he was shot, but since he was wearing full-body armor, he was alright except fat bruises.

However, the helicopter got hit pretty badly. It couldn't maintain flight and the pilot had to maneuver it down.

Morgan switched the camera to the spike-strip agent who showed them the helicopter. No fire, no smoke, no explosion like in the movies. Instead, a huge ass combat helicopter was parked in the middle of the road.

The SSA looked at Gabriel with a frown on his face.

"What?" Gabriel asked.

"Y-you are smiling at this carnage?"

Gabriel, who hadn't known he was smiling, said, "Sorry."

However, he couldn't stop smiling. Because nothing was more satisfying to watch than strong bad men stopped by stronger good men.

Chapter 42

May 12, 2019. 11:58 P.M.

The white Hummer passed through a town called Davenport in Iowa and got stuck behind a long line of vehicles. Leo, sitting in the passenger seat, turned the volume up on the dashboard TV.

"… emerging reports suggest that this atrocity is nothing like our city has ever witnessed," the pretty black girl said into a mike. "It begs the question, is Detroit exporting its crime?"

The camera cut to the newsroom where an anchor grimly said, "For those who haven't heard, Southfield PD has found body parts at a marshland near Holy Sepulchre, a historic cemetery in Oakland county. An anonymous tipster who has pointed us to this macabre obscenity also told us that the remains belong to a man named Thomas Brown. The involvement of a prominent Italian Mafia family is suspected. Brown was apparently burned to death by blowtorches and—"

Ryatt punched the steering wheel of the Hummer, making it honk. Leo grabbed the remote and turned off the TV.

They had first heard about Thomas at 11:00 a.m. MST, when they were studying a bank in Scottsbluff, Nebraska. Since live events and breaking news were unaffected by time zones, Ryatt calculated that it was 1:00 p.m. in Detroit when the news reported Thomas's murder.

They dropped everything and headed eastward with one thought in mind. Retribution.

Moving inch by inch, the traffic thinned as it climbed onto a bridge; a huge swarm of police officers were directing the influx at its entry. Giggling, Leo pulled his MAC-10 out from under the seat.

Ryatt shook his head, and he put it back. The pigs were not checking anyone, but regulating the vehicles to take only the left lane.

Once on the bridge, the traffic moved at a slightly better pace. First thing Ryatt noticed was the SWAT helicopter on the right lane. It was being hauled onto the back of an eighteen-wheeler.

Interest piqued, Ryatt observed the scene. A crane was standing on the riverbank and pulling an SUV from the water. A section of the bridge was broken on that side.

Ryatt tapped Leo's shoulder and motioned at the glovebox. Leo took out a pair of binoculars and handed them to Ryatt. He aimed them at the car in the river.

It had a Michigan plate.

Something didn't seem right.

"Search news from around this area," Ryatt said.

Leo pulled his phone and began working.

"Nothing from major networks," Leo said. "But a local YouTube channel, one Rapids Tribune, got something."

Leo played the video.

The teenager/reporter said that a high-speed pursuit took place on the bridge connecting Iowa and Illinois. The kid with his mobile camera tried to videotape the occupants of the SUVs, but the armed SWAT men did not allow him.

He did however manage to record the other two SUVs. One had its front crushed, the other one was peppered with bullet holes. Lolly went back in the video and paused it.

On closer inspection, he found they both had Michigan plates.

Could be Bugsy sending his men after Ryatt. First they got Thomas, tortured him, and got Ryatt's location. Then they sent goon squads after him. Did Thomas also spill the beans about Iris?

Suddenly out of breath, Ryatt pulled the car over and angry horns started blaring.

He took his cell out and opened a live monitoring app. Without Iris's knowledge, Ryatt had installed several cameras in their house, to keep an eye on his mom.

Living room was empty, so was the kitchen. He swiped it to the bedroom. No, she was not there either.

Horns were now mixed with drivers shouting. But Ryatt didn't move one bit. What had happened to Iris? Had Bugsy abducted her as well?

Just as he thought about calling her, he saw Iris getting out of the bathroom, toweling her hair.

Of course…

Taking a huge volume of air, he began driving again.

Ryatt had to admit. Some sort of guardian angel was intervening here. Not only intercepting the hit team, but also, somehow, keeping Iris safe.

But Ryatt couldn't delegate his responsibility of keeping himself and his mom safe any longer. To get the control back, he needed to eliminate the only threat in his life: Bugsy.

Chapter 43

May 13, 2019. 06:03 A.M.

In their eighteen plus hours on wheels, they switched driving between them to get the necessary sleep. Before entering Michigan, Leo changed the number plates.

Ryatt opened his duffel and took two lollipops from it. His mom had said that they weren't going to produce Zesty anymore. That batch was the last, and Ryatt decided he would use those two for Roman and Bugsy.

Leo drove straight to Calabria and parked at a street behind. So early in the morning, it was locked. But was it truly? Roman conducted his business from this shithole, meaning it must have many important documents, files, or hard drives. He wouldn't leave it unprotected.

Ryatt strolled to the bar's entrance, cupped the sides of his eyes and looked through the front door glass. No one was inside, but a ceiling fan was spinning over the bar counter.

Ryatt instructed Leo to bring the jimmy from the Hummer and break into the shop.

While Leo did the work, Ryatt scanned the neighborhood. The street was free of people. Maybe a few hobos here and a junkie there, but they wouldn't pay attention to two old men lingering in front of a shop.

Something moved at the corner of his eye.

He looked up at the building across the street. A hotel. Ryatt squinted and studied the second-story window closely. The drapes moved but it could be Ryatt's mind.

Discarding it as a false alarm, Ryatt turned on his heels. Leo had successfully pried the door open.

When inside the bar, Ryatt tiptoed towards the counter. And there, like he suspected, was a man lying on a mattress, down on the floor. Apparently guarding the bar, he parted his mouth and snored.

Ryatt crouched and wedged the Desert Eagle's muzzle into the guard's open maw.

But he did not wake up. Must be drunk.

Irritated, Ryatt shook the barrel and the metal grated the guard's teeth.

This time, he jumped and woke up in terror, hurting his throat.

Ryatt pointed his pistol at a telephone in the corner. "Call your fat boss and tell him that his bar's been broken into."

"Y-you... you are Lolly," the man said. His eyes widened in realization. "Fuck you, cunt."

"He chooses the hard way," Ryatt informed Leo and hooked his knuckles onto the guard's temple, disorienting him. Then he grabbed a towel under the bar table and bundled it up, before shoving it down the guard's mouth.

Leo bent over and put the muzzle of the MAC-10 under the guard's chin. Ryatt shook his head. Then he lowered the gun and put it under his armpit.

Ryatt thought for a few seconds. Not completely *non-fatal*, so he shook his head again. The MAC crept down to the guard's leg and the muzzle rested on a foot.

Ryatt nodded, and Leo squeezed the trigger.

It was just a fraction of a second but at least three to five bullets would have smashed their way through the ankle. The guard's eyes bulged and he let out a shrill, which the towel muffled. Ryatt let the loyal guardian writhe in pain for a good two minutes.

When he was exhausted, Ryatt grabbed his hair and slapped him. "Still prefer the hard way?"

The barkeeper trembled and shook his head.

Ryatt pulled him up and dragged him to the telephone. Before giving him the receiver, he called Leo over and told him to put the muzzle on the guard's zipper.

"Just a pair of things to think about if you want to warn Roman," Ryatt said.

The guard made the call and acted his best. Well, the fear and the breathlessness weren't acting.

"He's on his way," the guard said and dropped the receiver.

"Good boy." Ryatt dragged him back and they all nestled together under the bar counter, safely tucked away from the front door.

Fourteen minutes later, a bunch of angry footfalls pervaded the bar.

Ryatt filled his lungs and stood to his full height, pulling his gun out. Leo followed suit.

Roman's jaw dropped at the sight of Ryatt. He had two goons at his side, well-built beefcakes with ponytails. They were twins.

"Y-You…"

"M-m-me." Ryatt mocked. "Yes."

One of the ponytails slowly moved his hand towards his back.

"Not this again," Ryatt muttered and shook his head. "You wanna tell him, Rome?"

Roman did. "Don't, Levi! You'll be dead before you touch your gun." Then he addressed Ryatt. "What do you want?"

"Someone has to pay for what happened to Thomas."

Roman said, "No, I don't know—"

"Cut the crap!" Ryatt barked. "First, tell those monkeys to lose their guns. And it's choice time. You or Bugsy."

Roman's Adam Apple bobbed as he scratched the back of his head. Then he ordered the ponytails to drop the weapons, which they did. Leo skirted the table and picked them up.

"Come here." Ryatt led them to Roman's office and closed the hefty door behind. Should be soundproofed. Good.

Ryatt marched the weeping guard to a corner and stood him there. But he collapsed down and began tending to his mangled foot. Those types of wounds didn't upset Ryatt's stomach anymore. Perhaps he had evolved.

"You two gentlemen," Ryatt pointed at the ponytails, "sit beside your crying friend over there, and you, sir," Ryatt motioned at Roman, "take the chair."

No one obliged him despite his good manners.

Roman began, "Come on. I agreed that I'll help—"

The butt of the Desert Eagle knocked the words back into his mouth.

"Shut up and sit!"

Now everyone obliged the man with the gun.

Leo made a quick trip to the Hummer and brought back a bag. While Ryatt kept watch, he took a pair of zip ties and tied Roman to the chair.

"Big mistake," one of the goons said under his breath. "Wait till Don knows you're here."

Ryatt lifted his eyebrows at Leo who shrugged and pulled the MAC out. Not waiting for the confirmation, he casually shot the ponytail.

A burst of bullets shattered the head of the goon and sprayed its contents behind the wall.

"No!" the other ponytail screamed. They said twins could feel each other's pain. Though Ryatt wondered if it was true, he wouldn't ask the brother. Ryatt was not a sadist.

Leo was.

Amidst the living ponytail's wailing, the guard cried even more while Roman sat motionless, a smelly puddle forming under his chair. He knew what happened to people Ryatt and Leo had bound. He had seen it firsthand.

Ryatt sat on the table and put his shoe on Roman's broken knee. "Tell me what I want to know, and I promise on my mother's life, I won't do anything to you."

"Y-yes." Roman shivered.

"I want to know about Bugsy's mansion, how many men are there right now, the security codes, the dogs, the blind spots in the CCTV, and don't forget, I need the key, too. I know what happens if we tamper with the lock."

Roman said, "The key is in my pocket," and then gave out all the requested information. He also told them that there was a magnetic sensor fitted to his car, and that Bugsy's front gates would automatically read it and let them in.

Ryatt searched the pantry and found a glove. He wore it and inserted his hand into Roman's drenched pant pocket and pulled the wet key fob out.

Ryatt said, "Alright."

Roman said, "P-please untie me."

Ryatt walked away, not bothering to answer. Leo lifted the bag from the floor and dropped it on the table; the contents inside clanked menacingly.

Roman's eyes almost popped out as he shook in utter terror. "You promised you wouldn't do anything."

"I did, and *I* am not," Ryatt said and took out a lollipop from his pocket.

No amount of getting used to or evolution could have prepared his stomach for what came next.

* * *

Roman took an eternity to die. But Leo didn't stop doing stuff to him even after he was dead. Ryatt hadn't seen anything so animalistic and primal. He didn't think he would ever recover from the psychological trauma. But Leo didn't seem to mind, not one bit. He kept on doing what he did, sometimes with his bare hands.

The guard had in fact fainted when Leo was only halfway through. The living ponytail had become catatonic.

"Enough," Ryatt said. "Time to wrap it up."

While Leo cleaned up the evidence, Ryatt went to the Hummer and opened the tailgate. From inside, he took a pair of rubber gloves and pulled them over his hands.

Another flicker of movement on the second-story window of the hotel across the street caught his attention. But he was unable to find anyone or anything between the drapes.

It was just too dark.

Shrugging, he lifted two five-gallon gas cans from the Hummer and walked into the bar.

Chapter 44

May 13, 2019. 08:31 A.M.

Gabriel was sitting at the window, enjoying a cupcake. He munched, savoring the soft sugary goodness, as another wave of heat washed over him. On rare happy occasions, he treated himself with cakes for breakfast. Since the hotel had no chocolate cake, his favorite, he'd settled for cupcakes.

The reason for his festive mood was the three-story inferno raging from Calabria, dancing to the wind like an orange butterfly.

A gust of air fueled the fire and smeared smoke over Gabriel's face. Inhaling the blackness, he bit another cupcake in half. Just as he began appreciating the combined taste of sweetened wheat flour and fiery murderous rage, he heard sirens.

Ugh.

Closing the window, he stood up and walked into the bathroom. Like he suspected, his face was covered in soot and gray flakes. Though he washed it away, the stain felt permanent. Didn't matter, though. He blemished a good portion of his soul for revenge. And those who judged him for being no different than a criminal, they hadn't had a call from the coroner who stated that their dad had been bound to a chair and shot in the face. Now that Roman had possibly died an equally cruel death, justice was *almost* served. Karma was a bitch, so expecting its enforcer to be a pleasant, by-the-book snob was nonsensical.

As he came out of the bathroom, he noticed an envelope near the front door. He hadn't noticed it earlier. Someone must have slid it under during the night.

Gabriel carefully tore off the edge and shook the paper out. Three lines were typed on it. A user ID, a password, and a hyperlink.

Gabriel took out his phone and entered the web address but didn't press return.

"Stupid," Gabriel muttered and put the phone back in his pocket. He grabbed the jacket hanging from the wall and took the burner out.

In it, he logged onto the website. It was a bank in Switzerland.

Mildly aware of what was happening, he filled the user ID and password.

And pressed *Enter*.

The screen announced that Gabriel was now a multimillionaire.

Whistling, he put the envelope and burner into his rucksack. Then he swiftly wore the jacket he had kept ready and clipped the holster, before leaving.

Bill's room was closed. Let him sleep. Where Gabriel was heading now, it would become dangerous and ugly.

Chapter 45

May 13, 2019. 08:45 A.M.

The Chrysler eased to a stop in front of Bugsy's, and like Roman said, the intimidating gates parted automatically. In the meantime, Ryatt and Leo pulled their respective masks over their faces. The green zombie and red demon.

Though Ryatt had forgotten the mansion's color, he did remember its size. And it was gigantic as ever.

But not a single sentry on sight.

Bugsy should be lethargic with the security detail here because the news about what happened to his men in Illinois had not leaked to the national media.

Leo crossed himself and muttered Isaiah 54:17. His fingertips, nails, and skin around them, still pinkish from Roman's blood. Just a while ago, he had cut an eyeball out of a living man, but now he was all God-fearing like. Ryatt wondered, for the umpteenth time, how the cogs turned inside that little head of Leo's.

He stopped the car at the entrance; the security camera was pointed at their windshield. Leo observed it, too, and solved the conundrum with a bullet from his suppressor-fitted machine pistol.

The front door was thick, and that same sneaky lock was protecting it.

Ryatt pulled out Roman's key fob and selected the one that unlocked this door. Sweating behind the rubber, he operated the lock with the finesse of a burglar.

It unlocked with a click.

Weapon in hand, he went in and closed the door behind.

The house was still, as if time itself had frozen. Ryatt lay on the floor, so did Leo, presenting smaller targets just in case someone burst through.

No one did.

Ryatt crawled along the entryway, and when he reached the end of the wall, he peeked out on both sides. The hall was quiet, too, the silence so absolute that it rang in his ears.

He pushed himself up and sat on his haunches. Confident that they wouldn't confront CCTV, they removed their masks and crouched up the stairs.

A mechanical dentist-chair-like thing rested on the corner of the top step. Ryatt felt warm, looking at it.

He remembered that Bugsy's room was to the left. Just as he turned around on the landing, something shifted on the shiny banister.

A mini electrical-bomb went off in his stomach and a sickening sensation stunned him. Microseconds later, he heard the cocking of a gun; the click-clack of a round being chambered was robust. Must be a shotgun.

"Stop right there!" someone screamed behind them. "Don't move a muscle."

Ryatt could outdraw anyone and shoot them.

If they were in front of him.

"Reach for the skies!"

Ryatt did not obey. Better to die by a spray of pellets than whatever Bugsy and his men would do if they were to catch him alive.

"I said hands up!"

Out of the corner of his eye, he saw Leo stiffen.

"Don't move!"

Leo said, "Thank you, Ry. Thanks so much."

Then he smiled and winked, slowly turning towards the voice. *No, no, no.* Ryatt knew that look, the madness in his eyes. It was the same look when he set something on fire. When he flayed Roman's penis.

Leo giggled and dashed, and the explosion of the shotgun shook the corridor. It was so loud that it almost swallowed the series of gunshots from Leo's MAC-10.

Almost.

Ryatt turned on his feet in time to see Leo crash on the guy, and they both limply fell. Gun at ready, Ryatt sprinted towards them. He pulled Leo off the man who had several holes in his face.

And Leo, his best friend, was alive. But only barely. The buckshot tore Leo's tiny midsection, his shirt shredded and guzzling blood in rivulets. Leo caught Ryatt's wet eyes and tried to giggle, but it became a labored wheezing fit. His mousy face contorted one last time, in a demonic grimace, before the movements halted.

Ryatt stood straight, angling the Desert Eagle at Leo's dead murderer on the floor.

And he pulled the trigger. He pulled it many times, until the clip couldn't supply metal to feed his rage.

The man's head was obliterated. Almost flattened. His blood and bones, brains and hair, they all dotted the lower sections of the walls and Ryatt's pants.

Taking one last look at his late friend, Ryatt ejected the clip and pocketed it. Then he marched towards Bugsy's door, fed a new mag and chambered a round. But he knew full well that all the metal in the world would not be enough to settle his score with the rotten bastard inside.

"Time to end this." Ryatt kicked the door open.

Chapter 46

May 13, 2019. 09:20 A.M.

Gabriel parked the Camaro beside Bugsy's peripheral wall. He grabbed the shopping bag on the passenger seat, which contained a few new blankets, and exited the vehicle. He hopped onto the Camaro's hood, then onto the top. The metal sheet caved, but Bill wouldn't mind.

Looking around the avenue, he threw the spongy cloth over the spiraling barbed wires. They got hooked by the spikes and provided a comfortable ingress.

Gabriel wiped his palms across his jeans and leapt. His belly landed on the blankets, and he swung his legs over to the other side. Hugging the blankets, he looked down. A seven-foot drop. He loosened his ankles and legs, before letting go. As his feet touched the grass, he neutralized the force by maneuvering his knees as springs.

In a wink, he dived under the nearby shrubbery and observed the mansion from its cover. The CCTV camera above the front door was hanging down; bits of plastic and glass were strewn directly below.

Gabriel waited for a few moments. No gunshots. No shouting. Not even a TV.

Drawing his Glock, he ducked his head between his shoulders and crept to the door.

It's a weird looking lock.

Gabriel slowly wrapped his fingers around the doorknob.

An explosion shattered the quietness.

He jumped to the hedge flanking the door and crouched into a protective huddle. Then he pointed his gun… at nothing. He frantically turned left to right and right to left.

Nothing whatsoever.

Auditory hallucination? Fat chance. Gabriel never suffered from psychosis.

And then his stomach burned in searing pain. As if someone stabbed him with a red-hot knife.

"Mother…" Gabriel grabbed the hurt. It felt wet and sticky. And warm.

Dizzy, he looked down. A red blot was slowly spreading over his white shirt.

Chapter 47

May 13, 2019. 09:15 A.M.

Bugsy was sitting behind his table. Fat and sick, he looked like he was undergoing dialysis. And a pair of prosthetic arms jutted out from underneath his T-shirt.

Bugsy's hideous face curled in confusion. "H-how?"

Without answering, Ryatt strolled to the table. "*How?* I thought you always wanted to know the *why*."

The surprise on Bugsy's face dissolved, exposing calmness. "Oh, I figured out the *why* when I visited your home," Bugsy said. "Your mom. Iris…"

Ryatt's heart paused. He could feel his skin prickle and sweat exit his pores, and legs turn into noodles.

"Ironic name aside, she's one iron-spirited bitch. Didn't make a sound when we dry drowned her."

Ryatt's strength returned. "You w-waterboarded my mom?"

"Not only that." Bugsy laughed. "You want to know what I did to her forty-two years ago?"

"No!" Ryatt yelled. He had avoided thinking about those rumors on the streets even back then. Gun pointed at Bugsy, Ryatt said, "Shut the fuck up!"

Bugsy's beady eyes bore into Ryatt's skull, challenging him. His tongue wet his lips, mimicking an anxious viper. "I raped her."

Ryatt shut his ears. "You're lying!"

Bugsy frowned. "You know what? Yes. That's not the truth."

Ryatt let go, relieved.

Bugsy smirked. "*We* raped your mom."

"Wh-what?" Ryatt's world crashed around him; his pistol dropped to the floor.

"Come on. Don't get soft now. I'm not scared of death. Not after what you did to me. I clung to my life so that I could hurt you, and I've done that. Doesn't matter if I die," Bugsy said. "I'm an old, crippled dog with no barks left in me."

A gunshot snapped Ryatt out of it. Did it just come from the front door? Bugsy's back-up? Ryatt did not care if he lived or died. But he needed to punish Bugsy.

And fast.

Desperation hastening his actions, Ryatt locked the door and looked around the room. A minute later, he'd found a corkscrew, a knife, some pins. No, these were too lame.

Just as he decided to make do, he spotted the perfect devices of atonement, which could bring utmost misery.

Taking a breather, Ryatt said, "Know what? You may not have a bark left but you gotta have a lot of painful howls in you…" He ambled to the fireplace. Sitting on its ledge were two bottles of lighter fluid and a match box. "And I'm gonna squeeze the last of them out."

As Ryatt pocketed them all and neared him, Bugsy's eyes widened in terror. "Help!"

Leaning over the table, Ryatt grabbed Bugsy and dragged the pathetic sack of potatoes across the shiny wood. When he dropped him on the plush carpet, one of his prosthetic arms came loose but the other stayed fastened.

Ryatt squirted the liquid onto Bugsy's head. Few seconds later, he emptied the first bottle which he hurled at Bugsy's face before pulling the second one out.

When that was done, he let the old meat soak in naphtha and took a tour.

He came across an old phonograph on the showcase, its bronze speaker elegantly craning its neck. A dozen gramophone records were stacked beside it.

"Which is the best?" Ryatt asked.

"Help!"

Ryatt traced his finger over them and picked one at random. The disk said *Ana María Martínez - Violetas Imperiales*.

He gently fixed it on the turntable and wound the hand crank, after which he placed the stylus on the disk. An astounding soprano from an extremely good singer filled the room.

"Please..." Bugsy cried. "Take that record player. Worth millions in auction."

"*Millions?*" Ryatt asked.

"Yeah. It's from Italy. More than one hundred years old. Survived two world wars."

That got Ryatt thinking. It was more money than he had ever robbed in his career.

"Twenty-five years ago, Thomas told me to give up robbery. I should have listened to that big old fool. But instead, I told him— no, I *promised* him that we'd stop before I got anyone hurt. Now I've hurt him, Leo, even my mom, the only people who ever meant anything to me." Ryatt dabbed at the corner of his eye. "I robbed even when I was relatively rich, not because I needed to but I wanted to." Ryatt sniffled and retrieved the match box. "Greed. That's my sin. But it's not me who paid the price for it, but the people I love."

"No more sinning." Ryatt struck a match and flicked it. "No more suffering."

The blaze engulfed Bugsy with a satisfying swoosh. Screeching helplessly, he tried to roll, but it was impossible without legs and arms.

While Bugsy's yellow skin melted and peeled in patches, exposing bright red muscle tissues within, Ana's mesmerizing soprano brought a sense of serenity to the situation.

But with serenity came calmness, which gave Ryatt time to rest his mind. And it reiterated only one thing.

We raped your mom.

Unable to control the rage roiling inside, Ryatt grabbed the flaming prosthetic arm and ripped it out. The plastic scathed his hands, but he didn't care.

Screaming, Ryatt swung the arm down onto Bugsy, smashing his face in. Then again. Then again. Each impact dug a little of Bugsy's liquefied muscle and splashed it on the ceiling, while Ryatt repeatedly struck with the fervor of a deranged madman.

Ana climbed to a high note, the highest so far, and at exactly the same moment, Bugsy stopped twitching.

Panting, Ryatt tossed the disfigured arm onto the burning meat and sat on the table.

And he realized something. His anger was so pure and powerful that he hadn't needed to control his stomach with his lollipop, the last of its extinct kind.

While the flames crackled and smoked, Ryatt jumped down and walked towards the door. He felt tempted to nab the rare artifact worth millions. It was not the beautiful sound that attracted him but its monetary value. *Ugh.* His mom was probably in unimaginable pain, his only two friends gone, and he was thinking about dollars?

Disgusted with himself, his hand pulled out the pistol with lightning speed. He shot off seven bullets, blowing the player to kingdom come.

Then he collapsed to his knees and buried his face in his palms.

As he wept and warm tears streamed down his burned, bloody hands, he literally sensed the dark claws of the demon clutching his heart yield.

But it was too late for redemption, wasn't it?

Chapter 48

May 13, 2019. 09:32 A.M.

Embarrassed that he did not foresee the doors being booby-trapped, Gabriel had no option but to call in the cavalry. So that's what he did. His thumb, doused in blood like all its neighboring fingers, cut the call. SSA Morgan was sending the units. ETA: five minutes.

Might as well be an eternity away. Didn't matter, though. Gabriel heard the bloodcurdling squealing of a pig from inside. Meaning the devil finally met the end he so rightly deserved. Good. That was the reason he had come to Detroit. Now he would die gleefully. But arresting Lolly would be a cherry on top.

Gabriel heard shoes behind the door.

First he picked his Glock from the ground, then he applied pressure to the bullet wound with an elbow and pushed himself up, fighting the gravity.

"Fuck!" he cried.

The blood pooling on his midsection cascaded down his crotch, thighs, and eventually spread under his shoes.

The door flew open and a man came out, carrying someone on his shoulder, like a logger. Ryatt. That sense of déjà vu gripped Gabriel again. Ryatt was the man from Gabriel's *almost memory*. But he quickly recovered from its surreal clasp. Now was not the time.

They locked eyes.

"Detective Chase." Gabriel showed his NYPD shield. "You're under arrest."

"C-Chase?" Ryatt asked, shifting the guy on his shoulder, who Gabriel assumed was Leo. "Joshua's little boy?"

"Don't fucking say his name!" An unused energy surged through Gabriel. "My dad would have been alive if it weren't for you."

"Huh?" Ryatt asked, blinking like a squirrel. "I can guarantee you, son, I ain't got no part in his death."

"Oh, but you do," Gabriel said. "The one you killed in there," Gabriel motioned the Glock at Bugsy's front door, "he ordered my dad shot dead with a Desert Eagle, just so that I would go after *Lolly*."

"What the... how do you know?"

"My dad, he mentioned in his notebook that you're extremely efficient with your gun. But the crooks who tried to kill him missed several shots in a drive-by. That's when I began doubting. The slugs recovered from that Audi, and from my dad and his partner confirmed my suspicion. They didn't come from your Desert Eagle."

"Someone was trying to frame me real hard."

"Only Bugsy had anything to gain from it, on top of being the only person—outside of law enforcement that is—who knew that Lolly used a Desert Eagle."

Ryatt shook his head. "You don't have to concern yourself with that no more, kid. I roasted him to a crisp."

Gabriel smiled at Ryatt, weirdly thankful. "A classic cobra effect. The only thing I *slightly* regret is the fact that I pointed the Detroit Alliance in Thomas's direction."

"You set them after my friend?" Ryatt asked.

Gabriel nodded. "Once I uncovered your identity, Bugsy went after your mom. So imagine, what would have happened if I hadn't given them Thomas and arrested you instead? While you rotted in jail, Bugsy would have been alive and…"

"… hurt my mom to settle his little score with me." Ryatt looked at Gabriel, his tough world-weary face replaced with gratitude. "Thank you."

"I did it for Mrs. Durant," Gabriel said and held up his gun. However, his eyes darkened, aim slipped. But Ryatt, a gunslinger famous for his shooting skills, didn't even reach for his holster when Gabriel's gun arm slumped to his side.

"Come on, kid," Ryatt said. "Let me help you."

"Up yours." Gabriel coughed and he was sure he saw pink mist before his face.

"You're not very smart like your old man, are you?" Ryatt asked.

Gabriel smiled proudly. "Yup, that I can't deny."

"Why'd you come here without backup?"

"Because my dad sacrificed his life to catch you. So the infamous Lolly belonged exclusively to Detective Chase from the 122nd precinct, not the FBI or the DPD. And it doesn't matter which Chase catches you."

Ryatt shook his head. "Why you and your pops hate me so much? I'm not guilty, you know?"

"Not guilty?" Gabriel raised his eyebrows.

"You put a fat gazelle and a starving hyena in the same forest. A hyena's gotta do what a hyena's gotta do to survive. It's nature. So we are truly faultless because we've been given shitty lives and no opportunities. If anyone's guilty, it's that unfair God."

Gabriel laughed, but it ended in him coughing up blood again.

"You think it's funny? Why?" Ryatt asked.

"Because that's not how you compare things. You're interpreting it in an arbitrary manner that reinforces your inexcusable actions." Gabriel shook his head in contempt. He knew the whole slew of rhetoric criminals used to justify their crimes.

"What you prattling about?"

Gabriel sighed. "Truth of the matter is, you aren't a carnivorous hyena. You are a human. An omnivore. You have the ability to eat with or without murder. Maybe it's a test of your resolve. While Mrs. Durant didn't let the harsh world corrupt her and passed with flying colors, you failed miserably."

"W-what?"

"You think it's tough being bad? No, it's *tougher* being good. I've seen an eighty-year-old janitor. I've seen handicapped people winning the Olympics. I've seen single moms working two jobs." Gabriel wanted to laugh but he controlled himself.

Ryatt bit the tip of his lower lip, unable to answer.

"I don't have time for this." Gabriel clenched his teeth, trying to concentrate. "Drop your friend and kneel!"

Ryatt didn't drop Leo. He gently placed him down but refused to kneel. "Shoot me. I can't hurt my mom by going to prison."

"Should've thought about that when you pulled the trigger for the very first time, under that bridge." Unable to lift his gun arm, Gabriel dragged himself towards Ryatt, his shoes drawing crimson trails behind him.

"You may be fast with a gun," Gabriel whispered once he was near Ryatt, "but I'm fast with…"

Ryatt asked, "You're fast with what?"

Gabriel smiled. "This."

And he quickly slapped one end of a handcuff on Ryatt's wrist, the other locked to Gabriel's own.

Ryatt looked shocked, but that slowly transformed into a smile. "You don't remember me at all, do you junior?"

Appalled, Gabriel tried to open his mouth but it was cottony. His skin felt cold and clammy, and things were getting very confusing. The blood loss must have caught up with him.

Finally, gravity triumphed, the handcuff being the only thing slowing his plunge. He gained some of the consciousness back from the shock of the fall, and he lay still. The gun slipped from his numb fingers.

Ryatt, whose arm was pulled down, sat Indian style on the ground, beside Gabriel.

Did Ryatt say something just now? Something important? Gabriel couldn't recall. "I don't think I'm gonna be conscious for long."

"I agree. Give me the key and I'll take you to a hospital."

Shivering, Gabriel inserted his hand into the jeans pocket and brought out the handcuffs' key.

"That's it. Give it to me." Ryatt extended his arm.

Gabriel brought his shaking hand up. When it was near his face, he put the key into his mouth and swallowed it.

The last thing Gabriel saw before passing out was Ryatt laughing and shaking his head. "You're a stubborn bastard, just like your old man."

Chapter 49

May 13, 2019. 10:01 A.M.

Gabriel resurfaced from oblivion, then sank again, before gasping and waking once more. Gurney rolled, overhead lights flickered past, and white uniforms huddled over him. Ghosts. *Loud* ghosts.

Gabriel grabbed one and pulled it close. "Lolly?"

The ghost shouted. "Sir, please don't stress yourself. You've lost a lot of blood. We're taking you to the ICU."

"I know that," Gabriel said. "Where's the man who was cuffed to me?"

"W-we don't know," the ghost said. "You were dropped at the entrance."

"By whom?"

"An older African American gentleman in a Camaro…"

How the hell did Ryatt manage to unlock the handcuffs? Gabriel lifted his arm. The chains were there alright, but obviously not holding the most wanted bank robber in the US.

A thin metal wire protruded from the handcuffs' keyhole. Was… was that a paperclip?

Suddenly everything felt so utterly hopeless. All the work he and his dad had done was for nothing. Lolly had disappeared yet again. And Gabriel knew, this time he had escaped for good.

As his heart shriveled in agony, the blackness that enveloped him was actually a blessing.

Chapter 50

May 13, 2019. 10:30 A.M.

Ryatt drove across the city center, through the streets he had known as a kid and was hit with a dreary nostalgia.

The porno mag and VHS shop had been replaced by a fancy Apple Store. Fitting since it was technology that killed them.

Killed. Everyone and everything Ryatt knew ceased to exist. Thomas, Leo, Young Boys Inc., Bugsy, Roman, and the Detroit Alliance. Everything had died.

Everything except Ryatt and Iris. Only they survived the old Detroit.

When Ryatt had called his home phone earlier, his mom was unavailable. Seeing that the Chase boy had discovered Ryatt's noxious secret, the cops and the FBI couldn't be far behind. But Iris not answering the phone made little sense. They *should* have tapped the line and forced his mom to pick the call, so that they could track or trap him.

But they didn't.

Meaning Ryatt *might* have a bit of time left, until Gabriel gained consciousness. He must quickly take Iris and leave the state before that.

Five minutes later, he turned onto the cul-de-sac leading to the back of Goodwill. Chances of pigs watching this side were slim. No one knew about this route.

The rundown plot of vacant space that once festered with vermin was now a basketball court, and kids were shooting hoops.

Ryatt left the keys in the ignition, hoping some desperate boy would steal the car. He skirted the ground and crossed the path that snaked to the rear door. No hobo piss in the backyard anymore, but a small garden with daisies in it.

Ryatt unlocked the door with his key and stepped in.

Iris had renovated the shop in the early 2000s, tearing down the walls, making it a single space. What used to be their "kitchen" and "bedrooms" were now aisles and aisles of candies. However, she had a separate room for goods, where she also ate her lunch. It housed a portable stove and some utensils.

"Hello?" his mom called out from the billing counter in the front.

"It's me, Ma." Ryatt ambled inside.

Her demeanor suddenly changed. She stiffened for a moment and then galloped around the table, walking purposefully in his direction.

As she marched towards Ryatt, he spotted purple bruises on her wrists. Enraged, he wished to revive Bugsy, only to kill him again. Maybe when they met in hell, Ryatt would torture the son of a bitch for eternity.

Iris halted two feet from him and stared, her mouth tautened into a thin line.

It unnerved Ryatt, his stomach churning. He hadn't seen his mom so spiteful.

Her dry lips parted, her voice a whisper. "Are you Lolly?"

Ryatt did a double take, and that one moment of hesitation was all she needed.

Iris's face curled in disgust like she had just touched a hairy spider.

"Ma—"

She slapped him with all her energy. Her hand didn't miss his cheek even by a millimeter, rattling him to the core. His mom had never raised her voice to him let alone her arm.

Torrents of tears lined her wizened cheeks, and her voice broke. "All this time without sight, I've never felt blind. Not until now."

"I... I'm not—"

"Floridan Crocs never heard of any Ryatt," she said. "Then I called every team you've said you worked for during all these years. None of them knows you."

Ryatt had no clue how she did it, but her eyes were deadlocked on his. They pierced through his façade and glowered at his true self, which uselessly tried to scurry into some dark recess of his grotesque mind. While a cold chill shot through his spine, warm sweat droplets appeared on his forehead and above his upper lip. He sensed his Adam's apple bobbing, vainly attempting to dampen his parched throat by drily swallowing. He wanted to scram, to bolt from that stifling place, or to just cower at a corner, but he couldn't move his trembling legs.

"Wikipedia told me that your gang has killed fifty-two people and Lolly…" She sniffled. "*You* personally took thirty-four lives." Iris clenched her teeth and spoke in a grim tone. "Is. That. True?"

Ryatt nodded, unable to open his mouth. Another slap landed on the same cheek. This time, her righteous hand also caught his ear, making it ring.

"You know how many boys I saved from the streets?" Iris asked. "Thirty-fucking-four."

Ryatt closed his ears, wishing it was a nightmare. There was no universe or reality where he could imagine his purer-than-angel mom say that word.

"Thirty-four…" A guttural noise escaped from his mom but she instantly covered her mouth with a hand and inhaled slowly, her body shaking as she did.

Iris's shoulders, that had never shown weakness, finally slumped. She suddenly appeared so small, so fragile. So old.

What had he done?

Then he accepted the mind-shattering truth: he had destroyed what made Iris Iris.

"All my life's work is now meaningless." She looked around the shop. "While I was healing the world on one side, you were wounding it in the other."

Ryatt said, "Our life was unfair—"

Iris turned her head sideways, as if she did not even want to hear his voice. "Just… just don't." She stood there, pondering over something. After a while, she took a breath; her chest inflated once again, and shoulders settled back in their usual position of strength. She looked like she had come to a decision, and Ryatt braced himself for whatever she was gonna say.

She wet her lips. "Let's eat lunch. I'm hungry."

Not waiting for an answer, she walked past him and headed towards the storeroom.

Though he was confused by the anticlimax, he followed his mom like a subservient puppy.

As there was only one chair in this room, he sat on the floor.

She began cooking, and he resigned to look down at the carpet, again wishing it all to be a nightmare. He was never more scared in his life than that moment.

Each minute stretched into hours, and an eternity later, she placed two bowls in front of him. One yellow and one white, both brimming with ramen, the food he hadn't eaten in decades.

After she sat herself down, she picked the yellow bowl. Then she took a fork and began eating.

While she angrily munched the food, she asked, "You're too good for ramen? I'm sorry, this is all I could afford from my meager but honest income from this candy store. I'm never touching anything that came out of your cardinal sins. Not your house, not your car, and definitely not your steaks."

Ryatt's arms stretched automatically and picked the white bowl.

He coiled the ramen onto his fork and brought it to his face. The mere smell of it made him regurgitate. Nonetheless, he shoved a forkful into his mouth.

"Um... this tastes funny," Ryatt said as he munched. "It leaves a weird aftertaste. All sweet like."

"Stop complaining. Eat your meal!" she ordered. And he reluctantly obeyed.

After forcefully swallowing half of the food, his vision became watery and slow, like he was falling underwater.

The fork slipped from his numb fingers, worrying him. "Ma..." Ryatt tried to construct words but they slurred.

"Don't you dare call me that!" she spat, her lips quivering. "I wish I had never borne you in my womb."

Though Ryatt couldn't feel his tongue, his ears worked fine and her words hurt him like pins poked into the heart of a voodoo doll of him.

But more than the hurt, he was petrified. He felt like he was intoxicated, his head dizzy, and his mouth began drooling. As his heartbeat rose, he started hyperventilating.

And then everything darkened. The blackness brought along a horrible childhood memory, terrifying him.

"Ma!" he cried. "I can't see no more, Ma!"

"As much as I hate him, Bugsy *was* right," Iris said calmly. "I should have let you stay blind, when you said those exact words forty-two years ago."

Ryatt did not gracefully descend into water any longer. Everything moved irrationally, chaotically, robbing Ryatt of his balance, and he limply fell sideways.

He wrapped his hands around his throat and squeezed them because something clogged the airway. But to no avail. He could not draw a drop of air.

As he choked and kicked about on the floor, he tried to make peace with the fact. He was dying, and there was nothing he could do about it now.

Still convulsing, he brought a hand to his good eye and rubbed it frantically. He begged God to answer this one prayer. Just let him see his mom's angelic face one last time.

And God answered by giving him sight, albeit it lasted only for a second.

However, what Ryatt saw in that one second broke him into a million pieces. The last image burning into his soon-to-be-dilated pupils induced a pain so severe that it hurt his very soul.

His strong, superhero mom was holding the white bowl, taking a mouthful.

Chapter 51

May 18, 2019. 09:49 P.M.

Gabriel unlocked his room and shouldered the door open, holding a plastic bag that contained the things he had on him when they'd wheeled him into the ICU. He dropped it on the table and collapsed on the bed. The sudden motion made his abdomen throb.

"Goddamn it." He cupped the part of his belly where the suture was and pulled out a pill holder from his jacket. With his thumb, he flicked open the cap and shook a blue pill into his mouth.

The SNOM procedure benefited Gabriel in many ways. Hospital stay reduced to only six days, shorter bill, and most importantly, lesser scar tissue as they skipped laparoscopy.

When they discharged him, the attending physician had said, "You'll heal in weeks. But until then, stomach the pain, pun fully intended."

Gabriel did not lose an organ or have enough time to develop peritonitis because he was quickly taken to Level 1 trauma center. Thanks to Ryatt, Gabriel got off relatively and improbably scot-free. He had later learned that Ryatt had left his dead friend behind in Bugsy's mansion, to get Gabriel to hospital on time. Maybe, just maybe, there was a fraction of good in that heartless murderer after all.

Too bad he couldn't salvage that good in Ryatt and help him in some way. He was dead. The SWAT team that burst through Iris's candy store found both her and Ryatt lying dead on the floor, side by side. The pathologist wrote it down as 'homicidal poisoning with ethylene glycol', a common ingredient in antifreeze.

The SWAT team also found a letter beside Iris. It read: Please donate the reward money to Detroit Public School.

Since she was blind, it was written in a slanting line but the text couldn't be more intelligible.

Iris, even in death, cared about community service. Not only had she killed her son and made the world safer but also used the $500,000 bounty on his head for children's education.

Gabriel felt his eyes prickle. Why the emotion gushed out, he did not know. Could be the drugs kicking in. Or could have been Iris.

As the painkiller benumbed him and turned his head as light as a balloon, he made a rash decision.

He reached for his rucksack under the bed. Rummaging through it, he fished out the burner, which was still alive. A miracle as it hadn't been charged for six days.

When he entered the Swizz bank website, the browser remembered his credentials; so logging in was no problem.

He opened another tab and searched for the libraries in Detroit that were shutting down due to lack of funding. Once he notated them all, he switched back to the bank website. Without a moment's thought, he transferred the necessary amount to each one of them. And he still had almost a million dollars left, which he donated to the same public school Iris had.

When he finally crushed the burner into pieces, Gabriel had not a penny left of Bugsy's blood money.

Feeling good, he lay back and rested his eyes.

Just as he slipped out of reality, his cell phone rang, its ringtone muffled inside the hospital bag.

He grabbed the bag and took the cell phone out. To his surprise, it was not crusted with blood or grime. In fact, he observed that all his belongings were cleaned and smelled good.

Gabriel answered the call.

"You safely reached the hotel?" Conor asked.

"Yes, Mom," Gabriel said.

Conor chuckled. "Alright. Guess what? The DPD got the Camaro. It was abandoned at the back of Goodwill. A bunch of kids called 911 and reported that the key was still in the car."

"Hm," Gabriel said.

"I would've thought that the car might have gone missing."

"Not only you. Ryatt would've counted on it too when he left it there. Seems like you're both wrong about the world. At least about Detroit."

"Are you seriously lumping me with that sociopathic bank robber?" Conor asked.

"Sometimes you *seriously* talk like a sociopath." Gabriel yawned.

"Whatever," Conor said. "Anyway, the Camaro isn't the reason why I've called you."

"Uh-huh."

Conor's tone became grim. "I've gone through your psych eval." He cleared his throat. "Y-you have a genius level IQ but… um…"

"Don't mince words. What's up?" Gabriel asked innocently. But he thought he knew what was up, and it jittered him.

"You have trouble communicating?" Conor asked.

"I used to stutter, yes," Gabriel answered. "But I've worked through it. I haven't stuttered since high school."

"Come on, Gabe. You know we do backgrounds." Conor paused. "We talked to Victor."

Victor was Gabriel's captain from the 122nd precinct.

"What did he say?" he asked.

"That you had a breakdown during the Mr. Bunny investigation. You lashed out and... uh... you've had a hard time communicating."

"Mr. Bunny videotaped shooting my friend in the face and sent it to me. Try not stuttering after seeing something as traumatic as that," Gabriel said. "However, that was the only time I stuttered in my whole career as a homicide detective, because I lost so many people close to me to that animal."

"Yes, I agree. But you had some psychological problems as well. Substance abuse to be specific, and during that period, you were negligent of your health."

"I recovered and haven't drunk in a really long time," Gabriel lied. He mourned his dad's murder with cheap vodka.

"It's not just that," Conor said. "You know, our department has ways to put things together."

"What did they put together?" Gabriel asked, hoping they knew nothing about his little setback.

"Your problem with speech, your self-destructive behavior that borders on suicidal, and according to our research, you had late motor skill development. And you have poor sociability. I'm not saying this because you weren't able to maintain your marriage and stayed single after the divorce, but you punched me in the face when you came to talk to me about that cannibal you caught last month. Combine it with your extraordinary IQ and almost otherworldly persistence, it doesn't take an FBI psychologist to know what's up with you."

Oh boy.

No point in hiding the truth anymore. Gabriel sighed. "Fine. I'm aspergic."

"That explains a lot."

"W-what?"

"You went to special ed in elementary, where you met Casey, your late best friend, you know, who had autism?"

Gabriel frowned. "So what? Us tards in the spectrum stick together, uh?"

"Oh my... no. I didn't mean—"

"Then what *do* you mean?"

"Shouldn't have said that. What I mean is you're incredibly focused and determined. We all know how obsessed you are with justice."

"But my condition is still somehow a problem?" Gabriel asked. "Look, you wanna fire me, go ahead."

"No, why would I— I've seen you hunt down three ultraviolent criminals in the period of two months. You're a highly functional, crime-solving guru. A gem in the FBI's arsenal."

"What's the problem then?"

"You should have told me about your condition before. Or in your application."

"I'm not comfortable talking about it," Gabriel said. "You're right. I suffered from alcoholism, and still suffer nightmares. I don't know if those *psychological problems* are related to Asperger's. But my battles with liquor and nightmares *are* connected to scary things, sad things, that I'd rather forget."

"So you avoid thinking about them?"

"Honestly, I don't think about anything much. I don't care about sex, don't care if I have friends or money or respect. Frankly, there's not much I care about."

"Except solving crimes."

"Except solving crimes, yes," Gabriel said. "That's my routine, and that's what I'm gonna do until I die."

There was an uncomfortable silence on the line, making Gabriel hold his breath. Maybe the FBI did not take kindly to people like him.

"Good thing we got just the gig for you," Conor said. "Welcome aboard, *Agent* Chase."

Gabriel released his breath. "Thank y—"

"Excited about our very first case in BISKIT?" The pitch of Conor's voice increased, bordering on squealing.

"Yes," Gabriel said truthfully. Nothing was as satisfying as catching serial killers, especially internationally. Because serial killers were the personification of evil and fighting them was the reason he existed.

"Awesome. We've received a request from the CID in London."

"The UK?" Gabriel asked dumbly, feeling the excitement growing.

"Uh-huh," Conor affirmed. "Looks like a crazy guy up there mutilates his victims and puts them up for public display, taunting the authorities."

"Can you ask them to send us the case file?"

"They already did, and I've forwarded them to you, along with the flight ticket."

"Flight ticket?" Gabriel frowned. "I hope it's from JFK."

"I'm sorry. I-I didn't think you'd want to go back to New York. Didn't take you for the good-bye type."

"I'm not, but I need to drop Bill back, asshole," Gabriel said.

"Totally forgot about him."

"See. Sociopath," Gabriel said.

"Is not," Conor rebutted like a child. "I'll rearrange the travelling plans."

"Cool."

"Once you get to London, your new partner will meet you there."

Gabriel said, "Sounds good."

"Alright. Let me call you with a revised schedule." Conor hung up.

Gabriel gripped the phone with both hands and rested it on his forehead. Conor was not rude or condescending, but why would he want to bring Gabriel's condition up if he wasn't going to do anything about it? Probably to let Gabriel know that his secret was in the open. A power play. But it didn't matter. Gabriel always remembered what Joshua had said once when he'd come home crying because the bullies at school wouldn't stop calling him 'weirdo'. If people had a problem with his condition, it was just that.

Their problem.

Thanking his dad, Gabriel sat up and tossed the phone into the hospital bag. When the phone landed, something vivid and shiny was exposed from within. On closer inspection, he found that the item jutted out of his clothes, the ones he'd worn when arresting Ryatt.

Gabriel pulled his jeans out and what was in the pocket?

A Zesty.

Ryatt must have slipped it in when Gabriel was out cold.

He grabbed the candy and examined it. The déjà vu returned, and that melancholic sensation of familiarity crept into his mind, stunning his thoughts. The buried memory was somehow related to Ryatt. Gabriel was sure that he had seen him before.

But no matter how much he tried or squeezed his temples, he just couldn't remember.

Frustrated, he walked over to the window to get some much-needed fresh air.

Calabria, Roman's criminal hangout, was now a burned-out charcoal skeleton, cordoned by yellow crime scene tape.

Smiling, Gabriel closed his eyes and filled his lungs to their capacity a few times. But the oxygen did not ease the heckling memory. In fact, for some reason, staring out of an open window at darkness while holding Zesty intensified the uneasiness.

A strange urge to eat the lollipop overwhelmed Gabriel.

He pinched the corner of the Zesty's wrapper and pulled it loose. The yellow sphere was sprinkled with tiny red thingamajigs.

"Screw it," he muttered and stuck it in his mouth.

As the ginger candy melted between his cheek and teeth, the aroma it released boosted his ability to recall.

Wasn't the sense of smell a powerful tool to remember the associated incidents from the past, as it was linked more strongly to memory than other senses? It should be, because the déjà vu finally found its origin: a really old event from his childhood.

Gabriel's eyes widened in recognition and the world around froze in time. At last, he remembered where he'd seen Ryatt before.

If you enjoyed this book, please let others know by leaving a quick review on Amazon. Also, if you spot anything untoward in the paperback, get in touch. We strive for the best quality and appreciate reader feedback.

editor@thebookfolks.com

www.thebookfolks.com

More fiction by Nathan Senthil

Self-styled Mr. Bunny wants to be the most notorious killer in US history. With four high profile figures slowly hanging to their deaths, he's off to a good start. NYPD homicide detective Gabriel Chase much catch him, no matter at what cost. But who will have the last laugh?

When Detective Chase determines to pursue Mr. Bunny's tip-off that another serial killer is at large, he is met with disinterest from the authorities. Suddenly falling seriously out of favor with the FBI and suspended from his position, he endeavors to hunt him down alone. He is looking for a homicidal maniac who is cannibalizing his victims. But one who has learnt from the best how to evade the police. Chase will have to find a crack in his armor.

Other titles of interest

LATENT DAMAGE by Ian Robinson

When a respected member of the community is murdered, it is not the kind of knife crime London detectives DI Nash and DS Moretti are used to dealing with. Someone has an agenda and it is rotten to the core. But catching this killer will take all of their police skills and more.

NO AGE TO DIE by John Dean

When a dangerous convicted felon is released from prison, DCI Blizzard makes it clear he is unwelcome on his patch. But when a local church takes the man in, Blizzard has to deal with the community uproar. When a local youth is killed it will take all of the detective's skills to right a wrong.